ALSO BY RONIT MATALON

Bliss
The One Facing Us

THE SOUND OF OUR STEPS

THE SOUND OF OUR STEPS

A Novel

RONIT MATALON

Translated by Dalya Bilu

METROPOLITAN BOOKS
HENRY HOLT AND COMPANY
NEW YORK

Metropolitan Books
Henry Holt and Company, LLC
Publishers since 1866
175 Fifth Avenue
New York, New York 10010
www.henryholt.com

Metropolitan Books® and ® are registered trademarks of
Henry Holt and Company, LLC.

Copyright © 2008 by Ronit Matalon
Published by arrangement with the Institute for the Translation of Hebrew Literature
English-language translation copyright © 2015 by Dalya Bilu
All rights reserved.
Distributed in Canada by Raincoast Book Distribution Limited

Originally published in Israel in 2008 by Am Oved, Tel Aviv.

The excerpts from *The Lady of the Camellias* are taken from the Comédie d'Amour
series, Société des Beaux-Arts, Paris, London, and New York. No name of translator
or date of publication given.
The gardening excerpts are taken from the Hebrew website
http://www.ginun.co.il.

Library of Congress Cataloging-in-Publication Data

Matalon, Ronit.
    [Kol tse'adenu. English]
    The sound of our steps : a novel / Ronit Matalon; translated by Dalya Bilu.—
First U.S. Edition.
        pages cm
    Originally published in Israel in 2008 by Am Oved, Tel Aviv, entitled "Kol tse'adenu."
    ISBN 978-0-8050-9160-1 (hardback)—ISBN 978-1-4299-4766-4 (electronic book)
    1. Matalon, Ronit—Translation into English.   2. Jewish families—Fiction.
3. Tel Aviv (Israel)—Fiction.   4. Domestic fiction.   I. Bilu, Dalya, translator.
II. Title.
    PJ5054.M3274K6513 2015
    892.43'6—dc23   2014038264

Henry Holt books are available for special promotions and premiums.
For details contact: Director, Special Markets.

First U.S. Edition 2015
Designed by Meryl Sussman Levavi

Printed in the United States of America

1   3   5   7   9   10   8   6   4   2

To Ariel H.

What might have been and what has been
Point to one end, which is always present.
Footfalls echo in the memory. . . .

T. S. Eliot, Four Quartets

THE SOUND OF OUR STEPS

THE SOUND

THE SOUND OF her steps: not the heels tapping, the feet dragging, the clogs clattering or soles shuffling on the path leading to the house, no. First the absence of steps, the creeping dread in anticipation of her arrival, her entrance, the loaded silence, measured by a twelve-minute unit of time, heralded by the next-to-last bus stopping, the 11:30 bus from which she would descend.

Our mother didn't step, she skimmed. At great speed, in a total silence that split the balanced quiet of the street in two.

What did she put on her feet back then, which shoes, or to be more precise, how did she prepare for battle, how, with what? That sense of purpose she had, to the last detail, the sacred air of purpose, how she loved what was useful, necessary. I remember her last pair of shoes because I bought them; the earliest ones in my memory, less so.

I think she preferred shoes with laces. A bit of a heel, about two inches, no more. Maybe more, but just a bit.

I think they were brown or maybe black.

When they were brown she dyed them black. When they were black she turned them brown.

The brown didn't turn out too well, the black showed through.

She gave them to the shoemaker, Mustaki. ("How are you, *ya* Mustaki?")

A few times she gave them to Mustaki and then didn't wear them. ("That Mustaki made a total mess of the job.")

I think she didn't do the repairs to wear the shoes but to put things right, to clean up another corner of the world, to keep up her war against the disintegration of things. ("It's a good thing we've got him handy, that Mustaki, he doesn't take much.")

Small feet, size 6.

She was proud of them, her feet, but in secret. You knew she was proud when she talked about other feet, not small. ("She's got a pair on her, big as boats.")

THE STEPS, the approach, the return, the night. The return at night, after twelve hours' work. The return home, her bursting in. She burst through the door. The grating of the key in the lock took no more than a second, she must have taken the keys out on the way, when she got off the bus or even before. No, that's not right, the keys were in the plant pot next to the front door. We weren't worried about burglars. She wasn't worried so we weren't either: "What are they going to take? The tiles off the floor? Let them. We'll put down new ones."

But they broke in once anyway. Through the bedroom window. The police came to investigate. "Mother, what did the police say?" "Nothing. He looked. For half an hour he looked inside and out and then said, 'He came through the window.' 'Thanks a lot,' I said, 'so he came through the window, did he, that puts me at ease.'"

But she wasn't at ease. Her entrances, the way she burst through the front door, starved after long hungry hours of not-home, of longing for home, of keeping up appearances out in the world, which was not-home. The weariness corroded her like acid, a weariness of body, but more than that, the weariness of keeping up appearances, of not-home.

We listened for her entrances, for their violence, we knew every detail, step by step, yet we were still taken by surprise. The dread was the surprise.

In one wide-angled glance, from the semidarkness of the hallway, she took in the shack and the area around it, she registered, noted, and classified what she saw: a slight change in the placement of the vase on the oval table, shoes left on the carpet, a cup on the coffee table, someone slouching on the sofa, a squashed cushion, a chair out of alignment. Even before she put down her bag, she stood with it in the hallway, her eyes narrowed, jaw clenched, collecting evidence, coming up with evidence of collapse, of break-down, of the chaos of our home's disintegration. All the evidence confirmed it. She was the house. And any disturbance of the right and proper order signaled that the collapse had come or was about to. It was coming.

A few times she threw a plant or a vase (my brother Sammy ducked, the vase shattered on the wall above his head).

Or she swept the table with her forearm, knocking everything to the floor.

Or she smashed the dirty cups in the sink and bled from the splinters.

Or she kicked the leg of the table, hurting her toe.

Or she tossed a pot off the stove.

Or she took off her shoe and hurled it at the television.

Or she threw out our friends.

Or she hit us, with a broom, shoe, mop, hammer, the base of a lamp, a kitchen towel, her hands.

Or she screamed.

Her screaming, her entrance, the entrance was a scream. She always said, "I want to get in already." Not "come back" or "come in." There was nothing casual or assumed about her arrival, it was always an event, a dis-play of suffering. Again and again she would trumpet her entrance, her return. She proclaimed it, not so much to us but to herself, to the house. Her entrance was an effort to awaken the house to her, to rouse her heart in response. She restored it to herself after the hours of exile, of not-home, of not being able to scream.

In her good clothes, not fancy at all but good or proper, she stood in the semidark hallway (lit from the side by the yellow bulb in the bathroom) and took command of her domain, declared her sovereignty, banished whatever needed banishing, at least until order was restored, until her repossession of the house had been established. It only seemed that her yelling had any substance, that it said something. I could have said it was a cry of despair, but no: it was a cry of furious longing. That's what it was: the fury of longing.

Did you miss us, *ya bint*, did you miss us? (Her mother, Nona, called her "*ya bint*," daughter. She sometimes called herself *ya bint* when scolding her-self for something, but tenderly: "*Yallah*, get up already, *ya bint*, do some-thing.")

She never, almost never, said "I miss" anything. She did say "that's missing," "he's missing," "you were missing," "the house is missing."

Her screaming was the pit. We knew nothing of the pit, only what came before and what came after. We built a bridge over the pit as if it were a continuation of the land. This was repair work: before and after the pit.

We were closest, us and her, when we were in the pit: we no longer distinguished between her dread and our dread, the dread of hearing her say, "It's the end of the world." This was what she yelled: "It's the end of the world."

For a moment, in the jagged moment of her yelling, on the threshold of the house, between the outside and the inside, in the yellowish semi-dark of the passage, it was the end of the world. It ended because it had been reborn, with her return home. It dared to end because it was born again.

Before the pit came her steps, the steps we guessed at if we did not hear them. We held our breath in fear, in pity, in fear and pity. The pity was harder than the fear; step after step, five feet two inches, 143 pounds (in her thin times), twelve hours of work, four hundred plates in the Rosh Ha'ayin school cafeteria, twenty-something cauldrons, three hundred chairs arranged in the student center in the afternoons, after the cafeteria, a few pounds, a few pennies, an ironed handkerchief doused with cheap lavender water, the kind she bought by the pint.

There isn't a cat in the street. She said, "There isn't a cat in the street," instead of saying, "fear." The bus driver knew her. All the bus drivers on our local line knew her. The good ones let her off at the house, before the bus stop. The mean ones, one of them had ginger hair, only let her off at the stop. "It's the law." She hated the law and whoever made it. The law is whatever happens to suit him, she thought, and she said what she thought, too: "Your law is just what suits you, mister."

She always said what she thought, and more. Especially when she was worn out, parked on one of the seats in the empty rectangle of the bus in the ghostly light of the late night, or standing in the ghostly light of the dim hallway. The yelling was more than what she thought, and the nails.

Her words were nails. "Her words pierce your body like nails," my sister Corinne said, dropping her cigarette ash on the floor, listening for the steps.

The sound of her steps every night, night after night, for years. The ground she covered from the bus stop to the dirt path turning off to the left, leading to the house, and ending in a line of paving stones. The open square of the porch, the house. The front door with the two potbellied clay flowerpots painted green, sleeping toads.

She saw everything when she returned. She saw even before she saw, on the way, before she arrived, she saw what she hadn't yet seen: scenes of devastation, a desert. The thirsty lawn, the shriveled rose beds. Their dryness was her parched mouth. Even before she came in, with her coat, her bag, her packages, she fell on the sprinkler, the rake, the hoe ("Where's the bastard who took my hoe, where did my hoe go?")

She entered with black hands covered in earth, she paused on the threshold, the tense, thick air that she brought with her, that she created. The watchful look of the mistress of the house, the prison guard, her miraculous memory for the smallest details of objects and spaces and the relations between them: she never remembered people's names, only things. What did you miss, *ya bint*, what did you miss?

Perhaps it was not the house itself that she guarded, or the household objects and their arrangement, but the idea of the house that she pored over and over dozens if not hundreds of times, tested again and again the hope, the hope of home.

The entrance was the site of dashed hopes, of her injury, of her drama: she encountered the house only through her drama, slashing her veins in the presence of her lover, the house.

Our indifference, the complacency of our ignorant desecrations (our ignorance maddened her more than any knowledge) was to her an act of aggression. She wasn't striking out, she was reacting. The destruction she brought, great or small, was a declaration of love, of faith. This was the pit.

On the brink of the pit was the bathroom. The pit had no time, only space. We never knew how long it would last, only its dimensions in space. At a certain moment she would stop, abandon everything, disappear into the bathroom for a long moment, emerge with her face washed, her hands washed, after swallowing something, some pill or other.

A different stage would begin, the slow, calmer stage of her pallor.

In the gradual spread of her pallor, on her hands and face, the house would break out of its shell, stop being a stage, and become a home. The low table lamp cast a concentrated beam of light on the tablecloth, the carpet threadbare but acceptable. My sister searched for her tweezers.

We would look at her, now she let us look: we were afraid of her ferocity, but we were in awe of her pallor. This is her second entrance, her true arrival: she sat down on a kitchen stool, took off her shoes, dipped a piece of bread into tea with milk. There was other food but she didn't feel like it. This is what she felt like: yesterday's bread dipped in tea with milk.

Tea with Milk

TEA WITH MILK is what she drinks when she can't drink a thing, not a
thing. Tea with milk is the sign of emptiness, which has at its heart a
longing for comfort, a kind of babying that she usually denies herself but
now will accept: something warm, sweet, murky, and white like thin porridge, a colorless color of nothing forceful. That's it, tea with milk is what
she drinks when she refuses to speak forcefully: not "refuses," but dissolves
in the face of it.

Tea with milk is a rare moment of consent. Her consent to weakness,
softness, motherhood. She is most a mother when she's drinking tea with
milk, dunking a slice of yesterday's dry bread in it, fishing out the soggy
bits of bread with her fingers. Tea with milk gives her a sense of the true
proportions of what she has and, mainly, what she doesn't have. She
admires austere modesty, but as a matter of style, not substance, really
not substance.

Now I recall the oilcloth that covered the kitchen table with the aluminum legs, a square table with a new oilcloth. The cup makes a print on the
oilcloth, a round ring that she quickly wipes away, not getting up to do it,
just reaching for the sink, for a rag, and wiping. The pattern on the oilcloth:
symmetrical squares, symmetrical flowers, symmetrical lines. She hates the
material but puts up with it for its practicality. This is one of her great inner
dramas, the struggle between the aesthetic and the practical. She resolves

the conflict for a while when she changes the oilcloth on the kitchen table. Every two weeks a new one, spotlessly clean.

We sit on stools with aluminum legs, which she calls tabourettes ("put the tabourette back in its place when you get up"), doing nothing, saying nothing, a limited moment of grace while she puts off going to bed, going to sleep. She hasn't got the strength to go to bed, to perform the necessary acts preceding sleep, not because she's too tired to get up, but because it's hard for her to stop, to accept the big break that is sleep. Her sleep is short and intermittent; she puts it off longer and longer simply because she is afraid of it.

This is what hangs in the air among us in the kitchen as we sit on the tabourettes by the gleaming oilcloth in which our faces are outlined, abstract and featureless. This is what hangs in the air at night at the end of the day: her fear.

I see her on the tabourette, it is late, the hour seems to reach beyond the limits of time; from a distance of years of life and death. I see her there, in the kitchen of the shack, on the tabourette, in a state of complete surrender within the inevitable surrender of the end of the day's work, surrender within surrender. Her broad backside on the stool, still in the skirt with the broken zipper, overflowing the small round seat, her stomach overflowing onto her thighs, her breasts on her overflowing stomach. She is bowed, huddled, I should say, her short plump chin buried in her bosom, in her neck, her arms lying in her lap, without desire or will, touching her bare knees beneath her skirt. I don't remember the season, summer or winter or fall, but she leans over, hunched, as if she wants to warm herself at a heater at her feet. The features of her face are hidden from me, effaced in her bowing down, in the shrinking of her body. It is a picture of mourning. She is one keening.

It's quiet in the kitchen. The barred window is painted green. One of the cats that live in the yard pokes its head through the bars, looks in. On the other side of the kitchen, in the hallway, the clock keeps up its jolting, maddening tick. She bought it on twelve installments from a peddler who passed through the neighborhood (it turned out she paid four times more than it was worth). One night, when the clock was driving her crazy, she wrecked the mechanism and silenced it. In the morning we saw the wounded clock, still hanging on the wall. "I shut it up," she confessed matter-of-factly, a gleam in her eye. "I made it shut up at last."

AT LAST

A T LAST SHE came to me in a dream, after years when she hadn't. There
was a long, empty hall, a kind of barracks or a hut in some sort of camp,
a wing in an orphanage or old age home. I think an old age home. It
stretched on for miles, the hall, long and rather narrow, beds lined up on
both sides, with narrow regular intervals between each bed and the next.
Two long lines of iron beds, sheets gleaming white, not a bright color but a
terrible glare. She was in the last bed at the end of the hall. She was sitting
on the edge, dressed in a gown that was open at the back, the kind they give
you before an operation. Her legs dangled in the air, not reaching the floor,
like a little girl's. Her face was fresh, whole, as if her life had not yet begun,
as if she were on the threshold. I spoke to her: "I came to take you for the
holiday, come spend the holiday with us, come be with us."

She clasped her hands delicately, shook her head with reserved, almost
bureaucratic regret. "I won't," she said.

I was astonished: For the first time she was completely separate, in
some place, over there, that I couldn't even imagine, speaking through a
wall. "But why not?" I tried to keep hold of her. She smiled a weary, knowing kind of smile, resigned, and pointed to the end of the hall, not far from
her bed. My eyes followed her finger: an ageless man was standing there,
wearing faded but not shabby work clothes, holding some kind of tool in
his hand, a broom or a rake. He must be one of the workers here, I figured.

"I love him," she said in flat tone, through the wall, with a faint smile whose meaning I didn't understand. "He's poor, sick, lonely, he doesn't talk, he's younger than me. He's nothing. He won't amount to anything, but I'll stay with him. I won't come to the *familia*, finished."

Familia

THE FAMILY WAS almost *familia* but *familia* wasn't the same as the family, because of the dim, winding, two-way corridors that pass from one language to another. "The family" was only ever a kind of prosthesis attached to the body in place of the missing limb, which, despite the practiced, almost natural use she learned to make of it, never lost its strangeness, its twisted smile, just as her Hebraized name. (It was Lucette, but when she arrived in the country they told her, you're Levana. For years she would turn around whenever someone called her Levana, looking for the person with that name.) When she said "the family" instead of *familia* it was as if she were watching from the side, as if she had become, for a moment, the authorities.

There was no bitterness or ill feeling in this change, only the cheerful appearance of cooperation. She excelled in the cheerful appearance of cooperation, which was not an act but a deep truth, she would say. This was part of what she called our "mentality." "It's our mentality" she said, with a sigh that was both proud and resigned.

Among other things, "our mentality" involved the ability to adopt an appearance, to put on a face that a person showed to the world, which was not a negligible thing. She would say, "We eat with our eyes." Or "A person eats first with his eyes." Among other characteristics, this was the "mentality": she came from a culture of the gaze.

With all this business of the gaze, it's strange to remember how she was plagued all her life by eye troubles: her father, Grandfather Izak, suffered from bad eyes at a relatively young age, in his forties, due to severe diabetes.

Her mother, Nona Esther, lost more than 80 percent of her vision, making her almost blind.

Her first husband, my big brother's father, lost his left eye either to a disease or to a work accident, it's not clear which.

My brother Sammy was afflicted with herpes as a child and lost the sight in his left eye due to medical negligence.

She herself, in her sixties, suffered paralysis of half her face, which damaged her left eye.

The history of the *familia* and her place in it tiptoed around holes, pits of heavy, ambivalent silence: the eye troubles were there in the silence, the partial blindness, the flaws.

In my childhood our home was full of little plastic tubs containing dark lukewarm water; three or four tea bags floated in the liquid, and sodden dripping bits of cotton that someone—she, my brother, or my grandmother—would put on their eyelids as they half-reclined, stretching their necks with their Adam's apples sticking out as if for the slaughterer, using the corner of a towel to wipe the liquid trickling into their lips and chins. They hardly moved, pressed the cotton to their eyelids, waiting for relief with faces bathed in brown rivulets: silent eyeless weeping that seemed to well from their foreheads, the tears of gods or rocks, not of people.

I would sit on the carpet at their feet, each of them with the dripping tea compresses, and I'd watch their stillness, in suspense—it was the stillness of big wild animals laid low for a moment. When with effort they finally opened their eyes, blinking in the light, their eyelids were circled by dark rings, as if they had been punched or hadn't slept for nights. They would rise to their feet, swaying, dizzy from lying down for so long with their eyes closed. There was nothing healthy about this tortured procedure, but in her rushing impatience, she would quickly pronounce her eyes "Better," or "Better now," or, in moments of expansiveness but not waiting for the answer, "Better now?"

BETTER

S HE WAS "MY mother," a phrase that had the taste of something foreign, because among ourselves and sometimes to her face we called her "the mother"—the mother's coming, the mother's gone, the mother said, where's the mother? Maurice, too, especially Maurice (my father, another phrase with a foreign flavor) called her "the mother," but then he would say, "You know what the mother's like."

We knew what the mother was like. Our knowledge of her, which was made up of countless inner withdrawals, silent understandings and agreements, a weave of dread and love that kept changing its colors, had us riveted. Each of us in his own way was riveted by her, all our lives, anticipating her, but more accurately anticipating her changing from one thing to another. Those transformations of hers, the contradictions reversing themselves from one minute to the next, defined us and then defined us again.

In my imagination I sometimes saw the threads that tied us to her, both flexible and durable, like threads pulled from a lump of gum: the more you stretched them the thinner they grew, almost invisible but still holding to the original lump. This glue, the huge lump, stuck in your mouth, making it impossible to move your jaw; it crammed your mouth and pushed into your throat—this is connected to an image of sickness. To what happened when I was sick.

I was very sick with some kind of illness when I was four or five years

old. I had a very high fever that didn't go down for days, with the delirium
that went along with it. I lay in her bed, in her room, the bedroom. Hers
was the only room in the shack referred to with a certain ceremony as "the
bedroom." She allowed me to lie in her double bed, in which for years—
forever, in fact—there had been no mate. While I lay in bed she was at
work. She had two jobs: from early in the morning to midday she cleaned a
house in the affluent suburb of Savyon, and from early in the afternoon
until almost midnight she worked at the youth center in Petach Tikva,
where she acted for years as the house mother. At noon she came home for
an hour, "to put her head down," blink at two pages of Simenon in French,
change her clogs for the afternoon lace-ups, and grab a bite "standing up."

The days were mauve, with no day or night, as if they had been soaked
in a tub of dye; this period of profound illness was for me the time of childhood: there was no past or future, I was aware only of eternity, a heavy sleep
of the soul, an eternity that was nothing but a constant sense of suffocation. The walls of the bedroom were painted a soft lavender, a little faded:
this was her mauve period. For hours, days at a stretch, I lay in her bed with
my head on a pile of pillows arranged by Nona Esther, to make it easier for
me to breathe. Facing me were the white Formica doors of the clothes closet,
reflecting the pale light from the bedside lamps. On my right, to the right of
the bed, was the window looking out on the backyard. The Nona had closed
the blinds, but she opened one in a rage whenever she "dropped in" to see
how I was. Every day, one of them closed, one open in protest.

I was at the bottom of the ocean, on a bed of absolute loneliness: the
weight of the water above pressed heavily on my chest as I lay there
spread-eagled, not daring to move, to turn over. Things climbed up my
throat, heavy, viscous, and were pushed down again. Worst of all was the
window on the right, which looked into the darkness, into the backyard.
Out of the corner of my eye I saw them: enormous faces, flat, white, featureless, a circle of soft, whitish dough stuck to the windowpane, fixing eyeless
eyes on me, then turning into a giant, flat white pillow, laid on my face,
suffocating me. From above, above the surface of the water, came voices,
distant echoes of voices, a stifled quarrel between the mother and the
grandmother: she argued "*el bint*," and Nona replied imploringly "*el bint*,"
the child.

The flat white faces now turned into sheets of clinging plastic, sticking
to my face. I tried to move but I couldn't. Once in a while a hand was laid

on my forehead, not the palm, the back of the hand: it was hers. I felt the roughness and the flinching of the hand on my forehead, its flight from that spot. That split second of the back of her hand on my forehead, careful not to slide down to my cheek, was panic-stricken, full of the fear of death, of her question, "Better now?" And again, from the doorway, when she escaped back to work, "Better now?"

THE BACK OF HER HAND (1)

H ER HANDS WERE those of a laborer. Nona said, "A man's hands, look at the hands she's got, just like a man." Nona's own hands were so perfect they had attained the status of an ideal: white as white could be, almost unblemished, as if they had just been dipped in flour. The hauteur of her fingers, transcending the very idea of refinement, was breathtaking. I felt for Nona's hands constantly, as if I were seeking confirmation of something.

Hands, what they were and could be, were a hard, bitter stone stuck in the throat of their dreadful quarrels, the mutual insults, the symbolic and once even real slashing of veins, the harassment, the silence that went on for days and sometimes weeks (never longer than a month), the marginal and substantive complaints, the grievances aired and not aired (not many of those), the magnificent, bleeding wounds.

Nona said, "I left the real, sweet Lucette behind in Egypt." No, first she said, "She's got the hands of a man," and only afterward, "The real Lucette stayed in Egypt." Who was the real Lucette? Nona remembered her, or thought she did. "That mouth she's got on her, that tongue of hers, she never had that before. Nothing like that, opening that mouth of hers like she does now. She learned that over here. Like a doll she was, pretty as a doll with honey on her tongue, never mind what she said, only honey on her tongue. Yes Mother, no Mother, certainly Mother, only honey. And her cheeks, her skin. There was nothing like Lucette's skin: when she came into a room, the room lit up from the glow of that skin. Wherever she went, people turned their heads. *Basbusa* they called her in the street. *Basbusa*, that cake with sugar and butter, sweet as can be. She was *Basbusa* and her cousin Janette, her they called *Harisa*, a dry cake that sticks in your throat. The two of them would walk home from school together, and Lucette was *Basbusa* and she was *Harisa*."

These words in Nona's mouth, repeated again and again, tasted like the snitching of an informer: informing on the good, not the bad. She betrayed the good Lucette, the grace she once had, because the good one was in hiding, not the bad one. Something great, the loss of which was nothing short of catastrophic, had fled from sight during their emigration: femininity had been sacrificed to this rough place, to its new, rough, male humanity. At the heart of this femininity were the hands, and more, the care of them as a womanly asset, at once manifest and mysterious. For the lack of their care Nona blamed my mother perhaps more than for the fact of having a man's hands. That was it, that they hadn't been a man's hands at first, not at first. Nona might have resigned herself to a grace not granted, but not to a grace given and then ruined, again and again: "It's as if she does it on purpose, that stubborn mother of yours, on purpose."

THE BACK OF HER HAND (2)

THE BACK OF her hands were very dark, sunburned, and the palms were pink. Sometimes they looked like finger puppets in two colors, black and white, turning from side to side, two characters: the back that was also the palm, and the palm that was also the back. They were small, her hands, short, matching her small, round, compact body: *Basbusa*.

She worked with her hands only, she plunged them into everything: the loose and dry earth, the pail with the "blue" to bleach the sheets, the clay, the clogged toilet bowl, the dough, the mound of couscous, the garbage can in front of the house, where she had thrown something she regretted half an hour later, the cement, the nails, the fertilizer, a pile of tomatoes or green peas in the market, a can of olives, the fire water—a source of great delight (what exactly was "fire water"?).

"Put them in, put your hands in, don't stand there like a statue," she'd say.

Or worse: "He doesn't put his hand in, that one, he just glides over the top of things."

She rushed into physical matter with a passion, crazy to mix and merge with her very body. There was always "the goal," a sacred duty that she turned into pleasure, the work that she elevated to an absolute value. Wrong: she *was* the work, there was no elevation.

Her hands' agility, what's called dexterity, was beyond imagination, almost superhuman, like a cartoon animation: it wasn't just a characteristic, her agility, it was an entire category.

Watching the movements of her hands in the air and in the matter made you giddy: within seconds the distinctions between movements' actions dissolved, turning into a pale, centrifugal mist, with flashes of color flying around, one after the other.

This is how I saw it the first time, at a hallucinatory predawn hour that stretched on until eight in the morning.

She woke me the way she usually did, shaking my shoulders at first hesitantly and then vigorously. I was in her bed, perhaps I had fallen asleep there or perhaps I had crept into it during the night, indifferently and sleepily suffering her pushing me to the edge of the bed, her heavy grumbling at me to stop lying at an angle, stop killing her.

The square of her bedroom window, the semitransparent curtain drawn to one side, was still full of darkness, and the points of the cypresses, one taller than the other, were barely visible. For a while I sat on the bed, wide awake, staring into the darkness, which grew less threatening at the sound of the domestic racket she was making all over the shack. She had put on that dress of hers buttoned at the front, which later on, mainly in photographs, reminded me of a Soviet worker's uniform in a piston factory. She had three of them, the same cut in different colors, all inherited from her sister Marcelle in France: blue, mauve, and brown (my aunt was in the habit of buying almost everything in a particular style, if, in her opinion, it "fit her like a dream," an impression that lasted a few weeks at the most).

Her face was stern, trapped in a train of thought circling around some necessary chore to be performed in the day rapidly coming closer, something that was almost always connected to her great yet impossible desire to get the task of life under control. Within moments she stood me on my feet, on the bed, dressed me; in the blindness of hectic haste, my arm almost always was caught up outside the sleeve or crooked inside the sleeve. I was four and a bit.

When she crouched at the foot of the bed to lace my shoes, the square of the window was revealed to me again, but different: the dense darkness had given way to grays growing fainter, diluted by the pale light. We took the first bus to Petach Tikva, to what she referred to in her laconic way as

"Something I've got today": preparing five hundred sandwiches for summer day camps in the Petach Tikva area, an extra job in addition to her usual summer work.

We ran down a moldy staircase at the side of the municipality building into a big basement or shelter, skipping over cardboard boxes, piles of papers, office waste, clumsy garbage cans. The darkness down there was absolute; when she found the switch and turned on the light, it seemed as if the space were illuminated for the first time in its history, itself astonished by its new face. She threw her bag onto one of the dusty, broken chairs piled up at the side, suddenly lifting me with her hands and sitting me down on one of the long worktables. "Sit," she commanded, one of the only words she spoke during the two and a half hours we were there. The others were "We'll be done, *insh'allah*, by eight thirty."

There we were, the two of us, the long worktables, one facing the other, probably thrown out of some youth center; all around us concrete walls that had warts, strange, murky lumps; a wall clock that someone had seen fit to hang there; three huge plastic bags crammed with five hundred bread rolls, plastic containers with egg salad and pickled cucumbers, and four jars of chocolate spread. There was a single light. It dangled from a thin electric cord fixed in the ceiling, an opaque yellow globe, swollen, as if it were about to explode. The globe moved above her head all the time as she worked, above the worktable, swaying gently, left and right, as if a wind were blowing through the windowless concrete box. There was utter silence, full of suspense, movements, only movements, yellow shadows cast by the light swaying indifferently over her feverish head. I didn't dare bite into the roll she thrust into my hand, riveted as I was to the assembly line series of operations taking place before my eyes. There was no break, not a pause, in the trance that took hold of her, only that stirring of the air as testimony to the great movement rushing through it: she split the five hundred rolls with a knife, spread with egg salad, added two slices of pickled cucumber, wrapped, spread with chocolate spread, wrapped, again and again.

The hands of the clock on the wall behind her echoed the rhythms of anxiety welling up inside me, growing from moment to moment; the yellow globe swung over her head, keeping time to her hectic, desperate haste. "Will she make it? Will she make it?" I pleaded in my heart, feeling the tension stiffening my limbs and a sudden budding of hard tenderness, and with it a new sense of partnership: "Will we make it?"

The Back of Her Hand (3)

T HE EVENING BEFORE the morning she died, in the hospital, her hand resting on the fold in the sheet. She fondled the hem of the sheet between her finger and her thumb. The bluish veins branched in the darkness of her hand and lay on her face like a network of pipes on the surface of the ground, a vein pierced by the needle of the infusion. Fondling and fondling in a dreamy distraction. Fondling was never her thing, never. It was Nona's.

THE BACK OF HER HAND (4)

IT ISN'T TRUE, what Nona said, that she didn't take care of her hands on purpose, out of obscure vindictiveness toward the Nona, out of a kind of display of self-harm (not Nona's words). It isn't true: she actually "had her hands done."

From time to time, once every few months or in honor of a special occasion (a wedding, a holiday), she would go to Miriam, the manicurist, to have her hands done. "I'm going to do my hands," she would announce with a kind of suppressed pride, with the self-importance of someone trying to keep a secret but also eager for its discovery without her knowledge.

The time spent at Miriam's, in her apartment block in the neighborhood, was when she charged her batteries, while Miriam, as well as soaking her hands in a basin of warm water, slowly massaged the joints of her fingers. Miriam, and the time, and the basin, and "doing her hands" were the pauses she agreed to take from her life from time to time, to make room for "normal things" that she generally feared and held in contempt. Miriam had a way of drawing out her words in a kind of blandness that did not grant any moment any particular significance or seriousness, and this had an effect on her, blunting her usual proclivity for sharp cuts and sudden turns that could take your breath away. Hers, too.

"Dear oh dear, what's this I see here, Mrs. Levana?" Miriam investigated her hands with near- scientific curiosity, some new scratch or burn. Or: "So what do you say, Mrs. Levana? What do you say to these hands of yours? Are they a sight for sore eyes or what?" Slowly she would put on the spectacles hanging from her neck on a gilt chain, sending the mother a sidelong look full of irony and affection. Somehow she found herself revealing to Miriam, only to Miriam, the injuries sustained in her work accidents, like a little girl allowing her big sister to count and classify her wounds without judging them: the tragic halo and meaning of her wounds would dissolve under Miriam's eyes, turning them into a kind of game. If femininity were a kind of game, a forgiving, noncommittal wink—she could live with that.

When she came back from Miriam, she would hold her hands a little stiffly and self-consciously for a while, as if they were covered with wax, examining them from time to time. It was heartrending: from the back of her hand, ravaged by scratches, scars, burn marks, and swollen veins, emerged nails cut short as a boy's and painted a pinkish-orange; they did not belong, seemed quite perplexed.

There was a ring, too, which she transferred from her ring to her middle finger and back. Five interwoven coils of yellow and white gold without a stone, like a wedding or an engagement ring. Like.

We went to buy it together, she and I, from the goldsmith in Petach Tikva. No, we didn't go together, I trailed behind her while she did her chores, and suddenly, on an impulse, she went into the goldsmith's, next to the alley beside the big synagogue, and bought it, just like that, without thinking. Years and years after Maurice had evaporated from her life, at least in a day-to-day way, she bought herself a wedding ring, or something like a wedding ring. She never mentioned it, she wore it indifferently, lost it a few times and found it again in improbable places—hidden in the gravel of the path leading to the house, hanging by a thread from the bath drain, buried among shards of glass and sand in the dustpan—muttering to herself, "Look at that, just look, from God."

Miriam said, "Now, Mrs. Levana, while I do your hands, we'll put your beautiful ring away so it doesn't get spoiled."

She gave an embarrassed smile, a shy smile not from here and now, from a different place, a different heart (the photograph from Piazza San Marco with the pigeons), peeking in wonder at her hands, at the painted nails on which Miriam blew to dry them faster. For a few hours, after she had her hands done, they were not as rough—they lost the roughness, prickliness, that we felt when she touched us, if she touched us, a thin, invisible, almost prickly layer, like a patch of prickly pears to the north of the shack, on the way to the reservoir.

PIAZZA SAN MARCO: FIRST VISIT

THERE WERE THREE of us in the photograph: him, the mother, and me at the age of a year and ten months. (For years she said "two," later she corrected herself: "Never two. Maybe a year and ten months.") He was in Italy. He sent for her to come with the child, so he would see the child at last. They are kneeling before the pigeons, among the pigeons, the child between them, standing like a doll propped on her feet for a minute, supported from behind (the mother) so she wouldn't lose her balance and fall forward onto the paving stones, onto the pigeons. The tenuous, improbable balance is presumably connected to the odd gap between the child's upper body, swollen in the yellow coat—which looks as if it has been stuffed full of rags and cotton—and the skinny legs holding it up. The photograph is tinted in a pale green tending to yellow. Everything is bathed in the color: the square, the pigeons, the figures, the facades of the buildings behind them; the pigeons are blurred in the yellowish light, fading in a cloud of dust or plaster. He has one hand in his jacket pocket, the other held out to the pigeons, he looks at the photographer, smiles (what kind of a smile?). The mother doesn't smile. She is busy arranging the child in front of the camera, one hand supporting her from behind, the other, visible to us, holding the child's hand, with a solicitous expression regarding the child, as if to say, Look, look.

The photograph is split: three deep creases run down its right side, passing through Maurice, the square, the group of pigeons on the right. It looks as if it has been glued together, or as if it has been fished out of something, rescued despite itself, as if it has become fiction or was always fiction. A fictitious photograph. She says: "It was when I took you to Italy, for him to see you when you were about two years old." It never happened.

There Were Three of Us

THERE WERE THREE of us in the shack: my big brother, my big sister, and me, *el bint*, the child, the eternal third person. She herself wasn't another person, she was the shack. In one sense she took up no room, light as a feather, almost floating in space; in another she took up all the room. This lightness was, by the way, another of the rules of proper behavior that she had brought with her from over there, part of the "mentality." She would say, gravely knitting her brows (there wasn't much left of them, my sister plucked them with lethal diligence after she had finished annihilating her own): "Human beings should make themselves light, not weigh heavily on people."

But in the shack she wasn't a human being and we weren't people—all that pertained to the world outside and the way to behave in the world, to the need (the categorical imperative, in fact) to maintain a constant, effortful, near-paranoid sensitivity to the other person's "situation" in all its aspects: economic, social, cultural, legal, psychological.

She was this other person, she was not, as she said with her usual vehemence, *elbani-adam*, the human being: erasing the first person, the "I," was also part of the code of sensitivity.

Mostly she barked her reference to *elbani-adam* in Nona's direction, at what she perceived as callous selfishness that left no room for any other *elbani-adam*. This was one of the variety of forms that their indirect disputes took, quarrels based on codes and hints and semantic fields common to them both, which covered half a century and three continents. But it was impossible to trip Nona up with any talk of *elbani-adam* and how they should be, because, among other things, Nona believed she indisputably held the copyright to the proper behavior of *elbani-adam*, and, with the same relaxed firmness with which her enormous snow-white thighs rested on the armchair, she would repossess it, in a sleight of hand of sly, false agreement that drove the mother mad.

But the mother went on confronting her, sitting on the bed next to Nona's bed, or dragging in a stool from the kitchen, a seething bundle of nerves, her own thighs trembling as if attached to electrodes, looking for a fight and finding one.

"She only comes over to quarrel, that one. She shouldn't come. She sends my blood pressure right up," the Nona exclaimed in disgust. But when quiet descended for two or three days and the *asabiya*, the nervous one, failed to show up for her daily visit, Nona sent ingenuous messages. "Tell her I peeled the broad beans. Let her come and get them."

"I can take them," I volunteered.

"No, no. Let her come. The beans are ready."

And she would come, composed this time, and sit with Nona for longer than usual while they devoted themselves to soothing topics of conversation: condemnation of a common enemy, usually some unimportant sister-in-law nobody had seen for years.

I stretched out at their feet on the cool, newly washed floor, listening with one ear to the murmur of the conversation, which now spread out at the sides instead of rising to acrimonious heights; they sailed from subject to subject, conjuring up before me a crowded, busy, convoluted world, full of "relations" between men and women, women and their children, men and their parents, arabesques overlapping and intersecting one another, all etched on the silhouettes of women, both menacing and fragile, exchanging strength for weakness and weakness for strength. Nona's room (the quarter-shack) with the tiny kitchenette and the improvised shower above the toilet, with the army of loathsome green flies drawn by the two skinny cows belonging to the *amm*, our neighbor (nobody, perhaps not even he himself, knew his real name, he was always called *amm*, uncle, and his wife *amma*, aunt), the radio playing day and night, and the high iron bed reminiscent of a hospital—this was the natural site for this unending conversation, mythic and trivial at once, conducted between the two of them every day, during the course of which they erected and destroyed and agonized over entire worlds.

The floor tiles in Nona's quarter-shack went on sinking into the ground, and the closet leaned slightly to the side because of the sinking of the tiles (the mother once smashed its feet with a single hammer blow), and the moldy lump on the plywood ceiling went on swelling—"It's pregnant, that ceiling, soon it will bring us a baby"—and the words, words, words, of both of them and each of them grew smoky and charred with the pots Nona burned on the stove because of her forgetfulness and dreaminess, only to rise from the ashes and return, restored and replenished with the vitality of pain and beauty, as if to prove again that pain is trauma and beauty is, too. Especially beauty.

And as I lay there on the tiles, year after year, with my eyes closed but not in the least sleepy, dividing my attention between what was happening in the room and the sounds and whispers coming from behind the flimsy wall separating it from the apartment of the neighbors' daughter, Rachel Amsalem (Has she come, my darling, is she back already, my queen?), I had a hallucinatory vision, troubling and seductive, that I was adopted, a foundling, and that the entire conversation that took place next to me, with all its loops and labyrinths and changing, many-layered landscapes, all of them were nothing but a convoluted code pointing to this fact, leading to this simple fact, unequivocal and not convoluted at all. I was adopted. None of this was mine by virtue of blood and never would be. I didn't move, I dug my fingernail into the grooves between Nona's tiles, trying to scoop up dirt, to see my fingernail turn black. It was a strange moment of inner triumph, in which my foreignness, the possibility of being foreign, was a celebration, glittering, intimate, conflicting with nothing, at least as mysterious as the secret itself and just as silent.

Her One and Only

THE SHACK WAS her one and only, because that was what she decided, not with words, but with what gave them their validity: actions. The shack was one and we were three: my brother older than me by fourteen years, my sister by thirteen years, and the child ("Has the child eaten?" "Has the child come back?" "Have you seen the child?" "Keep your eye on the child, so she doesn't wander off," "The child is dead, she's dead, she's dead").

Between me and my sister stretched a train of dead children. The two-year-old baby who died in Cairo (Zizi, "When I had Zizi," she remembered), another one who died in her womb as a result of eclampsia in the eighth month, and abortions, between five and eight of them (when exactly, where?). "I got rid of them, I got rid of them like kittens and ran off to work," she said as if to herself, her gaze veiled and blank, looking into itself. There was no note of confession, admission, or guilt: it was a shrug, that's life, hardly the blink of an eye, on the strength of which she forced herself to bow before necessity, to break her own collarbone if need be, in order to "carry on," to get somewhere or other that held yet more of the same in store.

She set out and came home, set out and came home, diluting her deed ("I got rid of them") with dozens of other things she had done that day, refusing to give it any precedence, any priority. She simply put off feeling anything, as if to say, "Not now, later." But there was no later, no hour of distilled grief, sorrow that was not hindered or diluted: the whole of life, all the space, absorbed that "later"—every deed she did and thought she thought and joy she felt became drawers with double bottoms, in the depths of which lay that "later," ablaze inside the shack, prone to burst into flames at any second.

This is what drove her crazy in all the parched summer months of parched thorn fields surrounding the shack: the thought that it was about to go up in flames. When I saw her hostile narrowed eyes surveying the thorny gray expanse stretching out to the north of the shack, as far as the reservoir and beyond, the twitch at the corner of her mouth, the stance with legs apart and hands on her hips, like the leader of a street gang preparing for a fight with a rival gang, a ship's captain watching an approaching storm through his telescope, I understood (no, I knew) the meaning of the word "enemy."

She quarreled about the thorns with the council, the neighbors, with everything and everyone who refused to see the catastrophe as she did. At the heart of her intense panic was her wounded consciousness of the fragility, the flimsiness of the home, the shack: the wood, the thin plywood walls, the materials that could be consumed in a second. She never forgot them for a moment; she thought about them with profound compassion, with great, detailed concern, as if her pity were for them, for shack, not for herself, as if it were a being in its own right, an *elbani-adam*.

The terrible, blazing afternoon hour was the worst of the day, when she would "smell something," jump out of bed, interrupting her rest between one job and the next, race outside barefoot, wrapped in a housecoat. Standing on the burning asphalt of the street without feeling it, she stared at the faint puffs of smoke, this time from the thorn fields on the east, on the other side of the main road, wringing her hands. Sometimes she would shout: "Fire! Fire!" The street was empty. The road was empty. Inside the house I stopped my ears with my fingers so as not to hear her. The carpenter neighbor came out of the carpentry shop, reassured her. The carpenter's wife, Frieda, came out, poked her head through the bars of the gate, staring with eyes that remembered the nightmare so constantly that in the end they forgot it. She didn't reassure her, she was from the Holocaust.

For a long time the mother would stand there, gazing into the distance, at the red glare of a fire engine, and she went on gazing afterward, too, after the fire fighters had finished their work and driven away.

Once every few weeks she would take the initiative: she burned the thorns herself, the ones close to the shack, poured gasoline on them and set them alight. Terrified scorpions and lizards escaped from under the stones and thorns, fleeing in all directions. She stood there with the rake, black as a miner but with soot, conducting her own good fire. Once the flames got out of control, reached the path leading to the shack and took hold of the wooden fence. "You'll burn the house down in the end," my brother raged, throwing sand on the flames and looking for the hose: "In the end you'll destroy it with your nonsense." She looked as if she'd been woken from a dream. Distracted, wringing her hands, but this time in embarrassment, she justified herself in a small voice: "It's so it won't burn down because of the fire."

Sand

THERE WERE THREE of us in the shack: my big brother, my big sister, and me. She didn't count, she was the shack. Because she had no sense of history, there was no moment when the shack came to life: it had existed either forever or not at all, because she never stopped creating it. There were bits and pieces of reality and semifiction, secondhand leftovers of pioneering folklore: she remembered, for example, the sand dunes. She remembered them with acrimony, because they were still there and in her opinion had even spread.

Sometimes she referred to a time as "when we came"—just that. "When we came." Dates were beyond her: the year of her birth, like the month and the day, were shrouded in mist, because in Egypt her father had been negligent registering the arrival of his children. He would go to "the office" months and sometimes years after they were born, make up dates and towns of birth. She was registered as having been born in Livorno, Italy. She wasn't. But she had sentimental feelings for Livorno as the supposed town of her father's birth. When she wanted to make an impression she would say: "We're originally from Livorno." You might think she was trying to disguise her Middle-Eastern-Levantine background, but that would be nonsense: what she thought made an impression was not Middle Eastern or European, but the idea of being "originally" from somewhere. The idea that

we had origins, a pedigree, a foundation. The question of foundations both-
ered her greatly. She would say, "Him, he's got a good foundation."

"When the foundation is rotten, everything else is rotten." (The object
of this remark was usually Maurice.)

Or, "Don't clean from the top, start from the foundation."

Or, "How did you expect to turn out? We never had what's called a foundation."

A foundation moved her not only as an existential metaphor, but mainly
as concrete reality. Concrete to the marrow of her bones, she loathed the
vague, the clouded, and especially the convoluted. She lingered for hours
(hours? long enough) at the great caverns of building sites, excited and
wide-eyed as a child. staring at the cement mixers slowly making their way
down the mounds of earth to cast the foundations, at the great cranes topped
by a swaying glass cabin with a swaying man inside it, at the big trucks
of sand and gravel stopping the traffic, riveted by the curtains of pure
yellow sand streaming from the truck into the pit, which, unlike the sand
dunes surrounding the shack, were distant and beautiful, and above all
knew their place. The hated sand dunes did not know their place, they stood
in her path in every sense. Impossible to eradicate, the sand dunes defeated
all attempts to cover them up, to conceal or tame them, like the first layer
of paint in an oil painting, which peeps out of the subsequent layers, a
reminder of the past, forcing the past, the foundation, into the present.

The shack had no foundation, not really. It had been simply set down
in the dunes. Sometime at the beginning of the fifties, trucks arrived and
unloaded prefabricated shacks, putting them down at random on the sand
dunes in the new immigrants' transit camp: "When they got tired, they
stopped and put one down," she said.

The sands were all the same and the shacks were all the same. During
the long dark nights people got lost in the dunes, knocked on strange doors,
looking for their shack. People sometimes wandered lost in the moonlight
until three o'clock in the morning. Until Maurice arrived (he stayed then
for about half an hour) and came up with an idea: all the men, the heads of
households, would put a flagpole on their roofs and fly a petticoat or nightgown belonging to their wives. Nobody would get lost. And that's what happened. "Yes, believe me, that's what happened," said the mother, with a
grave, stern expression on her face that seemed to match a different thought

and a different story, which had apparently gone astray in her mind and ended up in the wrong neighborhood, at the wrong door, like the people in the story about the petticoats in the sand dunes, which of all the stories about Maurice was the one she chose to tell.

Three O'Clock in the Morning

THE CHILD WAS woven by a thousand visible and invisible threads into Nona's story, because the mother was silent. In the spaces of the silence left by the mother Nona talked and talked. The power of the imagination, which Nona possessed in plenty, did not defeat the power of memory, which she also possessed in abundance: she repeated the story, written and directed and acted in her mind, letter by letter, word by word, with the same pauses and stresses, the same theatrical pathos, the same transitions from language to language in exactly the same places, even the same technical hitches, a power outage that darkened the stage for a moment at exactly the same place in the plot.

Did the child sit on her lap while she told the story? No, the place on Nona's lap was taken by the ashtray. This was the time for her cigarette, after eating and before resting. The child sat at her feet, on the thin mat her uncle had once brought from the Bedouin market in Beersheba. The Nona couldn't see the colors that the child told her: red, yellow, blue, green, brown. The Nona practiced the colors with the child in French: *rouge, jaune, bleu, vert, brun*.

The child repeated the colors every day, even when the mat was no longer there: the mother threw it out one day in a rage after it got tangled up in Nona's feet, not for the first time, and she tripped and fell. "That's all

I need, a wheelchair," said the mother. Nona was silent, puffing on her cigarette without inhaling the smoke, the blank lenses of her glasses misting
over (by this stage she couldn't see a thing and the glasses were for show).
"*Indi karami*," the Nona said to the child after her silence came to an end,
after the mother left the room. "I have my self-respect."

The child couldn't understand the connection between the mat and
the "*karam*," Nona's self-respect. She asked, "But what's the connection. Tell
me what the connection is." Nona turned her head aside and hid her face:
the face that had been turned toward the child before was now turned
away, to look blankly at the glass panes in the front door. Perhaps the Nona
didn't understand the word "connection" or perhaps it was one of her
moments of deliberate deafness. In the end she said something. She said:
"Only God sees what I have in my heart." But that wasn't true. Everyone
saw. "Everyone" was the mother and the child, the child's brother and
her sister. "But Maurice," said the Nona, "he sees for himself, he's like me.
He's your father," she went on. "You remember that Maurice is your father?"
"Yes," said the child. "Tell me what you remember about him," she asked,
"tell me things." "I don't remember things," said the child. "You do remember
things about him, I know you do," said Nona, stretching out her hand to
touch the child on her forehead, but touching her eyelashes instead. "Whenever your heart sleeps for Maurice, wake it up, because he's your father
and his heart is awake for you. Do you understand?" "Yes," said the child,
and she pinched Nona on her right arm, which was both withered and
swollen. Nona had to have a special sleeve made for her dresses. "Make
room for me."

Now they were both sleeping in Nona's bed, covered up to the neck by
the heavy blanket. Nona slept on her back and the child slept on her side,
burying her forehead in Nona's arm, not the swollen one, the normal one,
smelling her elbow through noisy breath. "What a good smell," said the
child. "It's from the good soap they brought me, I kept it in my clothes. Until
yesterday, when I said to myself, *Yallah ya bint*, who are you keeping the
good things for, the dead?" the Nona explained as her eyelids closed, the
white, transparent lids covering her metallic blue eyes. "Don't sleep,"
the child requested. "I'm not sleeping, I'm resting," said Nona in a heavy
voice. The child waited a moment or two, footsteps pounded in the next-
door house to the right of Nona's quarter-shack, or to the left, in Rachel

Amsalem's father's house. "You're sleeping, you're sleeping," said the child. "No I'm not, I'm just closing my eyes for a bit, to let them rest," said the Nona with difficulty.

The child turned onto her back, distancing herself, marking a border between herself and the Nona with her finger on the mattress so their bodies wouldn't touch, a deep long moat between two now-hostile states. She examined the map of moldy stains on the dank ceiling: the fat one on the right was angry when they brought it food not from a can, it ate the *amm*'s cow but only the skin, without the meat, so it would have black cow fur on the inside, too, and whenever it wanted it could turn itself inside out and both sides would be the same, but its aunt on the left, who was browner, saw that everyone was running away from her—her fingers, head, arms were all running away—and she began shooting at them so they would come back quick, but only the fingers came back, all except the thumbs, which hid inside something and only came back after they had grown all by themselves in an envelope full of sugar.

A voice suddenly emerged on her right, from under the layers, as if from the depths of the floor. It was the Nona continuing some train of thought: "Maurice brought me that good soap. He knows how to bring all the good things." She paused for a moment: "When he wants to, he knows to bring the best things." She rubbed her stocking feet against the feet of child, who was now close under the blanket and lay her head on Nona's broad, soft, liquidy stomach. "You came out of my stomach, you did, said the Nona from far, far away, from the open air inside the room, and then added reluctantly, "It's as if you came out of my stomach."

The child sat up, "as if" at the beginning of a story, the beginning of the beginning. The Nona, too, raised herself heavily from lying to a sitting position, leaning against the two flat pillows propped up against the wall. The iron railing of the bed pressed against the base of her spine, but she didn't notice. The child leaned over to the side table, took a cigarette out of the packet, lit it, puffed on it once, and handed it to Nona with the ashtray. The Nona looked straight ahead, with great preparation and a certain veiling of her eyes: it wasn't the concentration of an effort to remember but of self-hypnosis.

Her voice was thick, hoarse, saturated with the vapors of a mix of grief and enthusiasm. "She got rid of them all before you came, the mother. Zizi in Egypt she didn't get rid of, he died on his own, but all the others that came afterward she got rid of like kittens, because Maurice left. How would she raise them? When you were in her stomach she wanted to get rid of you, too. "Enough," she said, "I've had enough." She fell silent, as if listening to the faint voice of the radio. "And what happened then?" asked the child, playing with the Nona's hand lying on the blanket, counting the hollows in the place where the fingers ended.

"And then I had a dream. One night before she was going to get rid of you I dreamed. In my dream the white man came to me. He came from the back, not from the front, he spoke to me and I didn't see his face, the words came from behind. Don't let her get rid of this baby, he said, this baby will bring good luck." She stopped again, gently withdrawing her hand from the child's grip, stroking her chin, her lids closing over her eyes, leaving a narrow slit. "Well?" asked the child.

"I went to her. I picked myself up and sat with her all night before she went to get rid of it, till three o'clock in the morning I sat with her and told her what the white man had said. I said to her, 'Have this baby for me, give it to me. It will bring us luck, you and me.' And she agreed. She cried and cried, and I cried with her, and she agreed, and that's how you came."

"And what happened afterward?" the child asked, disappointed. "Nothing, life," said the Nona. "As if you came out of my stomach."

The front door opened, forcing a ringing slap of air into Nona's sealed room. The mother appeared, one quick look, only for a second. "*Yallah*, home, enough for today," she said to the child, abruptly pulling off the blanket. "Get up, let's go." "Get up *ya habibti*," the frightened Nona hurried her. "Go to your house." The child laced her shoes with exquisite slowness, wet the laces with spit, and pulled them very straight before threading them into the holes, stealing a sidelong look at the mother's calves in their thick brown nylon stockings, the memory of whose slippery touch sent cold shivers down her spine. "Why is the child shivering, does she have a fever?" asked the mother from on high, in the dense air above the child's head that grew hot and cold by turns.

THE NIGHT BEFORE

THE NIGHT BEFORE the morning of her death, in the hospital. We gathered without coordinating in advance, coming together for a moment on common ground, because of a common concern—her. My brother in work clothes that were so ostentatiously work clothes as to be a cartoon of work clothes. My sister with the luxury of petit fours that my brother polished off in the blink of an eye and the casual luxury of her outfit, her platinum blond hair combed back with oil, her crocodile, or leopard, or something skin handbag. In those flat hospital room colors, in that visual bleakness, she appeared like a radiant strip of halogen, my sister Corinne.

"Why are you in work clothes? Didn't you go home to clean up a little?" the mother asks Sammy with obvious satisfaction, her face glowing: how she loves his work outfit, the demonstrative shabbiness, the declaration of manual labor. He understands what she is saying: he is the beloved son. My sister-in-law sent strawberries, warning him not to eat them on the way but he did. He lay the green plastic basket with the handful of remaining strawberries on the mother's sheet. "I'll wash them," Corinne said sternly, rebuking my brother with a look for not paying attention, not to the strawberries or to the dance of looks and hints that is going on. Oblivious he fished a dirty check folded in three from his trouser pocket and smoothed it out. "Sign it," he said to the mother, "I need a signature here." She signed. She had a habit of wetting the tip of the pen with her tongue, which left a little blob of blue ink behind. "Is it for that building materials guy?" she asked. My brother nodded with immense weariness, rubbing his eyes with grease-stained fingers. The pickup got stuck on the way; he left it in Gat Rimon and came here on foot. With the strawberries.

In the meantime my sister washed them and put them on one of the blue plastic hospital plates. She looked with revulsion at the permanent brown stains on the plastic, and placed a paper napkin on the plate to hide them. "It was a nice day today," said the mother. "I got up for a bit and saw that it was a nice day." A light cloud passed over her face. "Did you water the roses, so they won't dry up, poor things?" she asked my brother. He didn't answer, having fallen asleep on the armchair with his legs stretched out in front of him, his head tilted sideways, his mouth open. I sat on the edge of the bed and Corinne stood, stood, stood, looking at the mother in supplication, in boundless rage. "There's no doctor, we can never find the doctor here," she said. The mother examined a hexagonal cookie tin. "The way they know how to make these tins today," she marveled absentmindedly, stroking the tin with one hand while the other bunched the sheet in her fingers, bunched and let go. She gave off a kind of nervousness, but different, not the old kind, a nervousness of suspense and expectation in anticipation of something that held a big surprise for her, a prize. I looked at her with a certain apprehension, embarrassed by the new language of her body, the expression on her face: tension and tenderness, a suppressed gaiety, her cheeks seemed freshly ironed, glittering. She glittered with something, inside something, perhaps a promise. She held out the cookie tin to me: "Take."

I took one, sniffed absentmindedly, and bit into it. She looked at me. "*Allahu aalam*, you're just like your Nona. She'd sniff everything like that before she put it in her mouth. You remember how she used to drive me crazy by smelling everything like she was being poisoned?" she asked. Corinne came tapping on her high heels, bringing in dark tea from the kitchen. "Drink. It's good with those cookies." Her fingers were still bunching the sheet but not moving, in their muteness almost rebutting the animated gaiety of her look. "Why have you brought me tea, am I sick?" she said.

SHE SAID

OF MY BROTHER Sammy she said, "When he gets hurts, it's me who says ay."
My brother was her firstborn son, her portrait of herself from a different
geography, a different fate. She looked at him as if at dark water that reflected
someone if not exactly herself then some woman standing before her with
a face obliterated by sorrow. She looked at him with infinite yearning, with
dread, with longing for her dread, for her love. He was the "wound-child."
The child who was a wound. I said to her once, *"mon fils mon horreur"* (a quotation from a French translation of Akhmatova, I don't remember which
poem); she thought for a minute and repeated the words, holding them in
her mouth:

"Mon fils mon horreur. Yes."

This notion, "my son my dread," reached deep into her soul, deep into
the well where the hook on the end of the rope hits the hard cement at the
bottom, and the hook bangs on the cement, trying to get through to the
water beneath the water: the child who is the son, who is the dread, who is
the young girl. The son who is the girl.

She was a girl when she became pregnant, a child-mother, sixteen years
old. Nona married her off at fifteen to a man years older, wealthy, religiously
observant, from *harat el yahud*, the Jewish quarter in Cairo. There was a situation at home: Grandfather Izak lost the family property to gambling
debt, and Nona took the initiative and did something about it. "It was her

decision. My father didn't have a say in the matter," said the mother, when she said anything. The facts related to that marriage and to the circumstances of the marriage only came up in subordinate clauses to the main clauses spoken by others, not by her; they emerged from the flow and were submerged beneath it like the tips of basalt rocks, whose great bodies were sunk in the ambiguous waters of the phrase "apparently."

Apparently she was married against her will.

Apparently she was tortured.

Apparently she was beaten during her pregnancy.

Apparently she escaped from her husband's house in the dead of night, dressed only in her nightgown.

Apparently she was in the seventh month of her pregnancy with my brother when she ran away.

Apparently there was a scandal: Egypt, Cairo, a girl from a good family.

Apparently her husband divorced her, he never saw her again, he never acknowledged the child as his son.

Apparently Maurice (a close friend of her elder brother, a frequent visitor to her parents' home) was waiting only for this, for her, never mind her condition.

Apparently they got married, she and Maurice, when she was about to give birth.

Apparently "he was the only one who would have done such a thing," only Maurice: to not give a damn about convention or blood ties, to take the child as his son, to love him like a son, to raise him or not, just as he didn't raise his biological children, with no discrimination.

She banished the father of her son from her existence, just as he had banished her; she never mentioned his name, neither his given nor his family name. Faceless, good or bad—he was and remained anonymity incarnate: not even "a man" but "manhood" in the abstract. The reckoning of pain and rage sealed in his banishment was only the beginning, a pathway leading to something else. And this thing was her deep perception, physical and non-verbal, of the natural order of things. In the natural order of things there was an island. And an ocean surrounding it. And on the island were a mother and her son, a son and his mother, only them, a single soul. The son and the mother were the island, and all the visitors who came were nothing but a disturbance: the fathers, biological and non-biological, the children who were not the son, *mon fils mon horreur,* which became the name she gave herself, not the one she was given at birth.

We knew about the island and the worship of the island, which rubbed abrasively against our flesh but also took place far beyond it, high above the arithmetic of sibling rivalry, above the petty details of biography and circumstances of life, even above love itself. We knew what we needed to know: the mutual embrace of the mother and her son was the embrace of orphans, and the worship of the island was the worship of orphanhood, my brother's and her own, which were welded together.

Once, decades later, my brother's biological father turned up, via emissaries. In the middle of the Six-Day War two men arrived, apparently the father's brothers, standing at the end of the path leading to the shack, on the verge of the road. They stood and stood, in the end they sent the woman next door. They only wanted to know if he was alive, my brother; they thought they had seen his name in the lists of the dead. She didn't go to them, she went on digging vigorously in the rose bed behind the house, not stopping for a minute. "Tell them it's all right." She sent me.

THE ROSE GARDEN (1)

THERE WAS THE main path leading to the shack, but there were three more paths, coming from all directions, which meant you could reach the shack from the four points of the compass, but they were used mainly by animals, not people: stray dogs and cats, the mother hated the cats with all her heart—they were sly, impudent, thieving, bold, noisy, and they had kittens all the time. They overturned the garbage can at the entrance to the house. ("Damn that she-cat to hell, she's knocked over the garbage again.") It was a major concern, that garbage can next to the poplar tree, close to where the path met the asphalt road: she couldn't leave it alone. Early in the morning, still in her nightgown, she ran to the can, to examine the damage of the night and in the same breath to correct it: she raked up the trash scattered by the "she-cat" (one or many, the cats always took on the singular feminine form, "the she-cat," like a distillation of the satanic essence of the breed as a whole), washed the can down with the hose, leaving a little lake at the entrance to the house for us to tramp in, and finally weighed down the lid with a heavy brick she dragged from my brother's welding shop, securing it with a rope tied to the handles on either side. For a day or two there was quiet, the she-cat was defeated by these measures, but so was Nona. They shared the garbage can, she and the mother, in Nona's opinion at least. For long minutes at a time she stood in the blazing sun of the afternoon with her little garbage pail, waiting for someone, "some man," to remove the heavy brick from the lid. "I'll go to Jina's," she threatened.

"Go, *ya sitti*, go." The mother waved her arm. "It's a free country, everyone can throw out their garbage wherever they like." But she said it just for the purpose of argument: if only she could have (*inshallah ya rabb* if only I could), she would have cast every one of those people who "throw out their garbage wherever they like" into torture dungeons for the rest of their lives, or at least until they mended their ways. The corruption of the entire Jewish people, those being reborn in their land and those who weren't, was embodied in the garbage and in their relation to the garbage, the excretions that were thrown out of the house to pollute the surroundings. "I don't know what kind of people we are." She would shake her head with an affected expression of bewilderment on her face. "I really don't know what kind of people they are, these Jews, who spend a fortune on sofas and curtains in their homes, and don't care about all the garbage and the filth right outside their door."

"You, why should you care? What business is it of yours?" the Nona dared to call into question not the meaning of her words, but the spirit, definitely the spirit. Her reforming zeal, her crusading pathos, the way in which the mother instinctively saw almost every public issue as something personal, "her business"—all this gave rise in Nona to astonishment and revulsion at what she saw as common vulgarity and coarseness, unbecoming to a girl from a good family.

"You'll see," she whispered gloomily when the mother left the room to go to the toilet. "You'll see, one day they'll bury her in the garden, *fi elgnena*, with the hoe in her hand," she said, spitting out the words "*fi elgnena*" like a spoiled pistachio nut, smoothing the towel spread over her knees with her hand and staring at the rectangle of dazzling light, which stared back at her and spilled over onto the crooked tiles of the floor.

The door to her room stayed wide open; all day long until night fell, open to two branching paths: the main path leading to the road and the other path connecting her quarter-shack to our shack. The mother could cross the path in a moment, devouring it with her stride, it took me three minutes, and Nona ten: slowly making her way down the slope, stepping on the broken tiles, left over from some uprooted floor and stuck together here, careful not to let her dress snag on the thorns at the sides of the path. She buried her hands in the pockets of her dress, her fingers busy, rubbing and crushing the fabric; she would have three or four jasmine blossoms there, plucked from the hedge for the smell, and a handkerchief. She would proceed down the path, her fingers moving as she walked, and when she reached the edge of the mother's green lawn, the roses she had transplanted from the bed behind the shack to the front, to the right of the lawn, she would stop: the sprinkler. There she stood, the Nona, listening to the jets of the sprinkler, waiting for somebody to turn off the tap. The mother saw her from her porch, she did not move, she watched. Nona went on standing, wondering what to do. In the end she raised her voice: "Lucette, the sprinkler!" The mother did not move, trying to remove one of the thorns stuck in her fingers with tweezers. "Lucette!" Nona's voice rose hesitantly, then firmly, finally despairingly: "Lucette! Lucette!"

THE ROSE GARDEN (2)

I F ALL THE plants of the garden competed, the rose would defeat its rivals. For everything that the heart desires from a flower, the rose provides in abundance.

Beauty, delicacy, smell, and color. And not only its blooms. Its fruit is decorative, its foliage delicate, its bushes colorful, and its branches variegated.

The cultivation of the rose has always been challenging. It appears to be a special task, demanding careful attention, the combat of disease, plentiful watering, correct fertilization, professional pruning . . . on the other hand, a garden without roses is like a body without a soul. No other flower has given rise to so many legends. And no other plant has so many uses. From ancient times to our own day, the rose has been used for medicine and cosmetics, food and drink, and many other diverse purposes.

Roses are divided into a number of popular varieties:

Hybrid teas: these originated in a Chinese species imported to Europe by traders in tea, hence the name. When we speak of the classic rose, what we usually see is a rose of this type. It has tens of thousands of strains used for picking and other purposes.

Polyantha: the origins of this group are in various species and it is characterized by dense, herbaceous growth and low height. The inflorescence developing on the branches emerging from the base of the plant is plentiful and consists of clusters of many small flowers.

Floribunda: this is a species that combines characteristics of the hybrid tea with those of the polyantha. The number of clusters is small but the individual blooms are large and resemble those of the hybrid tea. They create an expanse of color in the garden but their flowers can also be picked for the vase.

Grandiflora : very similar to the floribunda and originating in the crossing of this species with the hybrid tea. They bear large flowers in small clusters.

Dwarf roses: they originate in the Chinese dwarf rose and other hybrids. They appear in all the other categories but their flowers are small and few.

Climbers: the classic climbers bloom once a year in large clusters consisting of small flowers. Their growth is vigorous and very strong. Flexible herbaceous growth. They are used to cover high fences, hedges, and out-of-the-way expanses.

THE ROSE GARDEN (3)

S HE FIRST PLANTED the floribunda, combining the characteristics of the
hybrid tea and the polyantha, behind the shack, in the long bed under
the windows of the hall and the living room, which she changed around
four times, and she changed the floribunda, too, after a few weeks, for
classic climbers blooming in large clusters, which changed places and
moved to the side of the shack, in the area between the shack and the
brick wall of the welding shop, until they failed to flourish and she moved
them back again to the back of the house, but this time to a new bed, to
the right of the lawn next to the laundry lines, instead of the polyantha,
which dried up completely and were thrown into the trash, or were
burned together with the hybrid teas that were planted in front of the
house, close to the path, in neat rows, where they bloomed once and never
again, crushed by the heavy branches of the mango tree, which she
sawed off to thin them out, and in their place she planted grandiflora
bushes, some of which were left where they were and some uprooted and
moved five yards away to the narrow strip of ground between the paving
stones of the porch and the lawn, and they, too, failed to flourish, and for
a while she tried to revive them in the big clay pots she bought from
Marko, until she gave up and exchanged them for dwarf roses of the

rambling variety, or the grandiflora polyantha hybrid tea, the Chinese or European species.

She wiped her hands covered with loose soil on the hem of her dress, sadly pursing her lips: "I don't understand why I never succeed with these roses."

THE GARDEN: "ELGNENA"

"ELGNENA" AS A tireless arena of experiment, substitution, and change. *Elgnena* as a battlefield.

Elgnena as unsuspended desire, eluding her the harder she tried to take hold of it.

Elgnena in place of suspended desire, her suspended desires.

Elgnena as the place where she tried to tame herself, in vain.

Elgnena as the place where she hardly learned anything, where she refused to learn.

Elgnena as an ancient, childish vision of purity, order, and beauty.

Elgnena as the defeat of order, purity, and beauty.

Elgnena as a playground, a sandbox, plastic blocks.

Elgnena as a constant yearning for the real, not as-if home, that she wanted to make for herself.

Elgnena as an invitation to climb a slippery mountain slope, to reach the peak, the rose garden.

Elgnena as a penal colony, a forced labor camp—for her, for her fellows.

Elgnena as a sanatorium.

Elgnena as a natural extension of the interior of the house, with the furniture and everything.

Elgnena is hers, only hers, hers.

Elgnena as an extorter of money, thousands and thousands of liras and shekels buried in its ground.

Elgnena as the main source of income for the owner of the plant nursery, Marko, who built a whole house from her horticultural ignorance.

Elgnena as a protest.

Elgnena as a protest against knowledge in favor of capricious, ignorant love, the opposite of knowledge.

Elgnena as a protest against the non-gardening neighbors.

Elgnena as a protest against herself.

Elgnena as a manifesto of love for the nature she never knew, never saw.

Elgnena as the aspiration for a life with a sky.

Elgnena as a pledge to something.

Elgnena instead of the yearning of the body, her body.

Elgnena instead of the body of a loving woman, her body in her imagination with the shutters closed.

Sky

S HE GAVE THE child to Nona, twenty days after she was born. This was
the agreement between them and also a necessity: that she would give
the baby to Nona and go back to work "after twenty days." She always
spoke about babies in days: twenty, forty. She would say, "When a baby
has forty days, it means he'll live. You have to wait for forty days."

The twenty days, however, turned into a scale with a number of
weights on it: that she had given the child to Nona, that she had gone to
work right after, that she was "like a lion" after the birth, after giving up
the child ("I was like a lion"), that she had been arrested for forty-eight
hours, together with the child ("the child had twenty days") because of
Maurice's debts, promissory notes he had made her sign before disappearing. They had let her go on the guarantee of Rabbi Nathaniel ("he was a
good man, *Allah yarhamo*") in whose Savyon home she worked. He brought
a fine gift for the child, a gift over the precise nature of which she and Nona
argued for years.

The mother said, "A gold bracelet with her initials on it." And Nona said,
"A blanket. He brought her a Bourbon-rose-colored blanket. It was my
brother Clement who sent the bracelet. Don't you remember, Lucette?"

She didn't remember, not exactly: going to bed with memory, delighting in its curves, were liberties available only to those who kept still, stayed
in one place, like the Nona. So at least she told herself: she had no time to

remember. She counted pain, too, even at the moment it happened, as a memory, a kind of illusion. She didn't believe in it.

Nona said that the child was sick. She got fatter and fatter with the quantities of semolina the Nona fed her, and Nona said that she didn't look right. There was something wrong with the child. Every day she pushed her in the carriage sent by Maurice's brother from Italy (was he the one who sent it?) to the clinic, for some kind of penicillin. If they didn't give her penicillin, or at least antibiotic pills, the Nona didn't sleep at night: "I didn't shut an eye," she said. They walked to the clinic along the long, roundabout asphalt road, not through the fields, lingering five or six times on the way. Nona liked to linger. Her eyes never tired of gazing at the perfectly matching clothes, for which she was responsible, from the color of the baby's hat, the trim of her socks, to the collar of her dress: then she still had her eyes. "Is there some celebration today that you dressed her up like that? What are you celebrating, Madame Esther?" people asked her in the street. They didn't ask, they stopped her: "People stopped me in the street to ask, 'Where's the party, Madame Esther?'" said Nona.

"Stop it," the mother scolded her, "stop dressing her up every day. Who do you think she is?" But Nona didn't listen and she didn't stop. She sank up to her neck in her double- and triple-entry bookkeeping of the Evil Eye and her measures to counteract the Evil Eye, until she became so confused by the figures and calculations that she drowned in them.

"The child is sick" was an antidote to the Evil Eye of remarks like "Where's the party, Madame Esther?" but not effective enough against the frontal attack of "What a little doll!" against which only antibiotics would serve, but even they were useless against the worst of all: "What a healthy child." Here only shots of penicillin would do. So far everything was simple. But the accounting became more complicated and labyrinthine, with no way out, when the doctor herself, under the Nona's urging to prescribe something, said: "What a healthy child." Nona was speechless. She "saw everything black": the impenetrable barrier separating the world of the demons from that of the angels came tumbling down, and from then on every angel was a demon in disguise and every demon sported the halo of an angel.

All this paled into insignificance beside the most perverse and uncontrollable of all: the Evil Eye that "elbani-adam," human beings, inflicted on themselves. This, the Nona thought, was the greatest catastrophe of all, the

Evil Eye that people gave themselves, with envious, annihilating looks sent by one to the soul of another.

Nona's head spun. For hours she lay in her high iron bed, a prey to her thoughts, her eyes open and absent.

At the foot of the bed, on the floor, the child crawled or tottered, playing with the white or red beans fallen from the jar. She was a little over a year old and she knew the songs. Once in a while the Nona checked to see if she was all right. She started singing "*au pres de ma blonde*" and the child continued "*qu'il fait bon fait bon fait bon.*"

And once, in a tale told in the present continuous, perhaps more than once, the Nona on the verge of falling asleep sang "*au pres de ma blonde*" and was greeted by silence. The child had quietly disappeared: put on her lace-trimmed bonnet, dragged her Bourbon-rose blanket behind her, slipped out of the half-open door, and crawled down the three concrete steps of the quarter-shack. It was midday, the dirt track at the entrance to the shack was boiling hot, the asphalt road blazed. The child walked down the middle of the road, barefoot, the pink train of the blanket trailing behind her, sweeping the asphalt. She went past Jina's house, the nursery, and the hill of sand and thorns opposite the bend in the road leading to Savyon, and reached the bus stop. There they found her, somebody found her. "Where are you going, Toni, in the middle of the road?" the somebody asked her. "I'm going for a walk," the child replied. He picked her up and carried her back to Madame Esther, who had simply fallen asleep after the opening sentence of "*au pres de ma blonde.*"

The mother knew about this from the neighbors, not from the Nona: the Nona "turned everything around" so it came out like nothing, as if it were nothing at all. "How can I be quiet when you let her wander round like that, how?" the mother raged. "You're never quiet, *ya sitti*, why should you be quiet now?" Nona retorted. But she spoke to the child, the Nona, in three languages: "It's a good thing he never found you, that one," she said. The child pricked up her ears: "At night he's as big as a house, but transparent. By day he's as small as a cat's tail, but he's still as big as big can be," the Nona continued. "Who?" asked the child. "The white man. He's been seen lots of times in the neighborhood, lots of people have seen him. Guetta's daughter who's deaf and started to stammer? It's all because she saw him and ran away." The Nona fell silent and took a puff of her cigarette. "What does he do?" asked the child. Nona thought for a minute:

"When you walked down the road, did you feel a wind, like a kind of hot wind next to your face?" The child nodded. "That was him. That's how he begins to swallow, with a wind, because of not having any teeth, he swallows with a dry tongue."

That night the child couldn't sleep. She lay next to the Nona, in the high iron bed, and after a few minutes she sat up, lay down, and sat up again, staring at the rectangle of glass on the door. Nona cooked her semolina, sang songs, counted the little pads on the tips of her fingers, put a damp towel with drops of valerian on her forehead.

When the mother returned from work on the last bus, she found the child on Nona's lap. The Nona's dress was open in the front: she had bared a huge white breast with a dark pink nipple, which lay between the child's lax lips. The mother stood and looked. Nailed to the spot, she stood and stared and suddenly came to her senses. Her eyes darted round the room and found the Bourbon-rose blanket neatly folded on a chair. She snatched up the blanket, pulled the sleepy child off Nona's wide nipple, wrapped her in the blanket, and charged outside, the child in her arms, flew down the dark path under the dark tent of the sky between the two houses, breathless, her heavy bag hanging from her arm swaying from side to side, hitting the backside of the child who was half asleep with her eyes open.

Eyes Open

ALL NIGHT SHE would lie with her eyes open, waiting for morning; she would switch on the bedside lamp and switch it off again, read another few pages until her eyelids drooped. She couldn't fall asleep with the light from the little lamp, and she couldn't do without it: the nights were an interrupted sequence of flickers of light, between which lay areas of darkness. At some point she reached a compromise in her bargaining between light and dark: she threw a towel over the lampshade, half covering it. The light was very dim but it was still there, veiled and orange. My brother, Sammy, was afraid the towel would catch fire in the night, when everyone was sleeping, when she was sleeping. "But I never go to sleep all the way," she argued, "my sleep is light as a feather." He looked at her suspiciously out of the corner of his eye, shaking his head in an affectation of shocked disapproval: "The things you do, God save us from the things you do."

Hand in hand they went, Hansel and Gretel, up and down in the land of the endlessly terrifying possibilities of conflagration: when she was at the bottom of the seesaw, he was on top, when she was on top, he was at the bottom. No less theatrical than she, and in some ways far more so, quick to take fire, rushing in his imagination to the scene of the catastrophe, not rooted to the spot like her, but on the contrary: full of eagerness, great enthusiasm behind every roar of fear. He lived in the movies. That's what she said: "He lives in the movies."

He did live at the movies, in the cinemas in the neighborhood or in Tel Aviv: matinees, first show, second show, the same film. Surfing in their third-row seats, he and his friends polished off whole cardboard trays of chocolate-coated banana candies, sliding down and falling asleep on one another's shoulders. Afterward, sitting in the car crowded like puppies, until three or four in the morning, they went over what had happened in the movie and what could have happened, acting out whole scenes, choking with laughter at their inventions. They parked on the dirt road leading to the shack, close to the rectangular orange building of the welding shop, among the construction pipes lying on the ground outside the building, ready for work the next day. Once in a while one of them left the car to pee in the thorn field and ran back so as not to miss anything. We heard them from inside the house, the mother and I: voices rising and falling in the dark, dissolving into a murmur, blaring forth again in wild shouts of laughter. Afterward silence fell. Her little bedside lamp went on again, and I heard the shuffle of slippers. She went out to them. From the kitchen window I saw her outside, on the dirt road: completely white in her white nightgown, knocking on the car windows: "Get up already, *yallah*." They rolled out, still half huddled in sleep, my brother first and two others behind him, and fell on the ground in a huddle, moaning as if they were dying. "Enough with the acting." She aimed a light kick at Sammy's shoulder. "You have work tomorrow, how are you going to get up?" He went on lying on his side in the sand for a little while longer, then he rose on all fours, and all the way he followed her on all fours, barking, drooling, and trying to bite her ankle to the sounds of giggling from behind. "What are you laughing at, at your own foolishness?" She pretended to be insulted, trying to suppress her laughter and to escape from Sammy, lifting up her long nightgown.

In a matter of moments all was quiet again; he threw himself onto the carpet at the foot of my bed and fell asleep in his clothes. "Get up and go to bed," she tried. "Get up." In the end she gave up, covered him with a blanket, and went back to bed, switching on the towel-cloaked light again. Her sleep was over. Until half past five she went on lying with her eyes open, fixed on the same book, the same page. I got out of bed, skipping over my brother's body, and went to lie next to her, but not close, on the edge of the bed. I closed my eyes, pretended to be asleep, feeling the lying tremor of my eyelids, the orange light of the lamp penetrating them. She lay on her back, staring at the gleaming Formica doors of the wall closet opposite her: "Why aren't you asleep, you?" she whispered. The purple walls of the room closed in on us, or so I imagined when I saw them through my eyelids, moving closer toward us, surrounding the bed on all sides, standing at our heads as if they were waiting for us. At my side I felt the movement of her thighs, slightly jolting the mattress. I felt that she wasn't sleeping, that she wasn't going to sleep. A delicate despair, lonely as the head of a pin in the wastes of the wilderness, rose from something in the rhythm of her breathing, the position of her body, a despair that didn't want anything, and wasn't addressed to anything, not even to herself. I heard her get up, open the shutters, lean out of the window, get dressed in yesterday's clothes hanging on the hook, bending down next to me, at the side of the bed, to straighten the pale green rug, the nephew of the dark green carpet on which my brother was sleeping at the foot of my bed.

The Same Book (1)

S HE READ. SHE would lay with her eyes open all night, switching the bedside lamp off and then switching it on again, returning to the same book lying on its back, open at the same page. What did she read? Almost always detective stories, always in French. She spoke Hebrew but she barely recognized the letters: women of her class in Cairo did not read and write Hebrew, only men, and not all of them. At some stage Grandfather Izak, her father, suddenly felt a pedagogical urge to hire a Hebrew teacher to teach her and her brothers at their house. They learned nothing. "We made his life a misery, poor man": they threw the Nona's feather comforters on him from the top of the stairs, they hid away, they smeared his glasses with flour and water paste, they glued the pages of his books together, they planned an engagement party for him and the neighbor's ugly daughter and invited the whole quarter. The teacher ran away. "I'll pay you not to have to teach them," he said to Grandfather Izak.

The story about the Hebrew teacher and his troubles filled the mother with satisfaction but not gloating. All the victims in the story were pitiable. "That poor teacher," she would say, "My poor father, may he rest in peace," and even "Poor Nona." Even Nona.

"Poor Nona" would take her out of school to look after her little brothers while she herself went to the mountains to stay at sanatoriums and convalescent homes. "One week I would go to school, one week she would take me out, decide that she was sick," the mother recalled resentfully. For years she swore that her hatred of doctors and medicine and illness came from all the fainting spells and weakness and swooning that attacked Nona as if she were the heroine of a nineteenth-century novel and sent her to bed for days on end. "The whole house would jump to attention, the whole house, because of her and her ailments."

The truth was that she actually liked two or three nineteenth-century novels, especially two of them by a father and son: Alexandre Dumas père and Alexandre Dumas fils. *The Three Musketeers* and *The Lady of the Camellias*. Every few months she would take out the old volumes that Maurice had once bought her and read them again. Alongside the ordinary "everyday" books, the dozens and hundreds of detective stories her sister sent from France, she had the ones she kept for best, the really good ones, the musketeers and the camellias. She knew both of them almost by heart, even with her memory, which was usually short, erratic, and irritable but expanded when she owed someone something, never mind what: then she remembered in minute detail exactly when, where, and how much, "down to the last penny."

She returned again and again to *The Lady of the Camellias* with a solemnity that was almost reverential; she spoke about her and even with her, in a low, discreet voice that became suddenly refined in the presence of the spectral tubercular thinness of the saintly courtesan Marguerite Gautier. When she told the story she would mainly dwell on one crucial, harrowing scene: Marguerite Gautier is crucified. She agrees to her own crucifixion, sacrificing herself for the sake of her beloved's future, for the sake of pure and absolute love, which triumphs over every interest and earthly desire. Her sacrifice is a secret, something between her and the father of her beloved, who demands that she leave his son alone, but more important, it is a secret that she shares only with God, not with society. Marguerite Gautier the courtesan is pure, white as snow. Society is dirty, the society that judges Marguerite and crucifies her is dirty. Marguerite Gautier is a victim of dirty society, "beautiful and white as an angel, poor thing," she said, her eyes filming over, perhaps with tears, perhaps because of the burning sensation in her left eye, her hand reaching for her cup of coffee, raising it to her mouth, but not to drink, only to rest her dry lips on its warm rim.

The Same Book (2)

S ATURDAY AFTERNOON, THE beginning of autumn, the living room dark
with the lamp in the north window already lit at four o'clock: she and
my sister, Corinne, sitting on the two sofas set at right angles, their feet
tucked up beneath them, on the low table a plate of cookies stuffed with
dates, drowning in lakes of white frosting. On the glass tabletop, around
the plate, are little mounds of powdered sugar. No one wipes the table. They
look sideways and down, not at each other, weeping for Marguerite Gautier.

The Same Book (3)

WHEN THE CHILD was five years old, Maurice turned up at the shack for the first time. For the first time she could denote an event in her own mind, a clear, perceived event, with a beginning, middle, and end; she could remember it through her own eyes, not through anyone else's, not in anyone else's language. The event had an order, a sequence, one thing followed another: he came in through the door, he slept there for three days, he left through the door when the three days were over. That was his back, when he left, receding down the path, clad in a rayon "wash-and-wear" shirt in a grayish-blue color, with two big pockets in the front. He didn't call her "the child" but Toni, which was more or less her name. "What's this 'the child'?" he said. " 'The child' is like 'the dog,' " he said, "or 'the cat.' "

In the book Maurice brought her there was a picture of a dog and also a cat. They were both black. The dog had his tail between his legs and his ears pricked up, and the cat had a tail that stood straight up in the air and jagged ears, as if they had been cut with zigzag scissors. The child outlined the jagged edges of the cat's ears with a red pen. "Why are you scribbling in the book?" asked Maurice, but he wasn't cross, he was distracted. He was thinking about something else. He told her the other thing he was thinking about: "This is the beginning," he tapped on the slender book with his long tanned finger, "it's the basis. And when you learn the letters you'll get to know the words. And afterward the sentences and after that the stories, everything that exists in this interesting world of ours."

Maurice sat, still in his jacket, on the sofa that the mother had in the meantime put in the hall, until she found it another place or another home, and the child sat next to him with her legs crossed, in her pajamas. After he came they brought her in her pajamas from Nona's quarter-shack, for him to see her. Before she had been sleeping in Nona's bed, but now she was wide awake, turning the pages of the little book from right to left. Maurice corrected her, turned the book around: "It's French, from left to right," he told her.

On the first page were the vowels, without pictures. They began with the vowels, Maurice started and she imitated him:

A, E, I, O, U.

The child managed the A, E, I very well, but not the O, U. The pronunciation of each letter, and especially the transition between them, was like balancing on skates or a rolling barrel. Maurice said that she had to practice every day, three times a day, like brushing her teeth. "But I don't brush my teeth," said the child. Maurice laughed: "She's got a mouth on her." The hall was yellow, the walls were yellow, and the light shed by the lampshade dangling from the ceiling was yellow, too, but a different, murky yellow: in some dreams the yellow poured over everything in sight, and the dream said, "This is me," letting the child know that she was dreaming.

Maurice sat on the edge of the sofa bed, his legs crossed, the halo of yellow lamplight above the silvery black of his hair, smoking. The mother stood with the kitchen towel in her hands, as if she had just popped in from the kitchen for a minute and was about to go back there, looking at both of them, listening to both of them. Afterward she sat on the armchair, next to the sofa bed, the kitchen towel still in her hand. They were all waiting, as if they were sitting in a dentist's waiting room. The silence that fell after the pronunciation of the vowels was measured in Maurice's cigarettes: cigarette by cigarette. The child looked at the pictures in the book, the letters, in silence. She didn't look at her mother: she knew how pale she was. And then the mother said in French: "Why did you come?"

He didn't know. Perhaps he shrugged his shoulders. His lean dark neck pressed into his chest, as if tightened by a coiled spring, leaving no gaps between the vertebrae. "Go to bed, *yallah*," the mother said to the child.

"Which bed?" asked the child. The mother's and Maurice's eyes locked, for a long moment they held fast. "My bed," said the mother, her gaze still gripped by his: "Get into my bed." The child went to bed, taking the book with the French letters with her, switched on the mother's bedside lamp, arranged the two pillows at her head, propped up against the headrest, and leaned against them to page through the book. Afterward the mother came and turned off the light, but she went on sitting up with her back against the pillows, holding the little book in her hands.

A faint, indirect light reached the room from the kitchen, where the two of them were sitting, the mother and Maurice: from the fluorescent light above the kitchen table the light crept toward the cubbyhole where she or her brother sometimes slept, turned into the side entrance leading to the bedroom, and came in from there, weak and crooked. Its weakness was the same as the sound, the voices coming from the kitchen, which sounded as sick as the light, and then they suddenly recovered, rose with renewed strength, and fell sick again, as weak as her hands holding the book, as her feet under the blanket, like the light, like the voices. Then a glass smashed. The child closed her eyes tightly, her face tense; she raised the pages of the book to her nose, to smell them. And then the noise of the toilet flushing. "But I can't, I can't, Lucette," Maurice's voice rose, vehement and pleading: "I can't, I can't."

In the morning the side of the bed next to the child was tidy, undisturbed, and Maurice was sitting on the porch, wearing the same clothes as yesterday, drinking his coffee and staring through his dark horn-rimmed glasses at the revolutions of the sprinkler. For a while she stood and looked, especially at the nail of his left pinkie, which was very long, curved, and yellowish. She went and sat on his lap, but with her back to him, as if she was sitting on a chair, her calves hanging over his, gazing like him at the turning sprinkler. His hands clasped her waist. The floor of the porch was flooded with water: the mother had doused it with the hose. Then she swept the water up with vigorous movements of the squeegee, spraying it in all directions, her nightgown soaked, clinging to her thighs and backside. Maurice shifted his legs, now he set his left leg on his right, and the child wobbled, almost fell off his knees, but steadied herself again. "I brought you another book but I forgot it on the bus. It's a pity I forgot it," said Maurice. The child was silent, passed her finger over his long, curved nail, over its tip. "But I'll send it to you by mail," said Maurice. "As soon as I get there

I'll send it, and you'll know that it's the same book." "What book is it?" asked the child, and the mother approached them with the squeegee and hit the legs of Maurice's chair with it. "Move," she said. They stood up and Maurice moved the chair to the corner of the porch, next to the two big potted plants, and dropped the ash of his cigarette into the pot. The child sat down on his lap again, but this time sideways, breathing in the smell of his clothes, his skin: tobacco, shaving lotion, and something else that smelled like roasted almonds. "The book is called *David Copperfield* and it was written by an English writer, Charles Dickens. It's the first book to read, because it's the best of all," said Maurice.

She peeked at his face as he said this, his face with the horn-rimmed dark glasses and the broad, drooping lower lip that quivered slightly, she wanted to see his face when he said "the best of all," and afterward, when she took her eyes from him and counted the paving stones on the path leading to Nona's house, she became confused and started counting again from the beginning. Then, too, she thought "the best of all, the best of all," shifting her gaze from the paving stones and the dizzying lines joining them, turning it to the roof, Nona's hot gray-tiled roof, which now seemed to be melting in the sun, about to explode at any minute into a thousand sparks and then to melt, to pour like heavy lava over the outer walls, over Nona's front door and three concrete steps, and the "best of all" poured too, the "best of all," which was a thought and words poured into her, melted and turned into a thing, a vapor, or spirit, or the air joining and separating the things that had a name.

The mother got dressed and went to work, said, "Good, I'm going," and went, leaving them alone. Until midday Maurice went on sitting on the porch with "the papers": flimsy pages, printed on both sides and marked in blue ink, which he took out of his bag with the slightly rusted buckle, which the child opened and closed, closed and opened. The coffee cups stood next to him, cup by cup, the cigarette butts sank into their fleshy, muddy dregs like the corpses of worms. Once or twice he took a break, went to Nona's to drink more coffee and listen to the radio. The child went with him, hand in hand down the path, as if he didn't know the way; she sat at their feet as they talked, and dreamed.

That was the first day, or the second, or the third. A glass was smashed. The mother collected the shards in her hands; they cut her. The Band-Aids she stuck on her hands were soaked with blood. Maurice's bag was on the lawn, wide open; all the flimsy papers, printed on both sides, were on the lawn. "Take your things and go," screamed the mother. Her hair stood on end, all her thick hair, cropped not to the roots, stood on end like in the picture in the alphabet book Maurice had brought, next to the word: *tête*, head.

There was something, on the first or second or third day, that began with the word "once," that followed from it.

Once the child went out of the mother's bedroom into the yellow hallway. It was midday, the hour between the mother's two jobs. The shocking silence in the house and outside it made the child leave the room, as if the world had suddenly emptied, retreated. She stood in the entrance to the hall and looked: Maurice was lying on his back, on the sofa bed, his eyes fixed on the ceiling, his Adam's apple sticking out, a cigarette in one hand. The mother, in her better work clothes for the afternoon job, was kneeling at the foot of the sofa bed, at his feet. Her forehead was buried in the upper part of his stomach, next to his diaphragm. His other hand, the one not holding the cigarette, stroked her head, not stroked, dug, stirring her thick hair, into the skin of her scalp.

The Same Book (4)

LA DAME AUX camélias

She always came to the Champs-Elysées alone in her carriage, in which she showed herself as little as possible, in winter wrapped in a large cashmere shawl, in summer dressed very quietly; and although she naturally met during her favorite drive many men whom she knew, if perchance she smiled on them, the smile was visible to them only, and a Duchess might have smiled thus.

She did not drive between the "round point" and the entrance to the Champs-Elysées, as was and is the practice of ladies like her: her pair of horses bore her rapidly to the Bois. There she left her carriage, walked for about an hour, entered it once more, and returned home at full speed.

All these circumstances, of which I have often been a witness, recurred to me, and I regretted the death of this girl, just as one regrets a complete destruction of some fine work of art.

In fact, it was impossible to meet with a more perfect beauty than Marguerite had been.

Tall, and at the same time very slender, she possessed to a superlative degree the art of hiding this forgetfulness of nature by simply arranging the dress she wore. Her cashmere shawl, the point of which reached the ground, allowed to be seen the large flounces of a silk dress; and the thick muff, which concealed her hands and rested upon her chest, was surrounded by drapery so skillfully arranged that, however fastidious the beholder might be, he could not help being pleased by the general aspect.

Her head was charming, and a marvel in itself. It was very small, and De Musset would have said that her mother must have taken particular pains to shape it thus.

A pair of black eyes, surmounted by brows so perfectly arched that they seemed as if penciled, shone in an oval countenance of indescribable charm. Imagine eyes with lashes so long that, when drooping, they cast a shadow on the rosy tint of her cheeks; a nose perfectly straight gave an intelligent expression to her face, while the nostrils were slightly expanded by the ardent aspirations of a passionate temperament; a mouth regular in form, with lips parted gracefully above teeth as white as milk; a complexion tinged with that velvety down that covers a peach that has never been touched; and you can form an idea of how that exquisite countenance looked.

Her hair as black as jet, and curling naturally or artificially, parted upon the forehead in two large bands, fastened at the back of her head, exposed the tips of her ears, in which sparkled two diamonds of the value of four or five thousand francs each.

How was it possible that the passionate life she led should have left Marguerite the virgin-like, nay, even childlike expression that characterized her countenance? We can only say that it was so, but we do not pretend to understand it.

Marguerite had a beautiful portrait of herself, drawn by Vidal, the only artist whose crayon could have reproduced her countenance. . . . Marguerite made it a point of going to all "first nights" at theaters, and passed nearly every evening either there or in the ballroom. Whenever a new piece was produced, she was sure to be present, with three things that she always carried with her, and which she placed in front of her box on the ground tier: her opera glass, a package of bonbons, and a bouquet of camellias.

Generally these camellias were white, sometimes they were red, but no one knew why she chose them of different colors, and the "habitués" of the Paris theaters and her own friends had observed this as well as myself.

Marguerite was never known to have any other flowers than camellias, and eventually she came to be known at Madame Barjon's, the florist from whom she purchased these flowers, as "the lady of the camellias," and that name stuck to her.

The Same Book (5)

I FOUND HER sitting in the hospital armchair, next to the bed, bathed ("I got up and washed myself very early, before everybody else"), wrapped in the green-and-blue wool tartan shawl I had brought her. The shiny white softness of her cheeks. She said that my sister, Corinne, had brought her a toasted bagel from the cafeteria downstairs and "these, too"—she indicated the bedside locker: six containers of Actimel yogurt in a cardboard tray.

"Your sister," she said in a half-complaining, half-gratified tone, "forces me to eat. I don't know what she wants, that one." I sat on the edge of the bed, my profile toward her. "But I'm not hungry," she said. "She doesn't understand that I'm not hungry." Her eyes glittered, an exaggerated, unnatural brilliance, as if from a high fever or great excitement.

The excitement, the near-electric conductor of her body under the big shawl that came down to her thighs.

"Don't force it," I said. "Don't force yourself to eat."

She examined the edges of the shawl intently, separating the tangled tassels from one another. "Nothing by force," she said.

We went down in the elevator to the inner courtyard of the hospital, next to the cafeteria: a dozen white plastic chairs scattered randomly over the clearing of lawn surrounded on three sides by glass walls and open to the sky above. In the middle of the courtyard was a tree that refused to grow, or that wasn't meant to in the first place. She thought she wanted coffee.

I fetched some. She took two sips and put the cup down on the dripping saucer, wiping it with the paper napkin. The mild sunlight of the beginning of December, behind the glass wall an entire family following one of their members on a gurney. "A lot of them come here from Kalkiliya," she said. "The one they brought last night to the bed next to me is from Kalkiliya. She didn't sleep all night." I moved my chair toward the narrow strip of shadow cast by the wall. Two dragonflies, one big and one medium-sized, came to rest on the used wrapping of something or other, some sandwich somebody had eaten. "I think a lot," she said, carefully prodding the sandy lawn with the toe of her slipper, "there are a lot of thoughts here at night." "What thoughts?" I asked. "You know, the way I was, this and that." She raised her eyes and looked in front of her, blinking. "How were you?" I asked, reluctantly, out of a sense of obligation. For a moment she was silent. "Like some sort of donkey, I think," she said, closing her eyes: "*Yallah*, let's get out of this sun."

We waited for the elevator, she held my elbow—just touching it, really, making the motions of leaning but not actually leaning.

She glanced at me briefly, like a passerby. "Don't you be like a donkey," she said.

The elevator opened its doors, two-thirds occupied by the lunch trolley. We could have squeezed into the remaining third, but we didn't want to. She didn't want to. "What have we got to do? We'll wait for the next one," she said, and stared up at the blinking lights showing the location of the elevator. I bent down to pick up the lighter that had fallen out of my pocket. I felt the shy tips of her fingers on the nape of my neck, heard her low, bashful voice above my head: "It's good that you're writing a book." "I'm not," I said. "Never mind"—she took back her fingers—"it's good."

THE SAME BOOK (6)

HER SISTER IN France crammed seventy-six detective paperbacks into sixty-five "items" of various shapes and sizes: women's plastic imitation leather handbags, copies of Louis Vuitton designer handbags made in Singapore. "How did I get all those *romans policiers* into the Louis Vuitton, how?" Aunt Marcelle beamed, delighted with herself, lighting another cigarette, forgetting the one slowly consuming itself in the ashtray. The mother waited for her "like the Messiah" to bring her "something to read" because that's what those *romans policiers* were, "something to read." The plots, the heroes, and the writers of these books in their dark, glossy, almost identical covers, were all fed into a giant blender and ground into a confused narrative with characters who came under the general heading of good guys and bad guys, with nothing to distinguish them from one another.

For long moments she stood in front of the low bookshelves in the bedroom, turning one of the paperbacks from side to side: "I really don't remember if I've read this one or not," she murmured, creasing her brow and returning the book to the shelf, pulling out two or three others and going back to the first one with a resigned sigh. The interval between the aunt's visits was measured by the number of times she had read and reread the "something to read": "When are you coming again, *ya bint sitin kalb*, you daughter of sixty dogs? I've already read the books you brought last time six times over," she complained to her sister over the phone.

She dragged the books over half the world, that sister: from France to India, from India to Nepal and Singapore, and from there to Israel, almost always arriving on a night flight and landing in the wee hours of the morning.

In the erratic light of the living-room chandelier, shaped like a ship's helm, spinning around itself and casting nervous epileptic shadows on the walls, the three of them—the mother, the aunt, and my sister, Corinne— stood sternly in front of the enormous open suitcases, examining the Louis Vuittons being extracted from the bolts of marvelous, glistening silk: Louis Vuitton for the morning, Louis Vuitton for the evening, Louis Vuitton for summer, Louis Vuitton in all shapes and sizes—school satchels, shopping bags, triangular, trapezoid, flattened balls. They wore magnificent Oriental robes embroidered in scarlet and gold, straight from the suitcase: the aunt in purple, my sister in white, and the mother in orange. The aunt and my sister, Corinne, smoked like crazy, stepped on the hems of their robes with the Louis Vuitton hanging from their shoulders or around their necks, talking business, business, while the mother tried to get in a timid word or two, but immediately withdrew in the face of the torrent of figures, economic forecasts, and hopes, like someone attempting again and again to jump off the sidewalk and hold on to a racing streetcar crowded with passengers.

They were working out the details of a business scheme with the Louis Vuittons, the aunt and my sister: this was the beginning. "Fetch a pencil and paper," commanded my sister; she drew a long, crooked line across the page and stuck the tip of the pencil in her mouth. Her lovely face, whose elusive, almost abstract, delicacy was impossible to capture and fix in the mind and always gave a disturbing impression of not being located in the face itself but somewhere else—her face now hardened, froze in one movement of intense tension, and seemed to withdraw, to absent itself: the force of her imagination took her far beyond the columns of figures, dismissing them and leaping over them toward some high, flickering reflection, exalted and fateful, of herself. Within a short space of time this absence turned into a strange, distracted rage: "Fetch a pencil and paper," she instructed me again, gathering her hair into a chignon above her nape, loosening the hairpins and gathering it up again.

The aunt sailed on. She unpacked rags and put them back, busy and serene as she received her public in the soft confusion of the Louis Vuittons, the coffee cups, the balls of cotton with which she cleaned her face, and the piles of books standing on the carpet. The Nona came in and sat down, the neighbor woman, my brother's worker from the welding shop, the brother from the kibbutz.

Corinne went to "put something on": at eleven o'clock, before the shops closed for the Sabbath, she and the aunt planned to drive to Tel Aviv, with the Louis Vuittons and what Corinne referred to as "the markup." The aunt nodded responsively whenever Corinne said "the markup," but on the way, sitting next to her in my brother's battered Chevrolet, she dared to ask: "But what is this markup, *ma chérie?*"

I sat in the back, watching over the enormous sack of Louis Vuittons so that it wouldn't fall off the seat whenever my sister braked. Her hands gripped the steering wheel with such force that the veins on the back of her hands stuck out and turned blue, forging their way forward, as if threatening the ringed fingers, a ring on every finger. "Just let me get out of the shit of the job I've got now," she said to the aunt, the cigarette hanging from the corner of her mouth, stained bright red by her lipstick. I looked at her nape exposed under the piled-up hair, gathered into the chignon that "always keeps its class," she would say, changing the color of her hair every two weeks at the hairdresser's where she worked in Petach Tikva, but never the chignon: she never touched the chignon even when the ends of her hair grew dry and brittle from the dye. Now her nape was reddish, almost scalded, as if a boiling hot towel had been laid on it. Marcelle was hungry, "dying of hunger," she said. She wanted to go to the Petach Tikva market first to eat fava beans. For months she had been dreaming of those fava beans, with the onions and the green chili peppers: she swallowed them whole without blinking an eye. We turned off to the market: in the side mirror I saw Corinne's face, stretching and stretching, thin and sharp as the blade of a knife. This delay cost her in blood, and her jutting cheekbones registered her hostility and sense of betrayal: the aunt was not with her, no, that woman was not with her.

Nervous and uncertain, she maneuvered the Chevrolet through the narrow street of the market where cars were parked on both sides and trucks were unloading their produce, scratching the left side and bumped on the right.

They left me in the backseat to guard the Louis Vuittons so they wouldn't have to drag the sack with them to the restaurant: the trunk was full of my brother's stuff, pipe sections, drills, and building scrap. I waited for them.

I laid my head on the sack and stretched out, my feet sticking through the open window. Someone passing tickled my bare feet. I looked up at the top balcony of the sooty restaurant building and watched two girls in short pajama pants sitting on the railing, one of them winding the other's long hair around her head and fixing it there with hairpins, one dark, oily band on top of another, shining in the sun.

I must have fallen asleep: Corinne's face leaned over me, suspicious and tortured. "It's already one o'clock," she said, "after one." She pushed me lightly aside to check if the Louis Vuittons were alright, her hands delving into the depths of the sack. For a moment her painted eyes met mine in a kind of hard, blank plea, and then she looked away again.

We set out again in the sweltering Chevrolet. Aunt Marcelle wasn't feeling well. The beans she had polished off had upset her stomach, she complained, trying to move the seat back so she could rest her head. On Dizengoff Street, near the Handbag Boutique, the Chevrolet gave up the ghost. In the middle of the street it came to a halt, indifferent to the hooting horns, the worst already behind it.

Corinne stormed out, catching the hem of her dress in the door as she slammed it behind her, dragged the sack of Louis Vuittons from the backseat, and ran across the street to the boutique. The aunt and I, still in the car, kept our eyes on her: her tanned calves on six-inch heels kicked out sideways, her broad backside encased in Bermuda pants rose and fell, the huge plastic sack suddenly came apart at the seams and burst open, scattering the Louis Vuittons over the road, under the wheels of the approaching cars. I ran to her, the aunt behind me. Corinne stood where she was, not moving, her legs now straight together, as if she were standing in the schoolyard in the morning lineup, staring at the road, at the Louis Vuittons on the road, covering her mouth with her hand. She went on standing there, moving her lips under her hand, even when Aunt Marcelle and I began collecting the Louis Vuittons from the road. I approached her. "What happened?" I asked. She took her hand from her lips, opened her mouth wide: the front tooth was missing and in its place was a black hole. "I think I swallowed my temporary crown," she said in a strangled voice.

The Same Book (7)

Among the things she bought with twelve or twenty-four payments: fridges, washing machines, stoves, sofas and dining tables and chairs, carpets, cabinets, heaters, an Olivetti typewriter, and, in the beginning, from a door-to-door salesman, the *Tarbut* encyclopedia and a series entitled The Young Technician for the child's brother, Sammy, when he studied welding for a few months (how few?) at the Max Fine school.

Once they liquidated the public library in Ramleh, and they brought the books to the student center where she worked. She let the child into a room on the top floor, which she called "the storeroom." The books were stacked one on top of the other, in towers that reached almost to the ceiling. "Choose and we'll take them with us when we go," she said to the child, and locked her in for a few hours, so "they" wouldn't know ("they" or "them up there": the authorities, the ones in charge, the powers that be. Even an anonymous petty clerk in the municipality was "them").

The child spent most of the time sitting between the stacks, peering at the spines of the books nearest to her in the almost absolute darkness of the room: there was a long, narrow strip of light in the gap between the two sheets of coarse black material draped over the windowpanes that were covered with black cardboard, torn here and there. The room had once been used as a darkroom for the photography club, and the windows had been sealed.

She sat on a pile of books, rested her cheek on her knees, and didn't touch anything. She had agreed to be in this darkness, interrupted only by the strip of soft, early-afternoon light, in the confines of the silence underscored by the muted sounds of the street below, which defined and fixed its contours, in the air dense with dust and the weight of the memory of long confinement, and the cramped, stifling corridors created by the towering stacks of books. A different kind of loneliness grew inside her, reserved, neither hot nor cold, a feeling of helplessness and resignation to the helplessness: nothingness was within reach, it was so close, so fierce, sapping her strength to want, the strength to say "I."

After about two hours there was the sound of a key turning in the door. The mother had come to see how she was getting on, bringing a loaf of sweet challah and a bottle of milk from the grocery next to the student center. Now the two of them sat in the darkness, dipping pieces of bread in the milk and eating. "Did you take what you want?" the mother asked. For a moment the child hesitated, then she pointed to a random, medium-sized pile of books: "Those," she lied.

The mother brought them home not all at once, four or five books at a time, stamped with the seal of the Ramleh Public Library. She put up two shelves opposite the child's bed, at eye level, and placed the books on them, arranged according to size, from tall to short. Years passed, almost three, until the child made them hers and read them. She tore out the first pages with the library's stamp on them, a mark branded on the books, a stain and sign of something, a germ of uncertainty and unease connected to the stifling gloom of the darkroom, the heaviness of the bread dipped in the cold milk, the strange smell, unlike anything else, that rose from the mother's parted thighs when she sat beside her, dipping the bread in the milk.

Every day on the radio at two o'clock in the afternoon, *The Wonderful Adventures of Nils*: if she could have, the child would have tied a rope around her neck and throttled herself to silence any sound of her breathing, to make room for those voices and those voices only. The painful void that came in the wake of the voices, after the end of the broadcast, the idleness of her hands. The child sat on the wet floor with the squeegee in her hand, next to the radio, and waited; perhaps they would change their minds. The floor was flooded with water, the mother's command forgotten. The child tottered over the slippery floor to look for the picture of the writer whose name they said in the *Tarbut* encyclopedia: Selma Lagerlof.

That was how the mother found her when she came home from work: sitting in the water, her trousers dripping, with the encyclopedia on her lap. The terrifying yell, the mother of all yells, would have shaken the windows had they been there—but they weren't, because in summer the mother removed them from their hinges so they wouldn't collect dust, leaving only the shutters. She took off her shoe, the mother, and shoe in hand approached the child, who dropped the book into the water, and ran outside barefoot, into the thorn field behind the welding shop. The mother chased her, she took Corinne's one-year-old son's iron rocking horse from the porch and ran after her in the thorn field, barefoot, waving the rocking horse in the air with her strong, furious arms. She came closer. The child heard the sound of her breathing, glanced behind, and ran faster. The mother, too, ran faster with the rocking horse and threw it at the child's back when she was six feet away from her. The child leaped sideways, a hairbreadth separating her from the iron horse lying on its side in the thorns at her feet, and went on running to the edge of the hill and the abandoned reservoir. Until evening fell she sat there on the concrete floor of the round reservoir, with the echo passing through its riddled walls, with the excrement and the newspapers at the other end next to the opening, and the round sky above her, a blue plate turning red.

In the evening the mother came and stood in the hole that was the entrance to the reservoir. "Come home now, enough," she said. The child didn't answer, she ran her fingers over the chalky side of the stone she was sitting on, examined her white finger smeared with chalk. "Come out of that dirt," said the mother, not moving, looking at the child; her face suddenly twisted to the left, squashed sideways as if someone had taken hold of her chin and cheek and twisted, squeezing out the sobs and pulling them sideways together with her chin: "I could have killed you. Thank God I didn't kill you," she said.

THE RESERVOIR

L IKE HER, I have no places that fill me with nostalgia, and the notion of going back "there," in thought or in reality, depresses and paralyzes me. I am prepared to know the face of nostalgia when I come across it, but not to remain there, not to put down roots. Roots—something else the mere idea of which distresses me.

A bulldozer drove over the stinking old reservoir, leveled the ground, and replaced the reservoir with a park. Brightly colored terraces. Waterfalls cascading in zigzags from the terraces. It's a good thing they removed the reservoir. I'm glad they replaced it. There is nothing vindictive in this: this is not the hoarse cry of memory demanding a reckoning. Memory stands on the escalator going up, and turns its face to look down at the bottom of the stairs, giddy with its erasure, the merging of the bottom and the top. There are no ghosts and no revelation in this merger, because everything— the future, the horizon of the present—is already happening. My sense of simultaneity (of the three dimensions of time, which are more than three) is my earliest sense of myself, more personal than my own name. There was never really a "there," and from the floor of the old reservoir on which I sat, I could see the reflection of someone gazing at me, inscribing me as I was inscribing her into the backward-looking future. I received the citizenship of being a guest in my own life. Since the beginning of time, the element of pathos in the world of objects has always manifested itself in nostalgia, in the yearning heart, which was born with the first gaze at the first object: the pathos of the reservoir. The future, in the guise of the yearning backward gaze, was also the past and the present, a memory that I must discard if I am to preserve it.

Our neighborhood ("Ours?" Yes, ours) was full of places and things that began as memories discarded at the moment of their birth, because they never, not from the first, carried any belief in the future. Everything seemed momentarily suspended, as if it would at any moment continue onward, without noticing either the suspension or moving on. There was a lot of air between the objects, between the memories, between the objects and memories of them. The reservoir gaping open at the top, riddled with holes at the sides, was full of air; even the concrete floor, with the changing reflection of the sky in the pools of rainwater, seemed to be floating in air. The reservoir's past, as a working functioning reservoir, interested nobody, not even the old people whose great past almost always overshadowed the smaller immediate past: it was as if the reservoir had been built from the start as an insignificant remnant of something that was insignificant in the first place.

But there were echoes in the ruined reservoir. We got a kick out of the echoes, Rachel Amsalem and I, she as a game and I as a nightmarish hallucination made real. We stood in the middle of the round floor, in the puddle of water, and called out to ourselves. Animal droppings lay on the bare parts of the concrete. Water lilies floated in the water. When we called out together I wanted to call just to myself, but when I went there alone something was lost; there was an echo but not the right echo, the one that was lonely but also had a sense of self. My loneliness required another pair of unseeing, disinterested eyes, indifferent as those of Rachel Amsalem: a blindfolded audience.

We did not keep on going to the reservoir for long, Rachel Amsalem and I: there was too much imagination there, which in the end impoverished the imagination. Our different and alien lonelinesses were increasingly deposited in other, hidden places: in the dank, shadowy areas alongside the bleeding dramas of our families and shacks, in the lies we told and the truths that pretended to be lies.

LIES

S HE, THE MOTHER, said that there were lies and there were lies. She had a special tone of voice for the phrase "and there are lies," not ironic but emphatic, like the exaggerated motions of the lips when speaking to a deaf-mute: the "and" said with a rising inflection and after it a sharp drop. This second kind of lie she called a "white lie." "But why is it white? What's white about it?" Corinne demanded. For her, the range of moral possibilities was subjugated to questions of fashion, what to wear where, how, and in what color. Apart from that, she was almost incapable of the sidestepping involved in the daily strategies of life: her inner drives, like her desire for theatrical expression, were so powerful and intense that they defeated the calculations of self-interest. Corinne told people "to their face" exactly what she "thought of them."

The contradiction between the delicacy of her face, which looked as if it had been woven from threads of air, and her proven ability to "open her mouth," and what a mouth, was almost scandalous. In the mother's crises, when they didn't cause her to collapse to the floor, and mainly when they didn't concern her, my sister was often the enthusiastic audience cheering her gladiator on from the balcony of the arena.

"Tell them, if they come again, that there's nobody home," the mother said to me. Corinne rummaged in the big wooden box where she kept the dozens of pairs of earrings she bought by weight at the central bus station.

"Don't say anything, don't answer them at all," she added. "But they ask," I tried again. "What do they ask? What have those people got to ask?" Corinne flared up, "Tell them he's dead. Dead. Do you understand? Dead."

The next day I returned to my post on the thorn hill, opposite the bus stop, waiting: not for them, for somebody. I sat on a patch of sand on the edge of the hill, forbidding myself to move, in muddy pants, wet with urine. Around me, buried in the ground, were my graves, four or five of them. I sat there after lunch working on them, every day anew, keenly aware of what was happening at the bus stop, not with my two normal eyes, which were fixed on the sand, but with some other, third eye. First I collected and piled up broken bottles and then flowers whose petals I had pulled off. Then came the digging. I dug a deep little hole in the ground that I had previously watered, and on the bottom I arranged the petals in a colorful spiral. On top of them I laid the broken base of the bottle: a transparent gravestone through which the petals were revealed. I covered the graves with sand, one after the other. Now I began an elaborate and mysterious procedure of uncovering and discovering: I dug in the ground again, as if at random, as if without the faintest idea of what lay buried there, suddenly discovering the cool, smooth glass, slowly scraping the sand until the petals were exposed, acting out the discovery and the surprise over and over with each grave.

In the dusky light of late afternoon the right bus stopped and the right people got off: he a short young man with a mustache, she in her last months of pregnancy, holding on to his elbow, bearing her huge body with difficulty on white, swollen legs. It took time for them to arrive, advancing with extraordinary slowness from the bus stop in the direction of our house. At the foot of the hill they stopped, paused, and considered for a moment. "Is your father at home?" the man finally asked. I shook my head. "Where is he?" he asked. "I don't know," I replied. "And your mother?" asked the woman. "Is your mother at home?" I covered the fourth or fifth hole with sand and didn't answer. I peeked at them out of the corner of my eye: the woman was sweating, she was dripping with sweat. The neck of her dress, from which a strip of gathered cloth stuck up, like a clown's ruff, was soaked through, plastered to the top of her chest. Anxiety trembled in the damp, still air between us like vapors. I wallowed luxuriously in the warm stream wetting my pants again, all the way down to the back of my knees. In the end they would leave. Again the woman took hold of his elbow; again she tottered on her swollen legs, giving him her handbag to hold. I waited a moment or two, watching their receding backs, and then I got to my feet, passed them, and ran as fast as I could toward the shack. I stood at the end of the path, hiding behind the garbage can, and waited. They reached the shack, this time for some reason via the neighbors' yard, and stood next to the low wooden fence separating the two houses.

"Maurice, Maurice," they called loudly, in chorus, the man in a deep baritone and the woman accompanying him in a rather squeaky voice, stressing the last syllable. Corinne came out of the shower, wrapped in a yellow bathrobe, her hands digging deep into the pockets; in a minute they would make a hole. The mother came out, too: "Why have you come again? He isn't here, I told you he wasn't here," she said in a lowered, almost confidential voice. "We were told that he's here, that he's been seen around here," the man insisted. "Who told you?" Corinne rushed into the fray. "Who's the liar who said that? Go look somewhere else. When you find him tell us, we want to know, too." The pregnant woman burst into tears and wiped her red face with the sleeve of her dress: "He took all our money, all of it. He talked and he talked and he talked, and my husband gave him all the money for the business deal. I haven't got anything to buy a bed for the baby, a bed for the baby." She smacked her stomach, rattling the gold bracelets on her wrist. The man came closer. He almost stuck his face into the mother's face: "I'll go to the police, let the police come and take you, thieves." I saw Corinne leap: she flew to the end of the porch, her robe came open, exposing her thighs, snatched up the broom, and began to hit—the man, the woman wailing behind him, the man again, the mother who placed herself between them, the neighbors' dumb dog who ran around them in circles, barking without stopping. The man seized Corinne by her hair and neck, while the wailing woman suddenly bent down and stuck her teeth into my sister's arm. The mother pulled the broom out of Corinne's hands and began to beat them herself. All the way to the road she chased them with the broom, yelling: "He's gone, gone, gone."

He's Gone (1)

W HERE WAS HE when he wasn't there? He was never "there," he flickered on and off, in the lives of others and in his own life, too.

He's Gone (2)

"What do you think? Was he a spy?" asked my brother, closing one eye, the good one, with a half smile, dying to take off, he just needed a bit of gas. "Who?" I made myself un-knowing, deliberately putting off what was coming anyway, with or without gas. "Maurice. In the neighborhood they said he was a spy." I laughed. He laughed, too, but only halfway. As a professional, he knew not to laugh with the audience. "Listen, I'm being serious now, he acted like a spy. Disappearing like that, where did he disappear to?" My brother creased his brow, settled down: "And the way he talked, too. He had that way of talking in hints. He never stopped hinting. Hints, hints, all the time hints," said my brother, covering his fourth banana with chocolate spread and taking a bite. "Eating all those bananas will make you sick," I warned him. He took no notice, carried on: "But the interesting thing is, who was he spying for?" "For himself," the mother contributed, "only him, him, and him." My brother leaned his elbows on the table, pressed his hands hard against his cheeks, and went on: "I, for instance, would break in a second. The minute they put me in the dungeon with the ropes to hang you from your feet, I'd tell them everything, spill all the secrets. Even before the dungeon I'd tell, just for a piece of chocolate or something." He stopped, reflecting for a minute: "But not him, he had a strong character, he wouldn't be broken by torture," said my brother, dwelling enjoyably on the word "torture." The mother wiped the table with a cloth, removed the basket of bananas from under his protesting eyes: "He wasn't a spy," she said, "he was a crook." "So how come they said he was a spy?" my brother persisted. "So what if they said?" She waved her arm. "People say all kinds of nonsense. If I listened to everything they said, hairs would grow on the palms of my hands." "So you, in other words, never sensed anything suspicious in his behavior?" "Anything suspicious?" she snorted contemptuously. "What are you talking about, anything suspicious? Everything about him was suspicious, he was suspicious from head to toe," she said. She might as well have been talking to the wall. My brother suddenly grinned from ear to ear: "What a character, that Maurice. Remember you told us how in Egypt, in the war, he and your brother bought silk parachutes from the British soldiers at bargain prices and went into business with about a thousand shirts they'd sewn, remember?"

A Portrait of Maurice by the Mother

"You could say he grew up in the street, from a child he hung out in the streets of Cairo. Cafés and cafés. His mother, poor woman, was an aristocrat, half-mad, the whole house was at sixes and sevens: you went in and saw everything heaped up in piles on the floor. His father would take women into her bed; he drove the poor thing crazy and then left. He was a lawyer, his father. His mother would send Maurice to his father's office to ask for money. He'd let him wait outside for days until he let him in. He'd sit there like a pauper with all the other paupers and wait for his father to give him money. His sister was highly educated and a bit off her rocker, too. What a life, with that mother and brother. She tried to kill herself once, the sister, she was as beautiful as Laila Mourad, the actress. He studied, didn't study, worked, didn't work, who knows what he did? He learned in the street, he learned in the cafés from those people who were communists, all day long politics, he didn't want to come here to Israel. I wanted to because of my brothers, and he came. As soon as we got off the ship in Haifa he got that obsession with the *Mizrahim* into his head, from the minute we landed. Discrimination. He was right, but he didn't do anything sensibly, he spoiled everything. Who didn't come to our house to talk to him? Yigal Allon himself, the minister of labor. But Maurice couldn't take the high road. Not him. They gave him a great job in the Labor Ministry, put him at the top, with his education and fine talk. So what did he do? Protested outside the Labor

Ministry, 'Bread and work.' So they fired him. How could you do such a thing? I asked him. Doesn't the bread you bring home come first? 'My principles,' he says. His principles. Nothing was good enough for him except for prime minister. Prime minister, that's what his majesty wanted to be. With all the fancy jobs they gave him, the respect people paid him in the beginning. And the papers. The whole house full of papers and more papers. No day and no night, the coffee and the cigarettes and the papers, the papers."

PAPERS

AFTER IMMIGRATING TO *the land of our fathers and settling in it, I never severed my connections with the country, even when I was abroad. I went abroad frequently, in my professional capacity as a journalist and scholar. These travels in the wide world helped me to broaden my knowledge and my horizons in every sense, both professionally and in the connections I succeeded in establishing with high-level people in the world. Even during the long period of my self-imposed exile I kept in constant touch with my comrades in thought and ideals. For the most part this connection was maintained by correspondence, but there were also visits from my friends from Israel. They came to meet me in various countries in Europe. I earned my living as an independent journalist working for various news agencies and European newspapers, especially in France. I also worked for the United Nations in Geneva. I set up a press and public relations agency in Italy, where among others I represented the government of the Shah of Persia at the independence celebrations of that country in Milan.*

The friends from Israel who came to visit me had one goal: to persuade me to leave everything and return to Israel. Their reasons were our sociopolitical and educational-economic situation, which was going from bad to worse, in the absence of any criticism worthy of the name. They all lamented the cessation of the publication of our social affairs organs HaMeorer *and* Kesher, *the only independent platforms for the ethnic Mizrahi groups in Israel.*

All their attempts to persuade me fell on deaf ears. I held to my opinion that it would be very difficult, very difficult indeed for me to bring about any change in our situation in Israel. The experience of the past was not encouraging. I was well aware that resistance to the Ben-Gurion regime and conducting any kind of opposition, however constructive, to the status quo would be suicidal on my part. There were two things that were forbidden to Mizrahi ethnic groups in Israel: 1) To establish any independent socio-political body, and 2) To take part independently in any kind of opposition. These things would be fought tooth and nail by all the political parties in the country as well as the so-called Sephardic leaders, the vassals of the said political parties. Together they had agreed to maintain the status quo in everything concerning our dire and worsening situation, as long as these "leaders" remained in the positions awarded them, which we regarded as that of puppets.

No man can defy his fate, and my fate determined that in spite of all my reservations, and in spite of the doubts and difficulties involved in my return to Israel, I returned there in October 1962.

Piazza San Marco: Second Visit

IT'S NOT THAT the photograph of her and Maurice with the child in the Piazza San Marco was chosen to be the one. It was the only one.

There weren't any others, any other family photographs, and the uniqueness of this one was the uniqueness of the so-called family, the trial moment of meeting, the trial meeting. She tried. She responded to his blandishments. She took the child whose birth he hadn't witnessed and made the journey to his world. She made the journey to his world for the first, the one and only, time in her life. A street photographer took a picture of them in Piazza San Marco in Venice and named an exorbitant price. But Maurice didn't care, he was lavish, extravagant. Was the mohair coat she wore in the photograph bought there? And the child's coat? He spent on them, that's what Corinne said, spent and spent. She listed, Corinne (greedily, admiringly, resentfully), all the things, one by one, everything the mother brought back with her: "the bottle-green mohair coat, the crystal necklace with the crystal bracelet, the pearl earrings, the suede evening bag in the shape of an envelope, the gold watch, the burgundy silk shawl, that scarf she always wore."

A Portrait of Corinne by the Mother

"WHEN SHE WAS born I couldn't touch her, she was like a goat. The wet nurse we had in Cairo held her in her arms, not me. She had a kind of fur all over her body, black hair like a goat. At the age of forty days all the hair fell off her body, in bits and pieces, and she turned into a beautiful baby."

Bits and Pieces

THERE WERE THREE of them in the shack: the big brother, the big sister, and the child. The mother didn't count, she was the shack; the shack didn't have a man in it, so she became the man. She spoke to them in her different languages, each time another one, which would come to an end and make room for a new language to carry on but not to replace it. That's the thing, there were no replacements, not real or symbolic, and the languages did not disappear, they didn't go away, they were only hidden for a while, to reemerge in a different composition, a different guise. This was what the mother called her "character," which was their lives—the earliest and most piercing of their lives, like two taps with a knife on a glass in the dark, one and then another one.

Corinne heard them best, the taps—she never stopped listening for them even when she was tuned in to a different station; something in her shivered. Where was she, Corinne, where was she really? The child remembered the movement of air she left behind her, coming and going, going and coming, brushing her hair in front of the oval mirror in the hall, when there was an oval mirror there, and gathering it at her nape. She remembered the expression on Corinne's face in front of the mirror: stern, clear-eyed, infinitely aware, not preening—the mirror was work. The child looked at her looking at herself in the mirror and said to herself: this is how you look into a mirror. Corinne said to the child: "I'm the one who gave you your name. Your name is Toni, not what they say." The child pricked up her ears, let the words linger in her mouth one by one: Corinne's speech was an event, a sudden crack of a whip. She kept quiet, or burst out, without transitional stages, but most of the time she kept quiet, gathering evidence, collecting firewood for the next outburst. There was nothing shy, embarrassed, or inhibited about her silence; on the contrary, it was proud and aggressive, a way of asserting her superiority and keeping others guessing. As far as she was concerned, speech was a kind of surrender, bending to another's will.

Corinne also said: "You were a bad baby. You bit and scratched. I would say, come to me, Toni, but you didn't want to, you bit." The two of them were on their way to Eva and her sisters, on the other side of the thorn field, to eat potato pancakes and cream. The child listened. "But why was I?" she asked Corinne. "That's how you came out," replied Corinne, going into Eva's house without knocking on the door. They sat there for hours, lounging on the big bed where they all slept and that stood on the porch with the crooked asbestos blinds, the empty, greasy plate that had contained the pancakes lying between them, among the piles of rags, clean and dirty laundry, dozens of empty bottles, and a green cage with a pair of tame parrots. Eva plucked her eyebrows, polished her nails, or tightened the buckle of a belt around her plump waist, and asked Corinne: "How's this?" Corinne didn't answer. She shot her a brief glance and blinked a couple of times, withdrawn into herself but still with that instinctive alertness, so sharp when it came to questions of "taste," which not only gave her more pleasure than anything else but also wounded her.

Her deep, feverish silence gave way incessantly to patterns and designs: at sixteen she cut up Sammy's army uniform and made herself a "safari suit" with three-quarter-length pants and a belt tied in front, and showed it off in the neighborhood where people thought it had been sent to her from a fashion house in Paris. That same year she left the hairdressing school where the mother had registered her. She thought they had nothing to teach her, and she went to work as an apprentice at a number of hairdressing salons, where she swept hair off the floor, suffered, and observed. She practiced at home on Eva and her sisters, Hannaleh and Riva, on the mother and the child. She liked cutting hair standing up and "dry," not the way they taught in the hairdressing school. This way, she argued, she could "really" see what she was doing. Tight-lipped, she held the scissors tensely, entirely given over to the desire to match what was before her to what she saw in her mind's eye, to what "could be": "Stand up straight"—she pinched the child on the nape of her neck—"don't move." The child's wavy black hair fell in thick bits and pieces to the floor, and Corinne pushed them aside with her bare foot. Hours after she had finished cutting her hair "*à la garçonne*," Corinne went on chasing her with the scissors in her hand "to trim something." "You have to be careful of that one when she's holding scissors in her hand," said the mother, but she herself wasn't careful; she, too, entrusted her head to Corinne, who forbade her to look in the mirror until she was finished, submitting to the categorical imperative of the beautiful, how it was to be achieved, and how exactly it was supposed to look—an imperative that she, Corinne, radiated from afar, unexplained and even full of contempt for explanations and justifications.

Once every two weeks Corinne dragged the child with her to the central bus station in Tel Aviv, to various wholesalers of hairdressing products and equipment, in order to "check things out." They went in and out of dark holes, cellars, and dusty basement apartments, crammed with giant plastic containers of shampoo and conditioners, rollers, and hair dryers. Corinne stepped on stiletto heels like stilts, her face turning greener by the minute. She bought the child *burekas* and orange juice, invariably arguing with the vendor over the change, mainly because she was impatient and got mixed up counting the coins. She didn't exchange a word with the child, and she always concluded the business survey with the purchase of three or four pairs of shoes in the cut-price shoe shops on Neve Sha'anan Street. When they returned home, getting off the bus at dusk after hours of futile wandering about, she went up to the tree next to the bus stop and vomited her heart out. The mother was sitting on the porch when they reached the shack. She hurried after them into the room, opened the boxes, and took out the bargain shoes one after the other, muttering, "She's opening a shoe shop here." Corinne had already taken off her clothes and was sitting at the kitchen table in her bathrobe, dunking pretzels in her coffee and soaking her swollen feet in a basin of lukewarm water. The next morning she marched off to the hairdressing salon, her feet plastered with Band-Aids and shod in one of the new pairs of shoes with the gilt buckles. "You'll ruin your feet," scolded the mother, "buy yourself clogs, like all the girls at the hairdresser's wear." "I'll die before I put my feet into those ugly things for washing floors," retorted Corinne, fixing the mother with her clear, pale look, full of contempt and defiance and entreaty: "You wear those clogs," she said.

Corinne Slept

Curled up on her side in the fetal position, her knees coming up to meet her chin. One hand buried between her thighs and the other under her cheek. Her eyelids transparent, still painted, she was too lazy to remove the eyeliner. The almost disintegrating towel she couldn't sleep without had slipped from her fingers, but it was still close to her face, lying on her neck. From close up you can see: a delicate trickle of saliva is dribbling from the right side of her mouth, wetting the towel.

In what bed was she sleeping, where? In what room and what metamorphosis of a room? Where was I sleeping?

First Portrait of Corinne in the Flying Shack

H ER FACE DIDN'T change at all, either when she was hanging behind the flying shack or underneath it, like a tail stuck in the wrong place, gripping the mother's ankles with two straight arms, her body horizontal, almost parallel to the ground below us, her chin thrust forward, into the air, and her eyes closed against the wind; the longer we went on flying the deeper they sank into her skull, making their way through the two tunnels intended for this purpose and popping out on the other side, through the hair flying in the wind, looking backward, staring at the air, remembering all the contacts we tried to forget.

We weren't in the least surprised; we went along with what was happening to us when it all began, or was about to begin, with little tremors foretelling the road opening before us: at first the door frames shook, especially the frame of the front door, twisting into itself and freeing itself of the wall only to rejoin it again a few minutes later, in order to take flight as a whole and not as a part, as the mother wished without even asking. She conducted the whole thing, that was clear, in a sleep that wasn't hers but ours; she conducted it all while sleeping our sleep, none of us in her own bed, shivering in our heavy blankets, silently counting the thuds of the legs of the bed on the tiles and the thudding of the tiles getting ready to join in the great flight. Everything was joined to everything else: the door frames to the walls, the walls to the floor tiles, the floor tiles to the panels, the panels to the cleaning rags, the kitchen utensils, the stove, the tables, the pictures, the sewing machines, the one they'd bought already and the one they were going to buy.

We flew as we were, doing nothing, following *"elmuhandis,"* the engineer, with our eyes shut, *elmuhandis* who was the mother, because that's what we called her—my brother first, he said it first and he flew first: *"Elmuhandis* is lifting the shack," he called and leaned out of the window, half his body outside in air that was getting thinner and thinner, high above the orange welding shop, the health clinic, above the thorns that covered the rectangle of land we left behind us, going up in flames at last, above the neighborhood and the shacks cut through by the curving asphalt road and the boys inside the shacks eating what they liked to eat in the blazing hours of the day with the beans in tomato sauce dripping from the half-loaf of bread they had stuffed after removing the soft inside, above the tapping of the heels of the girls on their way to the synagogue, above the Nona's quarter-shack trapped between Amsalem's half and the *amm's* quarter with the cows, and a special multipurpose cloud that screened the Friday afternoon Arabic movie with the character of the important man in the suit who was always called *elmuhandis*. And it was he who accompanied us, *elmuhandis*, in the movie in the cloud, orange, yellow, or gray-green, on our flight, bowing and straightening up, straightening up and bowing to the mother *elmuhandis*, who bowed back to him, *muhandis* to *muhandis*, he with a cigar-shaped lollypop, and she trying to put our shoes on our feet, snakeskin shoes she had brought from God knows where: pale green for Corinne and blue-black for me, long and black, entire snakes, with an opening in the middle for the foot, that writhed when we walked, but not too much, managing the corners nicely and lying in a long straight line when we took them off, Corinne next to her bed and me in the middle of the room, praying for them to be returned to the shop.

And with the special binoculars that only registered people, not landscapes, the mother *elmuhandis* looked down at everyone waving to us and throwing us black grapes that fell back into their open mouths. "They can say good-bye to the most beautiful house in the neighborhood," said the mother *elmuhandis*, "the most beautiful that ever was and ever will be," she said and pulled my brother away from the window with the elastic of his underpants, to prevent him from being sucked into the movie-cloud flying next to us, and packed him into white clothes on the carpet, white but not festive. The tiled roof rose and fell above our heads, rose and fell, as if the shack were doffing its hat to us, exposing a strip of sky whose color we were too exhausted to guess, not knowing if it was day or night, and mainly if it even mattered whether it was day or night, following the mother *elmuhandis* come what may, watching her peel her skin off in strips, move heavily with Corinne hanging onto her legs, clinging to her ankles without letting go, crawling flat on the floor behind her, between the two snakeshoes, and licking the mother's calves imploringly until the highest, sharpest, most dangerous air to which we rose, the glass air that started to crack the floor, ripping it open between the kitchen and the hall and sucking Corinne out, without any clothes on, her body flying through the glassy air and her hands on the ankles of *elmuhandis*, hanging on.

Snake (1)

S HE FEARED SNAKES more than fires, but only a little more: the two most obvious enemies of the shack posed completely different styles of destruction. She was afraid of fire, of its rapid and resolute powers of annihilation, but she respected its honesty, its lack of pretense. When it came to fire, what you saw was what you got. Unlike the snake: its slipperiness, its agility, its stealth, the thing that pretended to be something else, the personal promise of death it bore in its poison—all this sent cold shivers down her spine. She was appalled by the personal aim of the snake, the aim that had your name and your name only in its sights. The fire raged, it made no distinctions between things and people, it was impersonal and therefore not completely vengeful and vindictive; it didn't have a black heart. The fire she understood. Not the snake. "The black ones don't do anything, we only have black ones here," my brother Sammy reassured her. She listened suspiciously. "But the way it looks, just the way it looks, black or white," she said, and shivered.

SNAKE (2)

BOUT MAURICE SHE sometimes said he was "like a snake," in Arabic, which was much more snakelike: "*elthaaban*." "The *thaaban*," she said, "when you cut off its head the tail goes on playing," she said: "That's *elthaaban*, put him in the ground for a hundred years, and his tail goes on playing," she said, unconsciously combining two central images of Maurice: the twitching snake's tail and the tree with the crooked root, that even after a hundred years, wouldn't grow straight.

Maurice was thin, very thin, and over the years he grew even thinner: his dark cheeks were sucked in so much that they seemed to meet in the cavity of his mouth and join between his upper and lower jaws. The burning of his narrow brown eyes was like no other burning, as was the sweetness of his tongue: no one had ever talked like Maurice. No one swooned at that sweet tongue like Nona. "*El-lisan elhilweh*," she sighed yearningly once a day, with that veiling of her watery blue eyes: "That sweet tongue."

The substitution of a general idea for the particular name Maurice led no one astray but herself: this indirectness, too, as a rhetorical principle of the first order, was the essence of *el-lisan elhilweh*.

The mother detested *el-lisan elhilweh*, she saw it as an alliance against her, a many-armed octopus: "Why are you beating around the bush, just say what you want to say." The Nona drove her crazy. She would put on her sphinx expression, pretend to be sunk in reflection. "Everyone has his own opinion," she said at last, giving the agreed signal for the second or third act of the argument: what exactly was "his opinion?"

They quarreled most of the time and about everything under the sun: about food and money, intervention and nonintervention, the neighbors, sicknesses and cures, the political situation, manners and etiquette, a word spoken or not spoken, children, God, hypocrisy and sincerity, daughters-in-law and sons-in-law and cousins, the weather, the garden, the mainte-nance of the shack, "the child," my brother's friends, education in Israel and abroad, the length of Nona's hair, how often a person should shower, fast-ing on Yom Kippur, what exactly had happened "then," whether bears were vegetarians or carnivores.

But they really tore into each other about one thing only: him. He was the one underlying subject, hidden or half-revealed, waiting in the wings to make its appearance behind all the lurid masks in the theater of their bitter quarrels. It was all him and everything led to him, however remote, foreign, and ostensibly irrelevant.

Him and his *lisan elhilweh.*

Him and his tip-top suits, his Omar Sharif, *Doctor Zhivago* mustache.

Him and his jawful smile, gaping from ear to ear.

Him and his demented mother.

Him and his swindler father.

Him and his unhappy, abandoned sister.

Him and his lordliness.

Him and his cunning, slippery ways.

Him and his criminal friends.

Him and his important friends.

Him and his debts, past, present, and future.

Him and his extravagant, grandiose gestures.

Him and his politics.

Him and his limitless egoism.

Him and his desertions.

Him and the women he had and didn't have.

Him and the looming catastrophe—the catastrophe he was himself and that he brought upon others.

Him and his eternal, congenital vagrancy, the way in which the Nona embraced it. Around this there was absolute silence, around the dark cir-cle surrounding the figure of the vagrant. Maurice the vagrant was the hidden, secret subject of the hidden subject that was Maurice in general: the secret within the secret. When this figure appeared before their eyes, emerging from the churning froth of the talk "about him," the two of them were speechless, gazing wordlessly at the figure of the vagrant who did not look back at them: the elusive thing, hidden from the eye, waiting for its turn, was not the bitter reckoning of their bitter grievance, but their compassion.

Snake (3)

THE MOMENT WHEN the shack was the victim of a shocking mutilation that remained for many months, the moment when the shack stopped being what it was and became something else, as if something poisonous: even the story she told and retold about what happened and how, it became the horrifying thing itself, as if it wasn't a story about something that had already occurred, history, but a prophecy soon to fulfill itself through the mere pronouncement of the words.

It slithered into the house at noon: she didn't say "slithered"; the twisting arm, the hand moving from side to side, said it. Out of the corner of her eye she saw it: a yellowish rope, quick as lightning. She was standing in the garden, hoeing the rose bed, she didn't really believe she had seen it, she thought she was imagining things. But still, she put down the hoe and went inside. The house was quiet, spick-and-span, the floor still damp from the mop. For long moments she stood in the doorway and scanned the space in which she was familiar with every object, every stir or stillness, even the wind passing between the objects. There was no sign, but the very absence of a sign signaled a menacing meaning: it was there.

"There's a snake in the house," she announced in the welding shop. Sammy didn't hear, he was in the middle of welding. "There's a snake," she yelled. The three of them went into the house, Sammy, his worker, and she, stepping hesitantly as they peeked under the beds, behind the chests, in the corners of the rooms, behind the fridge, into the big plant pots. "There is," she insisted, "I saw it, I wasn't dreaming." "You were dreaming, you were," said Sammy, sticking his black fingers into the saucepan on the stove, fishing meatballs out of the sauce for himself and the worker. When they left she checked the house again, even pulling out the big linen drawer: "You were dreaming, *ya bint*, you were dreaming," she said to herself, and dropped onto the sofa in the hall, to rest awhile before she went to work, stared unseeingly at the book in her hands, and immediately shifted her gaze to the wall with the window in front of her: "You were dreaming, *ya bint*."

The faint breeze of early fall stirred the folds of the curtain, ruffling them a little: the curtain was new, striped in a spectrum of shades of yellow, from dark to pale. For a moment she closed her eyes, giddy with the wavy motion of the strips of yellow color sliding into each other, and immediately opened them again and saw it: hanging between two stripes on the curtain, "straight as a column," its tail curled around the curtain rod. She thought they looked at each other. "He looked at me," she said. She remained rooted to the spot for a moment longer, riveted by its alien gaze, and then she jumped up, burst out of the door, and flew to the welding shop at a speed that defied the force of gravity and the powers of speech. When the three of them returned to the house with hoes a profound silence met them, different from the one before: the yellow curtain still stirred, the snake still hung motionless on the curtain rod. It was the worker Binyamin who saw it, not Sammy: "There he is," he said. Sammy stood staring and blinking with his one good, seeing eye: "Where?" he asked. They began hitting with the hoes. She stood behind them, covering her eyes with her hands, peeping through her fingers, terrified. They beat the curtain, the window frame, the wall of the shack, in which a big hole immediately opened, revealing the shriveled rose beds and lawn of the end of summer, the wall of the welding shop, the clotheslines. She saw no more, she ran outside: she was not a witness to the decisive stage in the battle "against it."

We didn't go into the shack for a week, we slept on the floor in Nona's room, where she trampled on our arms and legs when she groped her way to the toilet at night. For a week the pallor never left the mother's face, the tremor never left her lower lip: "His head had already been cut off with the hoe, but the *thaaban* kept going without its head, he kept going with his tail and all the rest of him," she repeated what she had been told, what she hadn't seen.

July-Tammuz: The Month in the Garden

T HE MONTH OF *July is one of the hottest of the year and maintaining the fresh-ness of the plants and flowers during this season is no easy job.*

The life cycle of a number of plants ends in this season and they turn yellow and brown and lose their beauty and do not add to the charm of the garden. All we can do in this season to beautify and freshen the appearance of the garden is to plant annual flowering shrubs.

Annuals are purchased at nurseries in little cups that do not hold much growth substrate, and therefore when planting them care must be taken to dig a hole one and a half times the size of the cup, to return soil not tightly packed to the hole and fill it with water, to fit the size of the hole to the size of the roots, and then to insert the plant and water it immediately and go on watering every day in the evening or morning hours and even twice a day, until it takes hold in the ground. It should be noted that most of the annuals developed in the nursery in condi-tions of semi-shade, and the existing leaves will therefore wilt or shrivel in the glare of the sun, but with proper watering the plant will recover and become accustomed to the new conditions.

Lawns: in these hot days the lawn should be watered twice a week in order to prevent it from drying up. It should be mowed two or three times a month and fer-tilized once a month with small amounts of nitrogen-rich fertilizer. The blades of the lawn mower should be raised a little so that the lawn remains higher than in the spring. Mowing too low is liable to expose the roots and cause damage. At the same time, care should be taken to mow the lawn frequently. When the growth is too high the air cannot penetrate, causing the lawn to shrivel.

In this season of the year due to the increased humidity, the lawn should be regularly examined for various diseases of the leaves. The most common of these is wheat rust, which is characterized by the appearance of brown spots on the grass and which calls for spraying with Mancidan or Saparol.

Roses: all the wilted blooms should be removed. The ground around the roses should be padded in order to keep it wet and keep the roots cool. The roses should be given extra fertilization with soluble fertilizer. The rosebushes should be sprayed against pests and leaf diseases and it is recommended to spray regularly once every two weeks, or as required according to the nature of the garden. A good time for spraying is in the early hours of the morning.

A GOOD TIME

THE CHILD WAS told that she was growing up at a good time, and afterward this was corrected to a "better" time. The mother and the Nona said this sadly, and Corinne reluctantly, with a kind of shrug. "Corinne," they said, "didn't grow up at a good time. There were problems, issues, Corinne grew up in the middle of the problems." About Sammy they didn't say whether he grew up at a good time or a bad time: he was outside time, outside the shack that was the home in its first stammering decade, before the sadness. It was clear: the time was the shack, the home, the issues. "Sammy," they said, "was in the street all the time, he ran away from the issues." But the words "ran away" gave the game away. The child caught hold of it: "But why did he run away, Sammy?" she asked Nona. "He didn't run away," the Nona corrected, "he ran around. He didn't see. Corinne saw, she sat at home then. She saw everything, poor girl, everything that happened." "And she didn't run around?" asked the child. "She did, and how," pounced Nona, "and how she ran around. She was of the streets, *btaat elshwiri* she was. Just like you're *btaat elshwiri*, and if you don't stop I'll have your head. With us, girls don't run around in the street." "With us" meant the mother and Nona and Sammy. The three of them asked, "Where have you been?" and over and over again: "Where have you been *ya btaat elshwiri*?" But Sammy didn't scold. Unlike the two of them he had no opinion, good or bad, about *bitaat elshwiri*: in general he had no opinions, Sammy, only anxieties and fears, almost exclusively fantasies, anxieties, and fears.

He was fourteen when the child was born, he still liked wallowing in the dirt with his friends. "He would come home black as pitch," said the mother, and she would scrub him in the shower with the hard loofah until his skin was red. As soon as he saw her approaching with his good clothes, especially the ironed white shirts, he would burst out crying loudly: "Not nice clothes, not nice clothes." Nice clothes always ended up the same way, with furious beatings. This is how he came to identify freedom with tangible poverty and poverty with cheerfulness: there was no property to defend and nowhere downhill to go.

Years after the childhood distress of the "nice clothes" he would still feel overcome with anxiety when he saw a stack of fresh new shirts or trousers in the closet, and he made haste to throw half of them out or give them to his worker. The mother would run after him, rummage in the garbage can to salvage the garments, which he would just throw away again. "He's not normal, that boy," she said, but her face beamed: he was the one who was always in tune, by virtue of what he was and what he did or didn't do, with her hidden agendas, hidden even from herself. He was the one who read her instructions correctly. She said: "Look after the child when I'm not here, don't leave her alone with Nona."

He didn't. In the evenings, in his work clothes as an apprentice welder in the industrial part of Petah Tikva, he would barge into Nona's room, pinch her swollen arm, undo her braids plaited around her head, dip into the saucepan on the stove, eat standing up, and drop down exhausted: onto Nona's bed, next to the child, the carpet, the armchair, the concrete step on the threshold of the quarter-shack, or on the toilet seat, with the water running over his head in the improvised shower, a tiny alcove toilet with a shower tap stuck in the wall. "Let's wake him up, *ya bint*, he's fallen asleep in there," said the Nona, and the two of them called out: "Sammy! Sammy!"

Dragging his feet, a towel wrapped around his waist, he threw himself onto Nona's bed, making himself out to be more exhausted than he really was, but he was quickly chased off the bed and removed to the carpet. The bed was the stage, and the hour was the hour of the child's performance: "*Yallah*, get it over already so we can go to sleep," the Nona prompted her.

Almost every evening the child would stand on the bed in front of Nona and Sammy and sing "Tombe la Neige," until from behind the wall, from the Amsalems' house, the banging and the groaning would begin: Father Amsalem demanded quiet and got it, Rachel Amsalem split her sides laughing.

Sammy wanted to go out, his friends were waiting for him, sitting on the stone wall in front of the house. He waited for the child to fall asleep, lay next to her on the Nona's bed, and made up a story to distract her. She didn't listen to the words, only to the melody, forcing her eyes to stay open, staring at the steamy, hazy air that filled the windowless room and gave rise to a dense white mist. For a moment Sammy thought she had fallen asleep and he sat up silently, but she sat up, too: "I want to sleep in our house," she said. He wrapped her in a blanket, tucked it tightly around her in her pajamas, and the two of them went down the path joining Nona's quarter-shack to the mother's shack, leaving behind them the rectangle of opaque white glass set in the Nona's door, which the child looked at as they walked away. The mother's shack was clean, empty, and dark. The emptiness of hours was in the air and it didn't go away even now, undisturbed by their presence. Again Sammy lay next to her on the bed, one of the beds, again he told her a story, stopping every now and then, when his friends knocked on the door, to call out, "Just a minute." After an hour they made their way back again to Nona's. He carried her in his arms, lying on his shoulder, running along the path to the quarter-shack on top of the mild slope of the hill.

The Top of the Hill

I's POSSIBLE THAT the neighborhood was as flat as the palm of your hand. Perhaps we only imagined its hollows and curves, its slopes and wadis and hills, inventing a topography that didn't exist, or, more accurately, superimposing a mental topography on the physical one, referring to distortions and exaggerations of scale, to concepts that had been coined in relation to other places and had frozen in language and consciousness, with no connection to anything, addressing only themselves. We never actually said these words, we never said "hills," "hollows," "wadis," we were not acquainted with the words and what they represented. We said "up there" or "down there," we said "go up" but never "go down." For some reason we never said "go down."

There was the big "up there." Sammy said: "I'm going to up there." The big "up there," ten minutes' walk from the shack along the asphalt road or through the thorn fields, consisted of a cleared patch of land, worn wooden benches, two kiosks, a grocery store, and a cinema. But these details were just the framework for "up there," not the essence—that involved "everybody" hanging around and waiting for "everybody," the stories people told themselves or each other, pointless stories that went nowhere and wanted nothing but to create friction, a mild, gentle flame that never developed into a real fire. Their talk was the babble of babies. They lounged on the non-lawn or on the benches, Sammy and his friends, drowning in this gibberish until the wee hours, feeding each other. Then they went together to piss in the field, putting off as long as they could their parting from the place, from the thing that was the best of themselves. That was what "up there" once was: the place where the best of themselves was aired and aired again.

I wrote "once": I thought of "once," walking side by side with Sammy "up there," not hand in hand, to see the movie we had seen yesterday and the day before and the day before that, sitting in our regular places in the movie theater, the air fresh and empty, heartbreaking in its emptiness. Sammy tests me on the multiplication tables as we walk through the thorn field or along the asphalt road to up there. "Five times five, seven times eight, nine times six, four times three, five times nine, ten times twelve."

ONCE (1)

THE FURY THAT "once" prompted in her, the past, any wallowing in the past: "Once" she shook her fist at someone, never mind who; "Once it was. Now it's dead." With its good and bad, she saw the past as weights of concrete on her legs, impeding the movement of her forward-striving body, of her mind, which closed its eyes and hastened its steps as it passed the still faces of stone monsters. "Once" was the stone monsters, embodied in memories, in objects that held the memories and objects that held nothing, squatting like dead weights. She threw things out all the time, to make room: there was never enough room. She could never throw out enough to satisfy her.

She divided the human race into people who threw things out and people who didn't, who wallowed. The ones who threw things out were positive, optimistic, industrious, straightforward, clean inside and out, and full of consideration for others, not imposing their "mess" and torment. The non-throwers were the opposite: dreamy, lax, lazy, clinging, "sitting on their souls," muddy and muddying and missing the most important thing in life, clarity.

With that wild gleam in her eye that couldn't wait another minute, full of eagerness and passion, she said: "*Yallah*, parcel it up and throw it out already." Every two or three days, "*Yallah*, parcel it up and throw it out already": she was tidying up.

She emptied the closets. She emptied the storage space above the closets. She emptied the linen chest under the bed. She emptied the kitchen cupboards. She emptied the pantry. She emptied the glass-fronted sideboard and the chest of drawers with papers. She emptied her little storeroom next to my brother's welding shop. Before and inside the piles she carried out a ritual purification that lasted for hours, governed by the ostensibly simple principle of: "What do we need this for?" Immediate need was god: cruel, uncompromising, impatient, and brief. Anything slightly damaged, shabby, crippled, or for which the immediate need was not immediately evident was sent to the "parcel." The repeated sorting and sending to the "parcels" were a mirror image, a precise reflection of her mental map at a given moment, which could change a few days later: she never tired or despaired of this work of coordination between her outer and inner selves, of the indefatigable striving for a material reality whose features represented, with the greatest accuracy, the changing landscapes of her mind. She wanted to be "light, light," she wanted to acquire possessions not for the sake of accumulation but exclusively on the basis of need.

At midday (the sorting, like all important things, took place in the morning) the discarded possessions rested on the porch, bundled in big sheets, waiting for their final removal. She sat among the bundles, eating a little rice with beans, surveying them with the thoughtful frown that always presaged energetic action, trying to make up her mind. "Who to give them to?" Immediately after announcing, "I can't make up my mind who to give them to," she would untie the knots in the sheets, open the bundles, and sort out their contents again, this time according to the recipients summoned to come "now" to get their things.

In the evening, when she turned on the sprinklers, which would flood the porch, there were only two bundles left without owners. They were dragged to the garbage can in front of the shack, where they stood like two potbellied sentries on either side. Everything was fresh: the mown lawn; the moist leaves of the lemon tree, which only ever yielded hard lemons without any juice; the new tablecloth waiting in its wrapping in the closet for the old one to be thrown out; the dull gleam of the polished copper vessels now lined up in a different arrangement on the kitchen shelf; the empty white spaces in the exemplary closets; the clean nightgown she put on after bathing; her hair washed and her mind quiet.

But a sleepless night followed the quiet and clarity: four or five times the bedside lamp was switched on and off, the pages of her book rustled. In this quarrel between darkness and light hesitations, doubts, and regrets emerged and metastasized from hour to hour, until the dawn broke. At five in the morning she stood next to the garbage can in her nightgown, rummaging in the bundles and the can itself to salvage and retrieve things that had been restored to grace during the conflict of the night.

Suspended between the two fates, deprived of citizenship and papers, the retrieved objects lay on the porch while she moved them one by one from corner to corner, where they wouldn't catch her eye and remind her by their presence not of the sin of throwing them out but of the shame of changing her mind. Every morning, as she drank her coffee, she glanced at them out of the corner of her eye and looked away again, muttering to herself: "I always act and then regret it, act and regret, act and regret."

Once (2)

"Once": THE ENEMY of resilience, a luxury, the margins of the soul, the reserves. She had no reserves, no savings, real or symbolic. Alone, two adolescent children and a baby, a mother (hers) three quarters blind, a mother (Maurice's) three quarters crazy, up to her neck in debt. She said: "A person (*elbani-adam*) has to know his day-to-day, what his day-to-day is."

ONCE (3)

THE SECOND, THIRD, or fourth day before her death, in the hospital. I found her: the only days of her life when she was really there to be found, immobilized, situated where they had left her, only the light on her face changing and shifting with the passing of the hours. I found her crouching by the side of her bed, emptying the metal hospital locker. Tidying up a little, she said, downplaying the "little." Piled on the bed were bags of fruit, cookies, wet wipes, a box of chocolates, a towel, three pairs of underpants, a tube of Voltaren for the pain in her back, two or three books, nail scissors, a checkbook, opened envelopes of telephone and electricity bills, an empty, decorated, gilt cardboard box, very elegant. She looked inside it, turned it upside down: "What was in it?" she wondered, a smile of relief dawning on her face: "Those petit-fours your sister brought," she recalled.

She crammed the superfluous items into the box, pushing them down, making a parcel: "Take it when you go," she commanded. Again she crouched down next to the locker, trying to release the jammed door: "These hinges need to be oiled, nobody's oiled them for years. Go and bring a little oil from the kitchen," she said. "What oil?" I didn't understand. "Any oil will do, cooking oil, we'll oil these things a bit." Her face was pale, her neck too, a grayish pallor continuing from the faded gray mane of her hair. I brought a little oil in a plastic cup. She dipped a tissue in it and oiled the hinges, opening and closing the locker door: "You see?" she crowed. The family of the patient from Kalkiliya in the next bed looked at her in trepidation and awe. All of them were sitting on the bed: the father, three little girls, a two-year-old toddler, and a woman who appeared to be the patient's sister. "Just like the rest of the hospital, nothing works like it should," the mother confided in them. They were silent. The sick mother smiled at her with a certain effort, her face looking out over her husband's arm. "Come, I'll oil yours, too," the mother volunteered, "so you can open and close it at least." In the slippers that were too big for her, the big woolen shawl trailing behind her, she approached the next bed, growing paler with every step. The patient from Kalkilya's locker was empty. There were four bottles of cola and Kinley standing on top of the locker. She oiled the hinges, opened and closed the door a few times, and then put three of the bottles into the locker, leaving one on top. "That's better," she said, passing her hand over the white surface, wiping away the rings left by the bottles.

ONCE (4)

THE FIRST "ONCE," the first (perhaps) memory standing before every other first (like the tallest student in the class), not as a secret, but as a mold setting the shape of other memories, giving them their general appearance, mood, color: Sammy casting the three concrete steps leading to Nona's quarter-shack, to the new entrance on the other side of the quarter-shack.

They opened up a door in the back to make the access from the mother's shack more convenient. They cast the steps and the little concrete area above them. They paved the path winding from Nona's to the mother's house. The child watched Sammy casting the steps, installing the curving iron railing next to the steps for Nona to hold on to as she went down. She was one and a half and a bit: the warm touch of the flannel pants on her thighs, the sweater with the zipper in front, the smell of the wool with the smell of Nona's ointment that stuck to everything, her eyes almost completely covered by her bangs, and her white socks sliding into her boots, leaving a gap of exposed skin between the hem of her trousers and the top of her boots (from a photograph of the child sitting on the carpet at the foot of the bed in the mother's house).

The Nona stood and watched Sammy casting the concrete, too, the child clinging to her thigh. Then Sammy went to the welding shop, until the concrete hardened. Nona went inside to go about her business, deaf to the sound of the radio. Then came the call.

Once (5)

I CAN SUMMON the scene down to its last detail: he flew. He was fifteen and a half and barefoot. The call came from outside, from beyond the half-tarred road, beyond the row of single-story shacks, reaching him in the welding shop that isn't his, it's the neighbor's, a windowless orange building with a sliding iron door the width of the building and almost the height of the wall. The call was absorbed by the heavy door of the welding shop, where it echoed dully. I heard it unwillingly. I stood rooted to the spot, frozen into what I was doing, into what I was at the moment it came: "Sammy! Sammy!"

I was the omniscient narrator, I could anticipate the action step by step, propelled by the call: he was welding something when they called him. The call broke through the noise of the blowtorch. He ran to the house and there, at the entrance to Nona's shack, at the bottom of the concrete steps he himself had cast, he saw the child lying in a pool of blood.

He couldn't understand where the blood was coming from, whose it was. Nona said: "She opened her head. It's her blood from her head." He held out his arms straight in front of him. Nona laid the child on his outstretched arms. The child lay almost straight on his arms, her lower back a little curved, her head drooping toward the ground, past his right arm. They bandaged her head, taken a towel off the clothesline and wrapped it around her head. The towel didn't wrap well, it was too thick, it slipped off the narrow forehead, off the head. "The child will die," said the Nona. "If you don't take her she'll die." "I'm taking her," he said, staring at the bloody towel, at the flattened face covered to the lips by the towel, "I'm taking her." "She's dead, she'll die," repeated the Nona, "she'll die if you don't take her."

When his feet left the ground, racing toward the thorn field, he could feel the warm, swarming touch of the anthill he had trampled once before. He was barefoot, his arms stretched out in front of him, carrying the almost horizontal child with the heavy limbs of an unconscious body without a will of its own. Her big head, split at the temple, swung from side to side, and down toward the ground. The wet towel had slipped. His hands were covered in blood; his feet were covered in a mess of soil, blood, and grass. The path through the thorn field was hardly visible; the thorns had spread. He opened up the path with his legs, momentarily forging a passage that was immediately effaced again, conquered once more by the thorns after the bare, wounded feet departed, their skin cracked and burned by the blazing sand. He chose the shortest way to the top of the hill, to the clinic; he told himself that he was choosing the shortest way. From time to time he raised his eyes, to measure the distance to the top of the hill, which was blurring in the sun.

He didn't say "hill," or "blurring": the landscape was as plain as bread in the parched afternoon.

In the single-story shacks strewn over the plain, women and boys did things with bread. They took a whole loaf, scraped out the soft, white inside, and filled the space with beans in a spicy tomato sauce. That's what the boys liked to eat, that's what they were eating while he carried the flat child resting like a tray on his outstretched arms, his eyes suddenly falling on her Adam's apple projecting from her throat and pointing at the sun.

That was apparently the beginning: a sturdy boy carries a bleeding child in his arms. He is fifteen and a half and a bit, she is one and a half and a bit, his little sister.

Over the years the picture is rewound over and over again, someone rewinds it, not me, it's an anonymous memory that doesn't exclusively belong to anyone.

The boy and the bleeding child slowly leave the ground as his running carries them not forward but up, forward and up at the same time; slowly they take off, entering the low sky above the thorn field, above the single-story shacks, carried higher, above the taut black electric wires, the old water tower and next to it the new one, above the luxuriant orange groves of Kfar Maas and onward, to the high sky, above the clouds, where the two of them linger, the boy and the child, circling around in what looks from below like a monotonous dance in slow motion, the movement of their bodies skywriting white vapors against the murky blue of the hazy sky, huge trembling letters overlapping one another, erasing one another; only Nona knew how to read them as she looked up at the sky without seeing a thing. "The child's alive, she's not dead," said Nona, "she was dying but she didn't die. There was a miracle." "Not a miracle, not a miracle," said the mother. "There was an effort. The effort was the miracle."

A Portrait of Sammy Frightening Himself

ONE OF HIS eyes, the left one, is half shut, squinting anxiously and suspiciously at the other eye. His left leg limps a little in the wake of the eye, it, too, at a squint, nobody knows why. When he tells a story, to himself or others, he always exaggerates, crashing cymbals like the guy in the firemen's band. "Take a quarter of what he says and throw three-quarters out," says the mother, but she doesn't take her own advice, she listens to him wide-eyed until she catches herself and brings the two of them back to the dryness of the straight and narrow. "Stop with that nonsense of yours," she scolds, but not seriously, only as a reminder of the secret code agreed between them, which is also connected to the obscure dance about money: at least half of what he earns as an apprentice welder he spends on toys for the child; she condemns the waste, but turns a blind eye and still gives him money. He spends money on toys for himself as well, but not much, he invents things: he stays in the welding shop for hours after work, collecting scraps, old parts, and builds a tall circus bicycle of the kind he has long coveted—one giant wheel and behind it a little one. The first ride on this bicycle was also the last: he rode all the way from the welding shop in Petach Tikva to the neighborhood, about six miles, turned his head to look through the windows of a bus at the astonished passengers, and crashed. After that he built a joint bicycle for himself and his friends, welding five bicycles together in the backyard into a snake of a cycle that did very well on a straight path but collapsed and came crashing down on the bend in the road to "up there," throwing the happy riders off to the side of the road. And there was the bowling arcade he tried to construct behind the shack, then the huge electronic board with switches to calculate the multiplication tables, which he presented to the child's kindergarten (on the day of the presentation the teacher refrained from pulling the child's ear), and after that the reading machine, his tour de force, the most detailed and precise realization of his dream of idleness, the great sleep, life in bed, for which he never stopped pining. The reading machine was a rod that rose and fell, to which he welded a huge board with a tray at the bottom, and tubes dangling from its right and left sides: the person lying in bed could keep his hands under the covers, while the machine turned the pages for him; he held one of the tubes, one for drinking and one for smoking, in his mouth. The truth is that Sammy hardly ever read, in bed or anywhere else, but the machine united two fantasies: the fantasy of total rest and the fantasy of reading. He did read to the child from the animal book he had bought for himself, but only the first three lines, after which he tired and began to invent.

They lay side by side on the sofa bed in the yellow hallway, the clumsy machine almost squatting on their chests. On the board in front of them the book opened to the page about the lion, which was his favorite. From time to time Sammy paused in his story to suck sweet raspberry juice from the tube, red and dense as blood. "The lion is the king of the animals," he began to read wearily, in the tone of an insurance company brochure, and immediately abandoned the text. "And he followed me all the time, he kept after me with his teeth at my throat, but he didn't stick them in, whenever I moved I felt the points of his teeth on my throat and I was afraid to move, but if I stood still he would have gone for me, that's all he was waiting for, to tear me open and rip out a chunk of my butt," his voice rose and fell, dropping to a whisper that sent shivers through his body. Beneath the covers the child felt the shiver, and she, too, shivered. "What happened then?" she whispered. He closed his eyes, half asleep. "If you finish the yogurt I'll tell you." She didn't finish it, not before the reading machine and not after it, for hours she stirred it with a teaspoon, held the white stuff in her mouth, and spat it out in the sink behind Sammy's back. After that they got up and went to Levy's shop: a back room in his shack where he sold candy, building materials, pens and pencils, toilet paper, stockings, and toys. There was only one bit of floor clear of dusty goods to stand on in Levy's shop. And they stood on it. The child raised her eyes to the high shelves, to the dolls dressed in crimson brocade or faded blue, staring with dead glassy eyes from the top of cardboard boxes, pointed at them, and said: "That one, that one, and that one."

They Lay Side by Side in the Yellow Hallway

THEY LAY SIDE by side in the yellow hallway, which was yellow even when it wasn't and was defined by its changing yellowness—sometimes lemony and sometimes ripe egg-yolk yellow, falling to the floor from the point where the walls met the ceiling, so uniform in appearance as to look like another wall of yellowness. Sammy spoke into the yellowness, putting words in the air that bumped into each other aimlessly, merged in the yellowness that was not their lives but also was their lives. This is what the child thought, not in words but in the space that was love, in the absence of expectation, in the permission she had been given to drift, to pay no attention, to be aimless, which was love. And within the sheets or waterfalls of yellow, the child left Sammy precisely because he stayed, precisely because of the free-floating love and the fact that he stayed, the child left and drifted, she left Sammy and his story and went somewhere else, to a place where nothing fell from the point where the wall met the ceiling, to a place where one solid wall met another solid wall and the endless yellow of the hallway came to an end, turned into the little passage leading to the toilet, where there was a picture hanging on the wall that called to her again and again, precisely because of its mysterious silence, which, she felt, kept out the pouring yellow, blinding in its golden brightness. The picture, unlike the pouring yellow, did not say, "me, me," but "you, you."

She turned on her side, turning her back to Sammy, who didn't notice that she had turned her back to him, because this was the only way she could see the picture the way she wanted to see it, from the side and not head-on, looking in a way that both avoided it and dared to steal the sight—only this way was it possible to see the picture exactly as she had seen it the time before, with the same deep, dark, seething feeling that rose up in her but did not overflow because it stayed contained in the people in the picture, a murky promise. The longer the child looked, only from the side and with one eye open because the other one was squashed into the pillow, the more the wonder grew inside her, a sense of enormous oppression and enormous awakening at the same time; the weight of the oppression did not cancel out the awakening but magnified it, propelled her forward toward the picture and the three people in it, in whose presence there was something inexplicable and but also feverish, especially in the young woman in the white dress, sitting with her back to the other two, leaning against the wrought-iron railing of the balcony and looking straight ahead with blazing black eyes, dense with a fierce, glowing blackness whose gaze seemed to covet nothing at all in what it had settled on, nothing but the contemplation itself.

THE PICTURE: *LE BALCON* (1)

S HE COULDN'T PUT the toilet and the bathroom anywhere else because of
the plumbing, so the rooms changed around them in an ever-shifting
pattern like nervous dogs, maddened by the inexplicable immobility of a
scarecrow. In the endless rearrangement of the shack, the toilet and the
bathroom and the passage leading to them were the one constant element:
she contented herself with changing the ceramic tiles three or four times
and exchanging the plastic shower curtain for sliding doors and the reverse.
The picture was the right size for the wall of the little passage and so it
remained where it was: a reproduction of *Le Balcon* by Édouard Manet.
There was no lighting in the passage, and most of the time the picture
remained shrouded in darkness, fitfully illuminated when someone
switched on the light in the bathroom or the toilet or when a ray of light
from the yellow hallway suddenly revealed it.

Dogs (1)

SOMETIMES SHE SAID: I really need a dog here, to keep guard. From time to time someone brought her one or she acquired one: all of them pure-bred pedigrees: German shepherds, cocker spaniels, poodles, once even a Siberian husky. It's impossible to describe what Sammy called "her attitude" toward dogs, just impossible: shameless instrumentality, anxious concern that bordered on panic, cruelty. The first two weeks with "the dog" (she always called it "the dog," male or female, forgetting or ignoring its name) were a golden honeymoon. She was excited: "the dog" looked at her as if it understood everything. "The dog" was clever, bless it. "The dog" sensed everything—it waited for her, stood at the door and waited for her to come home from work. Sometimes she would scold it lovingly, with a kind of display of petting that consisted of clumsy pats on its head: "What do you want, *ya mshahwar*, you've already eaten, *mshahwar*, go to sleep, *mshahwar*, that's enough for today." ("*Mshahwar*," an exaggerated expression of affection: a combination of dumb, sooty, and black.)

And then the *mshahwar* didn't want to eat the special food she bought for it. None of the *mshahwars* would eat it. In astonishment, in worry, in budding resentment, she would watch the dog sniff the bowl and go away without touching the food. She said: "I don't know where I got this luck that none of them want to eat their food." For a day or two she maintained a firmly pedagogic stand vis-à-vis the canine resistance: "You won't get anything else *ya mshahwar,* you hear? You'll go without food." In the end she broke: she gave it bread and cheese, or fried chicken livers. These it ate eagerly, which enraged her and prompted her to put it back on the diet of dog food "as a matter of principle." And again she watched outraged as it sniffed, raised its tail, and went away without touching the food. This was the moment when "the dog" turned into a "he": "he" was stuck-up, selfish, spoiled, thought himself too good for her. "He's doing it to me on purpose," she said. Or with undisguised hostility: "Who does he think he is, that I'll spend so much money on him, *ibn el-fashari?*"

Nevertheless she brushed its coat every day and washed it once every two days, so it wouldn't have "that smell." It would take another few weeks, not many, for her to discover to her amazement that the dog was not a piece of furniture or an object and never would be. It moved. It chewed carpets, chairs, books, and the leaves of the potted plant. It shed fur and did its business on the new mat in the bedroom. (Five times she scrubbed it with vinegar and water and put it out to air on the lawn. The smell of the vinegar pervaded the shack for weeks.) It didn't impress the criminal cats that went on invading the kitchen and turning over the pots on the stove, and worst of all it destroyed her roses in the garden, digging up the soil around them. "This is no life," she said, chasing it with a slipper and hitting it until it hid under the sofa and refused to come out all day, despite her coaxing. "He's sulking," she announced bitterly, "his honor is sulking." And she went and planted a new plant to replace the one the dog had eaten.

The shack and its routines unraveled from day to day before her eyes; she unraveled: dejection and despair took the place of rage and insult. She gave up, looked for "someone to give him to," lobbied the possible recipients, and also believed with all her heart that "the problem is me, it's me that's crazy. I'm not suited to dogs. He's a good dog really."

The dogs were given away and passed from an uncle in Petach Tikva to a distant nephew in the north, from my brother to my sister, Corinne, and to my sister's neighbor. The ones that weren't given away were ruthlessly banished when the blood rose to her head: "Take him, take him," she thrust the dog into the arms of my uncle with the commercial van, cramming the dog's bowls, blanket, and food into a bag. "Let him out somewhere."

Dogs (2)

THERE WAS LENNY, one of a series of strays the child collected and brought home. When she talked about Lenny the mother's eyes clouded over: "I don't know what it was about that *mshahwar* Lenny that got into a person's heart like that." She gave him away shortly before the child was hospitalized with severe pneumonia, and then she went and brought him back. The next day he was run over by a car. She lay on top of him, on the road, covered with blood. It was impossible to pull her off the mangled body of the dog on the road.

Dogs (3)

Five mornings a week she cleaned the house of Rabbi Nathaniel and his wife, a childless couple, in the suburb of Savyon. If they summoned her to show up on a Friday, too, because of a reception or something of the kind, it was the end of the world: "My Friday is mine," she fumed, "It's mine, without my Friday I can't tell my head from my feet." But she went, she never said no to Nathaniel, everything about whose demeanor and person spoke of civility and good manners, even the surprisingly crooked parting in his scant, greasy hair. The madam wore checked suits, of linen or tweed: a checked skirt and a short jacket, nipped in at the waist, whose last button, the one lying on her bulging stomach, was left unbuttoned. She had that little dog, Cookie, a vociferous black poodle who wore a kind of little checked coat in winter and sat in a straw basket with a checked mattress. They kept mating her with male poodles and she kept littering puppies, black and curly like her. Rabbi Nathaniel patted her absentmindedly on her head; he didn't let her get to him, unlike his wife. Her pale, rice-paper-thin skin creased, her nostrils trembled with insult when she said: "Cookie didn't touch her food all day, Levana, you know she didn't touch it?" And the mother, impatient but resourceful, mixed Cookie's brown Bonzo dog biscuits with a little cream cheese, "to get it into her in a different way." "She gets sick and tired of the same thing every day, those little brown balls," she scolded-coaxed the madam. "You think she isn't sick of seeing the same thing all the time?"

The madam didn't answer, trapped in her own absentmindedness, which was different from the rabbi's and murkier, directed outward in nervous tension and even dread, especially when Corinne came to help the mother with the ironing. She, Corinne, sat on the spacious terrace of the spacious house, surrounded by fresh, sloping carpets of lawn, her calves resting on the chair opposite her and her golden thighs, where Cookie lounged, exposed, chatting with Rabbi Nathaniel about her "plans." With her smooth back exposed almost to the tailbone, framed by the long straps of her blue summer dress, one arm hugging the other shoulder, touching and not touching the slender earlobe with its earring sparkling with cheap stones, with her hair loosely, sensuously gathered above her nape, and above all, in the way she was sitting, with her ankles rubbing each other on the seat of the opposite chair, there was something brazen, not in a deliberate defiance, but precisely the opposite, in its utter naturalness, completely relaxed and apparently unself-conscious: the lordly naturalness of the mistress of the house or a child. And she saw it, Madam Cookie, she stood in the French window and she definitely saw it, her painted eyes widening in astonishment, and she rushed off to the walk-in closet and returned with an armful of garments and put them on the table in front of Corinne: "There are a few things here that I don't wear and I was going to throw them out, but perhaps you'd like them," she said. Corinne didn't move. She reached out with one hand to rummage casually in the pile, examined it with a cursory, sidelong look, and said: "They're not my style, thanks."

But the madam liked the "little one," liked her very much, once she even gave her one of Cookie's puppies. "Did you bring the little one with you?" she asked the mother, or complained: "Why didn't you bring the little one today?"

The child was then four years old, and the mother brought her, mainly for Rabbi Nathaniel, "who hasn't got any children, poor thing," and whose face lit up whenever he emerged from his study and found the child lying on her stomach on the marble floor of the vast kitchen, taking the brown Bonzo balls out of the bowl and putting them back in, occasionally slipping one into her mouth behind the back of the mother who was scrubbing something nearby. The rabbi held out his soft, padded hand to the child and said: "Let's go for a walk." They walked down the sloping lawn to the flat ground below, which was also covered with lawn, and the rabbi pointed to a dry stone basin and said: "There'll be goldfish here." Afterward he called

Madam Cookie and the mother to listen to the child singing in Hebrew, French, and a little in Arabic—the refrain from the Umm Kulthum song that Nona always sang—and how she recited a story she had heard on the radio at top speed and with proper emphasis, word for word. Rabbi Nathaniel picked her up in his arms, patted her lightly on the backside, and said solemnly: "This child will be the next Golda Meir when she grows up."

The child came to the spacious house with the sloping lawns because of the smell, which pervaded the interior and all the things revealed and concealed in it, even wafting from the bag of soup almonds in the pantry and the calendar hanging in the toilet. The smell had no discernible origin, no body and no words to name it: the smell was of absolute transparency, pure, refined, and imperceptible as the elusive flutter of a butterfly's wing on an eyebrow; it was different, odorless, the smell of an enlightened life, straight angles, calm orderliness, large-mindedness. The child wandered through the rooms after the mother, sniffed the tassels of a tablecloth, buttons, dusters, and pencils; she put one in her pocket to show Rachel Amsalem the smell. On Saturdays, early in the morning, she took Rachel Amsalem to the big house, to show her more. The iron gate was barred: Rabbi Nathaniel and his wife had gone to the synagogue. The little girls sat on the step and waited for them; they jumped up whenever they saw distant figures beyond the turn in the deserted street. It was noon when they returned, wearing white, arm in arm. "The child," said Madam Cookie in surprise and fished two caramel candies from her jacket pocket, holding them out. The little girls accompanied them to the house but didn't go in; they stayed on the terrace: each of them stroked Cookie once. Rabbi Nathaniel saw them to the gate, bowed down, and kissed the back of the child's hand: "And say Shabbat Shalom to Mrs. Levana," he said.

When the child returned Corinne was on the porch, smearing boiling hot wax on strips of white sheets to remove the hair from her legs. "Where were you?" she demanded. "I was waiting for Cookie," said the child and held out the candy: "They gave it to me," she added. Corinne threw down the strip of sheet in her hand, smacked the child's hand, and sent the candy flying, shook her by the shoulders: "What do you think you're doing standing at their gate like some beggar," she yelled. "Don't you dare do it again or I'll cut your face." She gripped the child's wrist and shook it up and down, until the strap of the plastic watch Sammy bought her at Levy's came undone.

Dogs (4)

S HE BABYSAT FOR Cookie when they went out at night. "You were at Nona's," she recalled for the child. She waited for them for hours on the armchair in the living room, with Cookie lying in her basket at her feet, with puppies or without. She fell asleep and woke up, fell asleep and woke up, her head falling heavily onto her chest, swaying from one shoulder to the other. Once, when she got up to have a drink of water, she stood and stared at the dog for a long time in the dim light of the room, and then she knelt down next to the basket, wrapped the checked blanket around Cookie's neck, and tightened her hands around it. "I almost strangled her," she said to the child.

ALMOST

RABBI NATHANIEL SAID: "Levana," and she said: "Yes." Rabbi Nathaniel said: "I want to talk to you about something." And she asked: "What do you want to talk to me about?" Rabbi Nathaniel said: 'You're alone with two adolescent children and the baby. Maurice won't come, and if he comes it will only mean trouble." And she said: "No, he won't come." Rabbi Nathaniel said: "It's hard for you. You have to worry about the two big ones so they won't get into trouble, God forbid." She said: "God forbid." Rabbi Nathaniel said: "I want you to know that we're here." And she said: "I know. May God bless you." Rabbi Nathaniel said: "How will Toni grow up, with your mother who can't see anything, or in the street." She said: "She isn't in the street, and she won't be in the street." Rabbi Nathaniel said: "She could be. You can't control her, you're not at home all day." She was silent. Rabbi Nathaniel said: "I want to suggest something to you, but don't misunderstand me." And she asked: "What?" Rabbi Nathaniel said: "I want to adopt the child, to give her a chance in life. That is to say, we do." She was silent. Rabbi Nathaniel said: "It doesn't mean that you'll stop being her mother. You'll always be her mother. She'll simply grow up in better circumstances." She was silent. Rabbi Nathaniel said: "Think about it. Don't answer me now. Take your time." She was silent. Rabbi Nathaniel said: "Just think about the good of the child, what's best for her." She was silent. Rabbi Nathaniel said: "You know that I love her as if she were my daughter. Almost my daughter."

She was silent. She talked to herself. She talked to Nona. She talked to Sammy. She was silent. She talked to herself. She talked to Rabbi Nathaniel: "You're a good man," she said to the rabbi. "But we don't give away children. Whatever happens, we don't do that, we don't give away our children."

PIAZZA SAN MARCO: THIRD VISIT

THERE'S NO SUCH thing. There's no such photograph. I won't make that
photograph speak, I won't force it to be there because it isn't there. There's
no such thing. Piazza San Marco or not, who knows if it's really Piazza San
Marco or some other piazza with pigeons, with photographers taking pictures of tourists and pigeons. Maurice a tourist? Who's a tourist? Who are
"the tourists"? By my calculation, she hadn't seen him for over two years
before Piazza San Marco: he left when she was pregnant, all of a sudden he
got up and left the country. He must have planned it without telling anyone, almost anyone. Got up and left. In terms of his wardrobe, he prepared very well indeed. After he left she received a bill for the suits he had
made by a tailor. Three suits. Silk shirts. Silk shirts? He wrote to her from
there after she gave birth, maybe a year after: "Bring me the child for me to
see her," he wrote. "Go," Nona urged her: "Go, who knows, *yimken yitadel*,
perhaps he'll return to his better self." That *yimken yitadel*: as if he'd ever
had a better self to return to.

   The photograph is disappearing at the edges, especially in the lower left
corner: this is the process of dissolution, a white mist that dissolves the colors, the contours, the figures. The flock of pigeons in the left-hand corner
has dissolved in this mist that has the sheen of water, a pool of water flooding the square, reflecting flashes of light and dazzling the eye. The dissolution, the white mist are the real thing, the truth. Of all the deceitful sights

in the photograph, the deceit of the so-called family, the deceit of a past that never happened, the thing that is least false, not false at all, is the hope. Her hope when she went there. Her hope when she lined up with him facing the pigeons, with the child. In the photograph she is the other woman, with the halo of the other woman, the hope of the other woman—a hope that is not complete blindness but complete clear-sightedness: then, perhaps only then, she stood and confronted face-to-face, trembling, she faced it—the fact, the hope, of being a woman.

LA DAME AUX CAMÉLIAS

"YES, I LOVE you, my own Armand," she murmured, throwing her arms around my neck; I love you as I never believed I could love. We will be happy, we will live quietly, and I shall forever abandon a life for which I now blush. But you will never reproach me with my past career?"

My tears prevented me from answering; I could only reply by pressing Marguerite to my heart. . . . Marguerite ceased to be the girl I had known. She avoided everything that could have recalled those scenes amongst which I had met her. Never did a wife or sister show to a husband or brother a greater affection or more care. Her morbid temperament took quickly every impression and was susceptible of every feeling. She had broken with all her friends and no longer had the same habits, used the same language, and spent as much money as formerly. People who saw us leave the house to go on the river in the charming little boat I had bought, would never have believed that this woman, dressed in white, wearing a large straw hat, and carrying on her arm a plain silk jacket to protect her against the cold and damp air, was the same Marguerite Gautier who only four months ago had been notorious for her extravagance and riotous way of living.

Alas! We made haste to be happy, as if we foresaw that it would not last long.

For two months we did not even visit Paris. No one came to see us except Prudence and this Julie Duprat, whose name I have already mentioned to you, and to whom Marguerite entrusted the touching diary, now in my possession.

I spent whole days at the feet of my mistress. We opened the windows which *looked out on the garden; and while the sunny summer made the flowers bud, even underneath the trees, we stood side by side and inhaled a breath of that real life which neither Marguerite nor myself had understood till then.*

This young woman displayed a childish astonishment at the smallest trifles, and on certain days would run about the garden like a girl of ten, chasing a butterfly or a dragonfly. This courtesan, on whose bouquets more money had been spent than could easily have supported a whole family, would sometimes sit down on the grass examining for a whole hour the simple flower whose name she bore.

On the Lawn

O N THE LAWN in front of the shack, on a sunny Saturday morning in winter, when the mild light, shrouded and indirect, and the shrouded, indirect warmth grant a general amnesty to everyone and everything: the shack
and everything belonging to it; the field, which is the field of thorns next to
Sammy's welding shop and beyond it, up to the white of the reservoir, which
is not white—only from a distance, in the flat, uniform grayness of the
thorns, does it look white; the shacks beyond the hill of thorns, which
seem to be planted on the slope of the hill, tilting like cups about to spill
their contents; the quarter-shack of the *amm* with the cows, next to Nona
sitting on the space above the concrete steps that she calls her porch and
talking to Rachel Amsalem's father, who is inside his house with only his
voice emerging from the window; the asphalt road with the long beds of
sand on either side; and the emptiness of the road that now seems happy
rather than sad; and the mother and Sammy and Corinne and I, who are
not sitting together on the yellowing lawn, and if we were then only for a
few minutes, leaving our impressions and other traces in the shape of cigarette stubs ground into the lawn by Sammy and Corinne, Corinne pretending to be asleep with her face to the wall, and Sammy really sleeping the
guiltless sleep of the just, undisturbed by dreams, a sleep complete and
satisfied, needing nothing, extending the stillness of the shack and its
rooms, which the mother and I were spewed out of, on our feet from six in

the morning, Sabbath or no Sabbath, she doing and doing and I watching or not, going back and forth, from Nona's porch to the mother's veranda and the yellowing lawn bordering the veranda, which propped up the mother with her legs stretched out in front of her, her feet encased in Sammy's short woolen socks, with the knitting she took up because all the women knitted, adding crooked row to crooked row, in despair and irritation because this knitting got on her nerves in the end, and with one eye open to the road and the street, to the pounding of the steps on the road and the paved path leading to the shack, and what might become of them at any minute, what could they be, which is the prophecy of the anxious heart and the muffled hope, the constant expectation of something that would shatter the silence of the garden, which was not actually blooming but which could be, someone's steps on the path, which could be the hasty steps of the neighbor who might have called to her, conferred with her for a few minutes, and whom she might have accompanied to the big road, leading to the big city, not the private road in the neighborhood, abandoning her knitting on the lawn and following him with pursed lips to the place he pointed out, where perhaps Maurice was waiting, after getting a ride from Tel Aviv, standing there in his crumpled suit, in which he had spent the night on somebody's sofa, waiting for her, leaning on the trunk of a tree in his dark horn-rimmed glasses, watching her coming as she stopped in her tracks five steps away from him on the other side of the road, saying in her heart what he could have said and said and said.

AND SAID

N0, HE DIDN'T make a good impression on Rabbi Nathaniel, Maurice, precisely because he tried so hard; he sat at the edge of the sofa in the
spacious house in Savyon, his legs crossed, and he "showed off," said the
mother, "how he showed off." She took him there one of the times when he
emerged from his darkness and came to the shack for a few days "on a trial
basis"; he wanted to find a refuge for a while and he found one, until he left
or was made to leave again. Why did she take him to Rabbi Nathaniel, why,
really?

They came like a couple, him and her, toward evening, sat on the sofa
in Rabbi Nathaniel's living room, which she had cleaned in the morning.
She dressed nicely, specially. He always dressed nicely, always stylish, never
mind the time of day, even when he didn't have a penny in his pocket. They
rang the doorbell: *ting-a-ling*. And again: *ting-a-ling*. Maurice's lean, carved
face shone under the entrance lamp like galvanized tin in the sun: he decided
to be alive there in the meeting because he wanted badly to die, to bury himself in the ground. He had to swallow a frog the size of an elephant at the
idea of this ghastly meeting and at the meeting itself: he was going to meet
his wife's "employers," the ones whose house she cleaned, his wife. "How
can you lower yourself like that?" he shouted once, not then: "How can you
go and be a housemaid?" "What am I going to live on?" she answered him.
"Where's the shame in it? It's shameful to steal, that's shameful, not to earn

a living by the sweat of your brow." She said what in her opinion she should have thought and felt, and which to some extent she did think and feel, but only to some extent. For her, shame came from another place: it wasn't the conceit of class or the pride of a girl from a good family that triggered it, but the pure generosity and warmheartedness, the generosity of Rabbi Nathaniel, that always left her speechless and ashamed.

They conversed, Rabbi Nathaniel and Maurice; they bandied words in an exchange that had the appearance of a conversation, during the course of which Rabbi Nathaniel asked questions and Maurice "twisted and turned," his narrow gleaming eyes glancing sideways at the reflection, at the giant imaginary mirror standing at their right, next to the long, non-imaginary sofa in the non-imaginary living room, in which were reflected not their figures, but the silvery metallic flashing of the swords in the imaginary duel silently taking place between them. The rabbi didn't say much, he mainly listened, laying his little traps, while Maurice said and said, and the more he sensed the net spreading at his feet, the more he talked: he talked about his journeys in the world and the people he met and became acquainted with, about his friendship with Picasso and his friendship with Yigal Allon, about his social and political views and about what he repeatedly referred to as his "philosophy, which is different." In this outpouring of himself he lost his footing and sank deeper and deeper, disappearing in front of the sharp, direct clarity in the look of the rabbi, this new protector of "his wife," whose frankness and friendliness he saw as pious, patronizing hypocrisy. He said nothing when they left and made their way to the neighborhood, but when they arrived at the shack he wouldn't go in. He got the last bus to Tel Aviv without even taking his shaving gear.

"I wrote about it," he said, years later.

Papers

T HE SUHBA, THE *political organization I established to deal with the issue of the ethnic Mizrahi groups and their situation, zealously carried out the resolution to take action to exhort and arouse our public and explain our problems to it. The staff of the organ HaMeorer, which I edited, and the intellectuals among us activated the rest of the members of the Suhba in the neighborhoods. Together and hand in hand they established a kind of national secretariat that took frequent action on a regular basis. The members of this secretariat met with me on an almost daily basis, and together we would analyze the situation and prepare for action. In the meantime, to our great regret, the economic condition of our community did not benefit from any positive developments and only deteriorated, especially from the point of view of morale and morals, which were severely impaired by the Ben-Gurionist propaganda and "education" policy. The persecution, the deception, and the anger increased the pressure on the masses of the Sephardie population, who were subject to virtual imprisonment. The press and the various propaganda agencies were still under the exclusive patronage of Ben-Gurionism, which forbade any publication of our activities and our very existence. This despite the fact that for our part we took care to send them all pamphlets and bulletins explaining our situation and our position on controversial questions. . . . After the many abortive attempts by the Ben-Gurionists to co-opt me with all kinds of corrupt bribes, and when they realized that I personally would not renounce the principles I believed in, whatever the cost, they turned their arrows on my family, the members of my household, and those dear to me.*

Knowing that my wife and my three children were the only property and assets I had left, they decided to take that, too, from me. In this way it was easier for them to carry out their ultimate design, which was to kill my soul through a method of mental torture culminating in spiritual and moral death. Therefore they chose my wife, my children, and the members of my household as the most convenient way of carrying out their dastardly design. In order to commit this murder, they aimed all their cannons of separation, intimidation, and slander at the walls of my home. They did this with a systematic cunning that would have shamed the vilest racists and anti-Semites. Because spiritual and moral death in its suffering and criminality is a far worse catastrophe than the murder of a man in cold blood.

Let me mention the fact that one of the cannons they employed in the execution of their design was a highly respected chief rabbi and well-known writer, who was also close to the government, the espionage agencies, the Jewish National Fund, the Labor Federation, the Jewish Agency, and so on and so forth. As mentioned above, this wealthy and respected rabbi was only one among the many agents who acted to destroy my family life and to sow separation and mistrust between me and the members of my household. Unfortunately for the important rabbi, I later came into possession of a document in his handwriting that confirms these accusations. This contemptible warfare, in which my wife served as the puppet whose strings were pulled by the Ben-Gurionists, left its mark on the letters I received from her in Athens as well. Every letter contained an ultimatum, admonishments, threats, and warnings, such as: 1) Since you have decided to continue along this path, you should return to Israel forthwith to finalize the divorce proceedings between us. 2) The rabbinate in Athens has been required to take legal steps against you, including your arrest, in order to return you to Israel for the purpose of granting me a divorce. 3) The children hate you, they are ashamed of your opinions, and they don't even want to know you. You have no chance of overcoming the situation, because there are important people supporting me and helping me to finish with you.

A Few Months After She Died

A FEW MONTHS after she died, in a nine-foot-square room in an assisted living facility for the elderly in the Hatikva quarter: Maurice's narrow eyes with their exaggerated glitter, which is now the glitter of the fear of death and not of vitality, try to crack the stiff scab of his face. As on all the days when he doesn't leave his room, he is dressed in long white flannel underpants and a long-sleeved flannel undershirt, and over them a burgundy-red sweater with a deep V-neck. This slightly Bohemian sweater with the boyish neck is the only marginal note to recall his previous existence.

The room is stuffy, closed, an electric heater emits white vapors at his feet, even though it's already May. "Your birthday's in May," he suddenly remembers, sending up a bubble in the dense, still water of his withdrawal. He says that he's been waiting for someone for an hour but the someone hasn't shown up: the social worker, the nurse from the clinic who's supposed to give him a shot, Dror, his messenger boy and disciple, or Solomon, that friend of his who brought him his last canary. Solomon breeds canaries in a giant cage in the yard of his house in Kfar Shalem, and from time to time he gives him a canary to keep him company. They were all eaten by the cats. He can't keep the room closed all day long, and when he sleeps they get in, break into the cage somehow, and eat the birds. "It's a pity about that one," he says. "She sang sweetly." His brown arms, horrifying in their thinness, grip the arms of the chair as if at any minute he would be uprooted and shot forward. There is an incomprehensible gap between the impression of strength radiating from the grip of the arms and the emptiness of the body, the sketch of a body hinted at underneath his clothes. He often closes his eyes in weariness, pain, sorrow, or for show. I prefer the fourth possibility. Again he takes off from the no-place of talking, which is the place we are standing in now, where we have always stood: "Nobody came to take me to her there in the hospital, not Sammy, not your sister, and not you. I asked and asked and nobody came," he says, staring at the coatrack opposite, where a wet towel is hanging, with an expression of wonder on his face, as if he has just noticed something he never noticed before. In this new tone of complaint (he never complained, even at his lowest hours, and there were plenty of them), which struck a note not of nagging but of dread, there is something chilling: flat, lacking intonation, gray, the unheroic, unembellished voice of the summing up of an unheroic, unembellished life. He is at the finishing line of his rhetoric. "And I didn't see her with my own eyes at the end," he says, his face—with his enormous mouth splitting it in the middle as if it had been cut in half with a knife—moves very slightly, a faint twitching of the left cheekbone under the dry, open eye.

AND I DIDN'T SEE HER

SHE WENT TO the market on Thursdays, taking me to help her: "Hold this for a minute," "Keep an eye on this for a minute," "Bring me the basket," "Go and stand in front of that woman," "In the meantime pick out the good ones, the good ones" (putting whatever I had chosen back in the barrow). Like almost everything else, the market was a battleground, but this time the battle was not only hers: over the money, over the quality, over the upper hand in the bargaining, over the line, over gaining access to the produce, over negotiating the crowds, over the seat near the door on the bus, over stopping "not at the station" but in front of the house, because of the heavy baskets. How contemptible and terrifying all this was: and the more contemptible, the more terrifying it was. I walked two steps behind her, so no one would associate me with her. The revolting beige plastic clogs she wore on her calloused feet with the polish peeling from the toenails ("I didn't have time for Miriam this month"), her battledress, a housecoat with buttons down the front, which was already faded and frayed by washing, the rings of sweat under her armpits, lengthening toward her waist, her impatience, her pushing and shoving, the haggling over pennies, and especially the insults she showered on the vendors, to their faces and behind their backs ("as ugly as his ugly mug, the tomatoes today"), which were accepted with surprising indifference, as part of the rules of the game.

Trailing behind her like a wooden horse on wheels pulled by a rope, falling to its side and dragged upside down, I dreamed my dreams. Next to the vendors' scales I dreamed, with the swollen string bag between my legs, standing in the middle of the alley and jostled on every side I dreamed, next to the chicken man, when the bag slipped from my hands, when she forgot her purse on the mountain of oranges, when I wet my feet in the puddle of muddy water that had washed the lettuce, the dill, the parsley, the coriander, and the mint.

I resisted. The dreaminess was my resistance. Slowly, secretly, and at some imperceptible point of balance between control and lack of control, between effort and relaxation, the absence that was my resistance swelled inside me, like a secret garden growing, deepening its roots: at first I slipped into the absence of daydreaming because it was second nature to me. Afterward, when the daydream faded, I pretended and continued to outwardly observe all the ritual requirements of absence (staring into space, passivity, chewing hair ends, deafness and silence when addressed). As I did so the pretense suddenly changed into something else, as if an electric current had been switched on, it stopped being a pretense, and the fake became real, even deeper and more comprehensive than before: what materialized from blurring the boundaries between pretending and not pretending, from my game of masks, was an absence of consciousness that was not only like sinking into a ready-made bed, but also something deliberately switched on in a convoluted inner process. In a matter of moments I could turn myself into stone or air: the market was my first training ground.

I couldn't see her. Far away, between the melon stall and the side of a van unloading produce, she suddenly disappeared from view. The basket was still stuck between my legs on the ground and on my cheek I suddenly felt the cool dampness of hair plastered to it. I said to myself that I should call out, but I couldn't: I knew I would not be heard in the terrible row, the noise of the engine, the crowds milling around among all the other cries, and even if anyone heard me, they wouldn't believe me, because I didn't believe myself. I looked at the vendor on my right: he crossed his arms on his chest, smoked a cigarette, looked at me but through me. I was transparent. I searched for the pattern of blue and brown diamonds on her dress in the crowd. When I looked up, to my surprise I saw the balcony of a residential apartment, a blanket thrown across the railing to air, normal life. I felt the pounding of my temples, I clenched my hands and opened them to stop the trembling and the strange tickling sensation crawling up from my ankles and advancing toward my neck. My sense of guilt was too great for me to feel its full force at that moment or any other moment, only the brief, ticklish touch of its hairy tail brushed past my face. In the emptiness and paralysis of my dread, the inanimateness of what could be called my "self," the recognition dawned on me, the beginning of a sharp pain that grew sharper, burning my chest, that it was she who had given up on me, that she wasn't looking for me and she never would. I leaped from my place, leaving the basket behind me, and charged down the alley, elbowing people out of my way with all my strength, until I arrived blind and breathless at the spice shop almost at the end of the market, which also sold loofahs of varying sizes and roughness. There was a little crowd gathered at the shop entrance. I came closer. She was sitting on a folding chair, her head falling a little backwards, pressing an ice cube to her neck, close to her chin. There was a faint, pale look in her eyes, and on her face, like the shadow cast by the lace veil of a hat, was a Corinne-like expression, fragile and delicate as glass. She smiled: "I was just going to buy the loofah when suddenly I didn't feel well," she apologized.

GATHERING

A T LEAST ONCE a week, when she got back from work at night, there was some kind of disturbance: neighbors, police, a doctor, the deputy head of the council, neighbors, the guy from the grocery, his brother who had dropped in to visit him and came along, too.

"The child!" the electric cables stretched above the street transmitted the voice, sending sparks flying as it passed through them with lightning speed, a rolling ball of fire. "The child!" growled the barrel at the side of the road, cracking the cast concrete beneath it. "The child!" spelled the stone fence in Spanish, checking the dictionary to be sure, "The child, the child," whispered the faded leaves of the Persian Lilac tree to the clicking of the knitting needles of the butterfly cocoons, "The child?" asked the electric saws in Yossi's carpentry shop, "The child!" asserted the empty dog kennel. "The child, the child, the child," repeated the cigarette stubs of the workers who had laid the road, waking up under the asphalt to the sound of her steps, rising out of the earth and turning into leaden spurs that broke through the asphalt and hit the soles of her shoes, waking them from their rubber sleep and rubber dreams with mirror writing: "eht dlihc, eht dlihc, eht dlihc."

"The child," said Nona over and over, wringing her hands which were shiny with the Veluta cream she had rubbed on them absentmindedly a few minutes before, only because the tube was lying next to the armchair. The child sat with her shampooed hair at the table covered with a green oilcloth in Nona's kitchenette eating a hard-boiled egg, only the white.

On the concrete landing at the top of Nona's steps, people were still gathered, but only the close neighbors, whose garrulous voices merged into a broad, monotonous murmur from which the words "Madame Esther, Madame Esther" emerged in varying tones at different pitches. The sharp dryness of the mother, who elbowed her way in with the bag hanging from her shoulder, was like a cold shower: everyone was gone in a matter of minutes. "What happened? Who died? What's all the fuss and bother about the child this time?" she asked. Nona decided to feel insulted: "If that's the way you're going to ask, I'd better not answer." She put on the expression of self-importance that always accompanied the sentence that hung in the air, spoken or unspoken: "I'll go to my corner and I won't bother anybody."

Her corner, however, was not only occupied by Sammy but had expanded to cover more territory: he had fallen asleep on her armchair with his outstretched legs on the bed, together with the cup and the plate from which he had eaten earlier, the last bite chewed in his sleep. Sammy was a good topic, a ladder to help her get down from the tree she had climbed: "He was so worried about the child, the poor boy almost had a heart attack," she said. "Get up," the mother shook his shoulder, "get up." She looked at Nona, at Sammy's sleep-stunned face and back again at Nona: "The two of you should be locked up," she said, "you and him both."

THE CHILD liked to hide, in other people's beds, for example, or huddled in the corner of the closet on the eiderdown, sniffing the sheets and the hem of the mother's winter coat, or under the bed, or in the deep narrow ditch Sammy dug behind the welding shop when he wanted to build a bowling alley, or on a bed of leaves in a little hollow in the depths of the orange grove, or curled up in an empty cardboard box in the neighbors' yard. She liked to curl up in very small spaces, to shrink the volume of her body so there wasn't a single slit of light between one limb and another.

For hours she would nestle in the hiding places that she didn't call hiding places, in the dense darkness that covered her to the top of her head, in the inside of the inside of the inside of something, wrapping and wrapped, distant and deep and muffled as the bottom of a submarine on the ocean bed, when all that could be seen through the glass was darkness and all that could be heard was the sound of breathing listening to itself, even in the inside of the inside of something, until even it, the breathing, turned from outside to deep inside, where there was no sound at all, only the utter silence that was darkness and the darkness that was silence. She didn't move: the echoes of Nona's calls, of Sammy's, of the siren, rolled like heavy stones high above her head, over the distant earth that was not her affair, no longer her affair, just as the panic, her own panic that swelled and shrunk like a bellows, was not her affair, she was separate and the panic was separate, wrapped in darkness like her, breathless, postponing the world from moment to moment, postponing the moment of responding and emerging from hiding, which, the more it was postponed, the more it receded into the distance, growing smaller and bigger at the same time.

The *amm* and *amma* in whose bed and between whom she lay with her head covered knew all this without knowing it. They shared the half-shack with Nona, wall to wall, they had one quarter and Nona one quarter, they kept cows and chickens in the yard, stirred a thick white paste on the out-side coal stove with a long stick, prepared *lafuf* and *mlawah* on the coals and wore "those clothes people once wore," said Sammy: the *amma* with her head wrapped in a black veil, a blue tattoo on her forehead, and a long embroidered tunic, the *amm* in rubber boots covered in mud and cow dung, with a thick salt-and-pepper beard and a white shirt belted with a girdle. They hardly ever spoke, not to other people and not to each other, seldom left the filthy, littered yard and the room that was like a closed seashell, opening a little to the outside world and immediately closing again, open-ing and closing: nine children they had lost in Yemen. The child crept into their room, into their bed, by day and by night, crawling through the air vent in the wall of Nona's shower and crawling wordlessly into their bed, under the mountains of embroidered cloths, the rugs and the blankets, in the sour staleness that hung permanently in the air together with the vapors of the smoke, the things boiling inside the room and outside in the yard, on the burning coals. The *amm* gave her fresh milk from the cows in a tin cup to drink, and the *amma* kneaded the *lafuf* into balls with her kohl-stained fingers and set them in front of her in a row. Outside the world, side by side, crowded together, the three of them lay in the bed, under the heavy piles of bedclothes, on the sheet wet with the child's urine, oblivious to the scandal kicked up by Nona and Sammy, fainting and yelling alternately, raising the roof.

They complemented each other, Nona and Sammy, in constructing a cathedral of imaginary calamities: she contributed the spirit, the inspiration, the directions and possibilities in general, while he translated the abstract ideas into concrete details, into technicalities, of "how exactly what could happen had in fact already happened." Most of all they trembled at the thought of the mother, swallowing the drops of valerian generously supplied by the Nona: what would the mother say, the sound of her steps.

And say she did, and how she said: "It's the two of you who frighten her with your fear, how will she come out of hiding with all the police and the brouhaha? You've frightened the child to death."

Sammy shook his head in disbelief: "You don't understand, she doesn't understand a thing," he spat to an invisible audience, rejecting in disgust the interpretation that in his opinion only showed up the fact of her cold-bloodedness, even though, an hour before, he had hung onto the policeman's sleeve, threatening him and imploring him to find the child forthwith, on the grounds that he was too much of a coward to do it himself.

He was afraid of Corinne: his blood froze when she walked through the room, her silence flicking at her side like a whip. "I can't talk to her," he complained more than once, trying to please her and always failing: she was the sole and exclusive agent of her own satisfaction, if there was any satisfaction to be had. Her arrangements, her rituals, her aesthetic fastidiousness, her ready contempt, her aristocracy, which was partly natural and partly a pose, the sharpness of her tongue when she opened her mouth, and her profound disapproval of "the gang" and "the neighborhood"—all these made him quail.

One afternoon the child played with Corinne's jewelry, all the dozens of pairs of earrings collected in the fancy carved wooden box. He came into the mother's bedroom and stood rooted to the spot: she had simply opened the box, found the key somewhere, spilled the contents onto the bed, and clipped the earrings onto her ears and the neck of her dress, like medals. Sammy saw black and red. "What are you doing?" he yelled, shaking the child's shoulders until her teeth rattled: "What are you doing? Do you want her to kill us?" The child widened her eyes and said nothing, while he went on shaking her violently to and fro until she fell back on the bed and lay there with her eyes open and empty. He stopped. All at once the convulsion that contorted his face and turned his eyes bloodred vanished, and a different convulsion of a different panic took its place. He leaned over the child:

"What's wrong with you?" He touched her shoulder lightly, "Talk." He raised her to her feet. "Talk," he pleaded, holding her cheeks and trying to force her jaws open: "Talk, talk," and then, in a growing panic, shaking her shoulders violently again: "Talk, talk!" he yelled, charged out of the shack, and flew barefoot to Nona's house: "She isn't talking."

For almost two hours he and Nona and the neighbors stood around her, crowded in the mother's bedroom, trying seduction, coaxing, threats, and a moment or two of feigned indifference ("Don't take any notice of her"). She stood rooted to the spot, a plank of wood. At some point he carried her on his back, frozen stiff, to Levy's shop, and begged her in growing desperation to choose whatever she wanted. They sent for the doctor. He went to fetch him, dragging him almost by force from his reception hours in the clinic, from his waiting patients.

The doctor gave her one look: "The one who needs a sedative is you," he said. Sammy lowered his blue work pants, his blue underpants that reached halfway down his thighs. "That shot he gave me was the size of the Flit cockroach spray, the needle was maybe a foot long," he recounted with a shudder.

ONE LOOK

THERE WAS THAT look of hers in all the photographs: a sternness aspiring to
a certain stateliness. She almost always posed in semi-profile, her eyes
fixed on some point or other beyond the lens of the camera, her chin slightly
raised, lips almost closed but not pursed, suggesting the shade of a shade of
a smile, perhaps ironic, perhaps hypocritical. Everything about her stance
in front of the camera proclaimed that she had collected herself in anticipation of what she assumed would be "the portrait," fateful and definitive
rather than a random picture. This one look that she kept for the camera
was an antidote to what was liable to emerge, to her annoyance, from the
photograph: herself as some nobody, just another woman who made no
impact on the visual imagination of the viewer. As if she was saying to the
camera: If that's gone, if that door to feminine Eros is closed, then let's go
with sternness, an imposing, slightly intimidating woman.

Corinne called it "impressive." Corinne loved saying "impressive," with
all the gravity of a considered judicial pronouncement, in a tone that she
kept for the rare occasions of this pronouncement from on high: "She comes
out impressive," said Corinne. She herself was the most enthusiastic cham-
pion of the mother's "impressiveness": this show of strength and even of
force, as a reaction to inner helplessness and demoralization, was in her
opinion the most appropriate armor for meeting the world, that "We'll show
them" posture of hers.

The appearance of the impressive woman started to emerge in photographs at the end of her thirties and the beginning of her forties, the time of the great renunciation. It was preceded by two completely different eras. The first one, that of the photographs in Egypt, shows Nona's "*basbusa*," *la jeune fille* down to the last detail and convention: there is no limit to the gentleness and the trusting, not to say gullible, innocence shining from that oval face with its creamy-velvety complexion, those lips like buds on the point of blooming, in the Levantine version of Hollywood produced by the Cairo studio portraits. Especially the wedding photograph, retouched and colored, with Maurice: the limp delicacy with which her hands in their pure white gloves hold the bouquet of pure white lilies, until it seems about to slip from them and drop to the ground (she was then in the seventh month of her pregnancy), the evasive turning aside of the body of someone who doesn't understand her role, who is not identified with it and is not playing it. She seems like the bridesmaid, not the bride.

Then comes the second era, the middle period of the first years of immigration and dismantling the portrait, every portrait: she has no face in the few photographs of that first decade in Israel. She is always bending over something, and even when she is not bending she is bowed. Her face appears in the photograph as the background, not the subject, lacking contours and dissolving like a puddle of milk on the surface of a tablecloth. The photograph in Piazza San Marco is from then, from the era of the portrait without a subject.

Piazza San Marco: Fourth Visit

More than an unalloyed so-called family photograph, this is a moment of unalloyed motherhood coming out of nowhere: her exposed hand, sticking out of the green coat and resting on the front of the child's body, keeping her from falling to the ground, to the square with the pigeons, while the other hand supports her back. Her face is turned to the child, not to the photographer, in semi-profile. The pleading intensity of her face as it is turned toward the child is like an act of theft: she has stolen this moment of family reunion and replaced it with motherhood, the moment belongs to the mother and child, to what they alone share.

She kneels by the child's side as if she always kneels, as if she bends down, first in her imagination and then in her body, to the height of a child. She didn't. She possessed a strange kind of panic and great impatience toward infantile neediness, which calls for a response made distinct by a thousand nuances, a thousand gestures and finely tuned attentions in which there is no room for *yallah*. And how could she live without saying *yallah*? She, who was built to be only the mother of large-scale, heavy undertakings, with bulldozers, rescue teams, helicopters, and cranes.

"Me, I never had the patience for babies," she said. "In Egypt, with Sammy and then Corinne, I would beg the cook to change places with me, for her to be with them and I would clean and cook," she said. "Doing nothing all day but take care of all those baby things drove me crazy," she said in moments of total honesty, which were also total lies. Babies died in her womb and in her hands. She was afraid of the babies' deaths and she was afraid of the fear. After twenty days, with urgency and a sense of relief, she handed the child over to Nona, like an explosive device.

THE GREEN COAT

PEOPLE SAID ABOUT her: a beautiful woman. She's a beautiful woman. Corinne added: "When she wants to. When she wants to, she can hold her own," said Corinne with a certain resentment, the residue of resentment she harbored not against anyone specific, but against the world in general, against disintegration, the decline and ruin inherent in things from the outset. She did not count what others considered beautiful ("Everyone says. So what if they do?"). Her thoughts on "beauty" were convoluted and obscure, while at the same time she strove for the clarity of an executioner: life or death. She detested the awkward efforts, whose clumsy stitches were visible from miles away, connected to the appearance of beauty. Not that she thought the appearance of beauty was rooted in anything casual or absent-minded. Not at all. Only for her striving for beauty took a different course, a different orientation, stemming first of all from one's inner bearing. "It's the way she wears it, how she carries herself," she explained, when she took the trouble to explain, giving the mother the benefit of her strict, slightly sour, discerning eye, snapping: "Put on the coat. It's better when you wear the coat." She was right. The moment the coat went on was a moment of metamorphosis, an immediate transformation from being a faded "nobody in particular," from her deliberate self-effacement, into a "lady." The coat and the moment of putting it on gave her a new and longer spine, which straightened her back not in a stiff and belligerent way but with a calm and powerful radiation of awareness of "Who she was," which suddenly came awake, from within.

The coats hung side by side in the depths of the closet, near the side, almost all of them hand-me-downs from her sister Marcelle, except for the green one, which wasn't green except in the photograph and according to Corinne. She was the one who said, "the bottle-green coat from Venice," and the mother after her, "the bottle-green," expunging "Venice." Corinne admired it always, she never tired of examining the big brass buttons and the part of the belt behind the buckle: "It's a good coat, this coat, at long last you've got something really good," she said to the mother, scolding her for putting it into the parcel to give away five or six times; each time she took it out for fear of the fuss Corinne would make, Corinne, whose fanaticism had detached the coat from its context, ripped out the threads of memories woven into it, and placed it on the lofty pedestal she reserved for "really beautiful" things.

It wasn't bottle-green, the coat: I carried out a thorough inspection of its olive-gray shade of mohair when I cut out a big rectangle of the fabric, from the hem to the pocket, to make a shoulder bag in handicraft class at school. Afterward, for fear of being found out, I crammed the remains of the coat into a plastic bag and buried it deep in the construction dumpster behind the shack.

HANDWRITING (1)

HER NON-WRITING, HER wounded handwriting, tormented by the Hebrew letters. Her shame at the wounded writing. At night, with the milky tea, the electric heater at the foot of the bed, the crust of bread dipped in the milky tea, the nightgown she put on as quick as she could in the cold room, slipping off her underwear once she was in the nightgown, still in her work shoes with the short socks, thinking of tomorrow, getting ready for tomorrow: postdated checks, payments on account, a debt due. At first her graying head bowed over the checkbook, her hand gripping the pen as if it had never held a pen before, writing the numbers in the box and then stopping, reflecting, waiting for the letters to reveal themselves. "Come and write these checks for me," she finally asked, but not in anger or impatience but complete surrender. At the bottom of the check she signed, wet her fingers, and handed over check after check: intervals of air separated each weak, ungainly letter. This gap between the letters, the white space she was careful to leave between them, was her acknowledgment of the strange language, of its foreignness: in French the letters are joined.

Handwriting (2)

THE SHACK WOULDN'T allow anyone to have nice handwriting, not that it forbade them, it simply exuded not-nice handwriting, because unlike the mother and her wishes, the shack wanted to freeze movement in time, to freeze our faltering, difficult beginnings, the lack of progress along the lengthwise axis of time hobbling the advance along the widthwise axis, the growth. Unlike the mother, the shack adhered to tradition, a tradition of eternal childhood, which it kept simmering on a low flame in the great storehouse of eternal childhood, that is, the attic above the shack, which we reached by a ladder from the outside and where the letters were folded askew inside the crammed cardboard boxes, where the bent screws and nails of old tables, the old sideboard, the shelves made of fiberboard, not wood, were exiled among the other things that belonged to the past—the past embodied in matter, in the mass of things that squatted on the plywood ceiling, making it bulge and sag over the living room and the other rooms.

The sagging, slightly dark bulge in the ceiling—a dark spot that defeated all the layers of paint that tried to cover it—rained down the age of six-seven, the letters of the age of six-seven, in a ceaseless shower, the precise notes of the choreography of the movement of the hand and the ungainliness of the movement, and the thing that was abandoned, the crooked abandoned letters that were abandoned precisely because they remained as they were, in the frozen quivering of the movement that is

never completed and never grows and remains behind in its awkwardness,
even when the speech is nice or as-if nice, Corinne's as-if nice speech, and
Sammy's don't-want-to-be nice speech, and the too-nice speech of the
child, who saw the fall of the letters, the imperative of the ungainly, not-
nice letters that was right like the groan was right, the groan of the shack
renewing itself and regretting its ceaseless renewal, trailing behind, dragging behind itself as it ran forward in the wake of the mother, who gave
birth to the command of the crooked letters and the unintelligible writing,
but gave birth to it from the rear, not the front, like a stepchild, and, without seeing, either the command or the denial of the command, nailing us
to the rain of crooked letters that were the duty of loyalty to the mother
and the mother's shame, which the shack remembered in every one of its
stages of accumulation, because it never stopped being itself for a moment
at every stage, in height, breadth, and length, carrying the one unchange-
able, remembering face, under all the other faces stamped on it, against
the mother's will or in obedience to it, remembering the debt of shame and
the debt of the handicap of the weak, limping handwriting, growing fainter
until it almost disappeared, and turned into a transparent thread tying
the four of us together.

HANDWRITING (3)

SAMMY DOESN'T WRITE because he doesn't write. There is no pen or pencil in the world that fits the non-grip of his knotty, swollen fingers: coarse, wounded skin on coarse, wounded skin, knotty layer upon knotty layer. He consumes whole tubes of Nona's Veluta and scarcely succeeds in bending his stiff fingers, only a little and only for a while, until they forget how to be soft and go back to being hard again. Sometimes they burn. Sometimes he wakes up at night from the burning of his hands. This goes together with the burning of his eye, which was penetrated by a chip from the welding. He lies in the light of the night lamp. There is the murmur of sick people in the room, murmuring shadows of sickness against the walls. Poultices soaked in tea on the burning eye and cool, greasy cream on the burning hands, but not the cream prescribed by the doctor, which he forgot to buy, lost the prescription. He hasn't got what's called a "touch." Only a scratch. "Better I don't touch," he says. And also: "Bring me a pencil to write something down." The pads of his fingers fail to grip the pencil. Again and again they try, and again it slips and drops. Someone else writes for him: me, or Corinne, or the worker, or me. He always complains: "How did you write it, tell me, how?" he cries, lounging in the chair, devouring the soft part of the bread and imagining out loud: "Just imagine if I was a tailor, threading those thin needles all day."

HANDWRITING (4)

E VERY MORNING, WHEN she went out earlier than early, she said to Sammy: "Make the child her sandwich for school, you hear?" He didn't hear, he covered his head with the thick blanket, his face scrunched up in pleasure. The child woke him, stood next to the bed dressed in the clothes that would have gotten her in big trouble if the mother had seen them: a fancy dress of bright colors, pulled out of the closet and patched together. He mumbled, pulled the blanket higher over his head so that his legs were exposed to the knee. At the big recess he'd turn up in the schoolyard with the sandwich he would have liked for himself, only the kind he would have liked for himself, wrapped in plastic and crammed into his pocket—two slices of bread, each about four inches thick, generously smeared with a pink paste of cream cheese and half a jar of strawberry jam. She threw it in the trash and bought herself a roll with sour pickles on credit at the kiosk next to the school, which she ate bite by bite: one bite for her, one for Havatzelet. Havatzelet pushed back her heavy black curls a little when she bent over the roll and held them loosely to her cheek. The child looked in wonder at Havatzelet's slender fingers gathering a tress of hair, her hollowed hand hovering for a moment over her cheek, touching and not touching. Everything Havatzelet did or said cast a stone into a lake, leaving circles of wonder on the surface of the water. But she didn't say much, and what she did say sounded like ground gravel: she was deaf and mute, Havatzelet, she sat in the front row to read the teacher's lips, with the child always at her side, watching with bated breath as the lines of the notebook filled with Havatzelet's writing, line after line, a pattern of embroidery.

The perfection of her handwriting was almost sublime, so superior that it left no room for envy, only gave rise to a desire to kneel in adoration: the letters were pure and clear even in their moments of greatest convolution, following each other neatly at a slight, even slant, continuing each other but not joined together, as if they had given birth to one another by breath or by sound, similar but not identical, attentive to their place in the word and at the same time to the broad tapestry of the line and the page, which was whole and symmetrical without being monotonous. The child brought Havatzelet gifts: Rosemarie chocolate, a bead bracelet she stole from Corinne, and the musical box in the form of a Swiss chalet that Maurice had once sent. Every day after school the two of them went to the child's house, where nobody was home, took off their clothes and draped themselves in the mother's ironed tablecloths and sheets, sipped the wine the child boiled in the coffeepot and served, because that was what the children drank in *Model Little Girls* by the Comtesse de Ségur. Their heads heavy with the hot wine, they stretched out on the lawn outside, still wrapped in the tablecloths and turbans, closing their eyes in consent when the pine tree shed its needles on their faces. Nona stood on her concrete steps and called to the child in a loud voice, but the child didn't answer, she went on listening to the ugly obscure speech emerging from Havatzelet's mouth, the words ground into a thick, coarse growl, strained, rising and falling, repulsive and fascinating at once, so foreign to her fragile wrists, to the etched, quivering lips that produced these sounds. She brought Havatzelet her notebook from her schoolbag, and opened it: "Write, Havatzelet, write," she requested, putting a sharpened pencil in her hand and almost forcing it onto the paper: "Write." Havatzelet wrote. There was a silence, which Nona's stubborn calls only emphasized. Once more the rows of pearls flowed from Havatzelet's hand, the slanting letters stretched their long necks like proud young colts.

The child kept on spoiling new notebooks. The first half of the first page, so fresh and pure, bore letters and words that tried to tame themselves, to aspire to emulate those of Havatzelet, but in the middle of the gleaming expanse of the page they collapsed, became themselves, broke with one jerk of the elbow the beautiful glass cage in which they had been placed, and galloped off wildly in all directions, distorted, clamorous, and blind as a famished mob falling on crusts of bread thrown to them on the road: one letter screeched, gaped with a black, toothless mouth or grew a monstrous growth on its forehead, another bent down to gather its scattered limbs, a third was spiky as a porcupine, a fourth lost the force of gravity and flew, while another bit its ankle with a sharp tooth. The child looked and saw filth: that's what it was, filth. At night, when she lay with her eyes open, adding penny to penny—the money she had stolen from Nona's purse and the money she would steal tomorrow from the mother to buy more new notebooks from Levy—assailed by the memory of the filthy writing from which there was no escape, she felt in full force the existence of the thing inside her and its constant expansion, the source of the contamination with which she was wholly infected, inside and out, expressed in the letters whose ugliness was evil, a sin that clung to her, that turned her into someone else and gave birth in her place to that other, corrupted child with the monstrous handwriting.

The spoiled notebooks with the writing on the first page piled up in the big drawer of the chest, covered with newspapers, but the mother found them and flew into a towering rage at the scandalous waste. The supply was cut off: she went to Levy and warned him not to sell the child any more notebooks. The child wrote in the spoiled notebooks at tremendous speed and almost with her eyes closed, so as not to see her handwriting, and only on one side of the page. Havatzelet evaporated overnight in the cold air now coming from the child, she was absorbed by the cement between the bricks of the child's inner fortress.

THE FIRST PAGE

THE PITS OF time, what were they, the pits of time? Wherever Maurice was, that was the pits of time. And also the rumors of where Maurice was. Now and then the mother threw a scrap into the pits of time: "Sammy found him sleeping on a bench in the street after his landlord threw him out."

Or: "He goes from one friend to another, sleeps on their living-room couches, until they get tired of him, too."

Or: "Did you find him, *ya* Sammy?" And again, lying on the couch, pale and muddled, half asleep, waiting for hours for Sammy to return from his search: "Did you find him?"

Once they put a notice in the paper, the mother and Sammy, small but on the first page: "Maurice, call home."

They needed him to get a passport for the child.

On the Couch

THE BEDROOM WAS tip-top, but sometimes she fell asleep on the living-room couch, like a babysitter waiting for the children's parents to come home, making this sleep and falling asleep something snatched, taken illegally, in parentheses, ready at any moment to get up and move on. In this way she managed her insomnia; she tricked it by moving from place to place. She wrapped herself in the airplane blanket that Aunt Marcelle once brought from one of her flights, and sometimes not even that: she covered herself only with the blue shawl knitted by someone, not her, keeping one eye open even in her sleep, alert to the footsteps outside, not hers.

Sleep on the couch was sentry sleep. She never stopped being the shack's sentry, its life. But anyone else sleeping on the couch drove her crazy. "*Yallah* get up and go to your beds," she upbraided Sammy or Corinne or me, sometimes keeping to herself the knowledge of what exactly were "your beds," after having changed the rooms and the beds or both of them around that very morning.

Her rearranging stopped at the threshold of the bedroom. She hardly touched the bedroom, but this "hardly," too, left wide margins of possibility for change and yearning: the bedspread, the color of the walls, the location of the chest, the position of the mirror, the coatrack, the curtain, the blinds, the framed tapestries with the roses she had once embroidered in a rare fit of feminine patience. Once the tapestries had been separated, looking at each other from opposite walls, once they hung side by side, or one above the other; another time they were reframed, with a wooden support behind them, and set slantwise on the chest, in semi-profile, sympathetic witnesses to the changing pastel shades of the room: pale mauve, mauve pink, peach pink, sky blue, porcelain, pale green (only for a week), and pale mauve again.

All these changes and small shifts did not upset the bedroom's status as a reserve, the kind of site that is visited but not invaded by life's daily events. The bedroom was a kind of dollhouse arranged and rearranged, with all the details required for the game carefully set in place, but for some reason the game never concludes, is suspended forever in expectation.

At midday, in the afternoon, and sometimes in the morning, whenever she wasn't there, I would lie on the double bed on the quilted bedspread without taking off my shoes, staring at the rippling of the semitransparent curtain in the breeze. The room was always pervaded by the smell of something new, not yet completely removed from its wrapping, peeping out, hovering like a halo over what stood heavy and muffled in the room: the mother's expectation. And something else stood there, too: forbidding expectation.

The room was the reserve for expectation and its prohibition, empty most of the hours of the day and night—a place of anticipation without anyone to anticipate.

Who was she waiting for? At first, the one whose name we were forbidden to mention, it conjured him up too vividly; afterward just "him," the great nameless "him," which detached from its subject turned into a disembodied longing, the glimmer of a different fate. Longings for longings.

The expectation that filled the room drove her from it: often she moved to the couch in the middle of the night, after she had stopped waiting for Sammy or Corinne, and the shack finally sank into its essential silence, which she loved so much, because then and only then she could hear the beating of its heart, when she was by herself, inside the walls and between the floor tiles, undisturbed.

THE MIDDLE OF THE NIGHT

NONA ANNOYED HER by saying: "*Yallah ya binti*, enough, it's the middle of the night, *nuss ellayl*." "What *nuss ellayl*, what do you mean *nuss ellayl*? It's eight o'clock," the child argued with her back to Nona, standing on the stool up against the rectangle of glass in the front door, between the white and the black, the dense cloudy white of the room and the heavy darkness outside, the tall waterfall of darkness sliding down Nona's concrete steps to the ground, toward the path leading to the shack, the cypress tree, the road, the houses on the other side.

Inside, in the windowless thirteen-by-sixteen-foot quarter-shack, Nona was always boiling something, fanning the hot, stifling haze rising from the pots, the tubs, from the jet of water boiling in the tiny, improvised shower, from the bonfire lit by the *amm* in his yard right under the narrow window of her kitchen, from her breath. She moved through the fog, the Nona, like a big ship stalled in the middle of the sea, waiting for a signal, arrested in its rocking, its heavy swaying from side to side in the white blindness. The radio played, but its playing was not a signal for anything different, only more of the same thing, more of the fog that had turned into a sound, embodied in the wheedling voice of Amm Hamdan delivering his daily sermon on the Arab-language station of Kol Yisrael: "*Ikhwani, ya wlad masr eltayyibeen*," my brothers, the good sons of Egypt.

The child strained her eyes at the darkness in front of her, wiping the vapors off the glass with her sleeve, waiting for a figure to appear, for the sound of the steps climbing the path that would turn into the figure. But the mother had not said exactly when she would come. She said: "Perhaps I'll finish early today." Or: "Perhaps I'll slip away early today." "She said perhaps," the child informed Nona, still with her back to her, "that perhaps she would slip away early today." "Perhaps," repeated Nona with her bitter sigh. "*Yimken*," she reflected for a moment and said again, "*Yimken*."

The child rubbed the toes of her bare feet together, suppressing the resentment welling up in her against the Nona, against her "*yimken*" and its heavy irony filling the room like the white haze, beating against the windowpane and stopping there, retreating from the darkness outside, which, for the time being, contained no "perhaps," but only unequivocal bleakness that was unlikely to give rise to anything except more darkness.

She tensed: another bus came down the road, stopped beyond the shack, at the bus stop. The darkness ripened now with juicy promise, like the seeds of a pomegranate. Now the child could make out the dark contours of the shack, Sammy's welding shop, and the garbage can, looming up in the dark.

A thin stream of cold air stole in under the door, freezing the child's feet and calves. Perhaps it was winter. *Yimken*. In winter there was more of everything: more darkness, more white haze, more long blanks between the expectation, more murmurs and imaginary sounds and false alarms, more urgency when the mother suddenly opened the door at last, poking the dripping umbrella in first and after it her dripping self, wrapped in a big shawl over her coat. The child fled to Nona's bed, pulled the blanket over her head, tucked her hands between her thighs when the mother pulled the blanket down, standing next to the bed still in her dripping coat: "Are you coming?" The child didn't answer; she shut her eyes tight, felt the transparency of her eyelids through which she saw the mother's face, high and distant, as if stripped of its skin. She didn't answer, and pulled the blanket up again. "Good," said the mother and left. The child jumped up and flew to the window: slowly and with difficulty, as if pushed from behind, the bulky, huddled figure of the mother advanced down the path leading to the shack and was swallowed up in the darkness close to the edge of the lawn, next to the cypress tree.

For a long time she went on standing there, staring at the spot that marked the verge of the disappearance and then the disappearance itself, and then she went back to Nona's bed and covered herself with the blanket. Nona lay down beside her, unbuttoning the child's sweater under the blanket, and laying her hand on the ribs that were shaken by weeping: "*Bitayeti leh ya omri*, why are you crying?" The child sat up, quickly pushed her feet into her shoes without tying the laces, raced in her pajamas down the dark path to the shack, straight through the unlocked door to the bedroom, to the mother's bed, and lay down next to her in the empty, solitary place. Her teeth chattered a little from the sharp transition between cold and heat, between the cool, flat freshness of the sheets—so different from the warm, deep hollows of the Nona's bedclothes, steeped in smells of urine, medical ointment, chamomile, and lavender water, and from the pity for Nona and Nona's loneliness inside those bedclothes. The mother switched off the bedside lamp and turned over on her side. Time passed; the child got out of bed in the middle of the night, every night, ran back up the path to Nona's quarter-shack, and knocked loudly on the shaky door with the glass: "It's me," she said.

The Cypress Tree (1)

THE CYPRESS TREE announced the shack, heralded it from far away, from the turn in the road to Savyon. Tall, calm, collected, it was the guard, the strict-yet-reasonable nanny of the wild, out-of-control child that was the shack. Corinne had brought it home with her from Arbor Day at school when she was small, and it was small, too, that's what they said.

The Cypress Tree (2)

IT SOMETIMES STUCK in her craw, that cypress tree, when she didn't appreciate it. Either she was praising it, or it stuck in her craw: obdurate, solid, hard to move. She had her reasons for why it did that: "Its roots spread in the ground and block the drains," she said.

Consultations took place on the sunny porch, what to do about the cypress tree and the roots. Taking part were Marco the gardener, Benny Levakar from the plumbers, Sammy, Nona, and her. Marco said that they had to lasso it with ropes from top to bottom and find the exact angle for it to fall. "Otherwise it could fall right onto your roof tiles, bring the whole house down, smash all the fancy lamps in your living room," he warned. She paled, wiped her hands on her housecoat even though they weren't even wet. "But there are special people for that," she argued nervously, "there are special people from the council for things like that." "Not from the council," intervened Benny Levakar, chewing his fifth date cookie, "It's the ones from the Beautiful Land of Israel that take down trees like this, it's only them that do it." Sammy was beside himself, against the whole idea in principle, even though he took part sporadically in the discussion, running back and forth from the porch to the welding shop: "But why take it down, why do you want to take it down, what's the point of taking it down?" he yelled. "What's the point?" she retorted, "Every second day the drains get blocked and you ask what's the point? He's blocked as the drains"—she turned to the others, waving her arm in Sammy's direction—"I explain to him and he doesn't take it in, the blockhead."

Sammy was given over to the skeptical, suspicious shaking of his head; he didn't hear a word, or else he heard exactly what he was supposed to hear, like they always heard each other's words: ready-made rhetorical flourishes in lovers' quarrels. He feared what he called her "extremism," the rash acts from which there was no going back, how he detested them! In a matter of minutes she would defeat him in their passionate debates over "doing or not doing," that almost always took place after she had already decided or done the deed, and he would withdraw, or pretend to, turning to some third party present in the room, or to some piece of furniture: "That's her problem, she's so extreme. Never consults anyone, just goes ahead and acts. Me, I take advice about everything, I like to hear what people have to say. Not her. She charges ahead, doesn't give a damn." Now he turned back to her, as if he had just remembered something, and opened a second round: "But why do you have to go to special people, pay them money? Can't we bring the tree down ourselves, me and the worker, in a couple of days? You have to deal with it now, right now?"

She really did. "Now" or "immediately" was her middle name. For her there was no pause between the thought or the wish and the act—the act was the simultaneous fruition of the wish and its fulfillment. Every delay, even the slightest, was an act of cruelty, a deliberate torment. She always acted alone—an entire Foreign Legion that deployed on its own behalf, to win. "That's me," she'd say after it was over, which was at one and the same time full of an arrogant sense of will that brooked no obstacle and arch amusement: "That's me. I don't wait, *ni un ni deux*. I act, and that's it."

But the cypress tree was not uprooted. "Something" stopped her. What was that "something"? She didn't know herself, she was apparently overcome by a rare sense of respect for inhibition, she couldn't dismiss it, and she uncharacteristically invented a false sentimental pretext: "Corinne brought it when she was small in an olive can and planted it. I remember how she planted it," she said. Corinne raised the two brown-penciled arches that were her eyebrows. "It wasn't me who brought it, it was Sammy," she said, in the indifferent voice of a court recorder. They could uproot the tree or not—it made no difference to her, because, every thing and every act were doomed from the outset to obey what was inherent and preordained—annihilation, catastrophe, and getting uglier all the time, canceling out the spectrum of difference between action and inaction, something and nothing.

THE CYPRESS TREE (3)

FOR WEEKS MAURICE hung from the top of the cypress tree, wearing his necktie but not hanging from it: a strong, thin, transparent rope was tied around his neck, holding him up so he appeared to be attached to the tree from behind. These were weeks of the year that never was, that wasn't counted among the years, since in some sense all the years existed not as a sum but an image. Up to now I've been rambling, but now for the facts: it wasn't the mother who hanged him. And he didn't hang himself. The thing happened of its own accord and came to light early one morning, the way things do. She, the mother, found him there, at the top of the cypress tree, at first the shoes: she saw them first, polished, toes turned out like those of a ballerina. She didn't recognize the light gray suit he was wearing, which caused her to heave a sigh of relief: at last he had something that she didn't know, that allowed him to disappear into the crowd. Will you have coffee, Maurice? she asked tenderly. He accepted. Every blue swollen vein in his dark drooping face accepted. She placed the little cup of coffee on the lawn, stuck a straw as long as a ladder inside it, and the three sparrows that came to her aid moved the straw carefully until it entered his mouth. When he finished the coffee he had to have another cup, and this time she didn't feel resentful and only put in too much sugar out of absentmindedness. He took a sip and made a grimace with his lips.

Amazing that she noticed the grimace of his lips in the general grimace of his face. "I like my coffee *mazbut, ya* Lucette," he said, "as if you don't know that I like it *mazbut*." She stopped him, listened for a moment to something, to sounds that reached her from above, like his voice: "We're talking so nicely, Maurice," she said, "at last we're talking really nicely," she said, and began to dig up the deep basin around the bottom of the cypress tree, to mark seats with the iron pegs she took from the welding shop. Each seat was marked by an iron peg and was an iron peg. He lit a cigarette, not with his dangling hands, which looked longer than ever, but by rubbing it against the coat of plastic that was beginning to cover him, heating up in the morning sun, which was already quite strong. "I've never been afraid of death, Lucette, you know that," he said, his eyes fixed on the tiled roof of the shack. "Of course you weren't afraid, why should you be afraid? You weren't afraid of life, why be afraid of death? It all comes from not believing in God," she said, counting us as we filed in front of her on the way to the basin: Corinne, Sammy, and me. We brushed our teeth in the saucers of sand she set before us and sat down on the pegs, each in his place under the cypress tree. We looked up at the feet swaying in the breeze inside the polished shoes.

Corinne started first, even though nobody asked her to, especially not the mother who was busy wrapping the chain of sheets tied together around our feet, tightening them in the loose soil. The coat of plastic began to cover his shoes, too, and through their soles we saw his feet, the bottoms of his narrow, relatively small feet, the feet of a boy or a small man. Corinne started first, she was the first to raise the candle she was holding high, until its violet flame lit his feet but didn't touch them. In the light of the flame she read aloud the lines, curves, and cross-hatchings printed there: *A mon seul désir, a mon seul désir*, she read very slowly, stressing every word for me and for Sammy, whose translation we understood even less than the source, blowing on our candles to put out the flame that refused to be put out, but went on burning all the time, with the low intensity of a flame on the point of going out. The mother came with the upholstery brush, climbed the ladder, and brushed his suit, to clean the dust falling from the branches of the cypress tree. "Let him keep his self-respect at least," she explained to us, took a pair of scissors out of her pocket to cut off a lock of his mop of silver hair, and scattered the fine hair over our heads. "You prayed for his rain, here it is," she said, knelt down next to us, in the basin, gathered up the hair that had fallen to the ground, separated each strand, and kissed them one by one, sticking the hair to the transparent words seared into the soles of his feet, *a mon seul désir.*

Now she gave the sign. Corinne was the first and we followed her: we raised our arms with the lit candles until they reached his feet and the words with the hair stuck on with spit.

A MON SEUL DÉSIR

HER VISIT TO me in winter in New York, perhaps a year before she died, the
thin fall coat that she wore in a shade of aubergine, which she bought at
a sale in the shopping center in the aunt's country town in France, "two
yards from the house." There were two things she never stopped doing: looking up at the heights of the buildings in amazement, until her neck hurt,
and searching the shops for all kinds of knickknacks for the house, such as
tins for spices, rice, and sugar, decorated with Christmas pictures, Santa
Claus with white snowflakes. She had set her heart on these, for some reason. We found only five little ones for spices, and she, according to her
calculations, needed three more: for tumeric, cumin, and bay leaves. We
strode down the cold city streets where the snow froze in a matter of hours
into a murky, slippery layer of ice. At first, perhaps, she brought up the rear,
panting a little: "Why are you walking so fast?" she complained, stopping for
a moment at the corner, where the wind was particularly vicious. She stood
still, wrapped her face in her woolen scarf right up to her eyes, spreading out
her fingers swollen with cold inside her gloves. "It's *jehennom* here," she said
in a tortured voice, through the two layers of scarf. "What do you like about
this hell?" We went into a diner to warm ourselves, ordered chicken soup
with noodles. She sank deep into the padded seat opposite me, with only
her very round shoulders and her neck appearing above the tabletop, turning the knife and fork wrapped in a paper napkin around and around.

The apathy with which she stared at the interior of the diner, at the door
to our right opening and closing, at the blurred snowflakes in the blurred
street beyond the windowpane, the new film clouding her eyes, in which
her pupils were bathed as if soaking in a pot of hot water, softening: she
looked as if she had no purpose. For the first time in her life without a purpose in the world, stripped of her purpose. A thought occurred to me: "Are
you sick?" I asked. She didn't answer, bent over her bowl of soup and blew
carefully, in respectful gratitude. I didn't know if she had heard me. She
wiped the corners of her mouth with the napkin, suddenly sat up straight
like a tortoise sticking its neck out of its shell: "Don't talk to me about sicknesses, you hear? I had enough of that with your uncle and aunt in France
before I came here," she shot out. Her eyes flamed, her whole face flamed to
the roots of the wavy silver hair above her narrow forehead. The visit with
her sister in France before she came here had upset her. They had gone to
Nice, she and Aunt Marcelle and her husband, to spend a few days there
with Uncle Marco and his wife, sitting on the handsome balcony overlooking the sea, playing cards. She didn't play cards, she was bored in half an
hour: it was only the competition with herself, with her own fate, that she
could engage. When they weren't playing cards, or eating, or watching
television, or reminiscing, they talked about sickness and medicine. "All
the time sickness and medicine, she talks about how many pills and vita-
mins she swallows a day, and he talks about how many medicines he
takes. They sit there with their bottles before eating, after eating, pills and
more pills," she said furiously, in deep disappointment. She tilted the soup
plate toward her, drank the last spoonfuls. Her face dimmed again. "Perhaps it's their age," I ventured, I looked at her, at the vague fog settling on
her face again, it frightened me—as if I were holding on to the hem of her
coat so she wouldn't slide down a cliff. "Don't tell me age, it's got nothing
to do with age," she argued, falling silent in the middle of the sentence.
When they brought the check (the argument about who was going to pay,
her arm violently pushing my wallet off the table, thrusting it back into
my bag), she remembered as if by the way: "I threw them out, I flushed
them all down the toilet. I didn't keep a thing," she said. "What?" I asked.
"That whole *amayat* of heart and blood pressure and cholesterol pills the
doctor gave me. I threw out the lot. No pill will ever pass my lips again,"
she announced triumphantly. "You're out of your mind," I said. "No, no."
She shook her head. "They're out of theirs." She wagged a warning finger

at me: "Don't tell a soul, you hear? Not Sammy, not your sister, no one. I haven't got the strength for their nagging."

We went on trudging through the frost, pretending to be tourists. She looked like someone sick with influenza who had come to work out of a sense of duty, determined to stick it out to the end of the day. We went up and down the Empire State Building. When we were going up or down, in the murky yellow light of the elevator that made her face even yellower, she told me about the tapestries, the wall hangings she had seen with Aunt Marcelle in the Cluny Museum, before they went to Nice. She loved those tapestries with the princess and that animal with the horn and the long neck, the unicorn. Afterward she and Aunt Marcelle sat in the little garden next to the museum, ate crepes, and looked at the brochure she had bought in the museum, as a souvenir. "She counts every penny, that Marcelle. Don't spend money on that," she said to the mother when she wanted to buy the brochure. "It's a waste of your money. That's what she's like: on the rags she buys in the market she spends and spends without a second thought, like a person who lets all the camels pass, and only says no to the female camel. When she comes he says, no, you won't pass." We left the building and emerged onto Fifth Avenue, into the stream of passersby hurrying from something to something else, where we were more foreign than ever: we didn't hurry, and we didn't enjoy dawdling either. It started to rain, and the rain came down harder, whirling around in the strong winds: our umbrellas broke and were cast into the trash cans to join their mangled sisters. We took shelter under an overhang of one of the buildings until the rain stopped or abated.

Dripping, wrapped in a thick shawl over her coat like a refugee, she rummaged in her handbag and fished out a lipstick with which she proceeded to paint her lips without looking in a mirror. It was a pink lipstick given to her by Corinne before the trip, which made her lips look like a congealed wound. "Those tapestries tell you what she says, that princess," she suddenly said out of the blue. "What princess?" I asked, confused. "The one in the tapestries in the museum, with that unicorn, but it's not so easy to understand what she's saying. *A mon seul désir*," she quoted with suppressed pleasure. "How do you say that in Hebrew?" she asked. "To my sole desire, or perhaps, my heart's desire, the thing I yearn for above all," I tried to translate. She went on, interrupting me. "Strange how you don't understand what she means when she says it. Do you know what she meant?"

She raised her eyes to me, narrowed against the wind, surrounded by wrinkles closing in from all sides in their pale of settlement, setting them apart from the rosy and smooth expanse of her cheeks. "I don't understand," I said.

RAIN

IN THE RAIN the shacks got lost, they lost the thread of the syntax that made them into a sentence, a residential neighborhood, and returned to their previous existence, in the time of the sand dunes, when they were scattered almost at random, each to itself, blind to the others, as if it were alone in the world. Before the rain we saw the nature that was strewn between the shacks as tame, subdued islands, a background to the shacks, not the foreground. In the rain nature emerged untamed; it exposed its true, uncompromising, jealous character. The mild slope of the hill between the shack and the old reservoir was no longer mild—it plunged. Water-falls rushed from the hill down toward the shack below, sweeping up every-thing in their path, flooding the brick wall the mother had built to arrest the erosion, streaming, to the lawn and then the porch, coming into the shack through the gap at the bottom of the door, through the towels and floor rags crammed into the gap to bar the water's way.

It was five or six in the morning, the hour of the flood when we woke up to it: the mother plied the mop. In her wet nightgown, plastered to her thighs, she beat the mop at the sides of the beds and under the beds, in the still-dark room, splashing in the water that flooded in from under the door and the water leaking from above in a trickle from the ceiling, coming in through the roof tiles, soaking the attic, and raining into the rooms. "Get up!" she yelled at Sammy in despair, "Get up! Water!" And he got up, threw the blanket over his shoulders, and went out with the hoe into the rain, to dig a drainage canal between the paved path leading to the shack and the steep thorny slope of the hill.

The child did nothing, she stood on the soaked carpet and watched. "Move," the mother scolded her, hitting her lightly on her ankles with the mop, "move already, lend a hand." She didn't move, she didn't lend a hand, looking at the flooded floor, at the old notebooks with the writing on the first page, which she had hidden under the bed, how they floated now wide open, facedown in the water, or faceup, with the ugly letters smudging and blurring, turning into a blue stain.

SAMMY IN THE RAIN

WHEN HE GOES out to work on construction sites in the rain, she's beside herself. And at night, too. She says: "At night, on the pipes, in the rain." He always works until nighttime on the building frames. If he has to start in the morning, he starts at noon; if at noon, then in the afternoon; if in the afternoon, then at night. But it makes no difference when he starts, he always keeps going till nighttime. "Do you have *constructzia* today?" she asks. "I do," he says, "only the guy from the building materials is holding me up. Give us a check for the building materials guy so I can get pipes out of him." "No checks," she says, "you never gave me back what you took two weeks ago, you'll get me into trouble with those checks." "Till tomorrow," he promises, bringing her handbag from the hall for her to take out the checkbook, "tomorrow I'll get my money from the contractor. I'll pay you back." "No," she says, snatching the bag from him, "your word is water in a sieve, that's how much I believe your promises. Your word isn't worth a damn, it's water in a sieve." "By tomorrow, I'm telling you," he begs. He grabs the checkbook, writes the sum down in his crooked writing, and gets it wrong, tears up the check, and writes another one, which she signs. "You'll get me into trouble, you," she says again.

But she's already implicated, waiting anxiously in the corner of the couch for the implication that has already in fact occurred, on the nights of the construction with the rain outside. She doesn't let the facts confuse her: the fact that she's here, deep in the heart of the warm room, huddled in a sweater and a blanket in the corner of the couch with the electric heater at her feet ("you have to sit right on top of it, that heater, to get warm, it's just for show, not worth a damn"), doesn't deny the cold, the terrible freezing cold outside that makes her teeth chatter. "He's up there on the *constructzia*, in the rain," she says. "Who knows where he is in this rain." It isn't only that she's there on the "*constructzia*" in her heart, she's there in her body, too, the body that is the heart, in the chattering of her teeth, in the shivering that seizes hold of her even when she covers herself with three layers and puts on two pairs of socks. Every half hour she goes out, in her nightgown, her robe and umbrella, to the path leading to the shack and from it to the road, to wait, to check a false hope. "Maybe he's already on his way back, that idiot. Maybe he already came back and he's sitting in the pickup, talking to the worker," she says.

Sometimes he really is there, in the pickup with the worker, waiting for the song on the tape to end, and then another one and another one, eating the steak sandwich they bought at the Tiger Inn and then five containers of Bavarian cream: three for Sammy, two for the worker. She knocks on the window, sticks her face to it, furious with relief: "Why don't you come inside, why?" "In a minute," he says, poking his head out of the door (the handle that opens the window broke a year ago), "In a minute I'm telling you, madam boss."

On other nights of pouring rain she can't stand it anymore: she throws off the blanket, switches off the heater, gets dressed in a minute, and takes three buses to the building site, to see how he is. She wanders in the dark between the skeletons of the silent, deserted buildings in the middle of some little town, searching for his building.

Sammy is at the top of the skeleton, 100 or 125 feet above ground, only his shirt on his back, pouring with water, welding something. For a moment he straightens up, swaying on the girder in the rain and bending down to his welding again. She stands at the foot of the building looking up, straining her eyes, seeing nothing but the sparks of the blowtorch shining in the rain.

On Other Rainy Nights

On other rainy nights nobody expected anyone, and the rustling sounds and voices outside were none of our business, evidence of nothing and signifying nothing, because "everybody" was already at home, all of us sprawled or semi-sprawled in the living room, competing for proximity to the heater—even Corinne, who on these nights suspended her usual care for her appearance and walked or lay around with her hair mussed, a single loose clip on her head that didn't hold anything up, wearing long white flannel underpants, and, draped over them, something between a shawl and an old blanket.

The room that was the living room seemed to be holding something, guarding the light that was shining on us indirectly, bringing exactly the right warmth of here and now, testifying that there was nothing missing, that we lacked for nothing. There we sat, close together, in the only space in the shack that was free of the rubble of the building site that was the shack: the mother was renovating, again, again she turned the house upside down to make it even more of a home. We sat among the dusty cardboard boxes that filled the living room, the furniture removed from other rooms (two in all), the groaning Friedman fridge ("Friedman is a good firm"), the standing and table lamps, the pictures taken for the time being off the walls and leaned against each other, according to height, the one from the little passage to the bathroom first in line, peering at us from the gap between the cardboard boxes: *Le balcon.*

The evening was endless, merging into the night without us noticing; we were confined to our places not like prisoners or the sick, but like people recovering from life, even if only for a few hours, this life of which the mother and Sammy and sometimes Corinne said: "Life, life, life."

Sammy wanted fried eggs even though he had already had two for his breakfast, but there was no bread to have with the eggs, except dry bread from yesterday. We went out to the starry sky of the kitchen, Corinne and the mother and I, the roofless room in the process of renovation, over which the sky spread dense with rain, split by lightning as if by a knife. The mother fried the eggs, Corinne held the umbrella over her head, over the stove, and I shone the flashlight on the sizzling frying pan. We used all the eggs in the fridge, maybe eight, and toasted the dry bread over the gas flame of the stove until it turned black. The water had already reached above our ankles, but it hadn't passed the low wall of cinder blocks placed between the entrance to the kitchen and the living room. There everything was still dry. We made our way back, with the pan and the bread and the plates, threading between the furniture and the cardboard boxes (the corner of Corinne's shawl caught on the chest and she almost tripped with the pan) to Sammy waiting sleepily for his eggs. We spread a towel on an empty rectangle of the carpet and sat cross-legged around the pan and the blackened bread and the washed scallions and sharp red peppers for Corinne. Sammy dipped first, leaned over and tore open the skin of the yellow yolk with the bread, and we followed him. Sammy explained something to us, but mainly to himself: the most important thing with fried eggs was to calculate the exact relation between the eggs and the bread, so that the bread was consumed at exactly the same pace. The bread wasn't all consumed; there was still some left after we had scooped up all the bits of egg in the pan. The mother brought the last piece of bread reverently to her lips and blessed it before she threw it into the trash can standing in the middle of the kitchen, in a puddle of rainwater.

THE PICTURE: *LE BALCON* (2)

T HE WISHES OF the three in the picture, that's what was so mysterious. What kept the child's eyes riveted to the picture for hours on end: what did they want? What did they really want?

In the way they sat and stood there was something both intentional and accidental at one and the same time, as if they had been caught in the middle of something—an event or an incident—that had happened again and again, since the beginning of time, and they experienced it as it happened but also presented it. The man stood gazing at some point in the distance, over the heads of the women, perhaps connected to them and perhaps in their company by chance. The expression on his face was mask-like, almost frozen, and he held his hands in front of him as if he were unable to move them, as if they were in plaster casts. The more the child looked at him, the more she understood: he was so connected to the two women, the elder and the younger, that he had no need to show it; the connection was taken for granted, part of the complete, natural randomness. The dark jacket he wore merged into the dark background behind him, only the triangle of his white shirt, the immobilized hands, and the pale skin of his face stood out in this darkness: he wasn't standing, he was emerging out of the darkness, the man with the narrow mustache, but as if bit by bit, not quite complete, like a ghost, but not an alien—a domestic ghost.

The older woman, dressed in white, and the young woman sitting next to her, she, too, dressed in white—were they there under compulsion or of their own free will, on the balcony with the green railing? Were they responding to the man with the immobilized hands, seeking to please him, or was he responding to them, agreeing to join them, as if they had called him out of some inner room, for the purposes of the picture, saying "Come here for a minute"? Was she sitting or standing, the older woman dressed in white, whose puffed-out skirts, blown up like a balloon, hid the contours of her body, the bend of her hips as she was sitting, if indeed she was? The child hated the older woman's expression; it disturbed her so much that in the end she loathed it, like the piece of a puzzle that refused to fit in, unsolved despite all attempts to place it: the older woman's face remained annoyingly enigmatic. She held her head slightly to the side, her fingers touching each other perhaps in affection, perhaps in some pretended meekness. Her whole attitude, standing or sitting, radiated a kind of meekness, an infuriating self-abnegation, or a pretense in order to keep a secret. There was a secret. The child knew it: she had a secret, the older woman; she was concealing herself on purpose, making herself pale and bloodless, to keep people away from her secret. And her partner in this secret was the black-haired young woman with the blazing eyes who set herself apart from them, from the man and the older woman, distanced herself from them demonstratively, almost defiantly. She is sitting in the billowing flounces of her white dress, but these flounces are not really hers; she consents to sit in them, to lend herself to them, but they are not really hers. What is she gazing at, and why does her gaze have to set her so far apart, to distance herself so much? What is she separating herself from, in her gaze? The young woman's powerful face shows the traces of a struggle, whose conclusion is this setting of herself apart, this demonstrative, apparent detachment—of this the child is sure: the detachment is only apparent, for the black-haired young woman sees everything, sees from behind even when she looks in front, she sees every twitch or shift in the expressions of the man at her back and the older woman on her left; she sees, she sees, filling the scene with her blazing, absent vision, a seething passivity full of blocked sorrow, a grief that blocking itself turned into a mire of oppression.

SORROW

THERE WAS ONE time when he came for a few days, he came in good faith, had not been thrown out of his life into the shack in the dead of night, from one abyss to another, but simply knocked on the door, in the normal way, not our house but on Nona's door. Holding a plastic bag in one hand and flowers (gladiolus) in the other, his briefcase tucked under his arm, Maurice stood in the doorway, looked at the child who was sitting right in front of him, on Nona's armchair facing the door. They looked at each other, he and the child, and didn't make a move. Nona was busy in the kitchenette, oblivious, while the child took in what he was wearing: a burgundy-colored shirt and beige trousers. Burgundy socks the same color as his shirt. Summer shoes with holes in them, but made on purpose, in a kind of close pattern, the leather supple as the shoes of a dancer. He didn't say a word and went on looking at her intensely, but the intensity of the gaze suddenly changed, becoming a slack, watery indifference, as if the puppeteer holding him up had loosened his grip. "Nona!" the child called.

They sent her to play with Rachel Amsalem, the Nona and Maurice. "Go, go and play *ya bint*," said Nona, wiping her glasses with the greasy towel, and Maurice smoked Nona's cigarettes, pulling a disgusted face as he smoked: "How can you smoke these cigarettes?" he complained, giving the child an absent look through the smoke and looking away again: "Go on, run along now. Afterward I'll give you something nice," he said. "Rachel isn't home," said the child, and she sat on the floor at their feet and played pick-up sticks with herself, putting the tips of her fingers on the points and pressing down hard until the sticks bent. The white gladiolus were lying on the white bed in two bunches wrapped in cellophane, long and dead: one bunch for the mother and one for the Nona. The child sank as she heard the words and refused to take in their meaning; time was reversed like a sock turned inside out. When Maurice got up to go to the toilet, Nona said that perhaps he would come home. "All the children have a father and a mother. Don't you want your father and mother to be together?" she asked in a wheedling voice. "No," said the child, "I don't." "Nobody's asking you." The Nona's face hardened. She crossed her legs: "It's only here in this country that people ask children about everything," she said, undid one yellow braid, and plaited it again, throwing it over her shoulder.

He wanted to do it "properly" this time, Maurice, to give and take, not to just drop on them. "I, *ya sitti*, didn't come to drop on anyone," he said to Nona in the end, after one of the ends in the conversation, which had a lot of ends, punctuated by heavy silences. This the child heard, "to drop." She peeked at him when he said it, at his wide lips distorted in disgust or pain: impossibly thin he stood on the edge of a well, his feet over the side, one little push to his back and he would fall, he had already fallen—swept inside as if he had been flung, not pushed, swallowed in a second into the mouth of the well.

That afternoon in the shack was full of politeness. The mother took off from work. They talked in the living room, couch facing couch, they talked in the kitchen, they talked on the porch, they talked again in the living room, carrying full or half-full cups of coffee. There was a new, solemn embarrassment in the shack, full of suppressed, agonizing expectation. The air grew denser and denser; it reached a point where it almost erupted, as if it had been filled with a pump, leaving room for nothing except his gaze, fixed on the mother and only on her, narrow and focused as the point of a pin and wide as the sea, brimming over—beyond his eagerness, hunger, supplication, yearning, and sorrow. When he retired to the bedroom to rest awhile, lying on the bed in his clothes, with a handkerchief soaked in cold water on his forehead because of a headache, the mother went to the Nona, to sit with her, shifting her thighs nervously on her chair. This time she spoke in a lowered voice, like a schoolgirl caught copying a test, drinking in Nona's words, which had the flavor and the tone of spells, of oaths: "*Tawli ruhek, tawli ruhek*," she repeated over and over again: "Be patient."

Corinne and Sammy had vanished, they were nowhere to be seen: one thing seemed irreconcilable with another. Things were somehow out of joint and the shack stopped being "home," stopped being itself: doors and windows were shut, closed to something. The child was impossible; whatever they said to her she answered, "No, no," she wanted nothing, not to come in or to go out. Maurice wanted to go out, he wanted them to get dressed up and take the bus to the cinema in Ramat Gan to see *Doctor Zhivago*. They went to call the child, behind Rachel Amsalem's house, in the thorns. There was an old tap there that didn't turn off, and she and Rachel crouched under the running water, in the mud, competing to see who could eat the most crammed into their mouths in spoonfuls and washed down with water. The mother dragged her away, pulled her by the arms and dragged her lying on her stomach as she dug her feet into the ground. The mother pushed her into the shower, filthy and crying, scrubbed her body, and shampooed her hair: twice she escaped wet and covered in lather and twice she was forced back under the boiling jet of water that stung her skin more than the mother's pinches and slaps.

Maurice sat in the living room, leafing through the newspaper, but a few times he came to peep into the shower, leaned against the door in his light gray suit, and looked at his face reflected in the mirror above the basin, smoothing his narrow mustache with his yellow finger: "But it's Dr. Zhivago," he said in surprise.

He liked Omar Sharif, he had even met him once, he told the mother on the bus, when the two of them sat on their bench in front of the child. His arm, she noted, encircled the mother's shoulders but didn't touch them, it rested on the back of the seat. The mother nodded, drinking him in, her shoulder blades moved under her dress: her back was a quivering map of feelers and open mouths, a tension of intent and intense devotion, intense tenderness. She had been taken, the mother: the child saw it with horror, how she was being taken.

For long moments before they entered the cinema they stood and licked the ice creams Maurice bought for them (he took a few pennies from the mother), they stared at the giant picture of Omar Sharif on the giant poster. He and the mother suddenly held hands, looking at the poster, not at each other, united in a profound agreement—Maurice and Omar Sharif were two peas in a pod.

Omar looked at Omar. No, Omar looked at the mother looking at Omar in the darkness of the movie hall, watching the screen only out of the corner of his eye while he looked at her, only at her, watching the screen but not really watching it, seeing through the Omar on the screen the Omar sitting next to her and gobbling her up.

They almost missed the last bus back to the neighborhood. The child fell asleep and Maurice carried her for a way in his arms, panting. It was night, but the next day had already begun, in the night, the tiny cog wheels of the next day.

The mother got up early to go to work, but the child didn't go to school; she said she had a stomachache, covered herself with the blanket, and scratched lines on the sheet with her fingernail as she listened to the sounds and noises made by Maurice in the shack, marking his passage from room to room, the metallic clatter: the mother's copperware that he overturned as he passed. The child got up, lay under the cypress tree, and pretended to read. She didn't say a word to him. She noted with hostility every move he made, every expression on his face. He told her he would prepare rice fit for a king, or a queen. He didn't ask her to come with him to the kitchen, but she went, sat down next to him, and asked if he believed in God. In the kitchen he was on wheels: pots, pans, ladles, boxes of spices, bits of parsley stuck to the counter and the floor, towels he kept taking out of the drawer because he forgot where he had put the one before. "I believe in man and in his free will, not in God," said Maurice. "There's nothing like the will of man." In the meantime he fried the ingredients for the rice fit for a king, or a queen: chicken livers, hearts, gizzards, onions, pine nuts. To the rice he added saffron. A wintry sun came in through the low kitchen window; light poured onto the floor. Maurice ate with his hands, scooping up rice and livers with his long dark fingers and putting the food in his mouth without dropping a single grain. Even his fingers, it seemed, stayed dry, not greasy. She did as he did: she gathered the rice in her fingers but she kneaded it a bit until it turned into a little ball, feeling his radiant smile shining on her, his whole smiling face spraying glowing sparks, like Sammy's blowtorch. "I believe that there's a God," said the child with her mouth full of rice. He took her hand, brought it to his lips, and kissed it, holding it for a long moment: "It's good that you believe, never mind in what, it's impossible to live without believing," said Maurice. That evening he stayed with her till late, at the table in the hall, until she finished her math homework, or almost finished it; he chain-smoked, with that smile from the afternoon, with the sparks of light, still on his face, waiting with gentle patience, not pressing her even when she sat for a long time daydreaming, chewing the tip of her pencil. He daydreamed, too, and woke up suddenly to the sound of his own voice: "What did you say, *ya omri?*"

When she came home from school the next day, he was no longer there. The shack was empty of him, of his few belongings. The mother didn't say anything. She read her book, lying on her side, curled up with her knees close to her stomach. The child threw down her schoolbag and flew outside, to the bus stop. She reached it breathless just as the bus was leaving. For a moment she was sure that in one of the windows she had glimpsed the edge of a burgundy sleeve and carefully combed dark hair, with a part on the side. She ran after the bus to the next stop, a little before the parched square of "up there."

Up There

S HE HAD THE little *"msandara"* and the big *"msandara"*: the little one was the storage space at the top of the clothes closet, the big one in the attic under the tiled roof of the shack. The big *msandara*, which was reached from outside, by a long ladder, she called "up there." There were differences between the little *msandara* and the great big up there, separated only by the tiles from the sky.

The little *msandara* at the top of the closet was a temporary hiding place, while the big one was a refugee or quarantine camp.

The little one was a lockup for objects that behaved badly but whose sentence had not yet been passed, while the big one was the penal colony to which they were exiled after being convicted (there were appeals).

The little one was crammed, without a crack of air between the objects, while the big one was two-thirds empty and full of air.

The little one was all immediacy and present tense, a direct and natural continuation of now, while the big one was all past tense: still, dark, full of cobwebs, dust, and lost glory.

The little one was visited every day, things were put in and taken out, while the big one only twice a week, and after a difficult journey.

The little one was the mother's flesh and bone, first person, an extension of the word "me," while the big one was the absolute other: she annexed it, but it refused to be part of her.

The little one was everyday, secular routine, while the big one was magic, a temple.

Everyone knew about the big "up there," they were accomplices, or witnesses, or something: the big "up there" was almost the only site in her life that she couldn't direct and create on her own, the way she preferred and was accustomed to, which demanded cooperation, linked arms, that "lend a hand" of hers.

The thing was that she hardly ever saw it, the big "up there," saw it with her own eyes, except for the few times when she took her courage in both hands and climbed the high ladder leading to the small opening with its little wooden door, and peered trembling inside, into the tall, empty darkness. She was afraid of heights. She—who hardly knew the meaning of fear ("for myself I'm not afraid")—became dizzy at the mere sight of the ladder leaning against the wall of the shack at an ominous slant. But she volunteered to hold it, gripping the lower rungs hard and pushing the ladder toward the wall and into the rose bed where its feet were planted, and urging on the climbers from below, her eyes on the ground: "Climb, climb!"

Everyone without exception was a possible addressee of those exhortations: Sammy, Corinne, me, Sammy's worker, the neighbor, Corinne's boyfriend, the man from the council who came to check the water meters, and once even the boy who came to collect money for what she called "the paralyzed children": first she gave him juice and cookies and then she sent him up the ladder. To be ready for the moment when somebody showed up, she arranged the objects intended for "up there" in a corner of the porch or on the back path, closest to the ladder, and watched brokenhearted as the volunteer trampled her roses (in anticipation of the destruction, she prepared new roses to plant, in season or out): a compelling necessity was at stake, overriding all other considerations.

The vast space above the ceiling, this dark upper domain spread over the entire area of the shack, was a perpetual invitation, a call: it called out to her to "take proper advantage" of it, but also to subdue it. As far as she was concerned, "up there" meant the possibility of extending her range of movement, enlarging its scope: she "showed" the narrow, rectangular opening to the attic what was what. Against the will of the opening, against the will of the "things" (sideboards, dining tables, bookshelves, chairs, and armchairs), she succeeded in accomplishing the impossible and shoving them through the narrow opening, in squaring the circle, but not for long: "up there" was no ordinary storeroom, it was a storeroom for stage sets, and what went in after a while came out again, visited the shack or other houses, and was taken back "up there" again, after the usual quarrel with Sammy about the ladder ("You're taking my things from work").

She dragged the heavy ladder herself, set it down next to the doorway to the attic, a little to the right, so that it would be possible to close the wooden door again with the crooked nail stuck in the frame. The upholstered and reupholstered armchair that had wandered from place to place until it was banished from the shack was now waiting below.

I climbed six rungs of the ladder and stopped, peering down over my shoulder, at the prints left in the rose bed by my shoes: the colors began to blur, the green merging with the brown. "Climb!" She smacked my calf, climbed one or two rungs herself, hoisting the armchair over her head. I took hold of the legs of the armchair and climbed with my back to the ladder. I saw a quarter of her face, distorted by effort and willpower, looking out from behind the back of the chair, below me. If I loosened my grip for a moment the armchair would slip and fall straight onto her head. "Climb!" She roared, but not at me, from pain: her knuckles were blue. We climbed heel to toe, the armchair between us, to the last rung, next to the opening. The armchair stuck in the doorway, its legs in the air. "It won't go in," I said in despair. "Yes it will," she fumed from below. "There's no such thing as won't. Use your brains and it will go in." I pulled the arms as hard as I could, swaying on the ladder, and freed the chair. We began again from the beginning, this time with the chair slightly at a slant, pushing one leg after the other, with little twists and turns, until the whole chair went in, lying on its side. I went in, too, closing the little wooden door behind me. I heard her muffled shouts, her instructions regarding the arrangement of the furniture, and I lay down on the plywood floor, crisscrossed by the heavy supporting beams of the shack.

Till evening fell I sat "up there," curled up in a corner on a pile of cushions that had once decorated the chairs in the dining nook. There was a magical silence, amplified by the darkness, a silence stretching from the low tiled roof above my head, from the long hall that was for the most part empty, left to its own devices, freed from the piles of objects assembled next to the opening, not policed, obedient to a secret inner order, to the logical disorder of a dream, but not my dream—I was a visitor in the dreams of my mother.

Planting Roses

THE ROSE SEEDLING is usually planted in the winter, when the temperatures are low and the growth of the rosebush is slowed down. This is the most suitable time for removing seedlings with exposed roots from the ground of the nursery and planting them in the garden. The physiological state of the seedling is then suitable for transference. Without causing physiological damage, it is important to plant roses with exposed roots, since this gives us the possibility of examining the root system and its shape, the degree of its branching, its health and relative size. This is also the time when there is a large selection of species in the nurseries, enabling you to select the popular species without compromising on the seedlings remaining in the nurseries or other distribution outlets. In the winter there is also no need for frequent watering of the young plant.

Of course, it is possible to plant roses in the late spring and summer, too, if the conditions of the terrain demand it. But in this case they must be planted with the earth around their roots. It is possible to plant selected seedlings in pots in the winter, in order to transfer them with their earth to the garden in summer. Planting in hot seasons must be carried out with great care, and be accompanied by frequent watering until they take root.

At the end of the planting the seedling should be held at the point of the grafting and lightly pulled to ensure that the "bud" of the graft is at the correct height. To straighten the roots after packing the earth, a wide basin should be dug around the plant. Watering is by a gentle stream at the side of the basin (in order not to *disrupt the earth clinging to the roots). The day after planting, the basin is filled in again. Some people make a mound to cover the place of the graft and the base of the branches in order to guard the seedling and the exposed arms from wind and dryness. The mound will be flattened by water from the hose after the plant has taken root.*

EXPOSED ARMS

A T THE AGE of seventeen Corinne got up and got married, left the shack only to return to it time and again, but with the halo of "the married woman with problems," which radiated even more powerfully than simply "the married woman." "Got up and got married" is exact, because most of the time, when she wasn't working or wandering, she spent lounging in the corner she claimed for her own, steeped in the still, silent waters of her visions, in the realms of infinite, stylish solitude where stylish faceless figures ignored each other or bowed stylishly to each other—all of them reflections of Corinne herself. Once in a while, when someone addressed her or when she thought someone addressed her, she shuddered and woke up: "What?" she demanded. "What?"

She married Mermel. His name was actually Sammy Mermelstein, but, in order not to confuse him with Sammy, everyone called him Mermel, a name invented by Nona, maliciously or innocently, because she couldn't pronounce his surname. She, Nona, objected violently to the idea of the marriage: "She's getting married to run away from home, poor girl. That's why she's getting married," she pronounced. The mother started jiggling her thighs, cascades of flesh shaking under her dress: "What do you mean 'run away'?" she fumed. "What has she got to run away from? Did anybody do anything to her?" She herself thought and also said that Corinne was getting married because of the dress. "It's that *msahwara* of a dress that she wants to wear. She's driven herself crazy with that dress," she said.

And the truth is that Mermel crossed the path of the dress and not the opposite: for months before she met him, maybe half a year, Corinne had strewn the rooms of the shack with pages torn out of drawing pads, full of sketches of that figure with the dress, which succeeded in living only up to its knees, where the hem of the dress dissolved into the whiteness of the fine paper. Corinne lacked any talent for drawing or sketching—or perhaps she actually had a great talent, because she took no notice at all of any rules of proportion or perspective, subjugating the body of the replicated woman completely to what she saw in her mind's eye, which seemed to see the world of things and creatures from upside down, like a child bending down and looking out with his head between his knees. Again and again she drew her, not obsessively but automatically and absentmindedly, gliding from unchanging sketch to sketch in the endless repetition of what was already fixed in her mind and wanted to fix itself as a fact in the world by means of one drawing after the other. The figure had no features, only the oval contours of a face, filled with cross-hatching pencil lines that reached the edge of her forehead and stopped, in honor of the hair combed back severely to the top of her head, where it was gathered up and shot out like a fountain in tongues of streaming, cascading curls. At the sides of the head, on a line with the chin, a pair of long earrings dangled, the shape of the spirals of her hair, which were not connected to anything since she had no ears or earlobes. The front of her body covered with what was the main thing—the dress—was flat as a board, and the slender, string-like straps of the dress hung on the round shoulders, dropping slightly downward and always at the same angle—two lines cutting across the exposed arms like scars.

The arms dangled lengthily at the sides of the figure down to the hem of the dress, and then bent to make long, flat hands, spread out horizontally on either side, like a pedestal fixing the figure to the floor and holding it up in the air. The mother looked at the dozens of drawings, turning them over, one after the other: "But what's so special about this dress? It's just a petticoat," she wondered. "That's exactly what's special about it." Corinne snatched the pages from her impatiently and wrote in her spidery hand in the middle of each dress "raw silk," underlining the words with two thick lines.

It was Sammy who first brought Mermel to the house: they met in military prison when they served for about half an hour in the army and were arrested again and again for being AWOL, or cheeking the officers, or something. The conversation between them was as follows: Mermel walked past Sammy in the holding cell and hissed, "Have you got a cigarette?" and an hour later Sammy walked past Mermel and pleaded, "Have you got a cigarette?" Later on they were both about to be released, but Mermel was immediately arrested again—in a rush to meet Corinne in her hairdressing salon he stole an army truck and drove straight into the wall of a nearby building. He didn't have a driver's license.

He worshipped Corinne, Mermel, as if she was some sacred object: sometimes, when he fixed his hungry gaze on her, seeing her and only her, it seemed that if he had to cut off his head with his own hands in order to preserve this worshipful stance toward her, he would cut it off. Her laconic coldness, the uncompromising, sinewy element inherent in everything she said or did, and everything she didn't say and didn't do, her haughtiness full of the restrained pathos of an exiled princess, and above all her beauty, unattainable and inconceivable even to herself—all these things hypnotized him. He brought her piles of brass and plastic jewelry that he bought by weight at the central bus station, flowers, fine chocolates that she didn't touch because she couldn't stand sweet things, stuffed animals, fans, handbags, stolen bottles of perfume, and once even a pair of Persian cats, male and female, which he asked for in exchange for a fitted closet he installed in some villa.

He was a carpenter by trade, but what he really did, according to the mother, was play cards. He spent hours in seedy gambling joints next to the market, betting the shirt on his back, until his parents turned up and made a scene in vociferous Yiddish—especially his mother, who had the control of her tear ducts down to a fine art and could bring herself to shed decorative tears at the drop of a hat, which infuriated Corinne and immediately ignited bitter exchanges between them: within a few weeks she learned to quarrel in Yiddish, Corinne; she picked up foreign languages out of thin air, with the accent and everything.

But Mermel was beautiful, tall and beautiful—the most beautiful, said Corinne, actually she didn't say, she screamed, covering her ears with her hands. Sammy and the mother sat or stood opposite her, while she curled up in the corner of the couch, her feet tucked under her, and lectured her. "I know him, he's not for you," Sammy drummed into her. "He's not for you,

I know him," and the mother repeated after him like an echo, "He knows him, Sammy knows him." Corinne's face was frozen, obliterated, as if it had been covered by the blurred and blurring cross-hatching on the faces of her drawings—all the muscles of her face were stiff while she pretended to listen, until she suddenly released her face and burst into that sharp, jagged scream, a terrible bellow loud enough to shake the rafters, pressing her hands to her ears: "But he's beautiful! He's beautiful! He's beautiful!"

CRYING

THE FILM THAT covered the mother's eyes from time to time wasn't tears, but an emotion that almost came to fruition and then held itself back. It was always accompanied by a certain tilting of her head, that filming of her eyes, not as if she wanted to hide, but as if she wanted to dim what was happening. We never saw her really cry. But we never really looked either: it wasn't "in her nature" to cry, it wasn't "in our nature" to look. It was in her nature to scorn whining, complaining that was like crying, to really hate it. She didn't put it in so many words, but she was vehement: at the bottom of the pit, in the blackest of the black, you didn't cry because you had leapt beyond the hurdle of crying, and as for all the rest, the intermediate degrees of shit, crying was putting on an act, or worse, falling into self-pity. What she did permit herself, however, was to shed a tear over "nonsense": *The Lady of the Camellias*, Egyptian films on television, the moment Enrico Macias's voice broke slightly when he sang "*soleil de mon pays perdu*," and at Corinne's wedding in particular.

Sammy organized playing the record on the gramophone, silencing the three members of the band in the functions hall with the grayish-pink curtains in Petach Tikva. The mother waited, going back and forth—from the rabbi's seat to implore him to delay the ceremony to the entrance to the hall, which opened onto a sidewalk full of garbage cans in the middle of the industrial zone.

She was wearing a long lavender-mauve dress, the color of her bedroom walls. This was what Corinne had decided, "lavender-mauve," angrily wiping the mother's eyelids, which Miriam had painted a peculiar phosphorescent blue. There she stood, the mother, in the lavender-mauve dress whose hem swept the filthy sidewalk, waiting for Maurice, taking off her gloves and putting them back on, scanning every passing cab in despair. For over two weeks they had tried to locate him, she and Sammy, to tell him about the wedding. In the end they found him, staying in a friend's house in south Tel Aviv. "Come, Maurice, you can't not come," she said. He twisted and turned until he finally confessed: he didn't have anything suitable to wear, he had left all his clothes in the rented flat he had abandoned in the dead of night because of the money he owed the landlord. He needed a new suit. They went together to the tailor, they chose material together: she bought him a suit.

At a quarter to nine, over an hour late, when she was back inside the hall, her dry cracked lips splitting the lipstick, he finally arrived, stood in the doorway looking in like someone who had landed there by accident, come to search for something or to ask for an address. Sammy had just set the needle on the song, brought the band's microphone up to the gramophone. She went to Maurice, to where he was standing, stepped alone on the green carpet to the strains of "*soleil de mon pays perdu*," wiping her damp eyes with the lavender-mauve gloves, almost the color of the dress; she tucked her arm firmly in his and almost dragged him toward the marriage canopy.

A Friend's House

MAURICE SAID HE would come on Friday morning and he did come, only not on that Friday but another one, the one after, or the one after that, when "it could be arranged." And the child wondered, when what could be arranged, what was the thing that had to be arranged, which appeared in her imagination in the plural: the things, the affairs. The things that piled up on top of one another, empty titles, giant boxes sealed with packing tape, containing something or not, obscure representatives of the obscure thing that was his life, his troubles, because that was what he said, "I'm in trouble up to my neck." When the two of them walked down the asphalt road with the orange grove on the right and the thorn field on the left, on the way to the bus stop to Tel Aviv, he said it: "I'm in trouble, but I'm getting out of it."

She waited for him from five in the morning, on the Friday he came and on the others when he didn't come. The mother said: "Why are you waiting for him at five in the morning? How do you think he's going to get here so early?" The child hated her, secretly she kicked the flowerpot in the corner of the hall and knocked it over on its side, pretended to bend down to pick up the broken pieces, but kicked them farther away with the toe of her shoe, toward the carpet. "Get out of the way"—the mother pushed her with the broom—"you're just making a mess." The child looked at the floor tiles, at the dirt collected in the cracks: "I'll go and live in Tel Aviv, too, and make a newspaper with him," she said. "With who? Who will you make a newspaper with?" asked the mother, going on to wipe the frame of the bathroom door. The child followed her: "With Maurice. I'll live with Maurice and we'll make a newspaper together." "Go, *salamat*, we'll cry over you, too," said the mother. "What are you waiting for? The door's open."

Dressed in her Tel Aviv clothes, the ones he had once brought her from Tel Aviv, she went to stand at the turn, to look in both the directions from which he could come: on the bus from Petach Tikva into the neighborhood, or the one from Tel Aviv that stopped at Kiron, and meant a long walk to the shack. He said: "I hate Petach Tikva, I'd rather walk than pass through Petach Tikva." She remembered those words now—"I hate Petach Tikva"—and what stood behind them and before them, the firm back of the words, what he called the "point of view," or "my point of view": that a human being, *elbani-adam*, did or didn't do things without any connection to efficiency or saving time, that the distress involved in "I hate Petach Tikva" rightly overcame petty considerations of efficiency. But he didn't say "petty," he said: "Petach Tikva isn't a town or a village, it's nothing. The only people who live there are the petit bourgeoisie who I can't stand." She walked at his side, on the gravel verges of the asphalt road, and tried to adapt herself to the rhythm and tone of his progress, which was neither slow nor fast, but something else, sideways, striving sideways. "What do they do, those people in Petach Tikva?" she asked. He wasn't listening. He had to have his coffee: "I have to have a cup of coffee," he said. They were almost there; they could see two-thirds of the cypress tree in front of the shack. The mother was waiting on the porch but she pretended that she wasn't waiting—she was busy sewing something and she didn't look up. He stood there, his briefcase under his arm, the plastic bag with a few dirty shirts for washing in his other hand: "I came to take the child for the day. I'm taking her to the Hilton," he said. "*Ya farhati*," she replied, still not raising her eyes, "A real treat. Enjoy yourselves." When the two of them left, returning to the asphalt road leading to the Tel Aviv bus stop, it was nearly ten o'clock, but Maurice said there was no hurry, he wasn't worried. He bought her a falafel at the commercial center opposite the bus stop, and he didn't see or pretended not to see her throwing away the bits of pickled cucumber from the salad, scattering a trail of cucumber slices behind them. "Am I allowed to throw them away?" she asked, and after a couple of minutes, with great satisfaction: "Am I allowed?" He shrugged his thin, hunched shoulders: "How can you order a person what to like and what to eat? Love isn't an order."

On the bus, sitting side by side, he told her where they were going and why. He said, "A friend of mine," stressing the words with imposing dignity, and repeating "A great friend of mine." His friend was a special doctor, called Dr. Berger, who had come to the Hilton from France, who cured people with special herbs and drugs of his own invention. He had only come for a few days, and Maurice translated what the patients said to him, and what he said to the patients. The child looked at him from the side as he spoke, at the narrow strips of his eyes, packed tight with shining sparks of radiance and flashes of lightning that rubbed against each other and ignited more sparks and flashes, especially when he said "my friend." "My friend," she knew, was the moment of his investiture, of his anointing with the priestly oil.

And what a place it was, the Hilton he took her to, walking quickly now, and the sea! At the bottom of the hill was the sea, the greenish blue of the sea—so alive and at the same time passive, spread out, full of vitality in its passivity, ceaselessly changing in its unchanging stillness, ordinary and at the same time mysterious, containing in some strange way the sense of the words "a great friend of mine," the dignity and the majesty, not of the friend but of the one who said "friend."

Maurice left her in the lobby, next to the windows that were walls looking out on the sea, more and more sea, saying that he would be back at lunchtime, when the doctor took a break.

She looked at the sea, she walked along the marble tiles of the lobby and looked at the sea, and even when she glanced at the people going in and out in their quiet, elegant clothes, she looked at the sea, and when she measured the wide corridors and sat on the velvet chairs in the lobby and on the long windowsill she still looked at the sea, visible at every moment and from every corner, filling the great room, the voices, the movements, the clatter of glasses and silver forks in the dining room (Maurice didn't return during the doctor's lunch break), the quiet fall of the blue satin curtains, the tapping of the high crystal heels of a woman covered in crystal who bent down to her when she fell asleep on the windowsill and stroked her cheek, the hunger, because at half past three she was hungry. Now a dusty glare covered the surface of the sea, the glare of the dust and the dazzle of the windowpanes and the silvery-white glare of the late afternoon sun on the water. Maurice emerged together with Dr. Berger. The child stared at the enormous signet ring on the doctor's finger. For some reason he examined her hands, the tips of her fingers, when Maurice said "*la petite*," this is my little one, and then the doctor thought for a minute, went back to the office where he received his patients, and gave her a present, notepaper and a ballpoint pen. Maurice stood straight, suddenly he straightened at the doctor's side, beaming like a bridegroom. And then they left the hotel, to make it on time to catch the last bus to the neighborhood, but also to drop in to "a friend's house" on the way, said Maurice, walking at her side, stopping every fifteen minutes to light a cigarette. They walked south, the sea on their right, but different, not communicative, withdrawn into itself and almost murderous in the sense of nothingness it prompted in her heart. Maurice sank, withdrawn into his shoulders, confined by the thoughts that trapped him like a fisherman's net; he didn't say a word. Among the stalls of the Carmel market, which were already beginning to close, they looked for the friend. Maurice thought he remembered something, but he didn't remember. In the end they found not the friend but a friend of his, the owner of a stall selling children's pajamas and underwear. Maurice took him aside, waving his arms and twisting his face, especially his wide mouth that twisted and gaped, pulling the rest of his face after it. Again they walked, this time down the side alleys of the market and farther south, to a broad commercial street with dark, hidden entrances to residential buildings. At one of them he stopped, said, "This is a friend's house," asked her to wait for him downstairs, in the street. The child waited. Once she went into the stairwell, looked up into the darkness, but the dark and the stench sent her back outside again. When he came out, his hair slightly mussed and with a new bundle of papers in a red file under his arm, with his briefcase, it was five o'clock. He gave the child a vegetable patty in a paper napkin, which the friend's wife had fried. "It's very tasty," he said. "Perhaps you'll think it's very tasty, too."

The bus was almost empty. It grew emptier from stop to stop, until they were the only passengers left: the child went to sit on another bench at the back of the bus, so that it wouldn't look empty. And Maurice still had to go back to Tel Aviv, not to Dr. Berger, to somewhere else, to somebody else. He didn't see a penny from Dr. Berger, "who took the money from the poor souls he promised to cure and ran away to France," said the mother.

PAPERS

THE SUHBA, A *group of comrades I established and led, shaped my private-family and sociopolitical personality for many years.* Saheb *is an Arabic word that means "friend, comrade."* Suhba: *the plural of* Saheb. *The Suhba elected me unanimously as its sociopolitical and cultural-spiritual leader. As a result of my election, I took it upon myself to perform faithfully and in a volunteer capacity this modest role, with all the responsibility it implies. I remember that the first thing upon which we were all agreed and the first condition undertaken by every* saheb *and sworn to by his oath of honor was: a prohibition on revealing or talking about the membership or the modes of operation of the Suhba. It should be noted that all the friends, without exception, adhered strictly to this obligation. I have declared in the past and I declare again that I take upon myself the consequences of the well-known existence of the Suhba. The Suhba became a household word among considerable sections of our broader public. It is also quite well-known to institutions, political parties, public figures, and leaders in Israel and abroad.*

The number of times I was questioned about the Suhba cannot be counted, nor can the number of times attempts were made to sabotage or destroy this body of friends. Some of the questions addressed to me were innocent; others were cunning, self-interested, diplomatic, and undiplomatic. To them all we had a simple answer: a saheb *is a friend and* suhba *are friends. Would you like to get to know them? To the extent that this answer did not satisfy the questioner, who was intent on discovering our sociopolitical principles, we added mockingly: We are not at liberty to discuss our friends and it would be immoral to do so. Did we ask you about your friends? Obviously neither the questions nor the answers interested the authorities and the Ben-Gurionist circles, who never stopped hounding us in order to crush and destroy us. In pursuit of this vile purpose they employed all the methods and means at their disposal, both aboveboard and underhand. Their first target was the head of the Suhba, your humble servant and the author of* The Solution? *Volumes would not suffice to recount all the tricks they played on me and describe all the obstacles they placed in my path. They even succeeded in sep-arating me from my family by means of libel, slander, and threats. This was the worst blow they inflicted on me, whose consequences and pain are still with me to this day.*

Well aware as I was of the degree of cruelty, immorality, lack of conscience, humanity, and democracy inherent in the behavior of those in power, I hid what-ever I could about the Suhba from them. First of all I resolutely refrained from officially confirming the existence of the organization in Israel or in the Diaspora, I refused to register the members, to hand out membership cards, to collect dues, and so on. This, in spite of all the "tempting" offers made to me personally and to many other members of the Suhba. It is probably due to these measures that I suc-ceeded in preventing the forces of division and material and moral corruption from doing their contemptible work in our ranks.

My firm position with regard to the social-organizational problem of the Suhba and my vigorous rejection of all complacency and sociopolitical conform-ism saved us from certain ruin. Experience teaches that destruction and disinte-gration were the fate of all the ethnic-Sephardic organizations that arose in the State of Israel, after Ben-Gurionism succeeded in destroying the Federation of Sephardim, which was second in size only to the General Federation of Labor. It may well be, too, that only thanks to this firm stance I saved many comrades from falling victim to the degeneracy and cowardice that unfortunately characterized so many public figures from among the Sephardim and members of Mizrahi eth-nic groups.

The Suhba was always active in thought and deed. It worked in various ways to deliver its message to the public at large. Hed HaMeorer, *the organ of the Suhba, reached all the leaders and important people in the country. The existence of the Suhba as an active organization could therefore not be cast in doubt. My friends and I were always there wherever and whenever our presence was needed and desired. Our center or headquarters operated on the move, like soldiers in the field; we lived among our public, suffering their poverty and their pain. It activated us and we informed it of its rights. Our center would assemble in one of the houses in the neighborhoods and finish its discussions in one of the streets or popular cafés in the marketplaces or suburbs. Sometimes we received a call when we were in the north, and that same day we traveled to the south, and vice versa. In most parts of the country we met friends and Suhba, and sometimes the distant friends came to us. They all wanted to know what was happening, asked questions, clarified issues, and wholeheartedly and generously volunteered their assistance. The membership of the Suhba was diverse, including native Israelis, Ashkenazim, and people from all the ethnic communities in the country. For our part we never questioned them about their political party affiliations. This question was of no interest to us. Every new* saheb *had to know one simple thing: that the Suhba was the Suhba of* The Solution? *The solution in which we believed was the solution to the problem of peace, both internal and external peace.*

These beliefs were proclaimed in a manifesto pasted up all over the country in the year 1964.

I owe appreciation, respect, and admiration to all those who accompanied the Suhba on its difficult path from the beginning to the present day. These dear friends, despite all the obstacles of poverty, oppression, cruelty, etc., set on their path by a certain doctrine, despite the planned policy of division, reaction, and lying propaganda that was their daily lot, were able to overcome all these things and continue on their path. They stood firm and walked tall in spite of all the obstacles, the dangers, the risks, and the suffering inflicted on them in their private lives and in every step of the way with me.

Piazza San Marco: Fifth Visit

THERE WERE TWO photographs of Piazza San Marco, one in his possession and one in hers. His conservation instincts were even weaker than hers, because of his personality and because of his history: his history was such that he almost always ran away, leaving everything behind except for a bundle of papers typed on his typewriter ("the memoirs I'm writing"), and afterward, when it vanished at some stage, on the little Olivetti that the mother once bought me as a gift.

He came one day ("one day"—the bubble of air in the bowl of time, the moment of his appearance, which was always "one day") and said that the apartment he was living in at the time had been broken into, they had smashed everything up, there was nothing left. He was a wreck: the color of his skin, the lines of his wide mouth with its sensuous lips, the nostrils, the inside of his shirt collar at the back of his neck—everything was gray. "I was up all night searching in the mess for that picture of the mother and you when you were little and you came to visit me in Italy. I don't care about anything except that picture, which I couldn't find," he said. His eyes filled. The little stick of ash of his cigarette held motionless in the air pointed down to the floor, dropping at the last minute on its way to the ashtray. "But what did they take?" I asked. He had nothing of value, and what he did have could be bundled up in a single sheet, which is what he did when he moved from one place to another. "I don't care about anything," he said again, reached for the plate of cookies, took one, and put it back again: "Only that picture of you and the mother, and the typewriter I work on. That typewriter is my work." His lower, drooping lip trembled a little: for a moment he looked to me like he sometimes looked to himself, without the effort to make an impression on the world. He made a living then from writing applications to the municipality, to government offices, and to the courts, especially for the owners of stalls in the Aliya market and the Carmel market. He had five or six of these clients. I gave him my typewriter.

In the coming days I told her about the burglary, the photograph of Piazza San Marco, the typewriter. This was during the course of an afternoon outing: we were sitting in a café in Dizengoff Circle that served croissants the size of challas (she said) and coffee in huge cups ("What is it with these cups? Do they want us to wash in them?" she said). I told her. Her face lengthened and tensed at once: she abandoned the coffee, the croissant, everything. As she listened, lengthening and tensing, she raised her finger to a corner of her eye and pulled it down: the sign of a lie, a liar, a barefaced lie. "Nobody broke into his apartment. It's a pity you gave him your typewriter." I didn't understand. "He told Sammy, Sammy knows," she said. "He organized the whole thing with some friend, to get the insurance money."

In the Coming Days

"In the coming days" were words for the continuous present, the knowledge gradually coming into being, not the future understanding locked up in the story of the past. "In the coming days" we didn't understand what we didn't understand. We didn't see what we didn't see. We couldn't see what we couldn't see. The story of life constantly coming into being covered the contours of consciousness, not like a blanket, but like ripples upon ripples, new circles made by the new stone thrown into the water in the midst of the previous circles made by the previous stone.

So "In the coming days" nothing was closed, there was no closure, and the bottom line of the story, all the stories, was the start of a new story, not completely different, but different enough. "In the coming days" made no promises and kept none, especially not fixing an object or a figure in the violent flux of time. In this blurring, in the perpetual coming into being, there was a lot of mercy: in spite of everything it allowed for an open fate, or the illusion of an open fate. "In the coming days" was another sign of open-ended fate and the illusion of open-ended fate that they both, he and she, in their different languages, different ways of managing the world, desired: *a mon seul désir*, the sole object of my desire.

If that petticoat had still been flying over the red tiled roof of the shack to proclaim its identity, if that petticoat had been the flag of the one identity that was forbidden, if something had been written on the flag of that one

forbidden identity, if what was written was a prayer whose words were forbidden, if the petticoat-flag-prayer had existed as an object in the world, then
it would have been an aspiration, taken on the amorphous shape of hope
pointing in a forbidden direction, so as not to foreclose or interfere with the
illusion of open-ended fate, not to stand in its way with an explicit meaning, fixed in time and place: *a mon seul désir*—to my sole desire.

The Tiled Roof

I T WASN'T ALL pale red, the roof, but patched with asymmetrical squares of tiles replaced here and there over the years, leaving dark brown-red stains among the faded pink. The mother was tormented by the patchwork of the roof but held back, because changing all the tiles would be a "headache." Never, it seems, was so much bitterness and resentment and suppressed rage invested in the word "headache" as when it shot out of her mouth in this meaning: an impossible or near-impossible task.

She had two tendencies that were not crystallized into a rigid ideology but remained as a toolbox from which she might have taken out a hammer or a screwdriver: a revolutionary-utopian spirit, which wanted to destroy the old and replace it with the new and perfect; and a reformist-liberal inclination, which aspired to improve and correct, even a little, the existing state of things.

For example, she sewed and hung curtains over the flaps of the tent in the immigrant transit camp where they were housed "when we arrived," she got hold of a rake somewhere or other and raked the ground: the surroundings of her own tent, and then of other tents. This was a "correction," which expressed in a profound sense what always outraged her: allowing a temporary and transient state to give free rein to mental and physical neglect, an excuse for letting go. This she found intolerable. In the bundle of aphorisms translated from Hebrew or French that she brought with her (another toolbox), there was one for this, too. "There is white poverty and black poverty," she would declare with dramatic pathos, and always twice in a row: "white poverty and black poverty." White poverty was poverty itself, while black was wallowing in it, in the dubious spiritual profits accruing from it, the self-indulgent liberties allowed themselves by those who had been beaten. Together with all this went the deep knowledge that home, the experience of home and the sense of home, were not things granted to *elbani-adam*, but something that he bestowed on himself, and not only once, but in a process of repeated reinforcement.

That was it—the process: she tore down and moved the walls of the shack as renewed confirmation of belonging, of home. An idea would suddenly sting her in the middle of something, never mind what, and then it wouldn't let her go; she would make everyone's life a misery. The moment when an idea would hit her registered on her face with a sudden stare at a wall, a window, a door, and her eyes would glaze, dreaming and scheming at once. "What do you say to moving that wall and opening things up a little"—she would turn to whoever was sitting next to her "at the time" ("he was with me at the time"): Sammy, or Uncle Robert. Which soon turned into "I wouldn't let him go until he did it": the hammers, the saws, and the drills were brought, the banging and drilling began, and the rooms and furniture to circle around. The hall turned into the living room, the living room into an enlarged hall with a kitchen, the passage opening once into the kitchen and once into the living room, the wall dividing the kitchen from the little windowless room that remained undefined, once Sammy's, once Corinne's, once mine, and once all three of ours, was moved forward and backward—enlarging the room at the expense of the kitchen and the opposite, and the same went for the porch, invading and then retreating from the territory of the kitchen and the entranceway. The ceilings were covered with decorative beams of wood that were removed two years later, after being painted for the third time, and the same went for the wallpaper, which was replaced or stripped off completely, together with the wall-to-wall carpet, which gave way to a straw mat laid on the new ceramic tiles, and the chandeliers ("What did you do to my *lustres?*") wandered from room to room and were reattached to the flimsy, sagging ceiling, pulling it down and bumping into tall heads—especially Mermel's, which was bruised again and again by the heavy chandelier in the living room and its twin in the dining nook.

She had "business" with those "at hand" (Sammy, Uncle Robert) and the tradesmen who were not "at hand" (painters, plasterers, carpenters, roofers, plumbers, and general renovators): checks were written in the middle of the night or the crack of dawn, and on the day the last payment was made, she was already writing new checks to pay for a new desire.

Sammy looked on and took part in all this with horror: it kept him awake at night. "If you move one more wall, you'll bring down the roof beam. The whole roof will fall on your head. When will you give it up, when?" he warned. "In the grave," she replied, sticking the hammer into his hand: "Do me a favor, knock this nail in for me." "This nail" was a way of belittling, ridiculing, and making light of a big or medium-sized operation: "What's all the fuss about, one little nail?" she would say dismissively, dismantling and afterward moving with his help the wall closet to its new place, arguing all the time about "the right way to do it." Sammy wasn't like her, he was "thorough." "When he does something, he makes such a thorough job of it you can never move it again," she said in admiration and hostility, stealing an anxious look despite herself at the sagging ceiling with the big damp stains that had defeated the whitewash, knowing what she refused to know: that above the ceaseless renewal lurked disintegration, the tiles that kept on cracking, first in one place and then another.

"Climb," she ordered Sammy, who climbed the ladder to the roof with the box of new tiles, to make repairs. He stood on the pointed top of the roof. We saw him from below swaying for a moment, his feet sinking into the disintegrating tiles, collapsing into the attic, and then the loud thud of his body on its flimsy floor, which was the ceiling. The heavy chandelier in the living room broke free of its chains, pulling pieces of wood and plaster with it, and shattered on the floor.

On the Floor (1)

M AURICE MADE AN effort when he came this time or that, but the mother
saw through him. "I see through him. All that so-called effort of his is
from self-interest. He thinks it's a hotel here," she said. But the child didn't
see the kind of effort Corinne talked about, she saw something different—
something close to abject submission. She saw him literally bow his head,
with his thighs apart, his head buried between his shoulders, and his eyes
fixed on the row of tiles at the bottom of the opposite wall: "Yes, *ya* Lucette,
right, *ya* Lucette, you're right, *ya* Lucette," he said to her when she raged
about something, *the* something, the fact that he didn't work like everyone
else. She wanted him to put bread on the table like everyone else. Go out in
the morning with some briefcase or other, not his usual one, and come back
in the evening, at regular hours. "Where's the shame in putting bread on
the table like a man?" she yelled. The curtain blew a little in the breeze. The
child sat under the window, behind the curtain, in the flower bed of the
backyard, and peeked into the room. And then he said, in French: "You
want to say that I'm not a man, is that what you want to say?" And she said:
"If you like." And then there was a kind of silence again: the mother was
seeking another way. The child looked inside and saw her looking for a
kinder way. And then she said in a voice that was almost gentle: "You had
a good job there in the Labor Ministry, with that director looking out for
you, if only you'd kept it, you." And then he said: "They're all corrupt there.

They're all thieves," and he didn't lift his head, still looking at the line of the tiles at the bottom of the opposite wall.

And then she said: "So you steal, too, Maurice, for your family. Why shouldn't you steal, too, like everyone else?" And he raised his eyes and looked into her face for a moment. The child saw the surprise on his face when he raised his eyes and looked at the mother as if he had just noticed her, suddenly intruding on his loneliness.

From outside, through the semitransparent curtain playing in the breeze, the child could see that picture, the picture of his loneliness, close her eyes at the sight to see it at last as it was. To see it without wanting to enter into it, just to stand on the threshold of the sight of that loneliness and observe its foreignness, which was made up of the alien letters of loneliness that denied the word "father," and made it impossible to pronounce or feel.

She went inside and sat down next to him, next to his bowed head, which was not terminally bowed: he had only laid down his arms for the time being. His fingers lay spread out on his very thin thigh, and she touched them, their long yellow nails. Now he looked at the mother—but differently, not with that former surprise, but with his face, his hollow cheeks, sinking into himself: "I can't be like everyone else, Lucette, I can't. If you want to kill me, kill me," he said.

"And she killed him, with his two left hands," said Corinne, sucking hard on her cigarette, her eyes narrowed watchfully. At six o'clock the next morning she woke him up, to drink his coffee quickly and "start work." In the middle of the hall she set up the ladder, ready with the trowel, the hammers, the paintbrush, the can of paint. She wanted him to fix the ceiling, waterproof it, and then paint it.

He took off his shirt, remaining in the white undershirt that emphasized the sharp angles of his lean, swarthy body, the body of a Sudanese boy. He covered his head with a bandana knotted at the four corners; his Adam's apple protruded when he raised his eyes to the ceiling, with the trowel in his hand and his tongue sticking out, touching the tip of his nose with exertion. Every fifteen minutes he needed a break, got down from the ladder, dirtying the shack with the prints of his feet and hands full of white paint: coffee, cigarette, coffee, cigarette. At midday, when she came home from work, there were maybe eight coffee cups standing at the bottom of the ladder, ashtrays full of stubs. The ceiling was still wounded, riddled with holes.

"And she threw him out. The blood went to her head from the mess."
Corinne sometimes told the story, when she emerged from her silence full
of stories, but not the specific story, and not specifically to the child—she
told the generalized story, which was a melting of all the stories together,
to a generalized audience consisting of herself or the child listening from the
side.

Maurice crossed the path, climbed to Nona's quarter-shack, slept over
there for two or three nights on the folding bed. The two of them got along;
they kept the same hours. The child liked being there with them. Listening
in the relaxed atmosphere to the conversation without edges, not from here
and not from now, from some "once upon a time," not exactly reminiscing,
but the echo of a spacious life with many entrances to many rooms. She lay
on the floor at their feet, on the striped rug over whose creases Nona
stumbled whenever she got up to fetch something from the kitchen. The
door to the quarter-shack was always open, to the high concrete landing, to the wind, to the smell of the honeysuckle, which Nona called *fula*,
jasmine. In a book the child read "time stood still," she said to Maurice, but
it wasn't right. Maurice said it wasn't right. It stands still and moves at
once, time, said Maurice, and he translated for Nona: "*elzaman, elzaman,*"
said Maurice.

On the Floor (2)

O N THE FLOOR in Nona's room, moments after Maurice was kicked out: how the mother threw herself down, first falling to her knees, appealing to someone or something, and then facedown on the floor, banging her forehead on the floor. "Seeing her is like seeing a building fall," said Nona, "a building."

FOREHEAD

SHE HAD A small forehead, a narrow strip between the line of her eyebrows and her hairline. A small nose. A small mouth. Small gaps between the small features of her face. The mother's smallness was praised both in Nona's quarter-shack and in the mother's shack as well: small was good. In Egypt, when a woman was small she was more of a woman. "Big" in a woman was shocking, in other words, like a man. Everything was determined by the feet, and by the limbs in general: big feet ("boats") and big hands dragged in their wake the curse of the big, the unwomanly. The child was scolded for having a big mouth, especially when she laughed. "Don't laugh," the Nona warned her. "You've got a mouth on you like Isma'il Yasin, God save us." Isma'il Yasin was an Egyptian comedian with a mouth that stretched from ear to ear, even when he wasn't laughing. "Tell me again who my mouth is like," the child asked Nona again and again, and she told her, and made both of them laugh.

She Said

S HE SAID WHAT was forbidden to say (she said it twice), forbidden to repeat (the child repeated it), forbidden to give any kind of force to, true or false (the Nona said: "It's a lie, a lie"), because of the fabric of life—which even if it was stuck together with spit and joined what couldn't be joined, even with spit, was still the fabric of life, stretching between those who were in the shack and those who weren't, filling the air between door and door, the mother's door and the Nona's door, imprinted on a person's face, the face by which each person knew himself.

From the moment she said it, hurled the words into the room, they tasted flat, or the opposite, so strong that nothing could follow them, only an emptiness that wasn't even silence, the silence of the Nona, but simply speechlessness—it was something unspeakable that you die with, not live with, that you take to the grave, because what she said, what she had to say, was a kind of grave.

The child invented the circumstances of this utterance, the place, and the time: she planted the circumstances, the place, and the time, exactly when Maurice left Nona's quarter-shack, after the mother kicked him out, and then fell on the floor.

She wanted the event to boil in her memory, she wanted the mother's words to boil in her heart, immediately and urgently, for the boiling to purify the awfulness of the words, to amount to extenuating circumstances. But then, when the mother threw herself down (Nona said: "she threw herself down"), perhaps she said something else out of the boiling of her heart, not "that," not the thing that had been gestating inside her for years, true or false, half-true or half-false, and emerged all at once, fully formed, perhaps in different circumstances, at another time and place (how many other places could there have been?): "I know everything, everything," said the mother. "Maurice told me everything," she said. "The Nona kept persuading him to go to bed with her," she said. "The woman who calls herself my mother wanted him to go to bed with her all those nights he came to her," she said. "Behind my back all that filth of his and hers," she said, "all that filth."

BETWEEN DOOR AND DOOR

BUNDLED IN THREE sheets tied at the corners, Corinne's clothes and her baby's things wandered between door and door: the door of the mother's shack and the door of Corinne's and Mermel's one-room apartment in the housing project for young couples on the way to Amishav. He would drop her off early in the morning, driving his silver Lark: first the bundles would land on the washed porch, and then Corinne with the baby, following Mermel with a closed face. "*Yallah* to your mother, *salamat*," said Mermel, because he had started to talk like them, the way they talked in the shack. The usual day began.

Usually the mother was watering the rosebushes, and she hurried to turn the tap off when she saw the silver Lark coming (he painted it silver in honor of Corinne, who thought and also said that this color, with its class, toned down the *hishik-hishik* of the Lark, which was altogether a gangster's car).

Mermel went on standing on the porch, very tall, with his shifty look and the car keys dangling from his finger, moving nervously from side to side as he spoke by means of and through the mother to Corinne, who by now had usually entered the shack. Through the noise of the electric saws in Moshe's carpentry shop across the road, and the beating of the iron in Sammy's welding shop, the whole neighborhood heard every word that was said: his voice was really something.

"Believe me, I don't understand your daughter," he usually said in the moments of ostensible appeasement and reconciliation that came and went in the stream of his volubility like tacking stitches in cloth: "Kill me if I understand what she wants."

"What does she want, what does she want?" Corinne's voice mocked him from inside the house: "What she wants is to cut off your head and stop your tongue from lying." The mother wanted them to explain to her, she made Mermel sit down on one of the wrought-iron chairs on the porch and explain to her, gaining time: "But explain what happened," she said, giving his finger a little slap, "and stop making a noise with those keys—it leads to quarrels."

"There's already a quarrel"—Corinne's voice rose from inside again— "don't listen to him, you hear? He's a gambler," and then, throughout the hour or more that Mermel unburdened himself into the open kitchen window, bursts of "he's a gambler" broke out from inside the house like rounds of fire from a machine gun—in the middle of his sentences, at the end, and in the very short pauses between them, without any connection to what he said or what he didn't say: "He's a gambler, he's a gambler."

At ten o'clock in the morning silence usually fell, the day-to-day silence of the shack, which was a low chorus of sounds and noises: the sprinkler, the washing machine, the radio, the dripping of a tap, the crackle of the noodles slightly seared in the pan before they were added to the Syrian rice for the meatballs with garlic and cumin that Corinne liked.

The bundles in the striped sheets ("American, the good sort," said the mother, who bought them for Corinne before she got married) stayed in the corner of the porch, static as Corinne: she, standing, sitting, walking around the shack or the yard—was actually lying down most of the time, her limbs outspread and eyes staring at the ceiling. Once every two days she was seized by a strange impulse of activity and fell on her clothes: dyed a blouse, cut up a skirt, or pulled the buttons off a jacket to replace them with others. And then she stared into space some more, as if she were still standing on the threshold of her life story, and not in the middle of it, her olive cheeks with their high cheekbones stretching up to the hollow temples, frightening in their fragility. "She isn't with us now, she's in her dreams," murmured the mother, cooing at the baby who tried in vain to attract Corinne's attention, climbing onto her lap and cupping her cheeks in his little hands, or banging loudly with a ladle on the saucepans he took out of the kitchen cupboard and then crawling into it, curling up on the empty bottom shelf. At night he screamed almost without a pause; the mother picked him up, walked around the dark neighborhood with him in her arms, patting him on his squirming buttocks, leading his insistent, ceaseless wailing up and down the streets. Around Corinne she walked on tiptoe, everyone tiptoed around her: the metallic brittleness she gave off and the unexpected bursts of rage filled the air around her with fear and pity. Corinne said that she wasn't waiting for Mermel, and as far as she was concerned he might as well be dead. "Don't say that," the mother protested, "he's the father of your child." "He isn't anybody's father, he's zero," retorted Corinne, got dressed up, put on high heels, and took the bus to the gambling joint next to the market to look for Mermel and ask him for money. It was morning, Mermel wasn't there, but his friends were. She overturned a table, she took a stack of bills and crammed them into her purse, after she tore their cards up one by one and threw the baize cloth out of the window, into the busy street of the market. On her way home she passed the pet shop next to the bus stop, and stood for a long time riveted to a pair of honey-colored Pekinese puppies, male and female, with certificates and pedigrees. She bought them both, with all the money she had taken from the club. On the bus home she held the puppies on her lap, under her buttoned coat. Their names were Pat and Patishon: Patishon was the plump and rather stupid male, Pat the bad-tempered female, who bared her sharp teeth and growled whenever anyone came near her, but didn't do anything.

"See what a scowling little face she's got," Corinne cooed, kissed her on her nose, and then kissed Patishon, too, so he wouldn't be jealous. She slept with them in her bed at night, fed them from her hand, delighting in their pink tongues lapping the soft bread dipped in milk from her palm, but was overcome by terrible anxiety whenever one of them disappeared from sight. "Where's Patti, where's Patishon?" she cried, morning, noon, and night, prowling wild-haired and swaying around the rooms of the shack and afterward the front and backyards, the baby crawling behind her with his diaper undone, his face smeared with grape juice and mud, wailing like her.

The mother grew more resentful from day to day, from the general upheaval of the invasion of the shack, and especially now, with this Pat and Patishon, which was "all she needed." They filled her with bafflement and hostility, these pedigreed pups: "They're like *bibelots*, so pretty you could put them on a shelf," she announced once a day to please Corinne, who beamed in gratification, but then she came out with the truth: she wanted to drown them, that's what she wanted, for them to stop standing "in front of her eyes" with their pampered little faces, those strange squashed faces of theirs, distracting Corinne, who was like "some kite" anyway, from the tasks of life. She told Corinne she should find a job: "Get up already. How long are you going to sit there without a penny to your name, cleaning up after those dogs all day?" she scolded her. Corinne held Pat and Patishon close on her chest, near her neck, burying her chin in their fur, her light brown eyes with their thick lashes gazing into the distance, wide open in astonishment and disbelief.

The mother brought her a notice she had torn down from one of the trees in Savyon, after reading the word "wanted": "Wanted, a saleswoman for a new book and record store in the commercial center." Corinne was silent. But she couldn't get enough of the advertisement; she read it again and again until she had to throw it away in the evening after Patishon overturned a cup of coffee on it.

The next day the two of them, she and the child, rode the bicycle to the commercial center. They arrived too early and sat and waited on the stone wall for the shop to open. Corinne smoked cigarettes halfway, and ground them out on the stone wall: "I don't want the owner of the shop to see me smoking," she said, lighting another cigarette. There was hardly anyone else in the commercial center: three times they circled the little square overgrown with yellow weeds, looked into the few display windows, to which Corinne, after a scrupulous examination, said as if to herself: "Anyone would think God knows what they were selling here. No style. Lousy taste."

At exactly four o'clock a plump little woman opened the door of the book and record shop, placing a stone in front of the door to keep it open, and turned on the light. Corinne didn't move; she examined the woman like a spider waiting for the right moment to ingest its insect: "Quick, tell me the names of books," she instructed the child without taking her eyes off the owner of the shop, whose silhouette was visible moving heavily behind the windowpane. "What names?" demanded the child in confusion. "Names, names"—Corinne pinched her arm—"If she asks me about books." "*Three Loves*," blurted the child. "More, more, tell me another two or three," urged Corinne. *Crime and Punishment*, *Angélique*, *The Foundling*," the child added quickly.

Corinne went into the shop, leaving the child to watch the bicycle, next to the stone wall. Behind the glass she saw Corinne sitting very straight on a high chair, hardly moving her lips when she talked, tightening the clip in her hair gathered in a chignon on her nape. "What did she say? Did she take you?" she asked as she walked back next to Corinne pushing the bicycle. "She said I was pretty," confessed Corinne reluctantly. "Is that all?" asked the child, disappointed. Corinne stopped and thought for a minute: "She gave me something to write at home, for some graphologist friend of hers to look at my handwriting and say if my personality is suitable."

They walked down the middle of the wide road with the darkness arching above them, trapped inside the vault made by the tall branches leaning toward each other and meeting high above their heads, sending a fateful shiver through the child, paralyzing and inexplicable, as if she and Corinne had been walking since time began under the high dome of the branches and would go on walking there forever, in this silence of knowledge that brought down all the barriers between past, present, and future, and planted her in a place beyond time, from which she looked neither forward nor backward but down from the heights. She looked sideways at Corinne, at her firm profile that lightened and darkened alternately; because of the shadows passing across her face or because of some inner shift, she saw how the despair that had previously settled on Corinne's face changed its nature and turned into something different—not the opposite of despair, not happiness, but a different despair, subtle and mysterious, resembling the height and darkness of the arch of the trees more than the shop and the owner of the shop in the commercial center.

WHEN THEY reached the part of the road next to the dirt track leading to the shack Corinne suddenly stopped, her eyes widening in terror: a dog fight. Three or four dogs attacking each other ferociously with dreadful barking, their bodies writhing on top of one another on the dirt track, merging into a single frantic mass, digging their teeth into each other's necks, hanging on and not letting go, their tails projecting for a moment from a single violent trembling body and then disappearing. Abruptly Corinne dropped the bicycle and raced to the scene, threw herself into the jumble of fighting dogs yelling, "Pat! Patishon!" The child stood nailed to the spot next to the bicycle lying on the ground. She saw Corinne's gleaming white blouse in the pile of dogs, her thigh, her arms trying to force open the jaws of one of the dogs locked on the neck of another. And then came the scream, or the shriek, a terrible, piercing sound that erupted from Corinne and quelled all the barking and howling. The dogs extricated themselves and fled. Corinne lay on the ground, bitten on her leg, close to the ankle. Back at the shack, Pat and Patishon lay in their basket, cuddled together.

Corinne spent most of the following days sitting on the porch, in the sun, her bandaged leg with the stitches resting on one of the wrought-iron chairs in front of her, her hand supporting her forehead bent over the white pages that she tore off the writing pad, crumpled, and threw away and tore off again, starting and restarting "that thing for the graphologist" in her handwriting that strained to be rounded but wasn't, like the writing of a child trying to write like a grown-up, or the opposite, an adult who wrote like a child: "I was born in the month of November under the sign of Scorpio. They say that scorpions die in the end from their own poison but I don't believe it. I have an aesthetic sense and in my opinion I have taste. Ever since I was a child I have been interested in everything regarding style in clothing and furniture and I wanted to be a designer. . . ." She stopped, recopied, stopped again, and started again with the hope of the new white page.

Mermel came to visit, having heard about the incident with the dogs and the bite. He parked the Lark on the dirt track and remained sitting in it until Corinne came out to him, and sat next to him on the front seat of the car. The mother came out to the porch a number of times and looked at the car from a distance, at their heads close to each other in the car, waiting. Mermel brought Corinne presents: a ring set with a pink opal and a pair of opal earrings to match. He left, but he arrived again toward evening, wearing a jacket and giving off a good smell. They went out to a "fancy restaurant" according to Mermel, and took the sleeping baby wrapped in a blanket, and Pat and Patishon in their basket, with them. The mother arranged the piles of clothes and shoes in the sheets, and tied them securely, to be ready for the next day, or the same day in the middle of the night, she didn't know: "He's buying her, that Corinne, he's buying her again with a few toys," she said.

The Sleeping Baby (1)

THE BABY SLEPT swaddled in layers of white cloth, layer of white on layer of white, white merging into white, the broad plump white of the dress of the woman holding him on her lap, into the white of her headdress whose edges fell onto her dress. What's called the "background," too, was white, or almost white: the space behind the woman holding the baby, which looked like a garden covered in snow, or the opposite, like an arid desert verging on whiteness, almost achieving it. And then the white was interrupted: the photograph was torn, half of it was cut off. It was from Egypt, the photograph. It had the color and the mood of Egypt and photographs of Egypt. The mother didn't look for it; she always came across it when she was looking for "some paper"—she would keep every single official document because she wasn't sure of what was written in it, "maybe something from the bailiff."

We sat on the floor, in front of the cabinet's open door: she took out papers and more papers, "tell me what this is," and "tell me what this is." And the sleeping baby invariably popped up in the end; buried in some pile, hidden under some paper or other, he was revealed—he wanted to be revealed, instantly silencing the noise of the day-to-day, of the bureaucratic business. She always looked at him as if for the first time, and began to cry, but soundlessly: "That was Zizi," she said, "and the one who's holding Zizi, she was his wet nurse. Because I didn't have milk for him."

She didn't know what had been torn from the photograph, who had been torn off, and why. Another time she did know, or thought she did: "It was Maurice who had his photo taken with him and the wet nurse on the day before he died," she said. She didn't remember who had torn Maurice from the picture: "It got torn. Stop asking me questions about ancient history, why it got torn. It got torn."

The story was born bit by bit, in installments, with years separating one part from the other, white spaces. "He died at the age of three months, because of Maurice," she said once, not in front of the picture, in its absence, after it was lost and no longer came to light among the papers. "Maurice fancied himself a gentleman. He didn't want to take Zizi to the hospital. Only the so-called lower classes went to the hospital. Maurice was stubborn. The baby died at home, of stubbornness, in the arms of the wet nurse."

The Sleeping Baby (2)

As soon as she saw Corinne's baby she asked about his sleep, why he wasn't sleeping. She wanted them to go to sleep already, the babies ("*Yallah, edardem ba'a*"), not only because their quiet sleep bore witness to their well-being and somewhat allayed her guilt over the world they had been brought into, which wasn't anything to write home about, but also so that they wouldn't get in the way of her overturning and reorganizing the house. How she would bend over a baby sleeping in his cradle or carriage, examining this great accomplishment with respect, even awe: "Look how he's sleeping!" On the other hand, a baby that went on sleeping too long gave rise to a panic that expanded exponentially: in a matter of seconds the baby went from a state of exemplary health to near death. Then even she would run to "the doctors," her usual aversion overcome by abject terror, and the Nona would celebrate a victory.

They both danced attendance on Corinne's baby, who always arrived at the shack with his bundles "just for an hour" and stayed for eight—a dance that consisted of arm-wrestling, open and disguised, over authority, and especially the source of authority. The dance steps obliged the mother, who secretly recognized the Nona as the source of authority on babies, to do whatever she could to avoid the humiliation of explicitly acknowledging this recognition, while Nona for her part spread her net of cunning tricks and verbal evasions under the mother's feet, without asking for recognition of her authority, not at all—as long as they did things her way.

Corinne's baby, who first slept and slept in his carriage on the sunny porch, his wrinkled red face ("like an old man's face," said Corinne) occasionally distorted by the grimace of a smile or momentary distress as he slept, suddenly woke up with shocking screams. What happened? What was it? "The end of the world, the end of the world," muttered the mother in despair, changed him, fed him, turned him on his stomach, his back, his side, walked him in his carriage and in her arms, stuck a suppository in his rectum, sang to him, scolded him, put him down in his carriage and ignored him for a few minutes, put a cold compress on his forehead, swung with him on the neighbors' creaking swing—and nothing. His screams only grew louder, his little arms and legs fought the air, he turned blue with crying and then red and then blue again, losing his breath. Nona sat in the corner of the porch in affected detachment, looking in front of her or not, and hardly seeing anything anyway, muttering as if to herself words that could be clearly overheard, clasping her long white fingers and waiting for the moment to ripen. The moment ripened: in her slippers and housecoat the mother ran to the clinic with him, to the doctor. The blood drained from her face on the way up the hill with the screaming baby and on the way down, with the still screaming baby: "I'd rather be a construction worker, it's easier, I swear," she said.

She sank into a chair next to the Nona, her eyes glazed, apathetically rocking the carriage with the screaming baby. Now the stage belonged to Nona; nobody could stop her. "You saw that this morning, when the neighbor dropped in, she said, what a lovely baby, you saw that?" the Nona said slowly and quietly. The mother nodded in agreement; she laid down her arms, surrendered unconditionally to what she called Nona's "old-fashioned nonsense." "And when she left the child turned over," the Nona continued, and fell silent. In the rich, saturated silence that descended between them the baby's crying sounded all the louder—still determined but a little hoarser, glazed like the look in the mother's eyes. "*Mafish fayida*, put salt *ya* Lucette." The mother dragged her feet to the kitchen, brought the big salt-cellar with the cooking salt, and began to sprinkle salt on the carriage, the blanket, and the baby's clothes. "On the head, on the head," urged Nona, "put salt on his head against the Evil Eye she gave him, *mafish fayida.*" She sprinkled salt on his head and inside his little hands. The weather changed, the sun withdrew from the sky and the porch, and the air darkened. They went inside with the salted baby, sat on either side of the carriage, and stared. "At that minute he slept, like from God. He calmed down in a minute," recounted the Nona.

THE SLEEPING BABY (3)

THE CHILD WASN'T simple-minded, but she sometimes thought, heard, and said things at a slant. Rachel Amsalem's big sister, Yaffa, told her that she made herself look simple-minded by believing everything people said. "What people?" asked the child. "Tell me what people?" They were sitting at the bus stop, waiting for the next bus. Perhaps the child's mother would be on it, bringing the waffles left over from the party at the student center, which the child had promised to give to Yaffa. Yaffa herself, on the other hand, was said to be a little simple: she was fifteen and she still played with dolls with the little girls, with the child and with Rachel. Their feet dangled in the air when they sat on the bench, shoulder to shoulder: the dogs had dug a deep ditch next to the bench, so that it was possible either to jump over it or to stumble into it. Yaffa did neither. When they wanted to get up, the child jumped first over the ditch, and Yaffa said, "Give me a hand." The child gave her a hand and Yaffa gathered up her long skirt so it wouldn't get in the way, closed her eyes, and took a long step forward, throwing the whole weight of her body onto the child and almost making her fall. She had a big body. She wore her mother's clothes: skirts to below the knee, blouses buttoned to the neck, and sleeves reaching past the elbows, thick brown nylon stockings. "Closed, closed, all closed up," the child's mother said about her, raising her hand to her throat in a gesture of suffocation. Yaffa's frizzy hair, coarse as steel wool, was stuck all over with dozens of

hairclips, to keep the curls from jumping up. From Friday night to Saturday night she straightened her hair in an *abu-aguela*, pulling it tight to one
side and then the other, with a scarf tied tightly around her head, singing
Sabbath songs out of tune in her choked, rusty voice, alone in the dark
half-room with the Sabbath candles, on and on until she was interrupted
by her brother David's despairing roar: "Enough, *ya rabbak*, enough! You're
sawing through my brains with those songs of yours!" and silence fell, settling on the Amsalem half-shack and crushing it, sinking it even farther
down into all the barrels, junk, old bicycles, and the cinder blocks they
wanted to use to extend their kitchen and got stuck in the middle.

They walked through the thorn field on the shortcut to the child's
house, which passed by the reservoir at the edge of the hill. The darkness
was shallow, full of sounds; faint lights shone from the distant shacks,
almost at the end of the horizon, as if from dying ships about to drown.
Yaffa told the child that God would punish her for lying, for saying that she
would bring her waffles and then not bringing them. "But I wasn't lying,"
protested the child. "I wasn't lying, I wasn't lying," she repeated, shudder-
ing a little at the sound of the metallic clatter of her own lying voice—not
the lie referred to by Yaffa but a different, far greater lie, hidden and forti-
fied as a secret, but a secret that was a lie, not the truth, a truth that was a
secret lie. In front of them shone the reservoir: a cat was walking along the
flat upper wall; it walked as if it were blind, swaying from side to side, but it
didn't slip. "So you don't want to play mother and baby?" asked the child,
picked up a long stick from the ground, and began beating the tall thorns
on either side of the path, on the right and the left. "Just a minute," said Yaffa,
and she stepped off the path, onto a clearing between the thorns, pulled
down her panties, squatted, and peed. The child looked at the strong jet
making its way onto the path and collecting in a puddle. "Don't you need
to pee?" asked Yaffa. The child shook her head, she held it in. "You never
need to pee," said Yaffa, pulling her nylon stockings up from her calves.

Her broad, expressionless face, dissolving into its own blurred expanses,
bent over the child: "Who's there in your house now?" she demanded to
know. "No one," said the child. They stood next to the reservoir and looked
at the big holes torn in the round stone wall, as if it had been smashed with
heavy hammers. The child averted her eyes from the dark holes and looked
at Yaffa, who also turned her face away in order not to see the footprints
left by the white man when he walked on the wall: the holes were his

footprints. "I'm dying of hunger," said Yaffa. They walked down the hillside, toward the pointed silhouette of the cypress, which was suddenly covered by a strange, alien film, which now passed through the child, too, turning into the nagging doubt of "perhaps": perhaps not here. But out loud she said, "Perhaps Sammy's at home."

"Sleeping?" asked Yaffa. "Sleeping," said the child.

The shack stood in its solitude in the garden, next to the cypress tree and in front of the row of young pines at the back. Since early in the afternoon, when the child came home and the mother left, it was completely alone. The mother left food for the child on the stove, meatballs and rice, rice and beans, or liver and rice, covered the saucepan with a towel, but the child ate two slices of bread with chocolate spread, forgot the knife smeared with chocolate spread on the counter, next to the cleaning rag soaked in soapy water, which had stiffened as it dried, into a strange shape with hollows and bumps, like a rock or a crystal. She sat on the stool in the kitchen, chewing the bread and looking at it, at the little flies hovering over it and sticking to it.

This was the empty time of the shack, the long hours unraveling into non-time, until the night when the emptiness was interrupted twice, first when Sammy came home, and then when the mother came home. When the child looked at the polished objects and furniture standing in the polished rooms, it seemed to her that they were breathing air into the still spaces made glassy by the emptiness, filling them with the vapors of their breath. Now it was hers, the whole shack was ostensibly at her disposal, without anyone to tell her what to do, but when she went from the kitchen to the living room and then to the little room and the mother's bedroom, she became a guest, interfering with the emptiness and the conduct of the emptiness, its welling and bubbling between the rooms, that fullness of the emptiness that turned into the presence of something, she didn't know what, which slowly, the more time passed, changed from disapproving to terrifying. She entered the rooms with her back to them, walking backward, so that whatever was in there wouldn't meet her at once, wouldn't fix its eyeless stare on her face. Outside, outside the shuttered shack, were the ordinary sounds of the day—marking the hours, creating the illusion that everything was normal: the carpentry shop, Nona calling every now and then from her concrete landing, the tractor digging something up in the thorn field. It was then, in the afternoon or early evening, that she slammed the door behind her and ran to Rachel Amsalem's half-shack, to wait for her. Yaffa, not Rachel, was there, sitting on the porch, cracking the thin skins of broad beans and humming quietly to herself. The child sat down next to her, waiting for her to finish, and collected the empty skins fallen to the floor, and as she skinned, hummed quietly, stopped humming, and started again, she told the child that her problem was that she had twelve faces. "Everybody says you've got twelve faces, that's why nobody wants to be friends with you," she said. The child was silent. She stared at a column of ants making its way to the anthill, in the corner of the porch, and wiped her eyes with her sleeve. "You don't have to cry because of that," said Yaffa, "you've got a really nice house."

She said it again: "Your house is really nice," when the two of them reached the shack, stood on the dark porch, and peeped into the kitchen window, from darkness to darkness. The child had forgotten her keys again, on the hall table. Yaffa waited by the front door until she ran to the living-room window, at the back, climbed in, and opened the door. Together they went from room to room and switched on the lights, also the standing lamps in the living room and the hall. Yaffa looked into the pots in the kitchen, fished a meatball in sauce out of one of them, and ate it. After that she looked at the shelves with the copperware, the glass figurines, and the music box in the shape of a wooden house, and peeked into the kitchen cupboards and the closet in the mother's bedroom. The child lined up the three bald dolls on the hall table: she had cut off their hair. "Anyone who doesn't behave herself today will sit in the thinking corner till lunch time and won't get a slice of bread," said Yaffa not in her own voice, but in the loud, jarring voice of the kindergarten teacher in the kindergarten where she sometimes helped the assistant. "But I'm the baby," protested the child. "All right," acquiesced Yaffa. She sat down on the couch in the hall, with the dolls next to her on the cushion, and the child curled up in her lap, covered herself in the dolls' blanket, and sucked her thumb. She closed her eyes, and brought her lips to Yaffa's breast: "The baby wants milk," she said. When she opened her left eye a crack and peeked, she saw Yaffa's broad face staring into space with its usual expression of good-tempered dullness and sleepy satisfaction. She put her hand on the child's forehead: "The baby has a fever. That's why he isn't sleeping," she said, and slid her hand over the child's face, feeling her cheeks and chin: "He's a sweet baby. If he stops desecrating the Sabbath people will stop saying that he has twelve faces."

Yaffa closed her eyes, her head swaying from side to side and her mouth hanging open as her hand slid down the child's body, down her ribs and then her stomach, slipped under the elastic of her trousers into her panties and farther down, where her fingers massaged the smooth lips of her vagina and poked inside. The child opened her eyes and looked at her in suspense. "The baby's asleep," she said.

She stopped abruptly and took her fingers out of the child's panties: "We'll play again later. Now go and bring what you brought last time and we'll go," she said. The child went to the room that was her room and took the savings bank off the shelf. With the slot angled downward she began fishing the coins out with a kitchen knife. Yaffa put them in her pocket. They went outside, leaving the lights on behind them. In Yosef's grocery shop, to the right of the bus stop, Yaffa bought a packet of sour tomatoes and paid with the coins in her pocket. They sat on the bus-stop bench and waited. Yaffa sucked the tomatoes one by one and then bit into them, examining her tooth marks on the tomato. She offered one to the child, too, but the child didn't want it. She wiped her hands in the darkness on her trousers as if they were stained with the sharp-sour juice of the tomatoes. The mother got off the bus, but she didn't bring waffles. She was carrying two bags full of books from the public library in Ramleh. Yaffa carried the bags for her as far as the dirt track winding up to the shack, dropping them on the ground and running home when the mother said: "Why are all those lights on? Who are they on for, the dead?"

The Sleeping Baby (4)

THE CHILD THOUGHT, heard, and said things at a slant in the viscous hours from noon to night, when she was inside the shack, hushing her breath against the pale, barely audible breath of the strange emptiness, or outside it, when she went around and around, from the front to the back of the shack, looking for an open window to climb through.

The keys were inside, lying on the dining table in the hall, on the white lace tablecloth the mother had soaked in tea, in obedience to Corinne's instructions, in order to dye it off-white, and it came out the color of tea. Through the window bars (Sammy installed them after a burglar once broke in—he didn't take anything but he turned the place upside down) she looked at them, how they lay next to the bald doll, almost touching her bent rubber leg, so close, eighteen inches away, but out of reach. For a long time she stood there, her feet sunk in the mother's flower bed with the new plants, her face pushed into the gap between the bars, hypnotized by the keys and the complacency of the keys, which at that moment was the compla-cency of the shack, its unapproachable lordliness, as if it had ejected her, expelled, rejected her—and not the other way around, when she had escaped from it before. And precisely because the keys were so close (when she reached in with her arm it touched the edge of the table), there was even something insulting in this closeness, and the intimacy implied by it—how could they have done this to her, to someone so close.

Through the window, from outside, the hall looked the same, complying in every detail with the picture she knew—and at the same time it looked a little different, as if it had been tilted a little sideways, as if it remained as it was, but with a transparent mask on its face. There was something strange about the curving legs of the dining table, with the ball in the middle, which she now, from her new point of view, noticed for the first time, and the narrow doorway leading from the hall to the little room opposite her looked allusive, promising, as if it hid many rooms behind it, countless passages and vestibules and rooms leading off one another. When she tilted her neck to the left she saw the edge of the picture in the bathroom passage, with the tip of the white dress of the sad woman standing to the left of the one with the burning look in her eyes, at whose presence the child now guessed, straining her neck sideways in the attempt to see another part of the picture retreating into the darkness, to the limits of her field of vision, suddenly jealous of the people painted there—the man with the mustache and the sad standing woman and the young woman with the witch's eyes—who stayed in the shack, who would always stay there, while she came and went, everybody came and went, and only they remained in the picture, would always remain the real inhabitants of the shack, the eternal witnesses of the real life of the shack that took place when there was nobody there.

The pail she was standing on sank a little deeper into the flower bed and noises came from the welding shop after a long period of quiet. She went there and found Sammy's worker, Binyamin, and asked him to force the door open, like last time. He said no: "Your mother nearly killed me last week for ruining her door, but I didn't ruin it. Come and look. I put the lock back just like new," he argued. They went together to the front door and Binyamin showed her how he had installed the lock. "You can't see a thing. Can you see anything?" he demanded triumphantly. The child shook her head politely and asked in despair: "But how am I going to get in?"

He went back to the welding shop and brought a long wire, hooked at the tip like a fishing rod, and the two of them stood in the flower bed again and threaded the wire through the window bars, toward the keys on the table. The wire wandered over the table like a blind man's cane, to the right and the left, searching. "What do I see there?" hummed Binyamin to himself, leading the wire in circles over the tablecloth as if he were trying to draw, not to trap something: "What do I see there? Somebody forgot a baby on the table. That's what I see. Left the baby sleeping and went away." "What baby?" demanded the child. Full of gratitude, she examined Binyamin's profile and climbed on the pail to get a closer look at the table. "That one, that one." He hit the naked doll lying next to the keys with the wire: "How do you leave a sleeping baby like that?" The child's eyes filled; she gripped the window bars with her fingers: "But I didn't leave him on purpose, I would never leave him, I only . . ." "I only, I only," Binyamin imitated her mockingly: "We've heard that before. Now he'll die with nobody to feed him. He'll die of hunger and not being covered." He reached the keys with the wire, almost succeeded in threading it through the key ring, but failed. The child felt the blood draining from her cheeks: "He won't die, he can't die," she said. "He'll die, he'll die," insisted Binyamin, finally succeeding in hooking the key ring on the wire: "He'll die because of you."

She let go of the window bars and sank to her knees in the flower bed, covering her face with her hands: "It's not because of me that he'll die," she sobbed.

"Don't cry," said Binyamin in alarm. "It was just a game. It isn't true. Did you think it was true?" She parted her fingers and looked through them at the broad leaves of the mango tree, the broad leaves spreading to the sides. Bitterness spread through her, terrible resentment, not at the lie, but at the breakdown of the partnership between herself and Binyamin with the lie about the sleeping baby. "It is true," she said coldly. "The baby's true."

Keys

THE BUNCH OF keys she always carried with her, the keys of the mother superior of a convent, which at their height reached maybe fifteen, attached to an iron ring. Each key—a vocation that became a door: the keys to the shack, the huge wrought-iron key to the door to Nona's quarter-shack, the two keys to Sammy's welding shop, the key to "her" little store-room next to the welding shop, the key to the main entrance of the student center, another four keys to other rooms in the student center, the three keys to Rabbi Nathaniel's villa—one for the front door, one for the side door, and one for the basement—the key to Corinne's one-room flat in the young couples housing project, the key to the bicycle lock, and another little one, to the lock of the attic, the *msandara* "up there," which was completely rusted and neither opened nor closed, and which she kept with her as a reminder that it had to be changed. "I have to get it changed, the *me'affan*" (the key? the lock? the entire door?), she would say whenever she came across it on the key ring, an expression of urgency, but also relief, almost happiness, crossing her face: there was something else to do, something that had not yet been done.

The keys left the ring over the course of the years, one by one or in droves: in the drawer of the hospital locker, after she died, the only keys left on the ring were the key to the shack and the key to the outside storeroom, which had been dismantled long ago and turned into a kind of cupboard, but which she kept on calling "the storeroom." The keys rested at the bottom of the plastic bag containing the things removed from the locker drawer, under the open envelopes of letters from the municipality and the National Insurance, which Sammy brought her from the shack. On one of the envelopes were scribbled in pencil two telephone numbers, which I didn't recognize. I rang them both. The first was answered by the automatic answering service of the local council, the second by the social worker in the sheltered housing for the elderly in south Tel Aviv, where Maurice lived.

I didn't know what to say. I asked her how he was. She knew me, the worker (he called her "the worker"), from my occasional visits; she was always lying in wait for me when I came out of his room: a born-again religious Jewess who kept a pack of cigarettes in her desk drawer, and quickly threw her cigarette stub out the window whenever anyone came into her office. Now, on the phone, she complained a little about Maurice: he didn't want to take part in activities, shut himself in his room all day, she reported. "He never took part in activities," I consoled her: "It's from way back." She was silent. I could almost sense the rich, dense texture of her silence on the other end of the line. "Strange," she said in the end, "that's exactly word for word what your mother said a week ago when she called to ask how he was. Word for word." She fell silent again. "She died, may she rest in peace, right?" "Right," I said. "Maurice has hardly touched his food since she died, may she rest in peace," she said.

I didn't touch the keys, I didn't have permission. Sammy had: he shoved them absentmindedly into the pocket of his work pants (with the hole), taking her death on himself and to himself with the same naturalness that he took her on himself and to himself when she was alive.

WORD FOR WORD

CORINNE REPEATED WORD for word what she had once heard from Aunt Marcelle, who had elaborated, not word for word, on something the Nona had once thrown out. This was in a moment of complete relaxation, of self-forgetfulness: for a moment Corinne forgot her daily schedule, raised her face to a different star. She really did raise her face when she said it—a face shining with passion and intense longing, steeped in the molten gold of the inspiration, the invention of the moment, the sudden birth of the inspiration of the moment: she was Maurice's daughter. Like him, she knew how to lend a quotation the force and inspiration of the invention of the moment, to turn the copy into the original by virtue of the belief, natural and unwilled as breath, that everything was original or everything was a copy, and what mattered was the emotional investment, or the depth of the emotional investment in what was said, what was taken, what was given. The dreaminess of her voice when she said what she said, repeating what she had heard but in her own way, steeped in longings that had no beginning or middle or end, translucent, open to infinity and opening with the conjunctive "and": "And he loved her so much, Maurice," she said, "and he loved the mother so much. And when he entered the room he looked only at her when he spoke, only she was there, nobody else but her. And he spoke only to her."

La Dame aux Camélias

B ut to return to the first day of this "liaison." When I came back to my rooms I was wild with delight; I remembered that the barriers placed by my imagination between Marguerite and myself had disappeared; that I was her lover and occupied, more or less, all her thoughts; that I had in my pocket the key of her room, and the right of making use of that key; and I was glad to live, proud of myself, and pleased with my lot in this world.

On a certain day a young man passes through a street; he brushes against a young woman, looks at her, turns round, and passes on; he does not know this woman; she has pleasures, passions, sorrows, which he does not share. He does not exist for her, and perhaps if he spoke to her she would make fun of him as Marguerite had made fun of me. Weeks, months, years flow on, and all at once, after they have each followed their destiny in various directions, the logic of fate brings them again face to face. Then this woman becomes the mistress of this man and loves him. How? Why? Their two existences now make but one; their intimacy had scarcely begun when it appears to them to have always existed, and every other event that happened before is effaced from the memory of this pair of lovers. We must acknowledge that this is strange.

As for me, I no longer remembered how I had lived before the preceding day. My whole being was steeped in joy at the recollection of the words exchanged during the first night. Either Marguerite was clever at deceiving, or she felt for me one of those sudden passions revealed in the first kiss, and which sometimes die as suddenly as they arise.

The more I reflected on it the more I said to myself that Marguerite had no cause to feign a passion which she did not feel; I also said to myself that women have two ways of loving, which may spring from one another: they love with the heart and with the senses. A woman often takes a lover, impelled to it by her temperament; and, without having expected it, she learns the mystery of immaterial love, and no longer lives except through her feelings; often a young girl who imagines marriage only to be the union of two pure affections receives the sudden revelation of physical love; this energetic conclusion of the most chaste impressions of the soul.

I fell asleep while occupied with these thoughts. My servant woke me and handed me a letter from Marguerite which contained the following words:

"THESE ARE my commands: Come this evening to the 'Vaudeville,' between the third and fourth acts—M.G."

I LOCKED the note in one of the drawers of my table, so as always to have the reality at hand, and as a proof that I was not dreaming, as I sometimes fancied I was.

She did not tell me to come and visit her in the daytime, so I did not dare to present myself at her house; but I was so anxious to meet her before the evening that I went to the Champs-Elysées where, as on the day before, I saw her pass and get out of her carriage.

I was at the "Vaudeville" at seven.

Never before had I entered a theatre so early.

All the boxes became gradually occupied except one on the grand tier near the stage, which remained empty.

The third act had begun. The door of this box, on which I kept my eyes almost constantly fixed, opened, and Marguerite appeared.

She immediately advanced to the front, glanced at the stalls, saw me, and thanked me with a look.

She seemed wonderfully handsome that evening.

Was I the cause of her looking so well? Did she love me enough to believe that the more beautiful she looked the happier I should be? I was not yet aware of it, but if such had been her intention she completely succeeded: for when the audience saw her they whispered among themselves, and the actor who was then on *the stage gazed at the woman who had disturbed the spectators by her mere appearance. And I had the key of her apartment, and in another three or four hours she would again be mine.*

People blame men who ruin themselves for actresses and demireps. What astonishes me is that men do not commit twenty times more follies for them . . .

Piazza San Marco: Sixth Visit

T HE THEATER OF the Piazza San Marco photograph was not a show put on
by Maurice, but the essential embodiment of his true nature, what he
considered to be his true nature, which he wanted to share with the mother.
The place to which he wanted to bring her, the Piazza San Marco, was the
recognition and acknowledgment of his true nature. How he had looked forward to it, made preparations: he changed his hotel room for a suite, hired
a girl beforehand to look after the child, borrowed money from the whole
world, and told the whole world about "my wife and daughter." "The whole
world" consisted of four or five journalists from foreign agencies he had met
in Geneva, when he worked as a translator in the United Nations. He wanted
everything to slide smoothly into this expansiveness, into the grand gestures; he wanted to persuade her at last of the truth of his world—the grandeur and the craving for grandeur—to "bring her back," as Nona said, to a
place where she had never really been.

They apparently arrived in winter or autumn, judging by the fine coats
that they put on and took off in the warm air of the fine restaurants, the
heated lobbies of the hotels where he held his meetings. He took her and the
child to his meetings: the mother nodded, sat with her thighs pressed
together in their silk stockings that rubbed against the hem of the mohair
coat, which she only took off when she started to sweat. He had bought her

the silk stockings. For the child he bought a ballerina dress with a skirt of ivory-colored lace.

But the child screamed all the time. The entire seven and a half days of Italy she screamed. "She never stopped crying, kept them on their feet and never gave them a moment's peace," said Corinne, who didn't get to go to Italy, with relish. They left her at home with Sammy, who wouldn't leave her alone: he pursued her with his one good eye, her and the boys who gave her rides on their bicycles, sitting in front on the crossbar.

ON THEIR FEET

NONA SAID: "FROM morning to night on your feet, in the end you'll fall. Who'll pick you up when you fall?" She said: "Only God will. Everybody's on their feet, not only me." Nona said: "What do I care about everybody? It's you I pity." She said: "Don't pity me. Keep your pity for the wretched of the earth." Nona said: "And who will take pity if not the mother? Will the wretched take pity? Those who are not pitied have no pity." She said: "Are you trying to say that I have no pity? Is that what you're trying to say?" Nona said: "I didn't mean you. I meant the world, *elaalam.*"

ELAALAM, THE WORLD (1)

THERE WAS NO room because of the mother's "day-to-day," and because "*elbani-adam* has to know his day-to-day," and because when she said "*elaalam*" it described the immensity of a self-contained whole from which nothing could be broken off, which eluded the grasp of thought or imagination, impossible to contain or conquer, crush or defeat.

This, more or less, was *elaalam*, all the space beyond the open door of the Nona's quarter-shack—because they always talked with the doors open wide to *elaalam*—in which floated shrouded things that did not announce themselves and had no exact address, and probably expected no one or nothing, because one way or another only *elbani-adam* himself, said Nona, had the duty of expectation and hidden hope, only he had eyes, according to Nona, that were stuck in the back of his head, looking backward, to the past, at what had perhaps once been and what "would be," and to a future that was conditioned on patience and time, patience and time, "*elsabr wa'el-zaman*," because that was what *elaalam* required, only that, but it was the only attitude unavailable to the mother and Maurice who refused, who wanted to skip forward; they skipped and fell, and failed the test of *elaalam*, because they had neither patience nor time, said the Nona, not to anyone in particular but to *elaalam* itself, which was the voices coming from the radio, and the voices behind the voices of the radio, which were Maurice himself—*elaalam* itself in its absence.

Maurice said "*elaalam*" loudly and aggressively, as a rebuke and even a demand, the sound of which the child remembered but not the words or the meaning, just like Maurice himself, who was mainly the sound of something that was apparently *elaalam*, an absent world that he confronted with infinity: infinite expectation, infinite absence, infinite *elaalam*.

ELAALAM (2)

"*ELAALAM, ELAALAM.*" THE Nona tried to share with Sammy, too, her usual gloom, which was a coat with reversible sides, one dark, one light, but he was absorbed in his own nonsense: sticking a button into the folds of flesh of her swollen arm, several times bigger than the other one, to see if it would stay there without falling while she spoke.

"Stop it, stop it, you'll never learn anything, you." She slapped his arm with the kitchen towel lying on her lap and he burst out laughing, rolling around on the mat at her feet, his knees close to his chin, swaying from side to side.

"Say it again, what you said before," he groaned. "What did I say?" she wondered, feeling the skin between her upper lip and her nose, to see if the five annoying hairs of her little mustache had grown back. "What did I say? Just say it in Hebrew, because of the Arabic you talk I can't understand a word. It's as broken as the Arabic of the Greeks in Cairo," she complained, echoing his roars of laughter with an occasional obligatory titter, but actually busy maintaining her self-respect, repeatedly straightening the voluminous folds of her dress as she restrained herself from bending down to scratch her ankle, which he was tickling with a stalk. "Come on, Nona, let's test your eyesight." He stood up, took a few steps backward, and held up his fingers: "How many?" "Three," she said crossly, stood up at last, and shuffled to the kitchen. "You know very well I haven't got my eyes. And you,

you start something and don't finish it," she muttered. "Yes you have, yes you have," he called after her, "you just pretend not to see." Sammy stopped abruptly, got into her bed in his work clothes, and covered himself with the blanket.

The bed was always made with the big blanket on top of it, day and night, receiving the child, Nona, and Sammy alternately, or all three at once: then Sammy lay with his head at the bottom of the bed and his feet between them or on top of them, and Nona pushed them away until he took them back and curled up in a ball. Sometimes the child ran her finger over the hard, rough skin of his sole, trying to tickle it, but he didn't feel a thing: "Even if you stuck a nail in, he wouldn't feel it"—Nona stated her opinion—"all he wants, that one, is to forget himself."

And he did forget himself—especially at work, stripping himself of everything that got in the way, confronting "the work" exposed, almost naked. He couldn't stand having a watch on his wrist—he would take it off and forget it, throw it out or give it away, together with the medallions the mother and Corinne would sometimes buy him for his birthday. "Maybe he'll grow up now." Most of the time he walked around the welding shop barefoot, forgetting where he had put his soaking wet shoes to dry, or simply taking them off and throwing them out because he didn't have laces, disdaining the greasy welding gloves and especially the mask. He welded without a mask to protect his eyes, dragging the mother or being dragged by her twice a week to the emergency room, to have the chips in his eyes removed: the bad, left eye, which had been damaged by herpes when he was a child, was completely ruined, and the good, right eye grew weaker and weaker. "If you don't put on that welding mask you can run to those hospitals alone," the mother threatened. He didn't listen; two days later he was welding without a mask again: "It's impossible to be accurate with that mask," he argued, "to get to the exact millimeter of the join."

He got the "millimeter of the join" into his head when he was still seventeen, working in Faiga's big welding shop in Kiryat Aryeh, before he went into business on his own. Faiga had an office on the top floor, above the hall where they worked, with a window the size of the wall: he stood in his office and looked down at the workers through his window, from time to time calling over the loudspeaker: "You there, come upstairs," or "You there, come upstairs to me." To Sammy he called, "You come up here to me" only once, but for good, not ill. He gave him a special design for a special cart without telling him what it was for, and Sammy worked on it for a week outside regular working hours, during which they put together big carts for bakeries, for taking the bread in and out of the ovens. When Sammy and one of the other workers who assisted him had finished making the special cart, Faiga summoned them to his office again, but not over the loudspeaker. He stood and watched them working for a long time in silence and in the end he said to them, "Come up here please." He offered them refreshments: wine and cookies. "Let's drink a toast," he said. Sammy was shy, but he didn't hold back; he polished off the whole plate of cookies. They were his favorites: two rounds of pastry with jam in the middle. "What's the special cart we made for?" he dared to ask Faiga. "For Eichmann. They put Eichmann's body on the cart you made," said Faiga. He held out his hand and shook their hands, pressing them for a long time: "Hats off to you, boys."

ELAALAM (3)

MAURICE WAS ELAALAM; intentionally or unintentionally he brought *elaa-lam* with him when he came.

He brought a Hebrew newspaper when he came (the child looked for the hidden child in the picture: "Where's the child?").

He brought a French newspaper, which was also *elaalam: Le Monde.*

He brought the newspapers he wrote in Hebrew and French, *HaMeorer The Wake-up Call* ("But what's it supposed to mean? Who's sleeping?" asked Sammy).

He brought out-of-season mangoes (the child exchanged a mango for ten cubes of sugar with Sima, whose father drank tea holding a cube of sugar in his mouth).

He brought a camera and photographs taken by a different camera than the one he brought.

He brought the profound, experienced sadness of a perception that was wiser than himself.

He brought Tel Aviv clothes for the child, exactly the right size even when years passed between one of his visits and the next.

He brought things that people had given him as presents.

He brought other opinions, saying: "A person should always listen to other opinions, not accept them, but listen to them," looking at the mother when he said "a person."

He brought a certain urban weariness, with a halo that was dull but still glinting.

And the hatred of parochialism. He, who never based his politics on hatred, only on honor.

And the longing for the remote and the foreign, the desire for the remote and the foreign, the desire for desire: *a mon seul désir*.

He brought a photographer, a friend from the Suhba, who photographed them all in the mother's living room: they crowded together on the couch, including Nona and Mermel, shoulder to shoulder; the picture came out almost black—they looked like the family of a wanted man.

He brought secrets, secrets about the secrets, and a certain knowledge he gave off that in *elaalam* there were always layers beneath layers, double meanings, drawers with countless double bottoms.

"Don't tell anyone about that cart you made for Eichmann, for that Revisionist you work for," he said to Sammy, with a grave expression. "But why?" asked Sammy. "What's the secret?" "Just don't tell anyone. Don't ask why. When you understand—you'll understand," said Maurice.

Elaalam (4)

A T THE END of the Egyptian movie on television, when she went on staring for a long time at the screen, still absorbed in the plot, she said: "That's *elaalam* for you. Look where people end up. They rolled around and around, him and her—what didn't they do and where didn't they roll?—and in the end they fell on one another."

Rolling

Twice a week they took the bus to Corinne's apartment in the young couples housing project to bring her things: two cardboard boxes full of canned food, rice, sugar, chocolate spread, noodles, cheese, margarine, cleaning agents. The mother said: "We'll bring her a few things. Until she gets rolling." About herself she always said that she was "rolling along." When people asked her how she was she said, "Rolling along." "Rolling" implied her ability to improvise, her endless inventiveness ("I took it from there and put it here") and also what was most important in her eyes: movement between different areas of shade, different and changing degrees of darkness. The very principle of movement itself, even pointless movement, in hope or the promise of hope.

Corinne, on the other hand, did not roll. At five o'clock in the afternoon she fell asleep in front of the television with the baby, wearing the same pregnancy dress for week after week, because of the fifty-five pounds she had gained during her pregnancy and had not yet lost: a blue dress ("Navy blue," said Corinne) shaped like a tent, with a white inset in the front that looked like a big baby's bib resting on her breasts. Mermel said that he could tell by the stains on the white bib what Corinne had eaten during the day: jam, meatball gravy, ice cream, or the baby's cornstarch porridge. She gave him a look through the honey-colored curtain of her uncombed, unwashed hair that silenced him at once. Even now, when she called to mind a sinking ship tilting on its side—with her heavy gait, shuffling in ugly slippers, in the tent dress, with the smudge of black eyeliner on her cheek, Mermel saw her as a great beauty and sent her anxious looks hungry for approval. But Corinne was sunk deep in a murky lake of disapproval, occasionally sending up her periscope to look out with a hostile eye, and then withdrawing it again. Most of all she scorned the "young couples": her apartment, the apartments next door, the thin walls, the stairwells, the other residents. "The people here are garbage," she burst out. "Where they got all this trash from is beyond me." The mother tried to dam the torrent: "They're just people like any others, like you and me, living their day-to-day," she argued weakly. "What do you mean like you and me?" Corinne cried, beside herself. "Tell me, what's the connection with you and me?" The mother said nothing ("better to keep quiet"), unloaded the cardboard boxes, and arranged their contents in the tiny kitchen cupboard with its peeling Formica coating, and opened the curtain to let in more light.

The child sat in the big fire engine Mermel had brought for the baby, put her book on the steering wheel, and read, as if to distance herself from Corinne's gaze, getting under her skin and peeling off layer after layer. "How come you turned that page so quickly? Have you finished reading it already?" asked Corinne suspiciously, and the child nodded. "So tell me what's written there. Let's see if you read it." The child told her what was written, but Corinne stopped listening and turned her eyes to the rubber band bunching the child's hair: "What's that ugly thing you put on your hair?" she demanded, and beckoned the child to come to her, on the sofa. She undid the pony tail, threw away the rubber band, brushed the child's thick hair, and ran her fingers through it: "That's how you should wear it all the time," she said, pulled the child's head onto her lap, and laid her hand on her cheek, feeling her cheekbone: "Are you the cleverest child in the school?" she asked, and went on running her fingers, the fingers of a blind woman, over her cheek, her forehead, her eyelids, her chin. "I don't know," said the child, without moving. "Of course you are," said Corinne, her voice as tender as her fingertips, "you're our princess. Just don't brag about it and spoil everything. You show them," she ordered in a stern voice. "Who?" asked the child, who was having a hard time breathing: Corinne's hand was blocking her nostrils. "All those spoiled nothings who think they're God knows what." She stood up abruptly, with a gesture of disgust, letting the child's head fall onto the sofa. Now she felt like having something good to eat. "Is there something good?" she asked the mother. The mother beamed. At last Corinne wanted something: "What, for instance?" she asked eagerly.

Corinne shuffled to the kitchen, opened and closed the cupboard doors, the fridge door, staring for a long time at the shelves. "You looked inside the fridge a minute ago, *ya binti*. No children were born there in the meantime," said the mother, unable to curb her tongue. She put on her coat and looked for her handbag. "Come with me," she said to the child. "Where are you going?" demanded Corinne tearfully, rubbing her neck, which had come out in a rash. "Why are you leaving already?" She took hold of the strap of the mother's bag. "I'll be back in a minute," promised the mother, and took a cab with the child to the confectioner's shop in the town center. "We'll get her the best cream cake in the shop for her birthday," she said to the child, her eyes fixed on the windshield of the cab. "But her birthday is in two weeks' time," said the child. "Never mind," dismissed the mother. "Two weeks more, two weeks less, what difference does it make?" She debated with the saleslady in the confectioner's for a long time, chose a layered cream cake, which was packed in a pink cardboard box with a green ribbon. "Pity the box isn't green and the ribbon pink," said the child regretfully, and hurried after the mother, who flew with the cake in her arms and pushed onto the bus with it before everybody else.

When they arrived, Corinne had made up her face at last, showered and scented herself and combed her hair, but put the navy blue dress with the white bib back on again. The mother set the tall box before her, on the folding aluminum table in the kitchen, without even taking off her coat, undid the ribbon with fumbling fingers. "For your birthday," she said to Corinne, her face rigid with emotion. Corinne fell silent, looked, and all at once her face shone with a pure white radiance, as dazzling as the mounds of whipped cream on the cake. She sent out a finger, stuck it in the mound of whipped cream in the center. "All real whipped cream, no margarine," stressed the mother, following the course of the finger covered in whipped cream to Corinne's mouth. Corinne held the cream in her mouth for a moment, and then her lips twisted in disgust, and she ran to the sink and spat it out. "Margarine," she said, "it's all margarine. That bitch from the confectioner's took you for a ride." The mother refused to believe her, tasted for herself, and immediately spat it out: "Margarine. She took the price for whipped cream from me; she swore it was whipped cream," she said.

Corinne put on her boots, packed herself in her coat, packed the cake in its box: "Come on, we're taking it back," she commanded. Again they rode to the confectioner's, with the baby in his carriage. The child stayed outside with him, next to the entrance. She saw the mother and Corinne setting the cake firmly on the counter, demanding the money back. They called the owner: she conferred with Corinne and the mother to one side, spread out her hands helplessly. They came out, and stood there furiously for a while, looking inside: the saleslady cut two slices from the margarine cake, put them on two plates, and served them to a couple sitting and drinking coffee. Corinne's eyes popped out of her head: "She's still got the nerve to sell it," she said, and burst back into the shop, with the mother behind her. The next minute their hands were digging into the cake standing on the counter, and throwing handfuls of the mess of dough and cream onto the shelf holding the cups above it: "Bastards," yelled Corinne. "Bastards. First you cheat people and then you carry on as if it was nothing."

As If It Were Nothing

A T LAST SHE came to me in a dream, after years when she hadn't. There was a coffin next to her, an expensive coffin, lined inside and out with dark blue velvet. She got into it as if it were nothing. She lay down on her back, her hands stretched out at her sides. "Close the lid," she demanded. I didn't move. I was trembling all over: her eyes were burning, surrounded by soot. "Close it!" she shouted. "Close the lid and throw away the basin already. Let me go!"

THE BASIN

THE BLUE BASIN was actually sky-blue, and not much different from the many other basins in the mother's shack and the Nona's quarter-shack, because both of them were firm believers in basins and their unique and various uses, and the particular purpose of each and every one of them, which was enshrined in law, the law of the ways and habits of life known only to members of the household, the unspoken rules of how things were done and how they should be done, with the right rhyme, rhythm, and meter that gave *elaalam* its form, context, and volume. The basin in which the sheets were soaked in bleach was not the basin in which the broad beans were skinned, even though they were similar, and the basin for the bean pods was not the basin where the clean socks were collected after the wash in order to facilitate matching the pairs, and then there was the basin in which the mother soaked her swollen feet, and the one where the semolina was mixed for the couscous, and the huge basin in which the Nona dipped the lower half of her body and splashed water on the upper half, and the one in which the baby eggplants were pickled, and the little one in which the strips of cotton wool were soaked in tea for Sammy's sick eyes, and the medium-sized green one in which the lace tablecloths were dyed in tea, and the other medium-sized one for cleaning the fixtures from the gas cooker in caustic soda, and the basin from the garden for collecting the twigs and the uprooted weeds, and the basin in which the bottles of cleaning agents were kept with the rag crammed between them, and the basin that was "not that one, that one"—they sent the child to fetch a basin from the little storeroom next to the welding shop and she brought that one and was told, "No, that one," and she said, "Which one?," and Nona said: "That one, that one. You, if they sent you to get water from the sea you'd come back and say there's no water," and the child laughed at what she said, even though she was crying, because there was burning, and she said, "But it's burning."

The burning came in the middle of the night, after she had crossed the path a number of times from the mother's shack to Nona's quarter-shack and back again, and fallen asleep on one of their beds next to one of their bodies for two or three hours, and woken up from the burning, pulled down the blanket, and sat up on her knees, writhing in pain, in silence.

On the pillow next to her lay a head, the mother's or the Nona's, and a mouth that mumbled into the pillow, in the dark, "Is it burning you there again?" and a hand went out in the darkness to the little bedside lamp and the little light went on, and whichever one of them it was pulled up her nightgown under the blanket and sat up and got out of bed and went to boil water in the kettle and to fetch the child's basin (which became the child's basin after Nona announced: "That's the child's basin"), which they hardly ever remembered where they had put it the last time, and they began to wander in the middle of the night in their nightgowns and housecoats on top of their nightgowns, from Nona's house to the mother's storeroom, saying to each other: "It's burning her again. Bring the basin."

And they brought it. They stood the basin on the mat at the foot of the bed in the near-total darkness, with only the bedside lamp illuminating a strip of wall and not the whole room, and poured boiling water into the basin and then cold water to make warm water into which they poured the purple-red alkaline grains, producing the pinkish-purple water for the inflammation of the urinary tract "that's driving the poor child mad," said the Nona, and the mother said: "Don't say 'poor child'—it's just an inflammation. It'll pass."

It didn't pass, and even if it did, a little, the child didn't want it to pass, and when the Nona or the mother asked her if it had passed she said no. The night passed, transporting the child soaking in the alkaline water with her eyes wide open, as if staring beyond the pain itself, the burning itself, in its changing degrees of intensity, and its gradual relief in the warm pink water that slowly cooled until it was completely cold, and nevertheless they didn't take her out of the basin. Next to her, high up on the bed, were the heavy breaths of the mother or the Nona, who sometimes turned from side to side. The child dipped her hands in the water, burying her cheeks between her knees, feeling her wet thighs, knowing that she existed, even if all around her, in the breathing darkness, the substantiality of the room was fading, the substantiality of the objects or of the people who were receding into the distance but were still present in some strange way, surrounding the nighttime house, which was reduced to the basin she was sitting in, and not coming in, circling around, leaving her in possession of what was hers, gradually forgetting her nocturnal summons, until it was almost dawn, when the mother or the Nona got heavily out of bed, brought a big bath towel, dried the almost frozen child, and said: "That's enough, enough for today."

Enough for Today (1)

UNTIL ALMOST MIDNIGHT she and Sammy sat on the living-room carpet and talked and talked and talked, close to each other, competing for the warmth of the electric heater, after the mother had switched off two of the glowing coils that Sammy had switched on, "eating up the electricity," and he had turned them on again, spreading his hands over the wire guard, touching and not touching. Perhaps he had tried to roast chestnuts on the heater and given up, charred them on the gas burner, and brought them back hot in his hands. "You could have put them on a plate," scolded the mother, but not seriously, her legs tucked under her so long that she couldn't move them when she wanted to get up, they were so numb. "Enough for today," she said, trying to stand up, staggering and almost falling: "Look how we've forgotten ourselves."

This was apparently happiness: on her face then was the relaxed absent-mindedness of forgetfulness, full of faith in time precisely because she had allowed it to be forgotten—and there was a different roundness then in all her movements: even her look was round, not wanting to change anything, and altogether not wanting but simply being, resting in the room and the furniture as if in blindness, in suspension of judgment: the look of parents at their children.

Enough for Today (2)

Until almost midnight she and Sammy sat on the living-room carpet, talking about it: it, it, and it—the welding shop. Row by row of cinder blocks it rose from the carpet at their feet, overshadowing the shack itself until it was almost invisible: for months and months, for the entire period of the "construction," the shack became a footnote, the launching pad for the rocket being sent into space—the welding shop.

For hours at a time they sat on the carpet and chewed over the idea of the welding shop: why and how, how much and where from, and again, how? Once she asked: "But how, *ya* Sammy?" and once he did: "But how, how?" These exchanges, which Sammy called "consultations," were not of content, but of tone, cadence, and music. They confirmed, argued, or drove each other crazy, but only because of the tone and by means of the tone, getting into a seven-minute quarrel over "his way of saying it" or "her way of saying it," always changing to the third person.

Sammy didn't want to be the third person, or the second person, "a hired worker": he wanted to be independent, the first person—he wanted it with all his might, and not so much because he coveted the real and imaginary power of the boss but because he dreamed of playing all by himself and deciding for himself. He, who until the age of four in Cairo didn't speak, because all his wishes were anticipated and fulfilled by at least six adults before he even opened his mouth, and who took so much pleasure in breaking his toys that Maurice hired a girl especially to "play with him," and in fact to smash them for him with a hammer—he played now with the mother with the biggest toy of them all—the welding shop.

They built it "hand in hand," the two of them. Since they had to scrape together the money for the construction from nowhere, they watched each other with an eagle eye, correcting each other like two strict teachers, giving back pages corrected in red ink. He ordered building materials—and she ran to the warehouse to correct the order. She ordered the cement mixer for early in the morning—and he put it off to later. She called in an electrician—and he called in another electrician, better and cheaper, who never showed up. But most of the time he was on the ladder and she handed him the blocks from below: between her morning job and her afternoon job, and sometimes at the expense of one of them, she handed him the blocks, between working in the garden and working in the shack, in the middle of her "chores" and at night by the light of the big projector. Until the start of the Sabbath they worked, or at the most until half an hour afterward, because Sammy refused to work on the Sabbath; he was terrified out of his wits: the *amm* told him that the business would not be blessed if he desecrated the Sabbath.

The mother scoffed at the idea of the blessing, but she accepted Sammy's work stoppage without blinking an eye, in the face of the stubborn, nonnegotiable element in Sammy's character: his panic. Mostly he panicked at what he called "strange," but what was actually bad, and bad meant whatever and whoever did not stand by his side and collaborate with him in his "consultations" as an actual or potential partner.

The whole neighborhood was his partner in building the welding shop, participating in the discussions that took place morning, noon, and night, now on the sandy floor of the roofless structure with its half-built walls, eating candies peeled from their cellophane or paper wrappings, offering sentences beginning "So what do you think if . . ." until the mother appeared in her nightgown and chased them all away: "Enough for today."

They left and Sammy did everything the opposite way, inventing methods that cost three times as much in the end: the construction stopped. "Everything's stuck," said the mother bitterly, reviewing the ruins of the garden every morning: the dead roses destroyed by cement and lime, the corroded lawn, the bed of new seedlings whose names she didn't know, crushed beneath the dumpster of building waste.

Again they sat on the living-room carpet until midnight: there was a new "What do you think about . . ."

He found extra work helping with the neighborhood soccer team, painted the lines of the field for the Saturday match, cleaned the clubhouse, and every Thursday he brought the mother two bags crammed with laundry: shirts, shorts, and dozens of socks stinking with sweat and full of sand, which went through the wash and left sand in the machine. On Fridays she sat the child and the Nona down to fold the soccer players' uniforms: the stink of the sweat still lingered in the socks, and Nona washed her hands at least three times with soap during the course of the folding, dismissing the child who stood dreaming with a sock in her hand and summoning her back again: "*Yallah* go, *yallah* come here."

In the welding shop they laid the cement floor but did not yet raise the roof: a dense, dark rectangle of sky, the stars stuck deep into it like tacks, lay squeezed between the cinder block walls. Sammy made himself a little tent of blankets "for the time being" as a shelter from the rain, in the middle of the roofless building. He wanted to build a snow sled for four people. "What snow are you talking about?" fumed the mother. "Where do you see snow?" He shook his head pityingly, took his sandwich, returned to his tent, and welded until one o'clock in morning, until she disconnected the electricity, went to the welding shop, and dragged him away. Grumbling, he shuffled behind her, half asleep, in his big work boots with the laces undone.

The child saw them from the kitchen window, in the dark: the mother's brisk barefoot steps, the outlines of her thick thighs showing through her nightgown when the light from the streetlamp fell on her, her short, sad neck crammed on top of her chest, the invisible threads that stretched from her to Sammy, encircling him as he shuffled, stooped, behind her with his curls white from plaster covering his eyes that could hardly see anyway, stopping for a minute to look back wearily at the blank rectangle of the welding shop and stretching his arm over his shoulder to scratch a spot at the top of his back, but not reaching it.

"Scratch me," he says, offering his back to the mother. "Where?" she asks. "Here, here." He raises his arm to his shoulder blades. They stand with their faces to the welding shop and their profiles to the shack, to the child: him in front and her behind him, absentmindedly scratching his back.

NIGHTGOWNS

THE PILE OF nightgowns in her closet, one on top of the other, in a straight line with the shelf: pale, white, or off-white, sometimes pastel, if flowered—then only little flowers, flannel for winter and cotton for summer (half-synthetic, drip-dry), never satin, or silk, or red, or black, or lace that wasn't a modest border at the neck, things only fit for a "madam."

They always gave off a feeling of freshness, a longing for freshness: in their appearance, their arrangement, their multiplication—always more and more of the same thing, over and over again. There was an element of obsession, a silent and secretive single-mindedness, in this craving for freshness that danced before her eyes: she, who never spent a penny on herself, bought more and more of these nightgowns, for "next to nothing," as she said, but still, she bought them. The nightgowns and the ritual putting on of the nightgowns turned into a symbol, a sign of the transition from the public to the private, the intimate, the shedding of her active, resourceful persona in favor of an abandonment—not chaotic, but orderly and anchored in law, the law of the nightgown.

The nightgowns and the language of the nightgowns drew a square whose four corners were herself, her sister, Marcelle, Corinne, and the Nona. The four of them knew the language of the nightgowns, bequeathed it to each other, and spoke it, to themselves and to each other: "I washed and put on my nightgown" was a statement whose real, deep meaning was clear only to them, a solemn, restrained echo that meant more or less, "I fired *elaalam* and retired in an orderly manner."

Endlessly they gave each other gifts of nightgowns and passed nightgowns on to each other ("I found this for you"), especially the mother and Aunt Marcelle, who announced the ceremony and carried it out, showering one after the other at let's say five o'clock in the afternoon, put on the long white orphanage nightgowns, and sat down at the kitchen table, ate bread and pickled turnips, and pretended to be playing cards: the aunt played *"crapette"* with herself and the mother looked on helplessly. "You're already in your nightgown?" Sammy asks in astonishment when he arrives, sits down next them at the kitchen table, and thrusts his arm deep into the pickle jar, as if unaware of Aunt Marcelle's hand affectionately rumpling his curls, but inclining his head slightly toward her in order to deepen the caress.

Sammy does not acknowledge the law of the nightgowns and disrupts it at every opportunity: "He always needs something urgently, that Sammy, when I'm already in my nightgown," the mother complains, but she complies anyway, gets up, goes out, gets herself dirty with the urgent request, comes back, and puts on a new, clean nightgown, but without the pristine thrill of the first one. Now he's in a big hurry; before he wasn't in a hurry but now he remembers that he is, the car standing on the road next to the shack refuses to start, it needs a little push. "Come on," he urges them both, "give me a little push." "But first we have to get dressed," Aunt Marcelle complains. "How can we go out like this?" They go out like that, in their nightgowns, and push the Chevrolet almost to the turn in the road, splitting their sides with laughter. Side by side they march down the middle of the road back to the shack. "How we laughed," says Aunt Marcelle, wiping her eyes and glancing sidelong at the mother. "How we laughed, didn't we, Lucette?" she asks, and her eyes suddenly become thoughtful, revealing a void of anxiety in the look behind the sidelong glance that for a moment recalls Corinne, flickering and vanishing into the darkness.

They return to the kitchen table, but not to the cards and the pickled turnips, but to a dish of oats, cooked for hours in milk and served with sugar, cinnamon, coconut, and chopped walnuts: according to tradition, the dish is prepared on the Saturday morning after a baby's first tooth comes out, because of the shape of the oats, which look like babies' teeth. Aunt

Marcelle wanted it now, without taking any baby or tooth into account: "What, aren't we people, too?" she demands, polishing off bowl after bowl. The white nightgowns are spotted now with little stains of mud, grease, the red juice of the pickled turnips, and the cinnamon-colored oats. The mother examines the soiled nightgowns sadly: "We'll put them in bleach, and if the stains don't come out—too bad, we'll throw them out and buy new ones," she cheers herself up.

Corinne, on the other hand, never threw out her nightgowns. In general, she didn't throw anything out—"she's got a whole museum there," said the mother: snow-white nightgowns, made of the finest pure cotton or the finest silk, simple-looking and expensive, lay starched in her closet with fragrant little bags of dried lavender between them. She collected them, gathering them one by one from fancy lingerie boutiques or secondhand shops, wore them once only, when she tried them on, and added them to her collection. From time to time she took them out of the closet, spread them out on the bed, examined them, folded them neatly, and returned them to the closet. "Who are you keeping them for?" demanded the mother, outraged by what in her eyes was the very essence and symbol of everything that had gone shockingly wrong in Corinne's life. "Until when?"

Corinne did not reply, not then and not ever. She went on sleeping or pretending to sleep on the couch in the shabby rags she wore in the house, her head on the baby's teddy bear, muttering, "in a minute, in a minute," to Mermel, who asked her for the third time to come to bed.

THE PICTURE: *LE BALCON* (3)

THE MOTHER MOVED the couch from the corner of the yellow hall, which even after it stopped being yellow recalled its first, original color, like hair roots that go on growing, peeping out under the dyed hair. After the couch migrated from its place, so did the child's gaze, the one kept exclusively for the picture and the way it could and should be looked at. In place of the couch stood an armchair, to its right a sideboard with long, narrow glass doors. Sitting on the armchair opposite the door to the shack (open or closed), she had to tilt her head to the left to see into the passage and the picture hanging there, to make an effort: seeing the picture now required a determined effort of will—and this changed everything, turned everything upside down. The three people on the balcony in the picture no longer drifted into her field of vision as in the days when she lay on her side on the couch and they invaded the corner of her eye; they had to be deliberately caught, fished by force out of the semidarkness of the passage.

There was something lost about the picture, trapped in its own crookedness, but unlike before, when a sidelong look from the corner of her eye brought the picture to her, made it hers, this gesture was now a pointless move, something that brought no gain. Once or twice the child tried to shake all this feeling off, to confront the picture "face-to-face," and she went and stood in the passage, switched on the light, and stared at the picture, eye to eye; she looked directly at it and almost immediately retreated from the only thing she succeeded in seeing: the loss of what she had seen before, mysterious and swarming with life. The people in the picture, the annoying man with the mustache, the timid standing woman, and the young woman with the blazing black look—all three of them seemed in the frontal gaze to be almost desiccated, as if their insides had been spooned out of them, leaving an empty shell.

And then, almost on the point of giving up, on the verge of the picture's slipping away, something was retrieved, hidden and elusive, as in a dream, but retrieved nevertheless: suddenly, for a split second, when she sat down on the armchair in the hall, the picture flickered on her right, caught in the corner of her eye, reflected in the long glass doors of the sideboard. Not all of it was reflected, only part, almost a third that was almost completely meaningless, appearing as patches of color of which the strongest and most resonant was the striking green of the iron railing, the green railing that defined the figures in their places, on the balcony, preventing them as it were from falling into a dark, deep void. Out of the deconstructed picture reflected in the glass—the patches of color that related to each other but did not make up a story that could be told, slashed by the vehement green of the iron railing—the main thing appeared again, what had been lost and returned in a different shape and form: the sense of the right, true estimation of the depth of the secret. The secret, the child felt, or thought she felt, that didn't belong to anyone and that nobody could claim to own, that wasn't stamped on anyone's seal, not even hers, and stemmed from the connections between things, from the invisible glue joining them together more than from the things themselves on their own. And then, a few minutes later, the reflection disappeared: somebody switched off the light in the kitchen.

SOMEBODY

S OMEBODY SAID THAT the mother had been without a man for nearly forty
years (not Corinne, who didn't permit herself to say it, not Sammy, who
wasn't capable of saying it, and not the Nona, who counted not in years but
in eternities). Somebody else—not the child, an abstraction of the child—
thought to himself, how can it be forty, when did those forty begin, and how
was it possible to count them, to draw a line from when they began to a
moment when it became possible to say "forty years," to say "without a
man"?

Because the child and Sammy and maybe also Corinne didn't think in
terms of "without a man," or even "a man," among other things, because
Maurice, who was presumably supposed to be the "man," was utterly and
completely Maurice, from top to toe, and not some man, with all the attri-
butes of a man, and the mother didn't think so either—she shuddered, her
shoulders shuddered at the inconceivable strangeness of the words that suddenly became hers, came out of her own mouth: "without a man."

Life went on under the mother's skin, where everyone rejected anything
that wasn't her, that wasn't her violent warmth, only her face, her speech,
the mother's speech, which meant silence on everything that wasn't the
mother.

But it came out once, "without a man," slipped out into the routine of
the soft Friday night hours that the child remembered, a witness to all the

hours as she sat at the kitchen table with the two of them, the mother and Sammy, crowded together: the mother on the stool between the table and the side of the fridge, Sammy on the stool between the table and the wall, and she between the two of them, but closer to Sammy, who ate all the soft part of her bread, slice after slice, because his teeth killed him when he ate the crust.

This is the time of the three of them, which is not absorbed by the rest of the week but floats on its surface, like a dumpling in soup, caught in the pale kitchen light, which sheds exactly the right amount of light, leaving a place for the shadows to exist. After the meal comes the lounging, each in his own shadow; each of them has his own sofa, except for the child, who lies on the carpet, watching the movement of the big living-room chandelier.

Sammy goes out with his friends, but later. The mother asks: "Are you going out with your friends?" and he says: "Later," gets up, and goes to bathe at last, splashing for a long time in the bathtub, singing to himself and falling asleep in the water until it's freezing cold. He comes out wrapped in a towel, his teeth chattering, and gets a big surprise.

Suddenly the mother is sitting *comme il faut* on the sofa, her legs crossed, dressed *comme il faut*: a cream-colored linen suit, skirt and jacket, a pearl necklace, her good shoes from Corinne's wedding, a narrow little handbag, for going out.

Sammy's wet curls cover his wide-eyed stare: "What's this?" he demands, tightening the towel around his waist. The mother uncrosses her legs and crosses them again: "I'm going out for a bit," she says in a voice that tries to sound as nonchalant as the shoe dangling from her foot and exposing her heel clad in a flimsy nylon stocking. "Who with?" He stands rooted to the spot in a puddle of water. The mother doesn't look at him; she turns her profile to the window: "Somebody who asked me to go out with him. He asked me a few times, and in the end I said yes."

Minutes pass. The child hears them from her place on the carpet, notices the almost imperceptible vibration of the mother's calves under the nylon stockings—the vibration of Sammy's shock, which becomes hers. "But why?" he demands. "Why?"

"What why?" She straightens up abruptly; her knee bumps into the corner of the table. "I'm going out, I told you, going out." She bends over her knee, rubs it with the stocking, and sits up straight again, but this time without crossing her legs, gripping her black handbag tightly, pressing it to her lap. The Arabic news is on the television, Sammy gets dressed and goes out. She stays like that for a while, rubbing her knee from time to time, until she gets up and goes to the telephone, dials a number, and speaks in a low voice, sits down again but without her shoes, and stares at the television. Afterward she disappears for a while into her bedroom and comes out dressed in her nightgown, covers herself with a blanket, and curls up in the corner of the sofa. Sammy returns, looks: "What, you didn't go out?" His curls are still wet, but combed to one side. He's eating sabras, taking them out of a paper bag, swallowing them almost without chewing, sliding them down his throat. "Here." He holds one out to the child. The mother doesn't move. The dark fringes of the blanket rest on her chin like a beard sloppily drawn with a pencil. There's a slight movement in her eyelids, a blink or a flutter: "I didn't feel like it in the end," she says.

BEARD

MAURICE HAD A beard when he came to photograph them with the photographer of his newspaper, sat them on the sofa in a row: "Like on the bus," said the mother. They called the child from Rachel Amsalem's to come and have her photograph taken, and she came with Rachel Amsalem, both of them wearing the same dress that Rachel's mother got from the woman she worked for, whose sister in America had identical twins. The child wanted herself and Rachel Amsalem to be identical twins, too, but like Rachel, a duplication of Rachel. "Let's be identical twins," she begged her, and she told Maurice, "We decided to be identical twins." And Maurice laughed, his whole narrow face, with the thick dark eyebrows sheltering the slits of light that were his eyes, with his delicate earlobes, laughed: "Good, *ya omri*, go ahead," he said. The child stood at a little distance from him, in the doorway of the room from which she made her announcement, even before she actually saw what she should have seen: his new, bearded face, which perhaps wasn't new at all, because the old one wasn't really settled in her mind, only flickered for a moment and disappeared again, taking with it, if not the beard itself, at least the possibility of the beard, the possibility of the tricks played by memory, not now—but then.

The child held tight to Rachel Amsalem's wrist, so that Rachel, too, would see exactly what she herself saw at exactly the same moment, so that their eyes would be the same eyes, their heartbeats—the same heartbeats:

the wispy white hairs of Maurice's beard, which looked as if they had been stuck to his chin and cheeks, without any relation to his mane of black hair, parted on the side, glistening with an almost oily glisten. They went to fetch Nona from her room and Sammy from the welding shop, because Maurice wanted "the whole family" in the photograph. "So there'll be one picture of everyone," he said to the photographer, and they waited, and waited: Sammy wanted to finish something.

The child sat in the middle of the sofa, seating Rachel Amsalem next to her. She buried Rachel's hand in her lap, feeling her strong, slender fingers, all the joints of her fingers, one by one: she was a tiger, Rachel Amsalem. Her short, supple brown body was all one smooth, taut muscle, conscious at any given moment of its suppleness and power, even in its most casual movements, of its ability to strike or to avoid being struck—with proud nobility, without a drop of sweat or undue exertion. She never leaned toward the other person beyond what was strictly necessary, only appraised him with her beautiful brown eyes, constantly seeking and quick to find the market price attached to everything and everyone. The child stared at her, riveted by the wide shadow cast by the span of her wings, her resolute, confident step, her soccer player thighs, and the captivating ease, feminine but at the same time boyish, with which she beat the boys in street fights and bicycle races: she waited for her all the time, but Rachel Amsalem never waited for her. Her heart, made of cast lead and slippery as a fish, had no expectations of the world. She acquiesced, now, too, sitting next to the child on the sofa, allowed her fingers to be played with, and accepted the warm look the child gave her, but she wasn't warmed.

"The photograph is only of the family. Rachel can wait until we're finished," said the mother, giving the two of them a disapproving look.

The child looked at Maurice, who was standing with his back to them, debating with the photographer. She stared for a long time at his stooped, slightly hunched back, waiting for him to turn around, to sense her eyes on him, and appear before her and Rachel Amsalem the way he was supposed to be, the way she thought of him, both unexpected and expected at the same time, repeating to herself, "But we're wearing the same dress," sharpening the words to make them penetrate his stooped back and dissolve inside him like a drug. Nona and Sammy came and sat down next to them. The mother sat with half her buttocks on the edge of the seat, as if about to stand up at any moment. Maurice stood beside her, next to the standard lamp, his head the height of the lampshade, rested his hand lightly on her shoulder, and looked at the photographer without removing his dark horn-rimmed glasses: "Family, not family, the child said she's family, her friend, so she's family. Why make an issue of it?" he muttered in the mother's direction, over her head, lowering his voice and blurring the words until they were barely audible, emerging incoherently from his mouth like a hum or a cough, in a language that wasn't clear, either Hebrew or Arabic, but the child heard.

PAPERS

I TOOK THE last El Al plane to Israel from Paris. . . . I remember that returning on the same flight with me were Mr. David Horowitz, governor of the Bank of Israel, and Mr. Shimon Peres, director of the Ministry of Defense. On my way back to the country, after an exile of six years, fate brought me face-to-face with one of the pillars of Ben-Gurionism and also with the man who pulled the strings of our country's economy.

I had no time to rest and contemplate what was happening around me in the country after such a long absence. The Suhba were eager to know what my plans were. They organized a big party to which they invited friends and comrades from all over the country. The party was held in a house in the Hatikva quarter. When I arrived there it seemed to me that I saw a lot of new comrades. However, it soon transpired that they knew me from before my journey and were well informed about me and about our struggle. In truth I saw a public that had kept its faith and dedication to our friendship and our cause and remained faithful to this day. After all the salamat and polite words, the people wanted to hear my impressions from my journeys abroad.

After stressing in my opening remarks my joy in being once again among the Suhba, and after pointing out the fact that during the entire period of my absence I had never abandoned my thought and concern for everything happening at home, and especially my concern for the situation of all our brothers in the cause . . . after this, I explained the activities I had undertaken abroad in order to get across the idea of a peaceful solution to our problems. I spoke about the personal meetings on both a narrow and a broad basis that I held on the subject with people of social, academic, and political standing in Europe. I stressed my meetings with the former secretary of the United Nations, Mr. Dag Hammarskjöld, and other personalities.

Members of the audience and I myself well remember that my remarks at the party gave rise to a long and lively argument, the gist of which was that the Suhba were not prepared to sit idly by and do nothing, the comrades having interpreted my words as evading responsibility and shirking the struggle for our rights. . . .

I have never contemplated evading my responsibility for the people I belong to and for the Suhba. And accordingly I vigorously rejected the opinions of the comrades about my future activities and as vigorously set forth my reasons for refusing to renew our publication, pointing out the obstacles that would stand in our way. I reminded them of the existence of an entire Israeli doctrine around which our policy is formulated. This doctrine, which I call Ben-Gurionism, is neither bourgeois capitalism nor working-class socialism, neither right nor left. It is not centrist or extremist, but conformist, faithful to the opinions of a single individual. This person was defined by Professor Yeshayahu Leibowitz as follows: "David Ben-Gurion is the greatest catastrophe visited on the Jewish people and the State of Israel from the day of its establishment." We know that this doctrine is anti-Sephardic in fact and in theory. And therefore it is neo-racist, neo-anti-Semitic in spirit and purpose. Since it dominates the ruling institutions almost exclusively, it guides and directs our lives here and also the life of a considerable part of Diaspora Jewry. It employs the terminology of Zionism and also rejects Zionism in favor of a messianic vision. It receives the encouragement and support of organizations, institutions, and Jewish personalities such as the Rothschilds. . . . It is well known that it also receives support and encouragement from non-Jewish elements in ruling circles in the United States, West Germany, and other countries.

To the extent that there are those who extol the form of democracy practiced in Israel, they are pulling the wool over the eyes of our public. How can they explain the fact that in our "democracy" the power lies exclusively in the hands of 40 percent of the Jewish population of the country, while the majority—in other words, 60 percent—does not have the right or the ability to determine any aspect of the political, economic, and educational lives of themselves and their children. This kind of democracy, to the extent that it exists in any other country, is a false democracy, racist and antisocial. If we wish to analyze the actions and consequences of the Ben-Gurionist democracy, one or even many articles will clearly not suffice.

And therefore bringing out a bimonthly publication that would occasionally deal with this or that issue would lead nowhere.

I could see one way to tackle the problem, which was to conduct a thorough research into the situation and write up the conclusions in a book. With these words I concluded my first appearance before the Suhba, at that party in the Hatikva quarter. I was ready and willing to devote myself to the writing of a book that would go into all the aspects of the problem and its solution. . . . I suggested that the book be written in French and called The Solution? *The question mark would hint that while we were bringing our views and suggestions regarding the situation to the attention of the public, the solution remained in its hands . . . in your hands . . . and in ours. And thus I began to write the book* The Solution?

From the day I undertook the writing of The Solution? *I decided to grow a beard and not to shave it until completing the task I had undertaken to carry out. How strange and amusing it was to see all the questions, reactions, and remarks to which something as small and common as growing a beard could give rise. For my part I took care that the Suhba would not make the true reason for my growing a beard public. I was amused by the questions and remarks addressed to me on every side and at every opportunity. I changed my answers according to the nature of the questioner, and the direction and intention of the question. This innocent amusement did not prevent me from devoting most of my time (from ten to eighteen hours a day) to my work on the draft of the book* The Solution?

I worked on the book for a whole year, and completed the task only in October 1965.

Piazza San Marco: Seventh Visit

Nona said, some time not on the calendar, that there never was and never would be in *elaalam* a love like that of Maurice and the mother, never, never, never, said Nona, staring at the photograph of the Piazza San Marco and seeing what she usually saw in photographs: a square of darkness, hearsay evidence of an event that may have taken place. She told the child to keep it as a memento. "So you'll have a memento that you were in Italy as a child," she said. The child looked and then turned the photograph over, held it between her fingertips again, looked and turned it over: there were those pigeons.

They gathered from all corners of the photograph, came closer, crowded together, advancing in a threatening mass, surrounding them on all sides; soon they would push the three people in the photograph to the wide steps behind them.

Maurice was friends with the pigeons, or at least he pretended to be: he held out his hand to them with seeds of something, whatever you give to pigeons. But the mother didn't hold out her hand to them. She held on to the child so she wouldn't collapse onto them and onto the square, held her tight and looked at her as if she wanted to encourage her to hold herself up, not to collapse, to help her in the holding. And the fog. The fog licking at the edges of the photograph and settling on the pigeons.

For years she looked from time to time and saw nothing but pigeons and fog, fog and pigeons. The photograph canceled itself out, erased its details, like the title of something, a perfunctory confirmation of something: "Oh yes, that's in Italy," the mother said whenever she came across it. "Oh yes, that's in Italy."

When did it open up? When did it agree to say something, to tell the story? When did one of the possibilities of the possible stories rise from it? When did they hear the word "hell" from the mother's lips, think they heard it, and the night before the morning in the photograph, the morning in Piazza San Marco, suddenly erupted?

It was a night in a hotel room, in the suite he took for the three of them. There were two rooms in the suite, one the bedroom and one the living room. They quarreled, Maurice and the mother, raised the roof with their yells. Maurice beat her, left marks all over her body, and disappeared. He locked her and the child up all night until the next morning in the empty room, the room she said was empty simply because "he" wasn't in it.

The Empty Room (1)

THE PARTY WE gave for her seventieth birthday at Sammy's almost-finished house, which took its inspiration from the White House (the pseudo-Greek columns alone took weeks: they built and demolished them, demolished and built again). We sat and planned, Corinne, Sammy, and I, in Sammy's kitchen with the dreamy, pale purple light filtering faintly through the purple lampshade, among the household goods packed in cardboard boxes for months, the entire period of the building, moved from place to place, growing a little shabbier with every move, their contents spilling out of limp, lolling cardboard tongues like those of exhausted animals. "But what's there to plan?" said Sammy dismissively. "There's nothing special to plan here. It's not as if we were doing it in Sinai, like I wanted." He lowered his voice to a melodramatic whisper, which reached a climax at the word "I" and then dropped down. Corinne didn't hear well because of the tall black turban that completely covered her ears, crushing the lobes inside it: the hairdresser had dyed her hair "baby-blond," which came out "the color of orangeade" and she had shaved her head in a fury. "What?" she asked again and again. "What did you say?" She was sitting right under the purple lampshade, in the turban that emphasized the lines of her tanned oval face with the sharp cheekbones and the arched eyebrows penciled in too high, rising to her forehead—and she looked like a beautiful, astonished Indian prince.

He forgot what he had said, leaned back in his chair, and began to bring

up memories of Sinai—actually a single memory from a single trip that
dragged the whole family with it and fed long hours of stories. He began
with the story of Yusuf the Bedouin's camel, which suddenly fell down dead
of a heart attack, but Corinne was impatient; she was in a hurry. "What's
the hurry?" he asked with a show of exaggerated, almost impersonal resentment: he hated it when people were in a hurry. People who were in a hurry
and, even worse, people who were "busy" were the tight-lipped, persecut-
ing agents of everything that embittered his life and spoiled its joy: "In Sinai
and Egypt they aren't in a hurry. You should see how they take their time,
slowly, slowly, slowly," he said, and he would have been happy to go on
saying "slowly" if Corinne hadn't sat up, straightened her long coatdress,
whose hem reached the dusty floor, and interrupted him with a brisk: "So
what's the plan?" His face fell: "Whatever you like. We'll have one of those
big parties everyone has," he said in a glum voice, sinking into a heavy
silence for a minute or two and suddenly waking to new life, his face bright-
ening: "The people you see there, you can't imagine. When I was in Cairo I
met someone from Holon with his wife—they won the lottery and went on
a trip around the world. They took an Egyptian kid along with them, maybe
fourteen years old, who filmed them with a video camera. Wherever they
go, never mind where, the kid with the video goes with them, and he says to
the camera: 'The time now is twenty-three minutes past two, and we're facing the pyramids, the time is thirty-six minutes past twelve and we're
facing the Eiffel Tower,' and so on all over the world, with the Egyptian kid
who sleeps in the same room with them, eats with them, everything,"
recounts Sammy, crumbling between his fingers one of the long slender
cigarettes Corinne left on the table. She took off, leaving behind her a sour-
sweet mist of perfume that mingled with the sharp smell of the turpen-
tine and the paint, but still remained distinct, coming and going. We went
on sitting at the dining table, which in the middle of all that mess was for
some reason covered with a spotless, imitation-cloth disposable tablecloth.

Sammy rubbed his increasingly reddening eye and tried to open it,
but it stayed half-closed. "Stop rubbing," I scolded him. He stopped for a
moment but his fingers went there of their own accord. "We'll bring Maurice to the mother's party," he said, mulling it over. I thought for a moment,
or perhaps the thought had already been in my mind: "On no account. It
will only destroy him. Her with all the celebrations in her honor, and him
with nothing," I said. "What do you mean?" Now he opened both eyes wide

in astonishment, one blue and unseeing, one red, half-seeing. "I mean that Maurice shouldn't know about it," I said. He went on staring at me: "Where do you get all that nonsense from, tell me. What's that supposed to mean, that he won't come? What's that supposed to mean?" he demanded indignantly. "It means that he isn't going to come," I retorted furiously. "You listen to me." We fought. I left the house, walking past the Greek columns, like Corinne. For the first time in our lives we fought.

On the evening of the party Corinne brought her early, and spoiled the surprise. But the mother didn't care about the surprise. She glowed, stood in the middle of Sammy's fifty-five-yard square, almost completely empty living room, and didn't know what to do with herself, fingering the collar of her blouse in embarrassment, but nevertheless noticing that the line of the skirting in the right-hand corner of the room wasn't straight. "Tell them to fix it," she said, looking for Sammy. "You hear? Tell them to take it apart and do it again." But Sammy wasn't there. He had gone to get Maurice from Hatikva. He phoned him three times: for some reason he couldn't find the way.

When he came back with Maurice, the first of the guests had started to arrive, clustering under the portico of the Greek columns, which had finally been finished, decorated with sparklers and chains of colored paper, to the annoyance of Sammy, who had no sooner returned than he climbed on a ladder and tore them down, so they wouldn't hide the splendor of the columns. Maurice entered, wearing one of Uncle Henri's dark blue suits from Lufthanse, which the mother had brought him from her last visit to Marcelle and Henri in France.

They stood facing each other, almost alone in the empty room, a few yards apart. Maurice stared at her and went on staring, tore the tissue paper from the package he had been holding under his arm, his nicotine-stained fingers trembling: the years of coffee and alcohol had wrought havoc on him. He took out a sheet of gauzy, semitransparent white cloth and spread it out before her, stretched between his arms like a matador's cape before a bull. It was a veil.

Then he approached her, laid the filmy white veil on her head—and there it lay, limp, unfastened, drooping down over her forehead and covering her eyes. "I brought it for you from Cairo, Lucette, the last time I was there," he said. Sammy passed through the room on his way to the lawn, carrying two cardboard boxes of cola: he was right.

The Empty Room (2)

Each of the rooms in the shack had an extension, invisible and empty, empty margins of the room itself, the empty part continuing from the full room, dense with the different air of a different knowledge. The empty room had a different time, lacking a plot and the development of a plot, but not in opposition to the humans or above them, on the contrary, more and more inside them.

When they all lay in their beds breathing the nocturnal breath of the full room, known to the eye and the body, they were joined by the clear breath of the empty room, not known to the eye and the body, born from a clarity that could hardly be borne—two or three outlines and a white space between them, which made the child giddy from contact with the truth, not the truth hidden in the full room, but the one evident yet still transparent as air in the empty room, which went on standing, after the shack was destroyed, defeated at last by the sadness and the weight of the years.

There was no need to go and see the ruins for herself, to lie about the boredom prompted by the sight of the destruction and call it loss. On the ground where the shack once stood, now leveled by a bulldozer in preparation for a new split-level villa, the bare, slender lines of the empty room arose in the air, conveying one of the main aspects of the truth, what the child in the fullness of time had come to consider the truth: that the secret, hidden from the eye yet transparent, was the good, not the bad, that the secret was love and not the absence of love, that the seductive carnival of suffering concealed a subtle revelation of the grace of joy like the empty room that told its own story: that what was captured in the empty room, hidden yet transparent, was not criminal or evil, but the opposite—grace.

The Empty Room (3)

I T DROVE THE mother crazy that the money changer on Lilienblum Street had cheated her when she changed dollars there, and that when she went to complain to the police, they made her "wait two hours for that so-called detective in some empty room in their police station at the end of the world." For days on end she ground herself down between these two millstones: the injustice on the one hand, and the folly of the people who were supposed to remedy it on the other.

She cooked up the story from beginning to end, leaving early in the morning, running around, coming home: not a word to anyone, until in the end she served up the finished product, the well-baked plot, but without the prologue, because she didn't have the patience to bother with the details of the self-evident. And the prologue was the "I prepared myself."

Her preparations commenced months before the date of her intended trip in July or August to visit her sister Marcelle in France. In her secret and continuous preparations, two tendencies vied: the excitement of a six-year-old at the prospect of the "airplane" and everything that accompanied it, and the deliberate calculations, mainly financial, of the manager of a small business, all her "taking it from here" and "putting it there."

In April the suitcase was taken down from the *msandara* and sat on the little mat in the bedroom for a week, at the end of which it was put back up, only to be taken down again at the end of April, filled, emptied, and in the

end thrown out and replaced by a new one, which was dragged off to have
the clasp repaired because it had been broken in the constant openings and
closings. Until the date of the journey the suitcase sat in the bedroom, where
it was moved from place to place: from the mat next to the bed to the corner of the room, near the coat hanger, and from there to under the bed, "so
I won't see it right in front of me." And then there were the plants, which to
her annoyance she was forced to wait until the very eve of the flight to cram
into her shoulder bag: Aunt Marcelle wanted plants. Especially she wanted
the detestable cactuses that injured the El Al security officers when they
searched her hand luggage.

In the middle of all this she took the bus to Lilienblum Street in Tel Aviv,
to buy dollars from the money changer—she was there at eight in the
morning. And he cheated her. Incredulously she counted the notes again
and again, going over everything: how he had counted the notes one by one
in front of her, once and once again, wetting his fingertip as he flipped
them over.

In her outrage there was also an element of admiration for something
she could not fail to appreciate: the dexterity, the wizardry of the sleight of
hand. When she repeated to herself "the crook" and went to complain to
the police, she both believed and did not quite believe her story, unable to
see herself finally in the role of the victim: the whole thing was more like
an invitation to a duel between two equal forces, he and she. But at the police
station she saw how the heroism of her sense of injustice, and the urgency
of remedying it, was reduced to three pages with carbon paper between
them and a bored police clerk, tired of interviewing people like her in an
empty room furnished with nothing but a desk and two chairs. She understood that they would not get her money back.

That night she slept even less than usual, and early in the morning she
returned to Lilienblum Street and stood at a little distance from the money
changers there, trying to identify the culprit. That morning he wasn't there,
but the next day, when she came again, she saw him, a fat man wearing a
beige sweater with a zip in front, a cigarette dangling from the corner of his
mouth as he led his customers to a secluded spot between two buildings
and counted out the notes. She skipped the next day, which she needed
to get organized: she went and bought a blond wig and enormous, dark
sunglasses, and borrowed Miriam the manicurist's red raincoat. Thus
disguised, she stood on the street corner and waited till noon, when he

arrived. She went up to him and asked to change money, insisting on staying in a busy spot crowded with passersby. "And then I showed him," she
recounted with a gleam in her eye: the minute he took the bundle of notes
from her and started to count them, she yelled, "Thief! Thief!," grabbed hold
of the collar of his sweater, and didn't let go even when people tried to separate them. He begged for his life, gave back all her money, and ran away.
"I got what was mine out of him," she said with a tired smile, smoothing or
skipping over something. Only years later the end of the story suddenly
appeared out of nowhere: after the fight with the money changer she lost
consciousness, overcome by the excitement and the effort. After a while she
found herself sprawled on the filthy pavement, strange faces bending over
her, her face and neck bathed in water, and when she opened her eyes she
couldn't see anything: the hair of the blond wig, sticky with mud and water,
was plastered over her face, covering it to the tip of her nose.

The Empty Room (4)

Rachel Amsalem put ideas in the child's head; the mother said so. "She puts ideas in your head all the time, that one," she said. She really did put in ideas, but she took them out quickly: in a matter of minutes she passed from one climate zone to another, from blazing heat to Arctic cold, pushing her agile hand into a crevice where she had buried something and immediately pulling it out again. They talked and talked, she and Rachel Amsalem—on the way to the synagogue on Saturday morning, on the way to the kiosk up there that had a machine where you played games for money that Rachel liked, and when they were just going for a walk on the way to nowhere. The child talked a lot but not importantly, and Rachel Amsalem talked a little but importantly, narrowing her eyes that were narrow anyway, narrow and slanting, slanting upward to her temples and the tight topknot at the top of her head: "So what are you trying to say?" she asked. The child didn't remember or didn't know what she was trying to say; she made something up to hang on a little longer to Rachel, who was always slipping away, disappearing into her own affairs.

In the synagogue, in the women's gallery that always gave off a sour, crowded smell, Rachel went to sit with her friends from the religious school, and the child sat by herself next to the grown-ups, on the bench closest to the torn lace curtain through which she peeked at the worshippers below. But she soon abandoned the monotonous backs wrapped in prayer shawls and fixed her eyes on the narrow door leading into the women's gallery, waiting for the woman who had no name, and if she had one the child didn't want to know it, because she was all appearance—an appearance that matched the murmuring prayers—and she waited for the moment of longed-for transparency that came with the woman's entrance.

The woman was always late, arriving in the middle of the service and sometimes just before the end, shrinking her thin thighs as she passed through the narrow space between the benches, looking for a seat, her hands resting on the hip bones jutting out under her tightly fitting skirt, as if she had a stomachache, neither greeting anyone nor inviting a greeting, as if she had taken a strict vow of silence. The child looked at her, she looked and looked, feeling the dimensions, the volume, and the texture of her own gaze as if it were a thing, changing its shape and going from the smooth blank flatness of a slate to the dizzy rings of a spiral, energized by the magnetic field of inquiry that was the woman's face.

It looked like nothing else, this face, as unique as a reproach that had put on a human form: her hollow cheeks, sunburned, nearly black, were cut. Almost the entire expanse of the face, from the chin to the eyes, was crisscrossed by symmetrical scars that had healed but still preserved the freshness of the cuts and their pink color, a little darker than the holes that punctured the skin between the scars, as if it had been pierced again and again by the prongs of a fork. On the bed of this wreckage the beaked nose and the eyes stood out, defiant, as if not belonging, especially the wide-open eyes with their broad, heavy lids, which rose and fell like the wings of a plane, bearing long lashes at their edges. Summer and winter she wrapped her head in a transparent nylon scarf, whitish or greenish, loosely tied under her chin, almost floating above her cheeks and not hiding them.

There was something disturbing, unclear, about this transparent head covering and the casual way the woman both did and did not wrap it around her wounded face: the more the child pondered its meaning, the more it evaded her grasp, refusing interpretation. Was the woman trying to hide her face with the transparent scarf but failing to do so because she was the victim of an illusion, seeing something different from what others saw, or was it the opposite, that she wasn't trying to hide it but display it, to thrust her face defiantly at the observer, with the scarf acting as a mocking gesture toward those who expected her to hide, a kind of theater, as if to say, "Here, take a good look"? Throughout the service the child kept her eyes fixed on the woman, waiting for something, some sign that would solve the riddle of her ruined face and how she bore this ruin, what she seemed to be saying to the world—only partially and obscurely, but somehow without involving shame, or outright brazenness either; there was something else, resolved at another, higher level—something that had left shame behind a long time ago but had not become shamelessness, and that radiated warmth, great affection, and intimacy, despite the evident disconnection between her and the others, who talked and talked about her.

Rachel Amsalem told the child what they said: they said that once, when she was younger, the woman had fallen holding a glass, and the shards had pierced her face and ruined it. "Who said that?" asked the child. Rachel shrugged her shoulders, she got bored quickly. She was walking with the child through the thorn field on the way to the shack, but not by her side; she skipped from one edge of the sandy path to the other, bending down every few minutes to get the sand out of her white socks, her taut body, strong and supple as a sinew, turning and twisting in superfluous move-ments, not confined to any purpose, given up to the joy of movement for its own sake.

Even when she was standing still Rachel Amsalem's body was charged, bursting with mobility and possibilities of movement. The child saw it: her father whipped her with his belt. Rachel Amsalem stood with her legs together and her father beat her with his belt on the calves, thighs, and arms while she stood there, not moving or blinking, open-eyed, only her taut skin jumping a little with every lash, with an imperceptible tremor, as if her skin were a kind of springy trampoline that sent the beating belt flying upward, repulsed simply by virtue of coming into contact with it.

Now Rachel wanted them to go to Savyon, to stroll down the empty streets. "But it's a graveyard there, without even a dog in the street," the child unthinkingly quoted the mother; nevertheless she went with her. Rachel explained on the way that they threw new toys into the trash cans there, they were so rich. "Who throws them?" the child asked doubtfully. "The people who live there," said Rachel, threading her hands under her skirt and pulling down her blouse: her budding breasts with their promi-nent nipples were flattened toward her diaphragm. The girls walked down the empty road, under the high, dim vault of the trees. On the edge of the pavement, near the gates of the big, still houses, stood the garbage cans, and they gave rise in the child to a kind of nervous greed and a feeling of disgust at the greed, as if she suddenly wanted to eat the mess she regurgitated from her mouth. When she glanced at Rachel, at her too-sharp profile, her heart fell for a moment into a crack that had suddenly opened up inside her: between believing Rachel and not really believing her, only wanting to believe her. A car pulled up outside one of the houses. They stood and looked: a tall woman wearing glasses got out, holding three or four shopping bags in her hands, with two little girls trailing behind her. Rachel gripped the child's wrist and pulled her toward them. "Here, I'll help you." She hurried up to the woman, almost forced two overflowing bags out of her arms, and stroked the head of one of the little girls with her free hand. They spoke English, the woman and her daughters; they walked up the paved path leading to the big house, the little girls behind them, Rachel leading the way, next to the woman, and the child bringing up the rear, shrinking at the sound of the new voice, high, almost shrill, coming from Rachel, an ingratiating, wheedling, obsequious voice. After they put the shopping bags down on the long kitchen table, Rachel asked the woman if they could play with the little girls: "Can we play with their hair?" she asked and undid the short honey-colored braids of one of them, and plaited them again, looking all the time out of the corner of her eye at the mother, to see what kind of impression she was making. The child did what Rachel did, knelt down on the kitchen floor next to the girls and pretended to be stirring something in a toy saucepan made of china. For a moment, over the heads of the little girls, her eyes caught the steely gleam of triumph in Rachel's look. The mother, holding a hesitant, absentminded smile on her face all the time, whether of approval or reluctant acceptance, set the table with four bowls of cornflakes and milk. But the child didn't want to eat; she shrugged her shoulders without saying anything and studied the miniature forks and teaspoons of the toy kitchen. Only when the mother left the kitchen for a while did she run to the table, quickly cram two spoons full of cornflakes with milk into her mouth, and return to her place on the floor. In the meantime the mother came back and told the little girls to go to their room, repeating the word "Sleep, sleep," and Rachel whispered to the child: "She wants us to look after them."

One of the little girls clung to Rachel and drew a flower on her hand in a blue marker, which looked like the long-stemmed tulips on the curtains in the room. A faint, filtered light penetrated the fully gathered curtains of the bedroom, wrapping the room in an additional layer of softness: the long, low shelves lined with furry animals and dolls, the rosy carpet, the blue bed covers with the piles of colorful cushions on them, the big round jar with two goldfish swimming in it on the chest of drawers. The child looked at Rachel and read it all on her face, the brass bed frames, the stuffed animals, every tulip of the pattern on the curtains, as if she were looking in a mirror. Now the mother was apparently telling the little girls to go and bathe, while at the same time glancing expectantly at Rachel and the child. "Come on, let's go," the child said to Rachel, who went up to the clothes rack, took down two pink bathrobes, and held them out to the mother.

The minute the mother and daughters disappeared into the bathroom at the end of the long corridor, Rachel Amsalem flew to the toy shelves and stuffed a teddy bear into her shirt. "Hurry up, take something and run," she said quickly to the child, and then she was gone. The heavy front door slammed loudly. For a long moment the child went on standing in the empty room, with the soft light and the curtains waving in the breeze. She heard the sound of water running in the bath and murmurs in English. There was a strange heaviness in her legs and head, as if they had been stuffed with cotton wool. As if hypnotized, she went up to the toy shelves, looked at the dead, glittering, glass eyes of the dolls, and her hand reached out of its own accord for a fire engine with two wheels missing. Silently she crept down the corridor, past the half-open bathroom door, closed the front door silently behind her, and walked down the paved path to the main road under the arching trees. For a moment or two she held the fire engine at a little distance from her body, and then she threw it into one of the garbage cans hidden discreetly behind the thick hedges. Rachel Amsalem was nowhere to be seen.

When she reached the main street of their neighborhood she suddenly saw the woman with the cut face and the transparent head scarf coming toward her, limping down the middle of the road. She was only wearing one shoe, holding the other one, which had lost its heel, in her hand. Her eyes— the prow of a ship looking far into the distance—were veiled in a film of blissful pleasure; air rose from her lips, like steam from an engine.

BATH

SAMMY SPENT HOURS in the bath, unlike the mother and Corinne. "That bath doesn't get anything off, all it does is leave the dirt in the water, dirt in dirt," denounced the mother, and Corinne's silhouette nodded vigorously, not Corinne herself, whose expression had set in some turn of thought two hours before. There was also the business of quick-quick. The mother bathed quick-quick, and she liked to say so: quickly and powerfully she scrubbed her skin with the "hard" loofah, quickly she rinsed herself off and got out of the soapy water, quickly she dried herself and put something on, as if she couldn't stand being naked a minute more than necessary.

Corinne, on the other hand, dried herself thoroughly, even the spaces between her toes, passing the tip of the towel between one toe and the next with the same pursing of her lips that a moment later accompanied the gathering of her wet hair into a tight knot on top of her head opposite the steamy mirror, leaving her face, with the eyebrows not yet penciled in, in an absolute nakedness that was beyond naked. The mother regarded Corinne's delicate, barefoot tread, the smell and the appearance of her cleanliness. "So you took a bath?" she inquired-confirmed, grateful for the symmetry that now existed between Corinne's beauty and her cleanliness, between her cleanliness and her beauty—a symmetry that she saw as the personification and essence of virtue, a moral category that resulted from "taking a bath," which actually meant a shower elevated to the dignity of a bath.

The bathroom was built onto the shack; it grew out of the wall into the yard like a wart, but with right angles. For months after it was built, with huge urgency, glittering with the glare of its green tiles, the mother breathed life into it; in other words, she thought about how to change or repurpose it: to move in the toilet, to uproot the bathtub and replace it with a washing machine and the laundry hamper, or to reduce its size and thereby enlarge the passageway, so that there would be more room. "But more room for what? To throw parties in the passageway?" demanded Sammy, looking for the tape measure to show her that all she would gain was two feet. "All that for two feet, two!?" he yelled. She was flustered. Her face showed signs of retreat. "All right," she conceded. "But you, your problem is that you get attached, you get attached to things."

He really did get attached, Sammy, to things as they were, as they had always been, since the beginning of time, which in his eyes ensured the stability of their future, so that things would go on in exactly the same way; if only he could, he vowed, he would screw, weld, or glue them to the floor, so nothing would move right or left, which appalled the mother even as a joke. With her "attachment" was expressed in the permission it gave her to change, shift, uproot, and rebuild: the possibility of change was the "attachment," the seal of belonging.

Nevertheless she left the bathroom alone, contenting herself with changes in the interior without moving the walls, and not because she was really persuaded by Sammy's "two feet," but because of Sammy himself: the bathtub was his sandbox.

He didn't spend his time there to get clean—the truth was that he quite liked dirt—but to play or to sleep, two activities that led to each other, or turned into the same thing: to play was to sleep. Soaking in the foamy water that had grown cold, sleep fell on him in the middle of his singing: we knew this by the long silence that descended on the bathroom. "He went to sleep," pronounced the mother in sorrow and wonder. "He simply went to sleep." Her hands were tied—all she could do was knock loudly on the door or send me, but she couldn't go in. This enforced inaction led her to moments of clumsy cunning: "Go and tell him that the contractor Gabai came, that he's waiting outside," she instructed me. I stood outside the closed door in the dark passage and recited the message in a bored voice:

I didn't want him to believe it. But Sammy reposed in realms beyond belief and disbelief: he didn't hear a thing. Even when the sirens went off in the Six-Day War he didn't hear a thing. Shaking, to the sound of the rising and falling sirens, we huddled in the dark bathroom passage, the mother, Corinne, and I, banging on the door: "There's a war on, Sammy, a war." Long minutes after the sirens stopped, he arrived at a run at the shelter he had dug in the yard, a towel wrapped around his waist, his bare feet coated with mud.

THE BEGINNING OF TIME

HOW RESTLESS SHE always became before a holiday meal, every holiday, all the holidays, since the beginning of time: she, who rarely said "always," and had only heard rumors of "the beginning of time," heard that there were people who had "their habits and customs from long ago."

The shack was spick-and-span hours ahead of time, you could eat from the floor, and her saucepans were closely guarded, especially from Sammy's greedy hands ("You've left nothing in the pot, two teaspoons is all").

There were hours left until evening, until "everybody" arrived: again and again she said to Nona, or to Sammy, or to the child, "everybody," almost believing it herself. A tight spring was coiled all along her short body: she tried to take a rest with the coiled spring; she lay on her side in bed with an open book, she got up and rearranged the cups and plates in the kitchen cupboard: what was on the bottom shelf went to the top and vice versa. But the spring was still there, almost nothing but the spring, even when she went around to Nona's and woke her from her afternoon nap to make coffee.

"*Yallah*, get up, make coffee," she prompted her, sat down in the armchair next to the radio and immediately turned it off: the talking gave her a headache. Nona smelled her. "I can smell her when she's in a state, I can smell her from the road," she said, and tried to come up with some innocuous thought, for example, that it was a good thing the holiday came just in time for the end of the artichoke season, because there was nothing so tasty as artichoke hearts with lemon and garlic. "It's the end of the season for them. The hearts came out big this time," the mother answered glumly, rubbing her bare feet against each other, staring hostilely at the chair standing in the middle of the room with the Nona's underclothes spread out on it to dry: "You have to put your underpants here for everyone to see? Would it hurt you to hang them up on the laundry line?" spat out the spring, while the mother suddenly rose to her feet, without finishing her coffee and escaped outdoors, leaving the Nona muttering, "*Ya tawli ya ruh*," be patient my soul.

In the noonday heat she circled the garden, dug something up, hoed soil that was already hoed, went to the welding shop to sharpen the pruning shears, pruned the parched rosebushes, decided to set up a rock garden next to the rose bed. She carted rocks in the wheelbarrow, one by one, from Marco's nearby plant nursery, and tried to uproot and transfer the giant cactus with the curling fleshy leaves that was standing in the way of the rock garden, struggling with it for a long time in the blazing sun, in complete silence, despairing and determined—her against the cactus.

"It can't be beat. It needs some man to get it out." She finally gave up, surveying the abandoned battleground around the cactus—the clods of earth, the ropes, the rakes, and the hoes lying on the ground. With her arms and legs scratched and slightly bleeding up to the thighs, with her hands pierced by the thorns of the cactus, she retired at last to the shower: exhaustion had defeated the coiled spring, the pain stretched to the limits had passed from the mind to the body.

Toward evening, shortly before "everybody" arrived, she went and stood by Sammy's head as he stretched out on the couch to rest: "Go fetch Maurice to come sit with us," she said.

And Sammy went, he searched and searched and didn't find him, or he found him in the end, and brought him after darkness descended, after the mother had turned on the gas to heat up the food and turned it off again, from time to time going out to the road where the breathless stillness of the holiday eve held sway.

Sammy came in first, and Maurice long moments after him, muddling his way in rather than walking—battling with the front door until he succeeded in opening it, standing in the dim passageway, next to the cupboard, his hair wet and combed back, mouthing a reluctant "Happy Holiday" in a low voice, with a distraction that was contagious, absorbed by the mother, sending a series of shocks through her, moving from her bloodless lips to her arms, to the dish in her hands, which fell and shattered into gravy-smeared splinters on the floor.

The splinters scattered, all the way to the end of the room, some almost underneath the carpet next to the window, where they were discovered and collected by the broom and the dustpan after everybody left.

PRUNING ROSES IN THE GARDEN

P RUNING ROSES IN the garden is essentially different from pruning roses in the hothouse. The form taken by the pruning stems first of all from the aims of the cultivation and our demands of the rose in the garden. When pruning we must take into account the intervals between the plants, the nature of the bush, and its function in the garden: whether it is a bush for cutting flowers, for blooming in the garden, as ground cover, or as a climber. While it is difficult to give a comprehensive or precise recipe for pruning, the underlying principles are the same for almost every type of rose, with small changes adapted to each group.

"Water branches": in most cases the rose in the garden is grafted. Close to the place of the graft, which is called the "heart of the rose" or the "apple of the rose," young new branches grow, starting out as strong, upright "water branches." These "water branches" can be easily recognized. In most cases they are thinner and more thorny, and they don't bear flowers. The regular removal of these branches will assist in the correct and healthy growth of the rose, and the production of a greater number of blooms. These branches must be removed as close as possible to their base, without harming the "heart of the rose."

In order to achieve the best results, the pruning should be performed in stages:

First all the superfluous branches should be removed, dry branches, "water branches," and branches from the upper body bearing flowers up to a height above which we do not wish to leave any branches in any case. Pruning a very *long-standing branch should be avoided unless we wish to replace it with a younger branch growing next to it, and it is very important to take care that this young branch is not a "water branch." The gardener should think twice before pruning a long-standing branch, something that is liable to cause it severe damage and even lead to its death. It is important to remember that the harm caused to the rose by not pruning is less than the damage of incorrect pruning, or pruning at the wrong time. To the extent that there is any doubt about the pruning of a certain branch, the gardener should leave it and remember that he can always prune it, if necessary, later on in the season.*

And lastly, an extremely important sentence that cannot be repeated often enough:

A branch that is pruned can never be returned!

MOUNTAIN OR PLAIN

"WHAT ARE WE, mountain or plain?" the child asked the mother, putting her hand through the hole in the wall to catch the tail of a passing cat. The mother hesitated for a minute, perhaps wondering what a "plain" was. "A mountain we're not," she said in the end.

The Hole in the Wall

There was a hole about the size of a tennis ball, but with jagged edges, in the wall of the shack, right next to the square window of the yellow hall. Through the hole you could see a section of the unplastered brick wall of the welding shop, the broad smooth leaves of the mango tree, and through them the green door of the mother's little storeroom stuck onto the welding shop, clinging to it like a baby tied to the back of its mother working in a rice paddy.

Sammy made the hole once when the blood went to his head because of the child and her homework. He remembered the homework at ten o'clock in the evening, after they had all been sitting for hours—Sammy, Sammy's friends, and the child—on the verge of the dirt road leading to the shack, talking nonsense and eating snacks, sweet, salty, and spicy, and then reversing the order and beginning again: spicy, salty, and sweet.

The mother had not yet come home from work but her warning filled the air, rising and falling with the inhalations and exhalations of the shack: "Remember, you, to see that the child does her homework," she said to him. And suddenly he remembered, dismayed: "What about your homework? Why didn't you remind me about your homework?"

Together they searched for her schoolbag, turned the shack upside down, and in the end they went to get it from Havatzelet, waking her parents who were already in bed: the child had forgotten it there on her way back from school. They sat at the dining table, under the low lampshade that spun slightly above their heads, tracing circles of light, and began taking things out of the schoolbag. Sammy took them out and the child watched: sandwiches wrapped in paper turning green with mold, a half-eaten rotten apple, hair clips and elastic bands, a lipstick of Corinne's that had melted and stained the inside of the bag with a thick red paste, mixed with flecks of tobacco from two cigarettes Rachel Amsalem had stolen from her brother and given the child to keep for her.

The math book lay at the bottom of the bag, crumpled and stained. Sammy sharpened the pinkie-sized stub of a pencil with a kitchen knife, because they couldn't find the sharpener, and read the question out loud— and they both waited, and waited: a fly buzzed with an ugly noise as it flew from one slat of the plastic blind on the opposite window to the next.

"Write it down," yelled Sammy, "Write down the sum you said." "But I didn't say anything," said the child, and wrote down a few figures anyway, and then rubbed them out with her thumb wetted with spit, because she couldn't find the eraser. A sooty stain with a damp little hole in the middle remained on the page. Sammy tore it out: they began again, but now they couldn't find the pencil. Sammy's eyes hurt. He covered them with the black airline eye-mask someone had once brought him and his hands groped over the tablecloth, the notebooks, and the books in search of the pencil. "You'll send me to my grave," he said, "to my grave," and told her to look for a pencil.

The child went from the bedroom to the living room; she stood in the doorway without switching on the light, staring into the darkness that stuck to her eyes even when she reached the kitchen where the light was on, gazed absentmindedly at the kitchen cupboard, stared blindly into the open fridge. "I couldn't find one," she told Sammy, and put up her hand to scratch the back of her head: the pencil was there, stuck in the elastic band of her ponytail. She pulled it out and handed it hesitantly to Sammy. All of a sudden Sammy jumped up, tore the mask from his eyes with a terrible roar, and punched the air violently in the direction of the wall. The roar came instantly to a stop, as if someone had choked it with a pillow: Sammy's hand stuck out, past the wall, into the yard. He looked in astonishment at the hole in the wall, at his fist that wasn't even scratched, and then at the child: "You see what you did?" he said.

GRAVE

TWO OR THREE weeks after she died, Corinne's telephone calls start, the ones that begin as if on the second or third page, after the blank page. A minute or so of silence announced the ritual like the muffled beat of a gong saying: kneel. Her voice seemed to come from her knees, a sound for which there are no adjectives.

"Is she in her grave, Toni?" she began. "It seems she's in her grave," I said. Again a silence, but different, animated: "But why?" "What do you mean, why?" I fixed my eyes on the window, on the balcony of the dental technician in the building next door, which had been turned into a laboratory: he was spraying a phosphorescent green substance onto a set of dentures. "Why did she die?" Corinne's voice came again. "She was sick," I replied. "I can't eat," she said. "I bought a grilled chicken and gave it all to the dog, the whole thing. It stank like a chicken with the plague." She fell silent, thought for a minute: "But she didn't show any signs."

The dental technician closed the top and bottom of the dentures, checked the fit. "But why did she die?" her voice pleaded. I held the earpiece away from my ear, which was suddenly burning. "Maurice is very sick. I'm going to see him," I said. Again a silence, longer than the previous ones, disturbed by the sounds of the television that she kept on twenty-four hours a day. "That day," said Corinne pensively, or the opposite, reaching for something with great concentration, undoing the loop of a sentence. "What day?" I asked. "The day when she was pregnant with you and they hit each other over him wanting to go abroad. The way she poured gasoline on herself and almost set herself on fire in the yard after he left the country, when she was pregnant with you," she said.

Second Portrait of Corinne in the Flying Shack

INTERESTING THAT THIS time Corinne was harnessed to the shack at the front, not the back: her never-ending hair, attached to the tiled roof like reins, suddenly stretched out and displayed the whole spectrum of its colors, changing areas of color from black, brown, chestnut, and orangeade-orange, all the way to baby-blond and white. And it was so much hers that it made us forget that perhaps it wasn't really hers, that she had cut it with her own hands from the heads of all the women in all the hairdressing salons where she had worked for years upon years. And now all that hair had come back, first sticking tress to tress, in nonchronological order, and then sticking to Corinne's head. It spread out upward, in front of us, like a long, narrow sheet of awning, carrying all the raindrops that turned into a shower of glass marbles as soon as they touched the sheet of hair, their color matching the color of the patch of hair they had landed on, colliding but not mixing.

From the front window of the shack, which was actually the kitchen window full of sky, we watched Corinne flying in a high, straight line, far away from us, at the end of the long sheet of hair that pulled her neck back with her chin thrust upward, straining our eyes in the direction of the event whose details we could only guess at, but we could not see clearly because of the distance, the haze, and the glassy dazzle of the marbles: apparently she had changed her clothes during her flight, and not by herself, but murmuring instructions to the flock of cranes gliding next to her, almost encircling her, opening and closing with their beaks the zips of skirts and dresses, buttoning and unbuttoning buttons, flying under her flapping skirt to tuck her shirt in nice and tight.

And Corinne tore a way for us through the sky, forging in her flight a narrow path exactly the size of her narrow body, but giving us an opening "to get a foot in," in the words of the mother, who stood at the kitchen window in the middle, between Sammy and me, marking in black ink on our bare shoulders the exact spot reached by her head, waiting a minute or two to grow a little, and marking the place again, leaving a row of close black lines that turned into a thick stripe on our shoulders.

There wasn't enough space but we didn't complain, the three of us crowding closer and closer to the window of the kitchen, which was the upper deck of the flying shack, feeling the shifting of the wall before us as it moved toward the flat porch vanishing into the great sea of the sky, ignoring, or at least pretending to ignore, the awkward attempts of the character from the bailiff's office to strum on Corinne's white grand piano—he refused to give up, went on and on hitting the keys, constantly changing his gloves—white for the white keys, black for the black—"just to make things clear" as he repeated, hurtling toward us on the piano stool, in the wake of the piano itself, as a result of the air pockets.

From time to time, we noticed, Corinne tried to turn her head back, even though it was stuck inside a cloud in the shape of a hair dryer, and to make eye contact with us and with the piano, to make sure that we were connected to her, and by the innermost threads of the internal alphabet, which had almost nothing in common with its accepted and in the end arbitrary order, especially with regard to Corinne, who always began with the Hebrew letter *het*: "dreamy" for me, "bullshit" for Sammy, and "spicy" for the mother, because of Corinne's love for spicy things.

When we reached the very top—and without panting, because the ascent to the highest of the high did not require any strain or effort on our part, on the contrary, the surrender of willpower—the parts of the shack began to fall away one after the other, first the walls, which responded to the stratospheric pressure of the good kind and simply dissolved, leaving us with nothing but the floor we stood on, which followed in the wake of Corinne's hair like a flying carpet, and in a certain sense played to our advantage, because the man from the bailiff's office found an article granting tax relief to people on a magic carpet—which we weren't really, but for taxation purposes we were, especially Corinne, who would have been ready for any arrangement that left her in possession of the white grand piano, which in its earthbound life filled almost the entire space of her new living room, standing in the middle of the room, on the carpet she bought especially in its honor, bearing the silver candlesticks wreathed with laurel leaves made of silk, also purchased in its honor "just to make an impression, impression, impression, who do you want to make an impression on?" cried the mother in the direction of Corinne, who was now flying far in front of us, vanishing into the dense sky until all that could be seen was the long, winding ribbon of hair, protruding from Corinne's head like a tongue stuck out impudently at the mother.

TONGUE

SAMMY DIDN'T LIKE it when the child touched the tip of her nose with her tongue: "Stop it"—he pulled a face—"don't do that." "But why?" she asked, taking advantage of the darkness in the street to do it again. "Maybe it will make you sick," he said. "It's a fact that most people don't do it." The child looked at him from below and from the side. She knew that he wasn't serious, but she hesitated: he had his own way of saying things, always with a kind of crooked shadow confusing laughter with fear, shifting clothes. They'd gone out, the two of them. After bathing and shaving he put on his only surviving jacket after he had got rid of all the others, and said, "Let's go out."

First they went "up there," to the movies, entering half an hour after the beginning of the movie they had seen the day before, and taking their regular seats: Sammy slid down in the seat, stretching his legs out in front of him, watched the movie, or dozed off, until he remembered something and had to go out, forcing everyone in the row to stand up. He went to get chocolate-banana Popsicles and came back. After fifteen minutes he went out again, for cola, and then again—this time to the toilet, after which he hung out on the plaza in front of the movie house with the others who were sitting on the steps and chatting, going in and out like him. In Westerns he only went out two or three times, and in "*Ichikidana*"—which is what he called the Indian movie—five or six times, because it was long, maybe two and a half hours long.

The child didn't budge, she sat on the edge of her seat, staring hypnotized at the screen even when Sammy pushed past her and hid it, hitting her knees to make her move. She sat next to Madame Guetta, her two daughters, and her mother-in-law, who also had permanent places, next to theirs, but who never bought anything at the kiosk: they kept on taking things out of the plastic shopping baskets between their legs, sandwiches with chicken, meat patties, or hard-boiled eggs, bottles of root beer, pretzels, cookies, and a plastic tub of eggplant and tomato salad. "Take, take." They pressed sandwiches and pretzels on the child, who almost always refused, and Madame Guetta fished strips of chicken out of the sandwich with her fingers and urged her to taste, poking her with her elbow: "Here, without bread, have it without bread." And nevertheless they all cried together—she, and Madame Guetta, and her mother-in-law, and her two daughters, who almost screamed, accompanying their weeping with mutual pinches on the arms and suddenly stopping, both together, when the singing stars got married in the end.

The child, however, didn't stop crying, she went on even harder, for a long time after the movie ended and the lights went on: the brief picture of happiness was immeasurably more painful than the long sorrows preceding it, eating into her heart as if it had been burned by acid. "Stop crying," Madame Guetta scolded her, "everyone's happy now in *Ichikidana*, there's nothing to cry about. Why are you still crying?"

Sammy dried her face with his sleeve, took a handful of pumpkin seeds mixed with empty shells out of his jacket pocket and gave them to her. They walked side by side down the dark, deserted road, to look for Moshe, Sammy's friend, in his parents' shack at the end of the neighborhood, at the bottom of the wadi, which looked like a hat someone had sat on. Next to the dirt path leading to his house they saw Moshe shuffling in front of them cuddling a wailing puppy in his arms; he found it next to the house, he explained, and his father was afraid of dogs. The three of them returned to the road on their way back "up there," to sit there for a while. Now they walked strung out across the road, the child in the middle with the puppy in her arms, and Moshe and Sammy on either side of her. Whenever the lights of a car flickered in the distance and the sounds of an engine reached their ears, Sammy and Moshe froze, looked at each other, and said, "Military

Police," ran off the road, and hid in the yard behind one of the shacks. They left the child at the side of the road, in front of the shack, to keep guard: "Don't say anything about us if they ask you," Sammy warned her before disappearing into the darkness after Moshe, taking off his shoes to run faster.

The child stood on the side of the road, on the curbstone marking the pavement that for the time being was only sand, pressed the puppy into the hollow between her shoulder and her neck, and waited. The Military Police patrol car slowed down, dazzling her with its headlights. The two policemen sitting in the front looked at her for a moment and went on driving slowly, cutting the dense darkness of the road into three rectangles with the two beams of light from the headlights.

SLOWLY (1)

AT FIRST SAMMY didn't want to stay in the army; he requested a transfer to the navy, and they told him that the only way to leave the Golani infantry brigade was on a stretcher, and he retorted, "I'll show you a stretcher," and bit the officer's leg. He painted the officer's dog black with boot polish, and cried that he was afraid of the dark and couldn't go to sleep without his mother, and made himself out to be so crazy that in the end he thought he really was crazy, and both he and the mother were afraid that he was actually losing his mind what with all the playacting and the jail, where he sat with Mermel and all the others, in and out, in and out, until they got rid of him for good, but afterward, when he wanted to go back—because the Six-Day War broke out and he was ashamed of being the only man on the bus and everywhere else, with the women and children and old people—the army didn't want him: he went to the town major and begged them to take him back for the war, and the town major took Sammy's file, opened it, and slowly turned the pages: "Look, if the Arabs reach Petach Tikva, we'll take you, but as long as they're not here, I don't think so," he said slowly and deliberately to Sammy.

Slowly (2)

THE SATURDAYS THAT fell on us like a thick blanket, the cypress tree congealed in the blue dust, when the mother said, "Everything's standing still," pressing her hand to her chest as if she couldn't breathe, going out to the yard, or the road, the neighbors, to see if everything was still standing still and coming back and confirming it, "Everything's standing still," lying down, getting up, sitting down, standing up, going out to look at the garden in the desolation of everything standing still, with the air dense as cement wiping out any distinction between indoors and outside, between the shack and what wasn't the shack, between going in and coming out, emptying action and movement of meaning, purpose, and reason, and "slowly eating up your soul, little by little, with a teaspoon," said the mother.

SLOWLY (3)

CORINNE HAD THIS idea of making cushions: "We'll buy material, I'll design them, you'll sew them, and we'll sell them to luxury shops," she said to the mother. "I'm not so good at sewing," the mother reminded her mildly, but there was nobody to talk to: Corinne had been whirled up and scattered to pieces with her inspired vision of the cushions, of "the killing." That's what she said: "I have to make a killing, to hold up my head." The "killing" meant money but it wasn't only money, it was decisive recognition by the world of Corinne's talent, her ability, and her inspiration—not just recognizing it with a smile and a handshake, but by bringing the world to its knees, by making it crawl to her at last. But the world was in no hurry to crawl, at any rate it wasn't so simple: when she wandered around those shops in North Tel Aviv, with their fake or not fake grandeur, to "get ideas," as she said, she would come back looking green and seasick. She hadn't missed a detail: she photographed it all in her mind, which had become a bloody battlefield where a bitter war raged among her conflicting emotions: contempt and disgust for the bad taste that pretended to be something else, admiration for the few "really" beautiful items and the nonchalance of the proprietors, inner urgency and certainty that she could do immeasurably better, and the black mood brought on by the awareness that all this, the whole "killing," was very far from being within her reach.

Impatient, pale, and taut as the mother's coiled spring on the eve of holiday meals, she went to buy fabrics in Nahalat Binyamin, not simply fabrics, but *the* fabrics: the great awe with which she said "the fabrics" was beyond measure; she spread them out before the mother, carefully folding and spreading them out again for herself, as if she were afraid of even a second of forgetfulness, needing to remind herself all over again. The "sets," as she called them, had been sketched beforehand on pads of white paper, and then passed on to the manufacturing department: for weeks the shack overflowed with the commotion of the enterprise, with the big nylon bags of stuffing with which all of them—Corinne and the mother and the child and the Nona and sometimes Mermel, too—filled the cushions, everywhere lengths and remnants of fabric lay about, threads and buttons, spools of satin ribbons, rolls of cellophane for packing, needles and pins, with the mother's old Singer sewing machine, always open, ruling the roost.

In Corinne's "sets" there was always one permanent motif and changing components "to play with," she said: one long sausage-shaped cushion of gold or crimson brocade, and next to it two or three little ones made of different fabrics, in a range of changing colors and shapes: round, square, rectangular, or heart-shaped. Corinne thought up the various combinations, stopping the mother at her sewing every hour or so, arranging the sausage and its offspring on the living-room couch, surveying them narrow-eyed from a distance and saying: "You see? That's exactly how the cushions should be thrown, they have to be thrown." The mother nodded vigorously at Corinne's "thrown," looking apprehensively at the light blazing in her eyes as they rested on the cushions, knowing without knowing: it wasn't cushions, "thrown" or not, that hung in the balance here, but a world, the entire notion of a world.

She returned to the sewing machine under the watchful eye of Corinne, who couldn't sew a straight line to save her life, but who knew exactly what the "clean seam" about which she endlessly nagged the mother should look like. The child picked up scraps of cloth, needles and pins, following the creation of the "sets" in a tense expectation that eventually turned into dull boredom.

She sat next to them, close to the sewing machine, listening with half an ear to the hum of the machine and the flow of their conversation, absorbed in what her fingers were doing under the table, as close as could be to them and at the same time far away and hidden from the eye: again and again she secretly stuck the needle into the flesh of her palm, very slowly, so as to locate the exact point of the threshold of pain, almost pain but not pain itself, each time conquering one more millimeter and coming closer to the area of sharp pain in the center of the palm and carefully sticking in the needle, leaving it poking up like a candle on a birthday cake and then pulling it out with a frozen, unchanging expression on her face, detached from the pain and unaffected by it, until a drop of blood welled up and she buried her hand between her thighs, rocking her body to and fro.

In the meantime Corinne and the mother completed the final finishing touches on the first twenty sets of cushions, packed them up neatly in the cellophane, arranged exactly in the order in which they were supposed to be placed on the sofas or the beds, crammed them onto the backseat of the silver Lark belonging to Mermel, who set off with Corinne to do the rounds of the exclusive Tel Aviv shops.

They came back in the early evening: Corinne with an expressionless face and Mermel with two pounds of smoked salmon, Russian caviar, and crystallized orange peel from one of the delicatessens next to the shops. "They fell on her cushions, ordered more," said Mermel, chewing salmon together with crystallized orange peel under the apprehensive eyes of the mother, who looked from him to Corinne. "Really?" she asked. "Everything's fine," snapped Corinne, and went to take a shower. She was afraid of the Evil Eye. The next day they sewed sets energetically: orders arrived. Corinne's food stuck in her throat she was so excited. She ate standing up, next to the sewing machine, tubs of yogurt and cream. A week later she drove off with Mermel again, with more sets; again they returned early in the evening. Corinne went to bed with her clothes on, and Mermel ate the remains of last week's salmon with old black bread smeared with butter. Corinne had quarreled with the owner of the shop, he said; she made a scene and took back the cushions. They had ruined her work, displayed the cushions wrong, sold them separately, undone the sets. "So what if they undid them?" wondered the mother the next day. "The main thing is they sold something." Corinne looked straight ahead with expressionless eyes: "Don't sew any more, okay? I don't need you to sew for me," she said.

SLOWLY (4)

LIKE THE SHACK, so, too, the trench Sammy dug next to the welding shop for the war deserved "first prize in the whole neighborhood," said the Nona admiringly, even though she didn't visit it much: she declared, and also stood by her word most of the time, that she would rather die from a "Muslim bomb" falling on her than spend hours with the "*asabayya*," the nervous wreck, the mother, in that place under the ground, twenty-one square feet, even though it was relatively nicer than most such places.

"So die," barked the mother. "We'll write your name on that stone where they write the names of the poor dead soldiers." The mother was really very nervous indeed because of the war, and because of her own character, which combined with the war: her huge anxiety, tireless resourcefulness, terrible grief, and absolute identification with the fighters and the spirit of battle induced in her a seething ferment. She took a course in first aid: they held a course in the neighborhood Labor Federation Center and she was the first to sign up. During the whole of the war she walked around with the first aid kit hanging from her shoulder or right by her head in her "light-light" sleep, dressed in her dark blue housecoat with the buttons down the front, "like a Soviet worker," which she didn't take off at night. She ordered everyone to sleep with their shoes on, at the first sound of the air-raid warning shining the light of the hundred-watt flashlight on their faces, which, according to Corinne, was capable of "waking the dead and killing them again with its blinding glare."

Sammy split his sides laughing—first thing in the morning he went with his spade to dig trenches in Savyon and the surrounding area with Moshe and Mermel, both of whom had also been rejected by the army— he fell apart whenever the mother walked past him with her brisk tread, off to her fighter-plane engine factory, with her first aid kit and the rake whose handle was broken and which she had replaced with a six-foot-long pole. "*Ya hadret elzabet*," he called her, "your honor the officer," instead of his old nickname, "*el muhandes*," the engineer.

For days on end she raced around like a weather vane, looking for a place to "volunteer." She went to the Labor Federation Center with Georgette and Bracha to "lend a hand" at the Soldiers Welfare Association, and left after a while because "all they do there is gossip all day long; not a soul in the neighborhood escapes those big mouths of theirs," but above all she devoted herself to improving the shelter.

She smoothed the sandy walls down with a spatula, hung sheets over them, organized a kitchenette with a hollow in the sand for the gas burner, laid down straw mats, made a bench to sit on and a cradle for Corinne's baby, relayed electricity from the welding-shop generator for lighting, and endlessly raked the floor.

There were no bounds to her delight and keenness when it transpired one morning that the army had decided to make use of Sammy's welding shop for the war effort: at half past five in the morning two army trucks drove down from the old reservoir hill loaded with damaged vehicle and tank parts. She stationed herself at the bottom of the hill, directed them to the welding shop, and opened the heavy iron door for them: Sammy was still sleeping. He shuffled up to the truck in his pajama pants whose belt was torn, holding them up with one hand.

In the brief breaks she afforded herself, she went to quarrel with Nona on the pretext of "going to sit with her awhile and have a cup of coffee," but suddenly stood up in the middle of the argument and walked out. "This time," said the offended Nona, "I'm finished with her, daughter or no daughter—I'm finished with her."

When the air-raid warning went off Nona remained sitting in her armchair, lighting the wrong end of her cigarette in the excitement of her resolute resistance, holding it between her lips with the filter burning like a brand. The mother hurried everyone into the bunker, bringing up the rear like a shepherd rounding up stray goats, glancing at Nona's open door and waiting a moment or two before entering the bunker herself, but Nona did not appear, or even come out to the concrete landing of her steps to look. "If she wants to stay there let her. Let a bomb fall on her in her stubbornness," spat the mother, sat down for a minute on the bench, and immediately got up again, rushed outside, and ran to Nona's place, to the sound of the sirens, which alternately deafened the yells coming from the quarter-shack and was deafened by them. She came back trembling with rage: "You go and get her," she ordered Sammy. Corinne, dying of fright both during the air-raid warnings and between them, sat pressing the baby's head to her bosom with one hand and the child with the other, muttering: "What a madhouse, what a madhouse." Ten minutes later Sammy crawled back to the bunker: "She has to get ready, she'll come soon," he announced with a smirk, the mischievous glint in his eye testifying that "she has to get ready" was an invention of his own, to madden the mother. When the all-clear sounded, they saw the Nona emerging from her room, descending the steps one by one, advancing slowly and haltingly down the path, in almost deliberate slow motion, "as if she's on a go-slow strike," stated the mother in astonishment, and surrendered, turned her back on the whole business, once again proving her utter hopelessness at conducting negotiations, which always opened with her taking the hard, uncompromising line of a tyrannical dictator only to blow up in a moment of impatience and disgust, when she washed her hands of the whole thing: "Let them take what they like. They can take the elastic from my panties, as long as they let me breathe," she said.

That same day Sammy dug a separate little bunker for Nona, next to the concrete steps of her quarter-shack. She only went down there twice, because the war ended—in a terrifying roar, which sent almost all the inhabitants of the street flying for their bunkers even though there was no alert: one of Nona's gas balloons blew up when she rashly threw a lighted match through the window.

Nona's little bunker was taken over by Rachel Amsalem and the child: they sat there for hours with the thirty pens in the shape of an umbrella that Rachel had slipped into her pockets from the booty her father the cook had brought back from the war. Rachel brought a map and showed the child what they had conquered, dictating the names of the places for her to write them down in the notebook the two of them had bought from Levy especially for this purpose, pausing between the names, knitting her brows in affected deliberation when the child pointed to the map and asked: "And did we conquer this?"

GAS

FROM TIME TO time she smelled something in the shack and coming from the shack, sniffing, passing between the rooms with her eyes fixed in front of her, hoping to catch sight of it. "I can smell something," she said, turning to the child, or Sammy, or Corinne. "Can't you smell it? There's something here, some smell." She bent over the unlit kerosene heater, checking for a leak, stuck her nose into the bed covers and the curtains, poked her head into the closets, the kitchen cupboards, the garbage pail, lay on the floor and peered under the beds, and in the end stopped next to the stove, the main suspect: gas.

One by one she sniffs the flames, dismantles the rings, and soaks them in the sink, shuts off the gas at the main, opens all the windows and the front door wide, and still she smells it: subtle, elusive, sly, coming and going, full of tactical retreats simply in order to get organized, gather strength, and attack again, suddenly hitting her in the face as she lies on her side in bed, persuading herself that there's nothing there. Again she hurries to the stove, goes outside to the gas balloons in the yard, shuts them both off, and goes back inside, sits down on the armchair next to the open window, with her book. She puts her hand to her neck, moves it from side to side as if she wants to get rid of something clutching her throat. "Can't you smell gas?" she asks Sammy. "There's a smell of gas." Sammy sniffs. "There's nothing," he says. "Just shut the window. It's cold."

"What do you mean, there's nothing?" she argues. "There's gas. Smell."
Sammy goes to the kitchen, opens and closes the gas tap, wets it with soapy
water to check if there's a leak; there's no leak. There's nothing. She stands
behind him, wringing her hands. "Am I dreaming?" she asks. "Am I imagining I can smell it?" "You're imagining," he says, and goes about his business, leaving her alone with "it." "Where are you going?" she asks in a panic,
following him to the door. "To work," he answers in astonishment. "Where
else have I got to go?" He slams the door behind him and she opens it again.
Now she is surrounded by a sweetish, viscous smell, fainter than before but
more poisonous: she feels nauseous. She goes to the bathroom basin and
tries to vomit, sticking her finger in her throat, but she doesn't vomit. "I don't
know how to vomit," she says, looking at the child riveted to the radio. "Was
I crazy smelling that gas all the time?" she asks her. The child doesn't answer,
kneeling by the radio and trying to learn the words of the song it's playing
by heart, registering the mother's calves next to her, with the hem of her
dress coming halfway down. "What gas?" she responds in the end. The
mother goes on standing next to her, without moving, casting a dense,
heavy shadow. The child raises her eyes and looks at her: her lower lip sags
loosely, the contours of her face seem to have blurred and suddenly spread,
overflowing their borders. For a moment she recovers, the mother. She
sprays the shack with an air purifier, finishing off almost the whole can,
escapes to the porch from the suffocating scent, and waits.

For hours she is locked into this dance with the smell—the elusive,
transparent monster, or at other moments a floating feather barely
brushing her face: the fear of going mad, which suddenly for no reason
goes away, vanishing like the smell of the gas. The shack comes back into
her possession again, but not for long; in her absence it is confiscated from
her again: when she isn't in it it's as if it isn't there, already extinct, or in
danger of extinction.

This is the gas of leaving the house: at least two times out of five she's
sure she's left something on the gas, forgotten to turn it off. Her face suddenly pales, she goes back, checks the switches and taps. Sometimes she
even goes back after taking the bus to work—she gets off with her knees
knocking, crosses the road, and waits for the bus going back to the neighborhood, or hitches a ride, when she's in luck: "I'm in luck today," she shouts
at Moshe, perched on his tractor, which passed by and took her home, on
his way to work at a building site.

In His Way

T HE CHILD SAW it: in his way, Maurice boiled with rage. It wasn't the mother's
kind of boiling—the brink of an explosion about to pour over her and
somebody else—it was the dull rage of the final, empty sobs of a baby who
despaired of its mother's coming, of a fatuous expectation, his face turned
blue in humiliation. He repeated this word several times—"humiliation."
He sat on the mother's porch with red eyes, as if he hadn't slept for two
weeks, trying to light a cigarette with a lighter that refused to light: "What
a humiliation. They humiliated them like dogs, worse than dogs," he said.

He turned up the day after the end of the war, dropped in for half an
hour to see how we were, and actually to borrow a few lira from Sammy.
He was waiting for him to come back from work. The mother served him
coffee but he didn't touch it. He forgot. After a couple of minutes he asked,
"Did you make me coffee *ya* Lucette?" Corinne sat next to him, at the table.
She didn't raise her eyes from the book without a cover the child had left
there, *The Diary of Anne Frank*, and the mother leaned against the doorpost
and watched: "What, are you in mourning?" she said. "Yes, I'm in mourning," said Maurice, "I really am in mourning for what happened and what's
going to happen." Corinne raised her eyes. "What happened?" she asked
drily. Maurice took off his horn-rimmed glasses for a moment, wiped the
lenses with the hem of his shirt, and said nothing. After a while, when his
voice came back, it sounded as if it were coming from under the earth,

hoarse and crushed: "The way they keep on showing how the Egyptian soldiers ran away without their shoes, they show it again and again, humiliating the other in his defeat. They can't see that there's a tomorrow, that
you have to talk to the people you humiliated. Some leadership." The mother
turned on the sprinkler, moved it a little so it wouldn't splash on the porch,
and got wet herself; her whole dress was soaked through, sticking to her
stomach and her buttocks. She went inside to change, wringing the hem of
her dress on her way. "What's wrong with the leadership? What have you
got against them? Would you have done any better?" Corinne spat out, and
turned over the book, which was completely wet. "Leadership"—Maurice
drew the word out—"great leadership. That dictator Dayan, and that Abba
Eban, when he speaks Hebrew he reminds me of the British Mandate. They'll
have to give back everything they conquered, every inch. What a catastrophe!" He stood up and started pacing the porch, almost slipping on the wet
tiles, hanging on to the back of Corinne's chair. She recoiled sideways; she
was cooking something up. The child looked at Corinne's face and knew
that something was cooking: her face was twisted, from chin to forehead,
hollowed and flattened at once, as if it were made of Play-Doh that had been
kneaded any old way, with no shape in mind. "Whose side are you on, ours
or theirs?" she demanded in a hostile tone. "Neither side"—Maurice raised
his voice—"I'm on the side of justice and logic and against all these victory
celebrations, that's what I am." Corinne jumped off her chair, threw the
book onto the lawn, and suddenly bent down, half-crouching and holding
both hands between her knees as if she were trying not to pee: "You're an
Arab, not a Jew, that's what you are, an Arab. Get out. Pick yourself up and
get out of here, you traitor," she yelled. The mother came out onto the porch:
"What? What?" she asked, looking from Corinne to Maurice. He took his
black bag with the zipper off the table, tucked it under his armpit, and left,
receding up the path with slow steps that tried to hurry, the little hump at
the top of his back hiding the nape of his neck.

The mother stood barefoot and looked at him, her toes digging into the
groove between the paving stones. "Now he hasn't got a penny for the bus,"
she said, went inside, and took two banknotes out of her bag. "Run after
him. Give this to him," she said to the child.

PAPERS

O N THE FIRST *day when the fighting broke out in our last war, the Sinai Cam-paign, I went to present myself at my IDF unit and complained that I hadn't received a call-up order. Being a simple soldier in the infantry I was sent straight to the quiet front with the Jordanians. The relative quiet on the Jordanian front gave me an opportunity to keep my ears open, to follow events, and to think seriously about the situation and the possible solutions. This led me to the conclusion that Ben-Gurionism, as a main factor in the Sinai war, had missed the chance and the most auspicious opportunity to obtain peace or make headway toward it.*

This conclusion was confirmed with time and I remain convinced of it to this day. The analysis leading to this conclusion is plainly objective and logical to any-one who understands the Arab mentality in general, and President Nasser's men-tality in particular.

After the announcement of the nationalization of the Suez Canal, Nasser knew that he was entering into an open conflict with the interests of two great powers, England and France. We had no interests in the Suez Canal like those of the English and the French. So what should we have done? Adopt a militaristic policy? Or per-haps plan a different policy at this auspicious opportunity that would lead to peace with Nasser? The Ben-Gurionist policy was and remained militaristic in spirit and purpose. This fact led me to conclude that the Sinai war distanced us from the way to peace when it was within our grasp, and brought us closer to the next war.

In the light of history and the evidence of the facts, the Sinai Campaign was a catastrophic political failure for all those who participated in it. It only increased the revulsion, the anger, and the hatred of Israel on the part of the Arab nations and particularly the Egyptian nation and its leader, Nasser. I dread to think of the results of this anger and hatred in the war to come. Our Ben-Gurionist propagandists never stopped boasting and ridiculing, in all the avenues of propaganda, the Egyptian army, the Egyptian nation, and its leader, Nasser. In exaggerated ways and a humiliating manner, we kept on describing the cowardice of the Egyptian solider who ran away barefoot leaving his shoes behind him. This contempt wounded the souls and the honor of all the Egyptians and the Arabs profoundly.

To my regret, we are continuing the same arrogant and contemptible vein of propaganda to this day. It seems, too, that we have learned nothing from the political cunning of our allies in this war, the English and the French. They were able to transcend their military victory and put it behind them, thereby proving themselves superior to us in political maturity. They were not slow in denouncing the war and those who led them into it, and who paid the price in their political careers for this superfluous war. Thus relations improved between these two powers and the Egyptians and political and economic ties between them were renewed.

And here in Israel? All we can do is go on arguing about the battles of the Sinai Campaign, reminisce fondly about the stories and legends and battles of the war, and invent more and more dubious facts about that war. Which shows that we are still worshipping the golden calf of the militaristic Ben-Gurionist doctrine that will lead us to the next war.

MORE AND MORE

THE CHILD WANTED Nona to tell her more and more about herself. "Tell me more," she begged, especially when the two of them went to town to sit in Café Milano almost every Tuesday afternoon, because Nona had to have a change of air. "Let's get a change of air," she said to her at two o'clock in the afternoon on a blazing *khamsin* day, setting the tub in the middle of the room, and taking off her slip, naked with the door open. "People can see you," cried the child in alarm, "they can see everything." "Let them see"— Nona tested the water in the tub with the toe of one foot and then the other—"What's there to see already? Didn't they see what I've got on their mothers when they were born?" With her silver hair gathered into a flat bun on top of her head, her vast hips, shiny-white and silky, the long neck rising from her chest, her breasts spreading out and rounding at the bottom—she looked like a huge china jug set on an unsteady surface and wobbling slightly. Afterward she sprinkled herself with half a bottle of eau de cologne, sneezing as she did so. "You're putting on too much scent," scolded the child, who also scented herself with eau de cologne, but the way Corinne did it: behind her ears and on her wrists. "That's because I haven't got my eyes," explained Nona, who sat in the armchair dressed and combed, her handbag on her lap, and waited for the appointed hour, the four o'clock bus.

The room was dark. There were no windows apart from the rectangle of light from the front door open onto the concrete landing overlooking the mother's shack at the bottom of the path, behind the thorns of the *amm*'s backyard, behind the brick fence of the welding shop, behind the cypress tree. The child went out to call Rachel Amsalem, so that she, too, could hear all the things Nona told her about herself, and found her next to the guava tree, sorting out the fallen fruit that wasn't rotten and collecting it. She came with the child reluctantly, cradling the guavas in front of her in her shirt. The two of them sat on the floor at the Nona's feet. "Well?" demanded the child, and looked at Nona expectantly, afraid that Rachel would get bored and run away. The Nona cleared her throat, and opened: "*Ya wai wai, ya baruch Adonai,*" she said in an unenthusiastic, perfunctory tone: her mind was on her "change of air." "Not like that," said the child in disappointment. "say it all from the beginning."

She began again: "You, *ya bint*, with you it's either *wai wai* or *baruch Adonai*—bless the Lord." The child roared with laughter and glanced at Rachel Amsalem who was sitting cross-legged with a blank, embarrassed expression of incomprehension on her face. "She said that I'm either *ay-ay-ay* or *baruch Adonai*, did you understand?" she pressed Rachel, and the Nona contributed: "That's what you say about someone who either sees every-thing black as black or white as white." Rachel barely smiled and took three caramels from the jar standing on the little table. The Nona went on to the next bit: "Pity the poor *madrub* who marries you. He probably wanted to hang himself, and went to get married instead, the *madrub.*" This was even funnier, and the child laughed till tears came to her eyes. Rachel laughed, too, but she whispered to the child: "What's a *madrub*?" The child wasn't sure what a *madrub* was and she looked at the Nona: "I don't know exactly," she said. Nona paused for a moment, lit her cigarette, took a puff without inhaling, and said the third part: "You, *ya bint, elriglen fil-khara wal-raas mtartara.*" Rachel Amsalem tensed at the word "*khara*"—shit. "What did she say?" The child couldn't answer, the laughter was choking her. "What are you laughing at? You laughed yesterday," the Nona scolded her, and she turned to Rachel and explained: "*Elriglen,*" you know what that is—feet. So the feet are in the shit but the head is up in the air, "*mtartara,*" going around and around," she explained.

Rachel Amsalem wasn't pleased about something. She arranged the guavas in her shirt and got up and left. The child saw her home. "Wasn't it funny, what she said about me?" She looked at her anxiously. "No," pronounced Rachel, kicking a stone with the toe of her shoe: "She insulted you and you laughed like an idiot." "She didn't insult me," protested the child. "Yes she did," insisted Rachel. "She said you were shit, that's what she said. Why isn't that insulting?" She stood still and stared straight into the child's face. From so close up her eyes seemed to squint, coming together toward her nose. The child was silent. She thought for a long time: "Because it was her who said it."

Time

Maurice's time was a time of absence: the past and the present had no headstone. This timelessness was flat, with no footholds to hold on to: when he came, when he went, what came first and what came afterward, when he stopped coming, at what age and what year—all this was not history but metaphysics.

His sudden appearances and disappearances were welded in the child's mind into the one great, burning appearance that consumed itself even as it was taking place, vanishing into the whiteness of absence. The longing was not an arrow sent into some future or past. It had no map: it was a longing for longings, for the white absence itself.

And then, at some point along the length or breadth of the flat expanse, he stopped appearing for a very long time, which was called "years"—and then he popped up, after the "years," emerging like the tip of a mountain that had been covered by the sea, when the child was eleven or twelve years old. This was his final appearance: after that there were meetings, but no appearances.

He didn't come to the shack; he could no longer just come to the shack and flee from it: that movement was over. He went to Corinne one afternoon and sent Mermel to tell the child to come and see him there, at Corinne's place.

It was after Purim but nevertheless Mermel found her on the lawn of the mother's shack in her costume, dressed as a nun, sitting up straight on one of the wrought-iron porch chairs and kissing the wooden cross covered by the mother in silver aluminum: Sammy's friend who couldn't make it on Purim was taking a photograph of her like this, and then another one of her standing between the rosebushes, holding an open Bible, the ends of the black head scarf flapping behind her back and the hem of the black dress hugging her calves, exposing the tops of her white socks that had slipped down into her shoes. Mermel peeled a banana and looked at her being photographed: "That's a nice costume," he said to the mother, putting off what he had come for. But she knew him only too well, especially his inability to keep his mouth shut: "What's up?" She gave him a look. "Out with it." Mermel squirmed a little and peeled another banana. "Maurice wants to see her," he said in the end.

Now the photographer told the child to pray. He sat her on the stone fence outside the welding shop. "But how?" she asked. "Like this." He put her hands together next to her stomach. "That's how they pray," he said. Instead of doing as he said, she did what she had once seen in a movie: she pressed the palms of her hands tightly together against her clavicle, closed her eyes devoutly, and mumbled something. Mermel stepped up to the stone fence, sat down beside her, and Sammy's friend photographed them both: Mermel eating a banana with his thighs open, and the child with her profile turned toward him, the black scarf covering half her face.

"He wants to see you," Mermel said to her. In the meantime the mother got dressed, locked the door of the shack, leaving the key for Sammy in the big flowerpot next to the door and forgetting the coffee cups on the porch table. "Take off that costume so people won't think you're crazy, walking around in a Purim costume after Purim," she said to the child. "No," replied the child, pulling her socks up to her knees. "What do you mean, no?" demanded the mother in astonishment, and thought for a minute: "Then you're not leaving the house, you're staying here." The child sat down on one of the wrought-iron chairs and held her tongue. The mother sat down on a chair herself: "We're not going anywhere. Let her not see her father," she announced to Mermel. "What do you care if she goes like that?" Mermel tried to persuade her. "She can go, I'm staying." The mother rose furiously to her feet and went inside. "You can't break that child," she muttered.

Mermel and the child went off, got into the silver Lark standing at the side of the road. When Mermel started the car, they saw the mother coming. She got in and sat down wordlessly on the front seat, and the child in her nun's costume moved to the back, pulling the white fabric swaddling her neck up to her chin, so as not to leave a scrap of skin showing. Nona, who grew up among the nuns in Cairo, said that it was forbidden to see their bare flesh except for their faces, the only part of themselves they were allowed to reveal. She didn't say "bare" but another word, pursing her lips, as if she had betrayed something against her will, and the child tried to remember what the word was, as she fingered the cross on her chest and stared at the orange groves of Gat Rimon, through which the Lark drove as if it were undoing some zip, which opened wider and wider as the car went on driving, cutting through the heavy density of the greenness.

On the front seat Mermel was telling the mother about various job offers he had received, repeating, "I've made up my mind to change, enough," dangling his left hand out of the window with the cigarette whose ash blew back in the child's direction. She heard the mother say, "If only, if only," and her voice sounded dull, veiled, as if it were emerging from layers of cloth.

She didn't come up to Corinne's apartment with them, the mother; she said that she would wait outside. "Where outside?" asked Mermel. "Outside," she said, turned toward the little playground in the sweltering lot next to the building, and sat down on a bench with her back to them.

The child went up. The child came down. The mother was no longer sitting on the bench; she was standing and waiting outside the stairwell. She had bought herself a jam tart at the nearby grocery store, but she had eaten only half and was looking for a garbage can to throw the rest away: "Too sweet," she said, examining the parcel the child was holding under her arm. "What did you get?" she asked. The child showed her: a white summer dress with red and blue polka dots and a low waist, red patent-leather shoes, and a package of finger biscuits dipped in chocolate. Mermel couldn't start the Lark. He said he would get hold of a friend to take them home, but the mother didn't have the patience to wait. "*Yallah*, we'll manage," she said, and started walking to the bus stop with the child, who almost tripped a few times, stepping on the hem of the black nun's habit, looking straight ahead without blinking an eye in the face of the amused astonishment of passersby.

Night fell as they waited for the bus, sitting on the gloomy bench. The mother took the dress out of its tissue paper again. "At least you got something out of him this time," she said to the child who looked across the road, at the housing project that was being built there: the ragged buildings were drowned in the darkness like dentures in a glass. She scratched the silver paper off the cross with her fingernails, until they were scratched with the sharp edges cutting into them.

Final Portrait of Corinne in the Flying Shack

We remained on our own, Corinne and I, on the flat porch of the flying shack, thrust up toward the clouds like a fingerless hand of a beggar, the clouds recoiled, retreating backward or forward—it was hard to tell— the closer the porch came, carrying just us trapped inside one of the big transparent marbles that had rolled off Corinne's hair and caught us inside it, inside the rich dense water that almost entirely filled it and was happily very warm. The mother and Sammy had abandoned us or been left by us, taking the flying shack with them and leaving us the porch as a favor or deposit on some unfriendly future to come, loading the shack onto Sammy's patched-together bicycle, which up in the air, for some reason, did not fall when turning but succeeded in flying "straight, straight ahead," obeying the mother's wishes.

We remained there, Corinne and I, me and Corinne, inside the fertile water in the marble, which provided us with all the necessary nutrients to keep us in precisely this state, neither growing nor diminishing, with our eyelids stuck to our eyes with spit, through which we saw each other as if reflected in curved mirrors, confirming our existence to each other, especially when Corinne leaned over me, and she leaned over me all the time, almost prostrating herself on me, as if the spherical conditions and the roundness of the water in the marble allowed it, in the absence of flatness.

The spiral rings of Corinne's breath on my face turned into shining glass toys as they left her mouth, into undefined hybrid animals grafted together, a head to a tail, and they grouped politely at one side and waited, while Corinne said what she said, and this is what she said: "I'll tell you the truth. Someone has to tell you the truth at last." I shut my eyes inside my closed eyelids and saw how Corinne's face so close to mine was sucked into the beam of my eyes, disintegrating and then reconstituted: "What truth?" I asked.

The glass animals whose beauty broke my heart stretched their necks and raised their heads together in the water of the marble, not to hear us better but to lick with their glass tongues the strawberries that began to sprout above them, at the rounded top of the marble. I noticed that Corinne was brushing her fingertips lightly over my face, a gesture that gradually grew more aggressive, pressing harder and harder on my cheeks, my forehead, and my chin, on the space between my upper lip and my nose: "The truth, the whole truth, and nothing but the truth about Maurice and who and what he is," said Corinne. "All right," I agreed, hoping that this would bring the matter to a quick end, "but tell me only with a sweet tongue, because without *ellisan elhilwa* I won't have a face left to show or hide."

Now Corinne left me alone, collected her toys, and licked them one by one, picked up from the round floor of our marble a pair of cymbals, which were actually the covers of emergency openings. Because that was what was written on them: "emergency openings." She fitted the cymbals onto her hands, brought them to the sides of my face, struck my cheeks with them for the first time, and said: "Maurice sucked our blood."

She struck the cymbals for the second time: "Maurice has poisoned our blood."

She struck the cymbals for the third time: "Maurice drank our blood."

She struck the cymbals for the fourth time: "Maurice drained our blood."

She struck the cymbals for the fifth time: "He is the blood. The blood must be spilled."

My head spun, or perhaps there was something else in me that spun. I was seized with a terrible thirst and I started to drink more and more of the water in the marble, grateful to the glass animals, which now came and surrounded me on all sides so that I could look clearly at their internal organs visible through their glass skin and copy the right answer. The right answer was: "So what should I do now?" And I said it quickly to Corinne who was busy with something else and hardly listened. She was feeling the cymbals, looking for the end of the wire, and she began to pull it and pull it. She unraveled the cymbals into a spool of gilded wire that she began to coil around my body, starting with my feet and moving up to my calves and thighs. "You don't love him, you can't love Maurice," she said in a rhythmic chant whenever she concluded coiling, tightening and tying the gilded wire of the cymbals around another part of my body: "You can't love him if you want to be ours," she said as she pushed the coils of wire together on my skin with her fingers, so there would be no strip of skin exposed, all of it covered with an impermeable layer of gilded wire: "Does it hurt you, Toni?" she asked, wiping her tears with her shoulder. I felt the blood stopping in my thighs, congealing in place. "But I love him and I always will." The glass animals sang in chorus, clustering around me, their food bags crammed with strawberries hanging and swaying on their necks, signaling me to join in the refrain: "But I love him and I always will." "No, no." Corinne shook her head, moving the spool up to my arms, coiling the gilded wire around my wrists and pulling hard to tighten it: "You mustn't love him. You don't love him." She straightened my arms to cover my elbows closely with the wire: "You mustn't, you mustn't, you mustn't," she muttered as she coiled. I could see the beads of sweat breaking out on her forehead even in the dark water of the marble, glittering like sapphires, and staying there on her forehead, radiant and solid, not trickling down, just like the tear drops that remained suspended from the corners of her eyes. "But I do love him," I tried again, gazing at the marble eyes of the beautiful glass animals kneeling next to me on the rounded floor and letting me stroke their pricked-up ears.

"*Yallah*," said Corinne, "we're finished for today." She gave me her hand and helped me up, clothing my body covered with wire, which now, close and smooth and complete, looked like a diving suit. We sat down, Corinne and I, against the rounded side of the marble and began rolling with it toward the edge of the flying porch, up to the place where the floor tiles stopped and gave way to the starry infinity of the nocturnal landscape of hills and lakes, which Corinne called "the sky."

THE GLASS ANIMALS

"COME WITH ME," Corinne nagged the mother for months. She wanted her to come to Cairo, to show her. "Show you what?" protested the mother. "What's there to show after all these years?" "Well, there's your house and all the places you said, Café Groppi and all of them," said Corinne, who despite herself eagerly swallowed all of Maurice's tales of Cairo, as told by Sammy: he traveled there once a month, Maurice, radiant with joy over the peace agreement. He had "his own affairs" there: the regular cafés where he met his friends, the renewal of old connections, cheap dental care by a Cairo dentist, books, newspapers, and nightclubs, buying and selling, and business schemes he dreamed up: the first was an agency for organized tours to Cairo under his guidance and inspiration, which he opened in his room in the Hatikva quarter, actually a reincarnation of the Suhba, only without the comrades, and the second, secret at least in definition—an attempt to export thousands of valium pills to Egypt, which suffered from a severe shortage of tranquilizers, as Maurice discovered to his regret ("What's all this 'to my regret' all the time?" asked Sammy).

But the mother didn't want to hear about it: "I have nothing to go for and nothing to show. The people I loved died or left, and what's the use of a place without its people? You go," she urged Corinne, to get her off her back, but Corinne nagged and nagged, and in the end she broke her. "She broke me," the mother announced. "When that one wants something she's got *uwwat ozraeen*, the strength of the devil."

They went for five days with three suitcases, the mother's one, and the two big ones belonging to Corinne, whose face showed the first sour signs of disappointment: the Mena House Hotel where she wanted to stay was too expensive, and she was obliged to compromise on the Marriott. "The Marriott's class, too. What's wrong with the Marriott? What are we, the prime minister, that we have to go to the Mena House?" The mother tried to mollify Corinne, who pursed her lips tighter and said, "All right, all right." Corinne's eyes widened with pleasure at the sight of the colonial-style room in the Marriott, but to the mother she went on saying, "All right, all right," and went with her, at least for the first two days, to all the places that everyone goes to: the pyramids, the museum, the Khan el-Khalili, and to the mother's old residential neighborhood in Sharre Elsakakini.

"What, is that all?" demanded Corinne, dismayed at the sight of neglect, the dirt, and, above all—the size. "The whole thing's no more than a street in south Tel Aviv," she said to the mother who stood rooted to the spot, looking around her: "Poor, poor Egypt, poor country, poor people," she said in a choked voice. Nevertheless, they went up to the apartment building where the mother thought they had lived before they left Cairo and knocked on one of the doors. An old woman opened the door, stared at them for a long moment in the gloom of the corridor, until suddenly, after a short exchange, her face shone. "*Umm* Sammy, *Umm* Sammy," she cried and took the mother into her arms. They sat with her in the miserable room with its closed shutters and drank coffee from sticky little cups. She patted the mother's thigh, held her hand: "Why did you leave us and go away?" she asked again and again. "Why did the Jews leave us alone with all the evil that came on us afterward and go away?" The mother unpinned the gold brooch with the amethyst stone from the lapel of her jacket and gave it to her, pinned it to the collar of her dress: "Keep us in your heart," she said.

Afterward the two of them went to sit for a while on the bank of the Nile. The mother was pensive, her eyes veiled: "Look how she remembered, *Umm* Sammy, *Umm* Sammy," she said over and over to Corinne, who was silent and morose, suddenly stung by a bee that left her ankle red and swollen and sore. She had had enough. In the coming days the mother roamed the streets of Cairo alone. Corinne didn't want to leave the hotel. She spent all day at

the pool or in the bar or in one of the halls of the lobby, and made friends
with a doctor and his wife and sister from Abu Dhabi.

She dressed herself up; morning, noon, and night, she dressed herself
up, making an appearance in the breakfast room or the restaurant, accompanied by the mother who was astonished every time anew, recoiling a
little from the admiring silence that greeted Corinne's beauty, the heads that
turned toward her or after her, full of an almost fearful wonder at the regal
halo shooting sparks like firecrackers around her oval face held high in
huge, inexplicable yearning, at the graceful refinement of her walk, at the
musical sweetness of her bell-like voice, and—above all—at the tension
aroused by this fragile beauty, so delicate and transparent, which seemed
to be held seamlessly together by means of her breath alone.

Between the pool and the thickly carpeted halls Corinne spent her time
in the souvenir shop of the hotel, buying and buying: beaten silver jewelry,
pure white kaftans, "handmade" embroidered tablecloths, and six or seven
colored glass figurines of not quite recognizable animals, which for some
reason mesmerized her. She bought two a day—dogs or cats that stretched
their necks and pricked up their ears in a manner that suggested something
between a giraffe and a deer. She arranged them on the dressing table in
the room, crowded together as if in a narrow pen, keeping a suspicious eye
on the mother when she brushed her hair in front of the mirror: "Be careful not to break them," she said.

And then the mother went out to sail on one of the tourist cruise boats
plying the Nile, giving up on Corinne and leaving her with the Abu Dhabis
in the hotel bar, with a frozen wedge of crystallized orange on the rim of
the tall glass of her San Francisco cocktail.

It was a very hot, humid morning, and the mother kept wiping her face,
which seemed to her to be covered with a layer of sweat and sand, sitting
on the boat next to a group of Israeli Palestinians from Umm al-Fahm on
holiday in Cairo, and chatting with them. The dark-haired bespectacled
young man next to her, with his arm around the shoulders of his young
bride, who was green and nauseous with seasickness, listened to the conversation, admiring the mother's fluent Egyptian Arabic. They spoke, he
and she, slowly and absentmindedly unraveling a bundle of threads of
origins and intersections. At a certain moment, she couldn't say exactly
when or how it came into being, she understood: Victor, this dark and

pleasant-mannered young man, was the son of Sammy's father from his second marriage after he came to Israel, Sammy's half brother. Now belly dancing began on the deck, accompanied by rhythmic hand clapping from the vacationers. The boat swayed. She and Victor looked at each other in amazement; her hands shook. They exchanged telephone numbers and addresses, promised to hold a family reunion at the mother's place, or Victor's place in Ashdod.

She returned from Cairo with the coiled spring, the mother, but this time it was different: a joyful anticipation about to burst its bonds, the thrill of suppressed delight tiptoeing around itself. Something had suddenly emerged from the viscous tar coating her former life, come back in a different form, purified by time, innocent as bread.

Sammy looked again at the note, at the address written down in Victor's handwriting: "And you say he's my brother, this Victor?" he asked again and again in embarrassment, in the anxious expectation that for the first time in his life had granted him the dubious asset of adulthood: a sleepless night. All night long he sat on the wrought-iron chair on the porch, dressed in his pajama pants, narrowing his burning eyes opposite the *amm*'s thorn field, which in its stubborn lonely neglect in the dark looked so hopeless and pitiful.

The next morning he called Victor and invited him to visit them on Saturday. Victor wasn't sure, and neither was the mother. She wanted to go and see her brother on the kibbutz, and she went. But in the end Victor came that Saturday. He sat in the wintry sun on the lawn of the mother's shack without the mother. Sammy barbequed meat; he burned his finger in his excitement. They sat side by side, Victor and Sammy, compared their damaged eyes: both had been infected with herpes in the left eye, at about the same age, and lost their sight in it. About "the father, may he be healthy," Sammy and Victor's father, they hardly spoke: he wanted nothing at all to do with Sammy or *Umm* Sammy.

In the evening the mother returned, saw the remnants of the luncheon party, and went off the rails: she overturned the barbeque grill, threw and broke the plates left in the sink, chased us with the broom: "You wanted to cut me out of the whole thing, do the whole dirty business behind my back," she yelled at us. "What dirty business?" asked Sammy on the point of tears, avoiding the broom and covering his face with his hand: "Why dirty? You wanted me to meet this brother, you brought the phone number and everything." She went inside, slamming the door and locking it behind her: "I didn't want anything, anything. Who gave you permission to get into my bones like this and decide behind my back?" she cried from behind the locked door.

For over a week she didn't speak to a soul, shut herself up in the shack, went only to the grocery store and back, slammed the phone down on Corinne, me, and Sammy. "But what's going to happen?" Sammy scratched his arms savagely, making the rash worse—eczema had broken out all over his body. His lips were gray, cracked with panic. He knocked on her door twice a day and she refused to open it. He crept around to the back window, tried to look inside and talk to her. She closed the blinds an inch from the tip of his nose: "Go away, I don't want to see anyone," she said.

The stone closing the cave of the past had been removed for a moment and then returned to its place with the same breathtaking and inexplicable suddenness with which it had agreed to move a little, to open and be opened.

One night Sammy implored me to come with him, to go to her together, he and I and Corinne. Perhaps the three of us would be able to get her to climb down. The shack was padded with darkness. Only in the passage a little light went on and off again a minute later, as soon as the sound of our steps rose from the flat porch surrounded by the pale, sickly patch of lawn whose baldness had been laid bare by the mower.

The Sound of Our Steps

Perhaps we were deafened to the sound of our steps in the rain at the time of the event, walking abreast along the road at night, at measured intervals, which enabled us to spread across the road, from sidewalk to sidewalk, stepping in time, at a measured pace, neither fast nor slow, but with precision—not like people escaping from something or someone, buffeted by the movement of the pendulum between the past and the future, between what had been and what would be, but like people who had been granted the grace of the moment, bathed for a moment from head to toe in the golden drizzle of the present, warmed by its humble furniture: the rain, the road, the night, the cat, the dirt path, a random sentence spoken or not, the crooked branch of a Persian lilac tree, the shack we passed without making anything of it, and walking on.

The mother marched in the center, if there could be said to be an actual center, walking between Sammy and me, keeping an ear out for Corinne, at Sammy's left, without turning her head to the side or being tempted in some other way to appear to be watching her, which was not necessary now, because everything was over—not "everything" in the sense of the course of life, but the "everything" of the skin's quiet knowledge, the skin that keeps watch through the inattention of the mind, the heart, circumstances, and fate.

We didn't drag our feet in any way, our bodies whole and determined even in the rain, not surrendering to the feebleness of defeated withdrawal, and not to false stiff-backed bravado either; no surrender was needed here, since there was no battle, no friction between what we were and what we weren't—man, object, or nature.

The glistening asphalt of the road expanded our hearts, especially since it stretched on and on, beyond the twists and turns in the road that hid more road, stretching out before us with all the beautiful, tremulous sadness of the unknown.

We stepped in the scandalous silence of a pact of love, be what it may, faithful at last to the same vision, the same oath, the same story that had resigned itself to being a thread, a remnant, a vestige, a flicker: the rain, the unforgettable experience of the rain.

It took us time to understand it, this experience, its particular and magical purpose as we walked: it came down our heads in fine, continuous threads, in tiny drops, and then, when it approached the surface of the road, about eighteen inches above the road, it changed direction and drifted upward again, not touching the ground at all, collecting in the air, at about the height of our knees, and turned into a thin, airy lake, flat as pita bread, with no dimension of depth, shedding an unworldly radiance, golden and transparent.

"*Allah yistor,*" God help us, said the mother, looking at our dry feet on the dry road, whose smooth glittering appearance came not from the rain but from the reflection cast by the thin lake of rainwater that lay above it like a polished glass roof, and she repeated "*Allah yistor,*" in a dry, matter-of-fact tone without dread, awe, or any other excessive emotion, since where we were at that moment and what we saw in the rain left no room for excess, or the hollowness of heart that gives rise to it. We walked for more than two hours, knowing the time by instinct and not by the clock, crossing the thin lake cutting the line of our knees, whose rainwater retraced its course and rose into the sky, back to the rain clouds, without diminishing or changing its volume or radius, so dedicated was it to the precise and unchanging mindfulness of its measure and its quality.

Clock

For three days before he died, Maurice listened around the clock to passages from the Koran read on the radio. Corinne said that he turned his back and died, waited for death with his face to the wall, "or else death was the wall," she said after thinking for a minute. She also said that after the mother died, he didn't want to live a minute longer, and he even said, to her or others, the words "the husband" is supposed to say: "After her I have nothing left," Corinne said that he said, and even if he didn't in so many words, explicitly and out loud, his whole being said it, giving a convoluted, arabesque meaning to the words "after her" with their inference to "before her," as if there really had been a "before," whose presence had vanished, and an "after."

It wasn't as if his hollowing out—his matchstick limbs eroded in his white flannel underwear—was completely a consequence of the death of the mother: it had been coming for a long time and was only waiting for her death to complete itself, to reach the remote and godforsaken suburbs of his body and fill them with emptiness.

In the democracy of suffering and diminishment decreed by old age, he could be considered a privileged citizen, because "he was used to it," said Corinne: for years he had been practicing solitude, illness in solitude, vagrancy, hardship, with "nobody to make him a cup of tea."

Actually there was. Two or three times a day the boy Dror dropped by his room in the Hatikva quarter, brought him things, delivered things for him, made tea, or, as Maurice liked to say, "a little tea."

"*Behayatak* a little tea," Maurice asked him, following his every movement in the kitchenette opening off the room, from his cognac-colored leather armchair, crisscrossed with cuts as if someone had slashed it with a razor blade. The east-facing window behind him bathed him in a dazzling glare: in this cage of shattered light, surrounding him like shards of broken glass, sitting up with effort in an unnatural stiffness that was liable to give way at any moment, his wild eyes planted in his face with a stony look, he resembled nothing so much as the portrait of Pope Innocent X in the series of the screaming popes by Francis Bacon.

The cut-up cognac-colored leather armchair, the boy Dror, another loyal acolyte, Salomon, for whom Maurice had once done some big favor in the past, his old typewriter, his "papers," the calendar that was also a wall clock, illustrated by a picture of a field of blazing poppies—a gift from the Migdal insurance company—had wandered with him for years from room to room, almost the only permanent features.

He sat for hours with his eyes fixed on the poppy field of the calendar, refusing the world with the firmness and politeness of his "*min fadlak*" and "*behayatak*," "if you please" and "do me a favor," words of politeness and request that were nothing but sentries guarding his inner non-world, silencing the inner conversation that had always gone on in his head but had stopped: it was a long, empty hall.

From time to time he left the hall that was his mind in the last months of his life, returning to it after a little while. In spite of everything he still found the will to gather up a little strength and go out: "I arranged to see him again," he reported wearily to Sammy.

"Him" was Sammy's uncle, the brother of the biological father from Cairo, who lived close to Maurice, "a few steps away." Maurice was trying to get the brother to soften the recalcitrant father, to persuade him to meet his son at last, for there to be a *sulha*, some kind of reconciliation. But there was no *sulha*: every week, when he met Maurice at the café in Aliya Street, the uncle brought only "small change," reporting in great embarrassment on slight shifts in the father's rigid position, which came to nothing. Maurice refused to give up. He mobilized all his cunning, his resourcefulness, his charm, his eloquence, to bring about the meeting between the father and son, for some kind of healing to take place—he was fighting, it seemed, to keep some promise he had not made to the mother but had promised himself for her sake, against her express wishes, and for her crushed, secret wish that had no voice and could not be put into words.

But the father didn't want to see Sammy until the day he died.

"He's a dry tree, that man, a blockhead." Maurice cursed him on one of the few times in his life that he cursed anybody except for the Ben-Gurionists, dragging himself off to meet the brother "for the last time," getting dressed in his gray raw silk suit with the burgundy waistcoat, in which he swam, like at the mother's funeral, when he wore it, too, collapsing and stumbling on the long dirt path in the cemetery, while Sammy and Mermel made a chair with their arms and carried Maurice between them, hoisting him high in the air like a birthday boy, or a big rag doll, when her body was cast into the pit.

Bordeaux

S HE CALLED ALL shades of red "Bordeaux," and not because she couldn't tell red from Bordeaux, but because she saw red as a kind of superfluous pause on the way, and she wanted it to hurry up and be Bordeaux. In addition, she liked rolling the word "Bordeaux" around her tongue. "It suits you, that Bordeaux dress," she said. "It's red," I corrected her. "Can't you see that it's red?" "You're right," agreed the mother, "you should always wear that Bordeaux."

She upholstered the sofas in burgundy ("It looks like a brothel," said Corinne), knitted a burgundy sweater for Sammy "for everyday," which she abandoned halfway through, painted one of the walls in the yellow hall burgundy, when there was "that fashion for colored walls," sewed a "*corniche*" for the bedroom curtain in burgundy, bought a bedside mat in burgundy, and countless tubes of gouache, a third of them red and black, to mix into burgundy, when she started to paint.

"I'm just painting a little, to pass the time," she said coyly. The easel stood on the porch with the big sheets of Bristol paper, and she started early in the morning "quickly-quickly": flowers, flowers, and more flowers. Flowers in the form of anemones, of roses, of cyclamens, of poppies. Even some of the cyclamens were painted in burgundy. From seven to eight in the morning she got through "maybe twenty." Then she hurried to remove the easel, the paints, the paintbrushes, in order to flood the porch with water and "begin the day."

This was the hour of Mustafa, the gardener who had worked for all the residents of the neighborhood until they all let him go, for fear of knife-wielding Palestinians. Only the mother went on employing him and occupying herself with him. "Let them fear for their ass if they want to. The only one I'm afraid of is God," she said. Every morning she was waiting for him with the coffee, and they began with a review of her work: "Nothing to write home about." She surveyed the paintings with a critical look. "Not so good this time, eh, *ya* Mustafa?" "Good," he disagreed. "Why do you say not good? Straight from Paradise they are, those flowers you paint."

On his face there was always a half-embarrassed, half-ironic smile, and his fingers were long and delicate and manicured as a pianist's. But the mother envisaged a different future for him. She wanted him to be a *muhami*: "You should be a lawyer, *ya* Mustafa, with brains and a tongue like yours, a *muhami*," she exhorted him. He walked behind her to the rose bed at the back, the disaster zone. "You see?" She pointed in despair at the wilted bushes, bending down and turning the soil over with her fingers: "It's all because of this lousy soil, sand and more sand, *mafish fayida*, there's nothing to be done with it." Mustafa knelt at her side, dug his fingers politely into the soil, not because he needed to verify anything, but in order to prove to her that his conclusions were based on empirical research. "Why do you say *mafish fayida*?" he said after a prolonged silence. "The soil is good, there's nothing wrong with the soil, very good soil." The mother spluttered: "How can you say such a thing?" "*Behayat elnabi*, by the life of the Prophet, the soil is good," vowed Mustafa, brought new rose plants, planted them, and urged her not to touch them. "Leave it with me," he said.

Now they visited the new roses, which had not yet bloomed, every morning after the coffee and the paintings: "Nothing," pronounced the mother bitterly, "these will die from the soil, too." Mustafa produced a metaphor of his own: "A man at work, does he like people standing over him all the time?" "He doesn't like it," the mother said reluctantly. "It's the same with the roses," concluded Mustafa. "They don't like people standing over them either. They, *ya sitti*, are also working."

A few days after this he stopped coming, because of the curfew, and he disappeared for long months. "I'm worried about Mustafa not coming. My heart is afraid for him. Who knows what happened to him?" the mother said repeatedly, and she persuaded Sammy to drive her to the village of Yaabad on the West Bank, to look for him. They set out in the morning in Sammy's pickup and arrived in the afternoon, losing their way among the stone barriers outside the Palestinian villages and the army roadblocks. Mustafa "lost his color" when he saw them: his wife had given birth to a new baby that morning, his fifth. They entered the only room of his house apart from the kitchenette, sat down on the long sofas, which opened up into beds at night, and looked around them: an entire wall of the room was covered with the mother's flower paintings.

They were stuck close together, rectangle next to rectangle, with no gaps between them, "like wallpaper," covering the wall from floor to ceiling, only it seemed that they had been altered a little.

The mother came closer. She almost pressed her nose to the wall and looked: on the areas of the pictures painted brown for the soil, Mustafa's daughters had stuck real reddish soil, on the green gouache of the leaves they had pasted green leaves from bushes and trees, and on the huge flowers painted burgundy, yellow, and purple—petals of red, yellow, and purple flowers, some of them fresh, most of them already wilted.

About The Author

Ronit Matalon, the author of *Bliss* and *The One Facing Us*, among other books, is one of Israel's foremost writers. Her work has been translated into six languages and honored with the prestigious Bernstein Award; the French publication of *The Sound of Our Steps* won the Prix Alberto-Benveniste. A journalist and critic, Matalon also teaches comparative literature and creative writing at Haifa University and at the Sam Spiegel Film School in Jerusalem.